SUNSET IN
OLD
SAVANNAH

BOOKS BY MARY ELLIS

〜

SECRETS OF THE SOUTH MYSTERIES
Midnight on the Mississippi
What Happened on Beale Street
Magnolia Moonlight
Sunset in Old Savannah

CIVIL WAR HEROINES
The Quaker and the Rebel
The Lady and the Officer

THE NEW BEGINNINGS SERIES
Living in Harmony
Love Comes to Paradise
A Little Bit of Charm

THE WAYNE COUNTY SERIES
Abigail's New Hope
A Marriage for Meghan

THE MILLER FAMILY SERIES
A Widow's Hope
Never Far from Home
The Way to a Man's Heart

STANDALONES
Sarah's Christmas Miracle
An Amish Family Reunion
A Plain Man
The Last Heiress

SUNSET IN OLD SAVANNAH

MARY ELLIS

HARVEST HOUSE PUBLISHERS
EUGENE, OREGON

Cover by Lucas Art and Design, Jenison, Michigan

Cover photos © Sean Pavone / iStock; Jon Bilous / Shutterstock; Joseph Leonardo / Wikimedia / Trolley / Flickr

SUNSET IN OLD SAVANNAH

Copyright © 2017 by Mary Ellis
Published by Harvest House Publishers
Eugene, Oregon 97402
www.harvesthousepublishers.com

ISBN 978-0-7369-6917-8 (pbk.)
ISBN 978-0-7369-6918-5 (eBook)

Library of Congress Cataloging-in-Publication Data

Names: Ellis, Mary, author.
Title: Sunset in Old Savannah / Mary Ellis.
Description: Eugene, Oregon : Harvest House Publishers, [2017]
Identifiers: LCCN 2016039331 (print) | LCCN 2016047408 (ebook) | ISBN
    9780736969178 (softcover) | ISBN 9780736969185 (ebook)
Subjects: LCSH: Murder—Investigation—Fiction. | Private
    investigators—Fiction. | Savannah (Ga.)—Fiction. | GSAFD: Christian
    fiction. | Mystery fiction.
Classification: LCC PS3626.E36 S87 2017 (print) | LCC PS3626.E36 (ebook) |
    DDC 813/.6—dc23
LC record available at https://lccn.loc.gov/2016039331

Printed in the United States of America

17 18 19 20 21 22 23 24 25 / BP-CD / 10 9 8 7 6 5 4 3 2 1

*This book is dedicated to the late Mary Sue Seymour,
who was my agent for eleven productive years.*

*You picked me up out of obscurity and took me to…
a place a tad less obscure.
I miss our friendship and your wonderful,
positive attitude.*

ACKNOWLEDGMENTS

Thanks to Catherine Neal, information officer for Chatham County, Georgia, and all the helpful folks manning the information booths throughout the historic section. What a pedestrian-friendly and bicycle-friendly and just-plain-friendly city Savannah is!

Thanks to the helpful dispatcher at Tybee Island Police Department. Although the island is relatively crime-free and hasn't had a murder in recent history, she was willing to help with my plentiful what-ifs.

Thanks to David Laux, licensed insurance agent, for your insurance help, and to author Casey Daniels, for brainstorming with me. Where would I be without friends?

Thanks to Twisted Sushi and Grill of Medina. Although several of the restaurants mentioned in the book are real, Tanaka's Culinary Creations is a figment of my imagination. I apologize in advance for any mistakes in my sushi making.

Thanks to my husband, Ken, who has accompanied me to Savannah many times. Researching with friends and family is so much more fun. I can't wait to go back!

Thanks to my agent, Julie Gwinn; my editors, Laura Weller and Kim Moore; and the wonderful staff at Harvest House Publishers. Where would I be without your hard work?

ONE

September

*I*f ever there was a perfect time for Beth Kirby to get out of town, it was now. While other parts of the country were enjoying the first crisp days of fall, the streets of Natchez, Mississippi, could melt the rubber off her worn-out tires. Her mother's hints that Beth should attend dance lessons with her and Dad at the community college had become insistent demands. After all, lots of eligible men were taking lessons these days. Rita's criteria would include any unmarried male between twenty-five and sixty who was still breathing without mechanical assistance. Then there was the obstruction of justice charge pending against her in district court. Despite her current partner's assurance, the DA wouldn't drop the second-degree felony until her former partner withdrew his complaint. And nasty Jack was living up to his reputation by taking his sweet time.

So why do I feel so uneasy? Beth parked in the shade and headed toward the back entrance of Price Investigations, only to be intercepted by her partner.

"I see you're here on time for a change." Michael Preston practically levitated out of his shoes with excitement.

"I'm always on time, give or take ten minutes." She stepped

around him. "Can we *not* act like sixth graders on a field trip to Graceland?"

Michael kept pace at her heels. "I thought you couldn't wait to get out of Natchez for a while. Are you homesick already?"

"Hardly, but I know better than to get my hopes up too soon." Beth pulled open the door and waved him in.

Always the gentleman, Michael refused to precede her inside. "You first, Miss Kirby."

"*One* of you should come in," said the office assistant. Maxine dragged Beth across the threshold by her sleeve. "Nate's chomping at the bit to deliver some good news."

Before she could free her arm from Maxine, Nate hollered from his office. "That you, Beth and Michael? Grab a cup of coffee and get in here."

"Donuts, Miss Maxine?" Michael produced a bag from behind his back. "Cream-filled with icing and chocolate sprinkles—your personal favorite."

Maxine snatched the bag from his fingers. "Be still, my beating heart."

Beth rolled her eyes as she filled her mug. "Bring me a donut too," she called over her shoulder. Belatedly, she remembered eating most of Nate's M&M's and then neglecting to replace the bag.

Their boss straightened in his upholstered leather chair, looking tan and well rested after his three-week vacation at the beach. "Make yourselves comfortable. I'm sorry that yesterday's staff meeting deteriorated into an impromptu celebration, complete with mystery guests from all over the state."

Beth took the chair closest to the door. "Never apologize for a party during work hours."

"It's not every day we hear a honeymoon was an unqualified success. A new baby on the way—congratulations, Nate." Michael leaned against the windowsill, two donuts in one hand, coffee in the other.

"He and Isabelle have been married for two years, Einstein. It's not like they're rookies." Recognizing the indelicate ground on which she trod, Beth swallowed a gulp of coffee and said, "I'm sorry. I didn't mean—"

"No problem," laughed Nate. "The pregnancy came as a pleasant surprise, but enough about that. While Isabelle and I were sightseeing, I found a case for both of you."

"Your wife said you were quite a hero in Mobile." Beth reached for Michael's second donut. "Chased some thug for three blocks, tackled him, and returned a little old lady's purse to her."

With his face turning a rosy shade, Nate waved off the praise. "I did what anyone would have done."

"I don't think so. Most bad guys pack loaded guns these days."

"Fortunately, this particular miscreant carried no weapon to ruin my honeymoon or the other couple's anniversary celebration. The woman's husband offered me a reward, but I refused. Instead, I gave them some of our business cards to pass out when they got home, in case their friends need a good PI."

"Is Mobile anywhere near Talladega?" asked Michael. "I'd love to see a NASCAR race."

"It's not, and the case isn't in Mobile." Nate took a tablet from his briefcase. "The couple I helped, Mr. and Mrs. Baer, had been vacationing in Mobile, but they live on the East Coast in Savannah. Thanks to the Baers talking up our talents, you two are going to a charming city steeped in history and home of the famous Oglethorpe Town Squares."

"Like in *Midnight in the Garden of Good and Evil*?" asked Mike. "I read that book years ago. A couple of scenes kept me up all night."

Beth swiveled to face her partner. "That book was fiction. Let's stick to reality. What kind of case?" she asked, turning back to Nate.

"Surveillance. A friend of Mrs. Baer hired our agency to check up on her husband. Take some pictures and discern the facts. But we are not to intervene. You'll create a file to present to her. What she does with it is her own business."

"Ugh," moaned Beth. "Spying on somebody's spouse? Sounds like a job for Sleaze Incorporated."

Nate's jaw twitched. "The last time I checked, Miss Kirby, my name was on the paychecks around here. Which means we need to generate cash flow so those aforementioned paychecks don't bounce."

"She didn't mean anything by that," said Michael. "Beth just talks without thinking. Could you throw me the donut bag, Miss Maxine?"

Beth would have loved to put her partner in his place, but unfortunately Michael was right. "Sorry, Nate. Spending time in jail affected my judgment."

"According to my sources, you were incarcerated for less than twenty-four hours. Your judgment was faulty long before that." Nate reached for another donut. "What you need—what you both need—is a vacation. This new client has offered a hefty fee, plus a generous per diem for expenses. I would go myself, but Isabelle is eager to sleep in her own bed. I heard that Savannah is a lovely city with plenty to see and do, so tie up loose ends here within the next few days. I'll handle anything that comes up while you're gone."

Michael scratched his scalp. "I'm confused. Are you giving us a free trip or a case to work?"

"It will be both. Plan to be gone a week to ten days, but the case shouldn't take longer than a few days. With the generous per diem, you can stay someplace nice and enjoy some R&R with all expenses paid."

Beth drained the last of her coffee. "It takes *two* PIs to snap grainy photos of a philandering husband?"

The legs of Nate's chair hit the floor with a bang. "First of all, those photos had better not be grainy. Second, we don't know that anybody is philandering. And if this assignment is beneath your dignity, Miss Kirby, you can always collect unemployment until something rolls in that meets your standards. What's the matter with you?"

From the corner of her eye, Beth caught Michael shaking his sandy-blond head. How on earth could she admit the truth—that she hated spying on people who might be stepping out? "My mother has been asking that question for years." Beth rose to her feet. "I would love to go to Savannah. Michael and I will do a great job. Our new client will be pleased as punch when we leave."

"That's better." Nate pushed his notes across the desk. "Here's the information you'll need. Keep in touch. Call me at least every other day."

"Are we driving or flying?"

"Your choice—fly and rent a car in Savannah or drive one of yours."

They spoke simultaneously. "Fly," said Michael.

"We'll drive separately," said Beth.

When the partners turned to face each other, Beth was quicker with an explanation. "Two cars will allow some personal free time. What if I want to go shopping while you search for the perfect workout gym?"

"Shopping for what—Cheetos and Diet Coke?" Michael quipped. "I've never known you to shop, Kirby."

Nate wrote out a check and tore it from the pad. "This is part of the advance. Work out the details on your own, and remember to save receipts. I'll tell Mrs. Evelyn Doyle you'll be there in a few days to introduce yourselves and outline the services we'll provide." Nate's forehead furrowed into deep creases. "Tell me now if this is a bad idea. If you two can't play nice, I'll send one of you on assignment while the other takes time off."

Michael shook his head like a balky mule. "We got along fine when you were gone, Nate. Beth and I will sort out any concerns she might have."

She glanced sideways to make sure Michael hadn't been replaced by a politician on the campaign trail. Considering she would be the one taking time off, Beth smiled as widely as her lips allowed. "Don't you worry about us. We'll do the agency proud without unnecessary gunplay or public embarrassment."

"Fine. When can you leave for Savannah?"

"I could be ready tomorrow—"

"We still have paperwork for the last case, Preston. Then there's the small matter of criminal charges still pending against me. I'd hate to flee across state lines as a fugitive. Additionally, my girl-friend's wedding is on Saturday. I don't want to miss it."

"Then plan to leave on Sunday. I'll let Mrs. Doyle know, and I'll call Chief McNeil and the Adams County district attorney to make sure all charges have been dropped. Now get out of here." Nate pointed at the door. "I don't want my crack detectives to hear me begging and pleading."

"Thanks, boss. I owe you one." Beth picked up the notebook.

"No, Miss Kirby. You owe me somewhere around one hundred fifty-seven." He motioned for his door to be closed.

On their way out, their assistant jumped to her feet as Michael passed her desk. "Let me know if I can print directions or set up hotel reservations."

Amazing what donuts on a regular basis can do around the office, thought Beth.

"You're a gem, Miss Maxine, but my new car has state-of-the-art GPS."

"If Michael tries to make a wrong turn, the car ignores him and does what's right." Beth winked at her.

The fiftysomething assistant's eyes grew round. "Is that true?"

"She's pulling your leg. Hold down the fort while Beth and I do the agency proud." Michael opened the door and waved Beth through like a trained dog.

"Don't take any wooden nickels," Beth said to Maxine.

"What's the matter with you?" Michael asked the moment the door closed behind them. "I thought you would be eager to get out of Natchez and away from Detective Lejeune. Now you have got a week to let things cool down."

"I am eager, but I don't like taking photos of someone cheating on his wife." Beth kept walking until they reached the street.

"You didn't do anything wrong. You need to get over this… hang-up you have."

"You're right. I was just expecting a better case, that's all." Beth lifted her hair off her neck. Only sixty seconds without air-conditioning, and it felt hot and heavy against her skin.

"A case is a case, Beth. You want to get something healthy to eat?" Michael asked, glancing at his watch.

"Thanks, but I need to get my oil changed and stop at the drug-store. Then I must figure out what to wear to meet some rich society lady."

"Pack some casual clothes too. Is there a Six Flags close to Savannah? I haven't been on a roller coaster in ages." Michael rubbed his palms together.

Beth laughed in spite of herself. "Why am I not surprised you love amusement parks? Okay, if there's an amusement park, we'll go. But you'd better not throw up on my shoes."

"Not this trained professional." He wiggled his eyebrows. "Are you sure we need two cars in Savannah? Parking could be expensive and hard to find. The more we economize, the more per diem we'll have for the fun stuff."

Beth pondered his logic. While the thought of traveling with a new partner made her teeth ache, Michael was right about parking in historic places. During her three visits to New Orleans's French Quarter, she received two tickets and had her car towed to the impound lot.

"You win. Pick me up at nine on Sunday and not a minute before. I'll need that long to pry myself loose from my parents. Whoever said, 'You can never go home again,' must have been talking about adult children."

"Your parents are great! I'm even getting used to Rita's cooking."

"Let's switch places for a month. I'd happily live above a law office across the street from Blues and Biscuits. Live music and good food—what else does a girl need?"

Michael started his car with the press of a button. "What does your gut say about our new client? Does Mrs. Doyle want us to lay groundwork for a lucrative divorce settlement?"

Beth focused on a freighter on the river. "Maybe she just wants to know what's going on."

"Nobody pays a hefty advance unless they're fairly certain about the outcome. It's really a shame, but for us, it's just another day in the exciting life of a PI."

"Yep. That's us, all right. Pick me up on Sunday, and save room in your car for my stuff. I'm not holding my suitcase on my lap for four states."

"Three states—Mississippi, Alabama, and Georgia." Michael ticked off the names on his fingers.

"Four. What about South Carolina?"

"You do realize Savannah is in Georgia."

"Um…of course I do. Just save me some room." Beth jumped into her car and drove away, feeling cranky for no particular reason. Yesterday she told their boss she could no longer work in Natchez. Today she was thumbing her nose at an all-expense-paid trip to a place she had always wanted to visit.

Maybe there is something wrong with me.

On the drive to a mediocre section of town, Beth tried to remember any head trauma suffered over the years. Yet every previous bicycling, white-water rafting, or rock climbing incident had injured an arm or leg, not her cranial capacity. Part of the problem was Michael Preston. Although his skills as a PI had improved tremendously, there was just something a little claustrophobic about him.

Beth walked into the kitchen of the small bungalow where she'd lived all her life and found her parents at the table, sipping coffee.

"Home so soon?"

"Any word about your new case?"

"Are you ready for lunch?"

As her parents hurled questions at a furious pace, Beth summarized the developments at Price Investigations in a few concise sentences. Then silence reigned as Rita Kirby digested the information and Stan Kirby rubbed his jaw sagely.

"Nate wants you to drive across country with a handsome young man and spend the next ten days in close proximity?" asked Rita. "He sees nothing amiss with that idea?"

Beth smiled, both at her mother's thought process and at her use of the word *amiss*. "Nate needs us in Savannah for a case, but if you'd like to call the folks at *Inside Edition*, I want a cut of the action."

Rita clucked her tongue. "Make all the jokes you want, missy, but mark my words. Your new partner may have other ideas in mind."

Beth pulled a Coke from the fridge. "Don't you worry; I'll have my guard up whenever Michael steps within ten feet of me."

"That's my girl!" said Stan. "We raised you right."

"Yes, you did." Beth kissed her mother's forehead and hurried up the steps before she exploded. She loved her parents and didn't want to argue, but moving back home hadn't been easy. With any luck, Mrs. Doyle would keep them busy until Christmas, tracking down missing dogs or spying on her neighbors.

She didn't need to worry about getting too close to someone at work again.

TWO

*D*espite the fact they only had to cross three states, the drive from Natchez to Savannah took more than eleven hours. Michael would have stopped several hours ago, but Beth had said, "Let's just get there. Then we can relax."

"Finally, we're here," he moaned as they passed the Welcome to Savannah sign. "Are you ready to relax now?"

"I'm ready to drop over dead. How is sitting in a car so exhausting?" Beth yawned.

"It's caused by oxygen depletion throughout the body due to inactivity. We should have stopped every hour and run in place for a few minutes."

Her second yawn was even louder than the first. "It was a rhetorical question, Preston. Let's just find a hotel."

Michael pulled into the exit lane and slowed his speed. "Looks like we have a Courtyard Suites, Holiday Inn Express, Best Western, Hilton Garden Suites—"

"Pick one. I don't care. We can find something different tomorrow if we need to."

Michael turned into Courtyard Suites, parked close to the registration desk, and got out. He pulled two suitcases from the trunk. "I'll get us rooms while you stretch your legs." When he returned with key cards in hand, Beth was sitting on a low brick wall, her feet in the fountain.

"Nate said this town is charming and historic." She kicked up a froth of water. "So far it looks like every place else in America."

"That's because we're still in the suburbs. Reserve your judgment until we reach downtown." Michael handed her a key and her bag. "You're in 208. Call me in the morning. We'll meet for breakfast."

"Thanks for doing the lion's share of the driving, Mike. Your car makes me nervous."

"Not a problem. Get some rest, Beth. Tomorrow we meet the client and go to work." Michael watched her trudge into the lobby like a middle-aged woman with bad knees. *What is going on with her?* Usually his partner had more energy than a hamster on its wheel.

During the drive, Beth had said little and must have read the same page in her book five times, but at least they hadn't bickered along the way. That would have driven him crazy. He usually enjoyed working with her, and she'd taught him well during his first month on the job. As partners, they brought different skills to the table.

Something had crawled up her pant leg, but whatever it was, it wasn't his problem. He loved working as a private investigator. He aimed to do a great job in Savannah and earn the trust and respect of his boss. Beth could either snap out of her funk or sulk alone. Michael planned to enjoy himself in one of America's most beautiful cities. His days of being a boring, weak, kick-sand-in-the-face accountant were long gone.

～

When Michael answered his phone the next morning, his

partner sounded as though she was in a better mood. "Good morning. Where are you? Are you ready to get something to eat?"

"I'm in the fitness room…finishing my workout," he said, panting. "They have a decent assortment of machines…and they're open twenty-four hours."

"Why did I even ask? I'm in the restaurant. Should I wait or go ahead and order?"

"I'll shower before we check out, so order me something healthy. I'm on my way."

When Michael found Beth in a back booth, she was sipping coffee and studying a map. "Are you getting a feel for the area?" He filled an empty mug from the carafe on the table.

Beth peered over the top of her magnifying glasses. "Nate said we were going to the East Coast, as in beach. The only waterfront I can find is a landing on the Savannah River."

"The Founding Fathers built the city upriver so commerce would be protected from the ravages of storms and tides. Savannah was designed with twenty-seven town squares, each uniquely landscaped. Twenty-two have survived." Michael flipped over her map and tapped his index finger. "There's the Atlantic Ocean, and the closest beach is on Tybee Island."

"Did you stay up all night reading tourist brochures?" Beth asked, refilling her mug.

"Pretty much. I'm so excited I couldn't sleep. I've never been to Georgia."

"Me neither. I thought Savannah was in South Carolina until yesterday."

"You were close. The Palmetto State is right across the river." Michael tapped his finger a second time as the server delivered their breakfast.

"Biscuits and gravy with cheesy grits," he muttered. "This is your idea of eating healthy?"

"Are you forgetting the orange slice?" Beth pointed at the fruit before adding a liberal amount of salt to her grits.

"Eat fast. I want to check out another place to stay before we call Mrs. Doyle."

"What's wrong with right here? We have free Wi-Fi and free parking. There's a pool, and the price includes breakfast."

"The rooms are fine, but I want to be in the historic district. We can run every morning at dawn, heading in a new direction until we've checked out every square."

"Or I can sleep in and you can text me photos."

"Suit yourself." Michael ate a spoonful of grits and grabbed the biscuit to eat plain. "See you in an hour in the lobby." After his shower, he found his partner in the lobby, punctual for the second time that day.

Beth scrambled to her feet. "I called Nate to let him know we're here, and I called my mother. She wants me to bring home a bowl of Savannah peas and carrots. Can you believe such a request?"

"Actually, I can, because you two share DNA." Michael picked up her suitcase and led the way outside. "I have narrowed our search to one likely candidate."

"You pick. The hotel is way more important to you." Beth climbed into the car's passenger side and rolled down the windows. "I will close my eyes until we get there."

Fifteen minutes later, Michael stopped in front of an elegant hotel facing the river. "We're here," he sang out.

"Homewood Inn and Suites. Part of the Hilton chain," she said, squinting at the sign. "Have you lost your mind? What kind of bite will this take from our expense allowance?"

"A tad over a hundred a night per room, including breakfast, but the location can't be beat. The city shuttle stops right in front for sightseeing. They have a gym, a heated pool, and a kitchen in every suite." Michael neglected to mention how large the *tad* was in this instance.

Beth lowered her sunglasses with one finger. "You do remember the part where Nate said we're on a case, right? Why do we need kitchens? Neither of us cooks, and I don't plan to learn anytime soon."

"Let's give it a chance. If you hate it, we can look at others." Michael pulled into a parking spot.

Beth climbed out, stretched, and let her gaze soar upward eight stories. "I'm willing to check out the rooftop, nothing more."

But after she saw the pool and lounging area with several fire pits, along with a view of half the city, Beth was hooked.

"What do you think, Miss Kirby?" Michael asked on the elevator ride down.

"Not a bad place to hang our hats. Let's see if they have any rooms left."

"They do. I put a hold on two this morning." Michael didn't dare meet her eye.

"My, aren't you the confident one. At least we're in the heart of downtown. Do you suppose Mrs. Doyle lives in one of those fancy mansions we passed? I love the wrought iron fences and flagstone courtyards, but could you imagine the upkeep on those places? My dad complains about cutting the grass once a week. Here, every inch of the yard is a manicured flower garden."

Michael waited until they reached the lobby to continue. "Most people probably have gardeners. About Mrs. Doyle…"

Beth's chin snapped up. "What about her? Are we fired already? She hasn't even met us yet!"

"Mrs. Doyle will see us at two o'clock, so we have lots of time. Turns out, however, that she lives on Tybee Island, not in the city."

"Then why are we *here*? Let's find something cheap on the beach. Neither of us needs a kitchen."

"This is where the action is, Beth. The lifeblood of the city. Something cheap on the beach is what you do with girlfriends."

They glared at each other for several moments before she relented. "All right. We can do that for a couple of nights. But if the location proves inconvenient, *I'll* find us something else. Remember, this is a partnership." Beth glanced at her watch. "You go check us in. I'm taking the newspaper up to the rooftop. After twelve hours in a car yesterday, I need some time alone."

Michael didn't argue. In fact, he understood perfectly. Hadn't his ex-fiancée often told him he was too demanding, too invasive? And toward the end, too much like gum stuck to her shoe? He had no desire to repeat the mistakes of his past. Instead, he waited in his room and then texted Beth when it was time to meet him at the car.

When she joined him, Beth didn't inquire about her suitcase or mention that she wanted to change clothes. He, on the other hand, had changed shirts three times.

"Won't you be hot in that sport coat?" she asked, climbing into his car.

"Maybe, but I wanted to make a good impression. Aren't you curious about your suitcase?"

"I figured you stuck it in my room. I always carry a toothbrush and toothpaste in my purse. Those and my hand sanitizer are all I need. Well, except for my Glock."

"You're *packing* to visit a sixty-year-old woman?" Michael turned on the car's GPS, already programmed with the address.

"Nope. It's still locked in the trunk. But why leave a weapon at home if you're licensed to carry?"

"Our assignment involves surveillance, not tracking down a dangerous fugitive," he murmured.

"A private investigator never knows what the case will entail. I believe in being prepared. In your case, however, leaving your gun at home was a prudent choice."

Because that's exactly where his weapon was, Michael let the comment pass and admired the scenery for the sixteen-mile drive along Highway 80.

Beth's wish to visit the beach was soon granted. Mrs. Doyle lived in a gated community that backed up to the glorious Atlantic Ocean. Michael stopped at the security booth at her enclave's entrance. "Michael Preston and Elizabeth Kirby," he said to the guard. "We're here to see Mrs. Evelyn Doyle."

After a few taps on his tablet, the guard pressed a button. "Go right in, sir, miss. Mrs. Doyle lives at the end of Oleander Lane on the left. She's expecting you."

Michael watched the man touch the brim of his hat in the rearview mirror. "Wow, a real live guard instead of a keypad on a metal post. Real estate just notched past the million-dollar mark."

Beth issued a sound similar to a snort. "Paying all that money for the privilege of living by water? How nice could the view be?"

"We're about to find out." Michael turned onto a wide drive leading to a house with an amazing amount of glass, considering how close it sat to the ocean. Unlike the formal, walled gardens in Old Savannah, this landscape contained mainly palmetto palms, huge clumps of pampas grass, and some kind of flowering vine that climbed over anything stationary.

When they knocked, surprisingly a small, silver-haired woman answered the door. Judging by her clothes, she was not hired help. "Mr. Preston, Miss Kirby?" she asked. "I'm Evelyn Doyle. Thank you for being so prompt."

"It's our pleasure," Michael said as they entered a tiled foyer with a soaring ceiling but no furniture. Art adorned the walls, some in groupings, some that took up an entire wall.

"You have quite a collection of prints." Beth leaned close to one sweeping panorama of wind and sky. "Are these all from the same person?"

"These are *paintings*, Miss Kirby, not prints. The one you're admiring is an Edward Droege, done right here on Tybee Island. In the living room I have a Mary Cassatt and a John Singer Sargent if you're partial to American impressionists. I also have a Wassily Kandinsky and a Marc Chagall if the Expressionists are more your cup of tea."

"Show me all of them. Lead the way," said Beth. She gave Michael a wink when Mrs. Doyle turned her back.

Mrs. Doyle led them past a gourmet kitchen on the left and a dining room suitable for dinner parties of twenty on the right. In the two-story living room at the rear of the house, it wasn't the artwork that commanded their attention. The entire back wall was an expanse of glass, from ceiling down to the high-polished wood floor. The ultracontemporary house sat on a bluff a dozen feet higher than the dune line, with views of the seacoast stretching for miles in both directions, unimpeded by other homes. Offshore, shrimp boats bobbed in the waves while gulls and pelicans soared on air currents and dived into the surf for fish.

"Wow," Beth said. The single word, although inadequate, was rather appropriate. "Do you ever get tired of this view?"

Mrs. Doyle joined her side. "Not yet, and I've lived here thirty-two years."

"Aren't you worried about a storm breaking all this glass? God forbid," Beth added hastily.

"When my husband had the house remodeled, he insisted on adding roll-down hurricane shutters. You can't see them from inside, but with the touch of a button, the house turns into a fortress."

"Would you mind demonstrating?"

"Not at all." Mrs. Doyle walked to a brass panel in the corner of the room and pressed a button. As promised, shutters rolled into place, obliterating every view of sea and sky. As the room darkened, the sound of the surf died away.

"Amazing. This certainly isn't a house you would ever want to leave," said Beth.

"The *house* isn't what I'm worried about, Miss Kirby, if that's what you're implying. I don't want to see my marriage of forty years end." Mrs. Doyle's tone turned icy.

Beth opened her mouth to comment, but Michael interrupted. "I'm sure that's not what my partner meant. We both simply love your home. Now, so we don't tie up your entire afternoon, tell us how Price Investigations can help."

"All right. Have a seat, please." Mrs. Doyle pointed at chairs and then perched on the arm of the sofa. "As long as you guarantee complete discretion, I'll get right to the point. Privacy is of utmost importance. That's why I dismissed my maid for the day. And that's why I brought in out-of-town investigators."

"You have our word," Michael replied, while Beth nodded her agreement.

"I believe my husband is having an affair. I don't think it's been going on very long, but I want it to stop. Get me photographs of his indiscretion so there can be no denial, along with names, dates, times, and background information on this…woman." Mrs. Doyle looked from one to the other.

"That shouldn't be difficult, ma'am," said Beth.

"Good. I've written down my husband's pertinent information, such as the make, model, and license number of his car, along with the address of his downtown office, the country club, our church, and a few other places Lamar frequents." She pulled a sheet from a drawer under the coffee table, along with a photograph of the two of them. "If you have any questions, call me on my cell. Never leave a message on the home phone or with a member of my staff." Mrs. Doyle rose stiffly to her feet.

Beth took the paper to skim. "Thank you. This should be enough to get started."

"You can trust us to protect your privacy." Michael extended his hand, which the woman clasped briefly.

Beth dropped their business card on the coffee table. "If you need to get ahold of us, our cell numbers are there. We'll be in touch in a few days. And you can be assured of our absolute discretion."

"Thank you. If you would be so kind as to see yourselves out…" For the first time, Mrs. Doyle's composure slipped. She sounded close to tears.

On their way to the door, Beth stopped abruptly and turned around. "I'm really sorry about this. No wife should have to go through such an ordeal."

Mrs. Doyle, looking like a wren perched on the sofa, smiled. "Thank you, Miss Kirby. It's kind of you to recognize what a loss this is for me."

"Call us if you need anything. And regarding your art collection? I like that painting that was done locally best." Beth hooked her thumb toward the foyer. "That seascape gives a feeling of freedom, that once the storm passes, a brand-new world will be left in its wake."

Mrs. Doyle hesitated, as though considering the painting in question. "Very true, as long as a Category 5 hurricane doesn't take away everything you hold dear."

THREE

I got the distinct impression Mrs. Doyle was no longer talking about the house," said Beth once they reached the car.

Michael started the engine and then reached for the document Beth was holding. "What are you talking about?"

"The hurricane she referred to as we were leaving."

Michael glanced up from his perusal of Lamar Doyle's particulars. "Why not? She just showed us the heavy-duty shutters that appear at the first sign of a storm."

Beth shook her head. "Never mind. I keep forgetting men don't think like women."

"Isn't that a good thing? Otherwise, the world would be very dull. Now that you've met the client, do you still feel that we work for Sleaze Incorporated?"

"Not so much. Mrs. Doyle deserves a major chunk of whatever assets they've amassed."

"You sure changed your tune. Was it the artwork that softened your heart?"

"She was really nice. And it's not fair when older women are put out to pasture after giving their best years to their families."

Michael looked about to comment but changed his mind. "Are you ready to find the dirt on Mr. Slimeball? According to

Google, Doyle's office is in the historical section, not far from our hotel. Can I pick a location or what?"

"You're downright amazing, but after spending yesterday in the car, let's take the afternoon off. There's no hurry. If the boss gave us a full week, I've no intention of wrapping up the case and twiddling my thumbs. Or worse, rushing back to Natchez."

"What about Six Flags?" Michael opted for a juvenile inflection.

"I checked. The closest amusement park is Wild Adventures in Valdosta. I made you a promise, but if you start whining, there will be no cotton candy once we get there." Beth unfolded her two-sided tourist map. "Since we're already on Tybee Island, let's walk the beach. I want to feel sand between my toes."

Fifteen minutes later, they parked the car and left their shoes, Michael's sport coat, and Beth's indispensable leather tote in the trunk. With pant legs rolled up, they crossed over the dunes on the boardwalk and headed toward the water.

"Tide must be going out," Michael declared. "Check out the dry mark on the sand."

"Try to relax for a few hours, Professor. There will be no quiz tomorrow." Beth shielded her eyes from the reflection off the sand.

"Wasn't that house beautiful? If I lived there, I'd never leave that living room." Michael pulled his sunglasses from his pocket.

"All the rooms probably have great views. The master suite is probably in one of the wings, with the guest rooms in the other." Beth marched into the surf up to her knees. "I have never been in a house that spectacular. Our last client owned a bigger home, but it's just wealthy suburbia by comparison. Mrs. Doyle's house is architecturally unique, situated on the best spot on the island."

"Could you imagine growing up here instead of in backwater Mississippi?"

"Natchez is a charming town on the Mississippi Delta. If you want to see backwater, you need to travel a hundred miles inland."

"I stand corrected, but tell me the truth. Ever dream about

living in a place like this when you were a little girl...or maybe last week?"

She laughed. "You can't covet what you don't know exists. I grew up believing that having my own bedroom made me akin to the Rockefellers. Of course, the fact I have no sisters played a role in that lucky twist. What about you? Any aspirations of creating your personal Biltmore to pass down to your heirs?"

Michael dug his hands in his pockets and stared out to sea. "Now that you mention it, I would like to move up the economic and social ladder."

"Do you ever *not* talk like a college professor?"

He smiled, looking over the top of his sunglasses. "This is me dumbing down the rhetoric, Kirby. Try to keep up."

"Okay, didn't know. Go on." As Beth started walking, Michael kept pace at her side.

"When I thought Rachel and I would get married, I crunched the numbers for our combined incomes and researched the best neighborhoods with the best schools. I had everything figured out except which college our future offspring would attend."

"*What?* You would let a son or daughter go somewhere other than Ole Miss or Mississippi State?"

"There's a whole world out there. Since I'm still single, I plan to broaden my horizons. My parents are content where they live, but I'm not settling for their brand of mediocrity."

Oddly, Beth felt a frisson of loss. They hadn't been partners for long, yet now that they'd adjusted to each other, she hated the thought of him leaving. "Sounds like you're putting Price Investigations in your rearview mirror."

"Not necessarily. I'd like to take our agency up a notch. We shouldn't confine ourselves to small-potato cases like that missing college girl last month, who sneaked off to Nashville for a bachelorette party. Now this month we're spying on a philandering husband? You're right. We are Sleaze Incorporated."

"Are you forgetting we solved a murder and the largest scam to hit Mississippi churches in decades? That wasn't small potatoes." Beth kicked water in his direction.

"Not at all. It was a great case, but how many of those will there be? Personally, I don't want to become a cop, and you already tried that once. Of course, you could always apply in a different town. It's not like you killed somebody."

"Hey, confine your ambitions to your own career. I'm happy working for Nate."

"I am too, for now. But maybe I can help take his agency to the next level. Bigger clients would offer more lucrative cases. I don't think Nate and Isabelle would mind getting rich along with me."

"Do you ever listen to yourself, Preston? Stick in a pin and let out some hot air."

Michael threw his head back and laughed. "Okay, I might sound puffed up, but there's no treading water in the business world. You're either actively advancing in your chosen career, or you'll soon be replaced by someone with more ambition. Nobody works for the same company for fifty years, receives a gold watch, and then retires to Orlando anymore."

"Golly, I hope Nate doesn't find out this half day off was my idea. He'll start interviewing for my replacement."

"He won't hear because I won't tell him." Michael slapped her on the back. "Now let's get something to eat. According to your map, there's a seafood house in the next marina, and I'm starving."

Beth was happy to halt their upwardly mobile conversation. Truth was, she tried not to think much about the future. Since leaving the Natchez Police Department in disgrace, all she wanted to do was work at something she enjoyed. Right now, right here, she was happy. There was no point in putting too much stock in the future. *What good did all those happily-ever-after plans do Mrs. Doyle?*

Once they climbed up to the deck overlooking the marsh and found a table, Beth started to relax. "Order me a bowl of she-crab soup while I wash up." When she returned, a huge bucket of peel-and-eat shrimp with melted butter and cocktail sauce sat in the center of the table.

"We needed something fast," he said.

"You did mention you were hungry." She tucked a napkin into her shirt.

"What does your gut instinct tell you about Evelyn Doyle?" Michael asked after several minutes of devouring shrimp. "Do you believe she's only interested in preserving her marriage?"

Beth wiped her hands on a napkin. "Hard to say. She wouldn't exactly pour out plans to filet the guy financially to people she just met."

"But we're the private investigators she just hired."

"Even so, a woman her age would have pride and a sense of dignity—maybe women of any age would in that position." As the server delivered a steaming bowl of soup, Beth leaned over and inhaled deeply. "What choice does she have? If her husband is having an affair, I can't see him coming home and her forgetting all about it."

Michael stopped eating. "One mistake and the marriage is over? What if Mr. Doyle regrets his behavior and wants to give their relationship another try?"

She shook her head. "A *mistake* is overdrawing the checking account or forgetting someone's birthday. Both can be excused after plenty of groveling and a few expensive gifts."

"I hate it when I can't tell if you're joking."

Beth picked up her soup spoon. "That's part of my charm. Anyway, neither of us has been married, so we're talking through our hats. Tomorrow we'll stake out his office and find out what Doyle is up to. Maybe it's all a big misunderstanding. Let's finish up here and get back to the hotel. I want to hit the pool and sip something fruity by the fire pit. I plan to enjoy myself if I'll soon be replaced by someone more ambitious."

Michael smiled. But during the drive back to mainland Savannah, Beth caught him looking at her oddly. Each glance implied that despite weeks of partnership in which they'd gotten along fairly well, they were still essentially strangers.

～

Michael had waited as long as he could. "Are you finally awake?" he asked when Beth picked up on the sixth ring.

"I'm not only up, I'm showered and putting the finishing touches on my *toilette.*"

"What's your *toilette*—brushing teeth and applying Chapstick?"

"Why the hurry, Preston? Nobody fools around before noon, and it's not even nine o'clock."

"I can't wait to tell you what I found out. Meet me in the Lodge. I'll pick out breakfast today—nutrition in keeping with my training for the Ironman. The competition is less than two months away."

"I'll be down in ten minutes. Make sure there's coffee." Beth ended the call and then appeared twenty minutes later.

Because her wavy red hair was still damp down her back, Michael was fairly certain he had woken her up. In a long print skirt, cotton top, and high-heeled sandals, Beth looked dressed for a garden party. "Why the fancy outfit?" he asked. "We're staking out Doyle's office, not infiltrating a ladies' bridge club."

Beth reached for the coffee and filled her cup. "These clothes are cool and comfortable. Should I choose to apply for a job or request an insurance quote, I'm ready. Is *this* our entire breakfast?"

"Yogurt and hard-boiled egg for protein, whole-wheat bread

for carbs, and, of course, fresh fruit. Everything we need to start the day."

Beth nibbled a piece of dry toast. "Impress me with what you've already done this morning."

"Twenty minutes in the gym, followed by a two-mile run to learn the best route to Mr. Doyle's office, and a quick shower. While waiting, I learned that he works at Town and Country Insurance Agency, the largest agency in the state of Georgia. They insure thousands of clients for billions of dollars."

"Well done, early bird." Beth spooned up some blueberry yogurt.

"Mr. Doyle works there as an employee."

She met his gaze. "He doesn't own the agency?"

"Exactly. How does your run-of-the-mill agent afford a house on Tybee Island? Mrs. Doyle didn't appear to work for a living."

"Maybe they got money the old-fashioned way—they inherited it. Why didn't we think of that?" Beth smacked her forehead with her palm.

"Maybe, but why wouldn't he buy an agency?" Michael finished his fruit and pushed away the bowl.

"Look, I know you're a great forensic accountant, but forget about the money trail for now. We need to figure out if Mrs. Doyle has competition or not. Stay focused." Beth scraped the inside of the container.

"I'm way ahead of you. During my run, I found the employee parking lot. It's small with less than a dozen spaces. Hopefully, Doyle has earned one of those premier spots." Michael snapped a lid on his to-go mug. "I'm ready when you are."

"Can't I finish my gourmet cuisine? Like I said, not much happens in the marital infidelity world before lunch. I hope you have lots of reading material."

Michael was glad he let Beth finish breakfast, because as usual she was right. After he determined Doyle was inside the building on the ninth floor, he kept his eye on the late-model Lexus from inside his cramped car for three hours. Beth, on the other hand, read a paperback and sipped Snapple across the street from the front entrance. Her park bench under a shady live oak was definitely a cooler vantage point. Just about the time he needed to find a men's room, Beth texted him a message: "Mr. Doyle just left the building on foot, heading east. I'm going to follow him."

Michael hopped out of the car and rounded the building. A restroom break could wait. This would be his first surveillance on foot, and he didn't want to miss it. One thing he knew for sure—Lamar Doyle couldn't outrun him. He easily caught up to Beth midway down the block. Dressed in her summery outfit, she looked like an office worker on her way to lunch.

"He's twenty feet ahead in a charcoal suit," she said.

"Are you sure that's him?" Michael fell in step beside her. "That man's hair is grayer than in the photo."

She barely glanced up as they passed two elderly women. "It's him. Mrs. Doyle said the photo was taken at their twenty-fifth anniversary. They've been married almost forty years. And slow down. We don't want to run the guy over."

"Savannah residents walk even slower than people in Natchez." Michael skirted around a young mother pushing a stroller.

"Perhaps their plans for the future don't include major coronaries at fifty."

"Mine either. That's why I exercise and eat right."

"You sound like an infomercial." Beth grabbed his arm as Mr. Doyle turned into a Cool Beans coffee shop on East Congress Street. "Good, we can recaffeinate. Now stop staring at him." She gave his arm a pinch.

"Get in line. I'm heading to the restroom."

When Michael returned, Beth was on her way to a table with two large lattes and two pecan rolls. Doyle sat in a booth reading the *Savannah Morning News*. A croissant sandwich sat untouched in front of him.

"Thanks for the coffee," Michael whispered.

Beth leaned forward and bobbed her head toward their target. "While you were indisposed, Doyle held up the line by making small talk with the Cappuccino Girl." She fluttered her eyelashes. "I thought his smile was going to crack his face in half."

Michael assessed the woman at the milk steamer. "You can't be serious. She's half his age. Besides, every guy flirts with pretty girls while standing in line. It's just a way to pass the time."

"I don't think so. Doyle called her by name, twice."

Michael studied the front counter. "All the employees wear name tags. Since Mr. Doyle's office is five minutes away, he's probably here often. You of all people should understand. Aren't you a regular at that chicken and biscuit joint?"

"Let's wait and see. So far he hasn't touched the sandwich he bought. He might be waiting for someone."

Michael picked off the pecan topping. "It could be a client. What middle-aged man would rendezvous at Cool Beans?"

"Lamar Doyle, that's who." Beth's gaze flickered over his shoulder.

Helpless to stop himself, Michael turned and stared until she dug her nails into his hand. The pretty cappuccino creator had sat down in the same booth as Doyle. With a sandwich identical to his, she was having lunch with him. "Okay, they apparently know each other, but that doesn't mean they're romantic. She could be the daughter of his best friend."

Beth rolled her eyes. "Could you get us more napkins? I sense a big mess about to happen."

Michael hopped up with his pecan roll and headed to the service bar. From his new vantage point, he could watch the pair unnoticed. Not that it made much difference. Neither Doyle nor the employee was paying attention to their surroundings. As

Michael studied the calorie count of baked goods, the pair shared a meal. There were no stolen kisses or holding hands under the table, but the woman kept touching Doyle—a pat on his arm, a brush of their fingertips. His gaze on the woman didn't seem like fatherly affection for a family friend. Feeling uneasy, Michael threw his roll in the trash on his way back to the table.

"Isn't that sweet? Doyle eats lunch here so she doesn't spend her break time alone." Beth made a noise similar to a growl.

"Did you catch her name?" he asked. For a moment, he forgot he was a professional investigator and not a garden-variety voyeur.

"Bonnie. Doubtlessly, she dots the *i* with a tiny heart. I took several photos with my phone when they weren't looking. Actually, I could have stood on the table clicking off shots like celebrity paparazzi and they wouldn't have noticed." Beth balled up her sticky wrapper. "For part two of today's surveillance, I say we split into shifts. Why don't you follow him back to the office to make sure he doesn't duck out early? You can continue researching the scoundrel on your laptop."

Because Beth had more experience and seniority, Michael didn't mind taking orders. "Fine. What will you do?"

"I'm going to walk back to the hotel and hit the pool. I have a sudden urge to wash slime off my skin. I'll take over later whenever you're ready." She pushed up to her feet. "Text me if anything good happens."

Michael watched her leave the coffee shop as though an infectious disease hung in the air. Maybe ghosts from her past refused to stay buried. Or maybe she was just being practical. As she had said in Natchez, this piece-of-cake assignment didn't need two PIs.

Soon Bonnie returned to her post at the milk steamer, while Doyle strolled back to his office with a definite spring in his step. By Michael's watch, he'd been gone only forty-five minutes.

While their person of interest cold-called clients or crunched the numbers for annuities, Michael googled him from the comfort of his car. The only photographs he found of the man online were with Evelyn. Doyle served on the boards of a barrier island preservation society and the Savannah Historical Society. He was a member of several civic organizations, the All Saints Episcopal Church, and the island's country club. He graduated from Duke with a degree in business management and a minor in economics. The guy was no dummy, unless you considered how he managed his midlife crisis. He had never been arrested, declared bankruptcy, or been named in a civil suit. Other than one speeding ticket four years ago, he was an exemplary citizen.

When the confines of the Dodge Charger grew claustrophobic, Michael stepped out to stretch and almost missed Doyle exiting the building. He had changed clothes since lunch. When Doyle drove out of the parking lot in a big hurry, Michael had no difficulty keeping up. Old Town traffic snarled to a stop at every intersection. Fortunately, Doyle's destination was on the far side of Forsyth Park in a neighborhood called the Victorian District, according to a brass plaque. Instead of carved stone and fancy brickwork, these homes were rambling, pastel structures trimmed in white with gingerbread curlicues.

When traffic again slowed to a crawl, he punched in Beth's number. "Where are you?" he asked. "Doyle is on the move, and not in the direction of Tybee Island."

"I'm at the hotel, ready to go, but you have our only set of wheels. I knew we should have brought two cars."

"Yours wouldn't have made the trip. After he reaches his destination, should I come pick you up?"

Beth huffed. "Don't be ridiculous. He could go somewhere else in the meantime. Tell me where you are, and I'll take a taxi. The sooner we get the goods on him, the sooner you ride the roller coasters. Is he alone?"

Michael narrowly missed a parked car as he pulled into the

valet line at an expensive-looking bistro. "Not anymore. He just left his car with the valet at a restaurant at the opposite end of the historic district. Guess who was waiting at the front door."

"Little Miss Latte? Was she still wearing her cute smock?"

Michael didn't need much time to assess Bonnie's attire. There was very little of it—high heels and a short dress in teal green. "Nope. My granny would describe her outfit as 'dressed for trouble.' Not that I'm the Savannah fashion police."

"Stay focused, Preston. Text me the address and keep them in your sights. I'll be there as soon as I redo my makeup and change clothes three more times. I will *not* be outdone by Latte Girl."

After she ended the call, Michael laughed at the mental image. Not that his partner wasn't attractive, but Beth's beauty was down-home and down-to-earth, more jeans and T-shirt than high fashion or Victoria's Secret. Despite her deplorable diet, she was trim and fit thanks to strenuous workouts. Unlike him, Beth had always been athletic, whereas he had only recently joined the fitness ranks after being glued to his computer for years.

Unfortunately, the valet took his sweet time relieving him of his car, so when Michael entered the restaurant, Lamar and Bonnie were nowhere in sight. He dodged the maître d' with a polite "I believe my party has already been seated" and wandered through the crowd. Several older men with young women, none of them familiar, sat at dimly lit tables. In a panic, Michael walked to the bar area where people of all ages milled, waiting for tables.

"Excuse me," he said to the bartender. "I'm meeting someone. Is there another bar besides this?"

"Try the rooftop. She might be up there." The bartender pointed toward the stairs.

Michael sucked in a deep breath. Bolting up the steps in a place this posh would only draw attention. Even a novice like him knew that wouldn't be a good idea. He asked the maître d' to watch for his companion, Miss Kirby, and headed upstairs. On

the roof, couches were clustered around low tables for private conversations under the stars.

Spotting his prey near the railing, Michael slipped into a seat
at the bar where he could spy from a safe distance.

"What are you having, sir?"

Oddly, the question took him by surprise. "Do you have a special house drink?" he asked, seldom one to imbibe.

"Do you like grapefruit juice?" the bartender asked.

After he nodded, the man mixed up a frosty beverage that
Michael had yet to taste when Beth arrived twenty minutes later.

"Pretty swanky place," she said, climbing onto a stool. "I'm
glad you left word at the front desk. It annoys me when I can't
find my *date*."

"No problem. I've been looking forward to seeing you all day."
Michael looped his arm around the back of her chair.

"Where are they? And what's this?" Beth picked up his drink
and sniffed.

"They are at eleven o'clock over your left shoulder. And that's
called a Crowd Pleaser. I haven't tried it yet."

Beth turned slowly on the stool until she spotted Lamar and
Bonnie. "Looks like if the rest of the patrons disappeared, they
would be none the wiser." She sipped Michael's drink through the
straw. "My, that's refreshing."

"It also has alcohol in it, so go easy."

Beth set down the glass and pulled out a digital camera. "I did
a little research too. Bonnie's last name is Mulroney, and she has
only worked at Cool Beans for six months. Her previous work
history is spotty—mainly fast-food joints. How can she support
herself in Savannah unless she relies heavily on the generosity of
rich men?" Beth dropped her voice to a whisper as the bartender
wandered to their end.

Michael sat so he could watch the pair but discovered he didn't
enjoy this part of the job. Having been played a fool by a woman,

he found that seeing Doyle step out on Evelyn left him sick to his stomach.

Beth picked up the camera and sashayed over to the railing. "Come over here, honey, and see the view." Her drawl was thick and exaggerated.

Michael joined her side. "Take a picture from every angle," he encouraged.

Beth clicked off several shots of ordinary trees and houses as they worked their way toward the couple. "Isn't Savannah just the perfect spot for a honeymoon?" She grabbed hold of his arm. "Stop staring at them," she hissed in his ear.

Michael knew Beth was right, but he couldn't believe how brazen Doyle acted in public. How did he know one of his friends wouldn't be dining here? Or did people in love lose all common sense? "Let's get one of the two of us," he suggested once they were in position.

"I can't wait to send these to Mom." Beth snaked her arm around his waist and snapped off several selfies. Except that the angle of her camera caught the couple behind them instead.

Michael felt discombobulated by the close proximity of his partner, but the moment soon passed. Doyle rose to his feet, dropped money on the table, and headed down the stairs with his arm tightly around Bonnie.

"Notice Doyle used cash so there would be no paper trail," Beth whispered on their way back to the bar.

Michael took out a twenty to pay for his grapefruit cocktail and followed the lovebirds downstairs. "I should have put our name in for a table." But since he hadn't, while Doyle and Bonnie enjoyed gourmet cuisine, he and Beth dined on scrimpy appetizers with copious amounts of iced tea.

Two hours later, Doyle stood and pulled more cash from his wallet. "They're finally done," said Michael. "I'll head to the valet desk for the car while you pay our tab. Keep your eye on them."

"Don't worry about me." Beth popped the last blue cheese–stuffed olive in her mouth. A few minutes later, after she joined her partner in his car, she wasn't smiling. "Do you have any idea how much our *dinner* cost?"

"Relax. It was a legitimate business expense. Here comes Doyle's car now. Look at those two—not even remotely subtle."

"I hope this evening ends soon. No offense, but I've seen enough of your car's interior to last a lifetime." Beth readjusted the seat.

"None taken." Michael followed the Lexus, keeping another car between them at all times. "Looks like you're about to get your wish."

Doyle drove down a residential street, still within the historic section, and parked in front of a huge three-story mansion that had been converted into apartments. Bonnie hopped out and waited on the sidewalk with open arms.

Beth withdrew a second camera with a telephoto lens from her bag just as Doyle locked both arms around Bonnie's waist. "Yuck," Beth muttered, snapping one photo after another of the two kissing. "I feel slimy just watching them."

"You're not kidding." Michael checked the time and jotted down the address as they entered the building. "As much as I'd love to head back to the hotel, we need to document how long he's inside."

"Wake me when this is over." Beth slouched down in the bucket seat and closed her eyes. Within ten minutes, Michael heard her soft snore, indicating she'd fallen asleep despite the vehicle's confinement.

Michael wouldn't have been able to sleep if his life depended on it. As darkness settled in around them, his mind raced with ideas as to what they should do next. Considering his previous missteps, he wanted to shine on this case.

Ninety minutes later, Doyle bolted out the front door. He

jumped into his car and drove down Habersham well above the speed limit. Michael waited to wake Beth until the philanderer turned onto President Street and headed toward the Islands Expressway.

"He's on his way to Tybee." He nudged her awake with his elbow.

Beth straightened in the seat and rubbed her neck. "Good. Let's go back to the Homewood. I need a serious desliming before hitting the sack."

"Should we call Mrs. Doyle?" Michael spoke without thinking.

"Are you crazy? We're paid to gather information. What the client chooses to do with it isn't our business."

So much for impressing her with how far I've come.

FOUR

*B*eth rubbed the back of her neck where a kink had formed. "Can you believe that guy? Headed merrily on his way home, to his exclusive neighborhood, no less." She gulped down half a bottle of water. "What do you suppose he'll tell the missus—that he had to work late at the office? Or maybe he had to entertain clients at the fancy little bistro? That way, on the off chance a mutual friend spotted him at dinner, he'll have a ready alibi."

"I thought we were paid to gather information and not form opinions. You're sending mixed signals to the new trainee."

Beth blew out her breath. "I'm entitled to an opinion, the same as you. We're just not allowed to voice them to the client. If you had a brain, you'd know that. And we're certainly not allowed to influence behavior, which is what we'd be doing if we called Mrs. Doyle in the middle of the night to say, 'Check your husband's collar for lipstick,' or 'That perfume you smell isn't from the car's air freshener.'"

Michael braked to turn onto River Street. "If we're simply expressing opinions, you seem to have changed yours in a hurry, Kirby."

She pressed a palm against her forehead where a headache

had taken hold. "Maybe, but seeing that guy in action turned my stomach. So brazen, so arrogant. He has it made with a society wife on the island where he's a pillar of the community. Mrs. Doyle is well educated, well connected, and not bad looking. She probably saves sea turtles in her spare time. We know she supports the arts. Then her husband keeps a size 2 blonde in town in a loft apartment for when policy riders and sales meetings become too dull. The best of both worlds."

Michael pulled into the last spot in the lot. "His behavior seems to have hit a nerve."

Beth turned in the seat. "It would hit a nerve with any self-respecting female. I can't believe Miss Mulroney thinks so little of herself that she'd barter herself for free rent and two-hundred-dollar dinners."

Michael held up a hand. "Okay, but right now we don't know that Mr. Doyle pays for Miss Mulroney's apartment. You're making assumptions—something you taught me not to do." He pressed the button to lower the windows. The breeze off the river was humid, with a slight smell of diesel from the freighters that passed twenty-four hours a day.

"You know what, Mikey? This workday is officially over. Before I throttle you with my bare hands, I'm going to my room and locking the door. Don't call me in the morning, and don't get me any quinoa with dried pea pods for breakfast. I'll call *you* once I'm ready for day four in paradise." Beth opened the door and swung her legs out of the car.

"Wait, Beth. I didn't mean to get under your skin. I was just making conversation."

"I'm too tired for polite conversation." She climbed out of the low car, slammed the door, and leaned in through the window. "Nate promised this trip would be a reward for a job well done on the last case. So far it's been more like three days in a Navajo sweat lodge."

Michael appeared to be fighting back a smile. "Get some rest. You'll feel better and the world will look different tomorrow."

Beth marched toward the entrance without waiting for him. She'd had enough of Pollyanna for one day.

The next morning, after fifty sit-ups in her room, forty laps in the pool, and a long, hot shower, Beth did indeed feel better. When she spotted her partner in the breakfast room, she felt guilty from her scalp to her toes. She strolled over with her tail between her legs and sat down.

Michael was sipping coffee and reading the newspaper. "Good morning, Miss Kirby," he said without glancing up.

"Good morning. I'm sorry for the things I said last night." She sighed as she filled her mug with coffee.

"Which part exactly? When you accused me of having no brain or when you threatened to choke me to death?"

She cringed. "All of the above, and please don't tell Nate about the threat. I'm already on thin ice with him."

Michael finally met her eye. "The list of what not to tell the boss keeps growing. However, you could have thrown me under the bus tons of times and didn't, so my lips are sealed." He pointed toward the buffet. "Let's pick out our breakfast. Unfortunately, quinoa and pea pods aren't available or I would already be gulping them down."

"Seriously, I was out of line and I apologize. You have the best brain in Mississippi."

"We have a low population state." Michael's face softened, not that his features were ever unyielding. "But I accept your apology, so let's move on."

"No, we should talk about this. I had an epiphany last night when I couldn't sleep."

"You slept just fine in my car. I heard you snoring." He arched an eyebrow at her as they made their way to the buffet. "Tell me about your epiphany."

"You were right. Watching Lamar in action affected me. I thought Mrs. Doyle hired us to pave the way to a substantial divorce settlement. Now I think she's entitled to every dime her creepy husband has."

"This might not be about money, Beth," he said on the way back to the table. He'd taken his usual fruit, egg, and yogurt, while she chose cinnamon oatmeal with a slice of ham—sort of halfway between healthy and a heart attack on a plate.

"Maybe not, but I don't like him pulling the wool over her eyes."

He nodded in agreement. "What's on our agenda for today?"

"Since you're a forensic accountant, find out the particulars on the apartment on Bull Street. I'll dig up the dirt on Bonnie at the coffee shop. Usually coworkers love to gossip if given half a chance."

"I'm one step ahead of you. My sleepless hours are from five through seven." Michael finished his hard-boiled egg in three bites. "Lamar Doyle does indeed pay for that apartment. It's not owned by Town and Country Insurance. He probably writes it off as a business expense from an account his wife isn't aware of."

"That explains Bonnie's ability to pay the rent from a coffee shop paycheck." Beth stirred sugar into her chicory-flavored coffee. "Make copies of everything for Mrs. Doyle. They'll come in handy should she want to take the guy to the cleaners. Track down any secret bank accounts. Doyle might be paying all Bonnie's bills or have additional women on the side. Who knows how deep his pockets are?"

Michael frowned. "You do realize hacking into bank accounts is illegal—"

"Stay within the gray areas of the law. We have Mrs. Doyle's signed permission to delve into their private affairs. Finances of a married couple would fall into that category. Stay away from any accounts connected to his employer. The file we're compiling will be for civil or domestic court, not criminal. There won't be any defense attorney eager to toss out evidence on a whim." Beth took a spoonful of oatmeal. "I'm no expert on divorce, but my guess is the Doyles will want to settle out of court and stay out of the newspapers. The more ammunition Mrs. Doyle has, the better off she'll be in negotiations."

"Wow, for a woman who doesn't like hunting, you sound like you're gunning for a bear."

"I've finally found a varmint worthy of bringing out my gun collection for. We have a two o'clock meeting with our client at her home. I've already printed out eight-by-tens of those photos from last night. With what you discover today, we should have an impressive file to present. She can either keep us on retainer to maintain surveillance or simply call her lawyer to begin proceedings." Beth plucked a strawberry from his bowl as she popped to her feet. "I'm on my way to talk to Bonnie's fellow baristas."

Michael pulled her down by the arm. "Sit. You're not going anywhere until you eat your oatmeal. Consider it your penance for last night. I won't have you skipping healthy food and pigging out on donuts later."

"Yes, Dad," Beth said as the server checked their carafe. The woman glanced from one to the other curiously.

Michael smiled—a sure sign that she was forgiven. For the life of her, Beth couldn't understand how she could be cross with him. Maybe she didn't deserve a partner so nice.

~~

After finishing breakfast at a time of day when most people were thinking about lunch, Beth changed into her most youthful outfit. She wanted to look as if she needed a job without having the savvy to dress properly for an interview. In capris, a tank top, and a silky cardigan, she marched down to the coffee shop in high-heeled sandals. She could have driven, but Michael's flashy car stood out from the pack, which wouldn't help on future stakeouts.

Beth plastered on a vapid expression and stood in line for a caramel apple latte with extra whipped cream. Fortuitously, Miss Loose Morals was nowhere in sight. Two young women manned the espresso machines, while an older woman took orders and accepted payment. "Excuse me, ma'am," Beth drawled while paying for her coffee with cash. "Y'all accepting applications here?" She tried to look as earnest as possible.

"Yes, we're always hiring. But the manager's not in today." The woman pulled a single sheet from under the counter. "Please fill this out completely, either here or at home. Leave it at the register, and then Mrs. Fletcher will give you a call." The woman offered a patient smile.

"Thanks. Could I borrow one of your pens?"

"Here, but make sure I get it back." Her smile slipped a notch.

Beth took the pen, the application, and her latte to a table in the center of the room. From there she could study everyone who entered and exited. More importantly, she knew exactly when one of the young employees went on break. When the girl manning the pastry counter slouched into a booth with a cold drink and sandwich, Beth scribbled in a few lines on the application and sauntered toward her.

"Hi. Mind if I ask you a few questions?" She held up the application with a sheepish grin.

"Have a seat." Crystal Callahan, according to her name tag, pointed at the other bench.

"Thanks. I only filled out one of these in my life, and it's been three years since my last job." Beth slurped her latte. "Do ya think they'll wonder 'bout that?"

Crystal shrugged. "The boss might ask what you've been doing."

"I was living in Florida. My boyfriend made oodles of money. My work motto is 'If I don't need to, I don't want to.'"

The girl lifted her soft drink in salute. "I'll drink to that. What happened to your boyfriend?"

"I'd rather not say, but I did leave Jacksonville in a big hurry." Beth dropped her voice to a whisper.

"Well, this is a great place to meet a new guy. Better than the mall or the gym or a bar. Look around. Lots of great-looking men stop in every day." Crystal leaned forward as though to impart an important secret. "I'd forget about the young ones if I were you. Set your sights on mature men."

Beth looked confused. "Why would I want some old guy?"

"Who do you think has all the money? Not some young lawyer just out of college. He's up to his eyeballs in student loans."

"Yeah, but a lawyer has a great future."

"Depends on what you're looking for. I don't want to sit around for five years to see if he'll propose." Crystal shrugged a second time. "Someone I know is doing it right. She latched onto some old guy from Tybee. You can't believe the apartment he put her up in, and he gave her a credit card for whatever she needs. She has the weekends for her friends since he's with his wife."

"He's *married*?" Beth didn't need to feign a scandalized expression.

"Well…yes." Crystal sounded only mildly abashed. "That way she has enough time for what she wants to do." She took a bite of her sandwich. "If she gets pregnant, she would get child support checks for the next eighteen years. Her job here would just be mad money."

Beth stood, her stomach churning with disgust. "I'd better let you finish your lunch."

"Fill out that application and call Mrs. Fletcher. You're not bad looking. This could be a stepping-stone to something big." Crystal winked one overly made-up eye.

Beth mumbled her thanks and walked out the door, tossing the rest of her latte in the trash. She couldn't wait to get away from her *mentor* and back to the hotel. Was this a new career goal for some young women—latching onto a rich baby daddy? Revulsion turned the caramel apple concoction into something that felt more like battery acid.

FIVE

Shortly after one o'clock, Michael picked up Beth in front of the hotel. With the file safely tucked in his briefcase, he was eager for this particular meeting to be over. Facing their client with evidence that her husband had been unfaithful couldn't possibly go well. *What if Mrs. Doyle starts crying? What would be proper decorum?* He couldn't picture his mother or grandmother in such a predicament. He decided to let Beth take the lead during any emotional episodes.

"Ready to go, partner?" he asked as she climbed into the passenger seat. She had changed into a long skirt and sleeveless blouse.

"As much as I ever will be. What did you find out?"

"I found Lamar Doyle's secret checking account. He keeps less than ten grand in it and uses it to pay for the apartment, its utilities, and a credit card with Bonnie Mulroney as an authorized user. American Express sends the bill to his office."

"Yeah, I heard that Bonnie has a slush fund for clothes, shoes, and pedicures." Beth pulled a sour face.

Michael glanced sideways at her. "Somebody at the coffee shop actually talked to you?"

"Why not? After all, I'm a prospective employee trying to get the lay of the land at my new job."

"You applied at Cool Beans? Don't use me as a reference. I'd have to mention your combative attitude late at night." He couldn't stop chuckling.

"I picked up an application and talked to Cappuccino Girl, Crystal, on her lunch break. But after hearing her blueprint for financial advancement, I won't be interviewing anytime soon." Beth peered out the side window. "Crystal thinks Bonnie should get pregnant so she can have a reliable *income* for the next eighteen years from child support. Sleaze Incorporated just sank to a new low."

"Oh no. I didn't expect Bonnie to be madly in love with Doyle, but the woman is motivated solely by money? This is worse than we thought." Michael turned onto the Islands Expressway.

"Honestly, I'm ashamed of the low morals of certain members of my gender."

"I'm sure they are not indicative of most women in Savannah."

She glanced in his direction. "We can only hope. But now I must include Bonnie's potential aspirations as part of our evidence for Mrs. Doyle. Do you have the file ready?"

He nodded. "We have pictures of them at the coffee shop, during drinks on the rooftop, the candlelit dinner, and the kiss on the doorstep. I made copies of his lease agreement and proof that he has another checking account, although I'm not happy about that."

"He's a married man with a lifetime of joint finances with his wife. Who's to say the account didn't turn up in a normal search of their social security numbers? Everyone knows there is no longer any privacy online."

"I also have copies of the utility bills and the American Express card for the last several months. We can rest assured Mrs. Doyle doesn't buy her clothes at Abercrombie and Fitch or Forever 21, and her music from iTunes. Nor does she wear perfume called Pink Sugar."

Beth wrinkled her nose. "This better be enough proof for our client. I truly don't want to climb a tree with a telephoto lens to take candid shots of those two. I'm a nice girl from a good Christian family."

"What would you do? Tell Nate we quit and we're on our way home? All part of the job, partner."

"Let's hope it doesn't come to that." Beth leaned her head back and closed her eyes.

Not knowing what else to say, Michael turned on the radio to mitigate the tension in the air. When they pulled into Mrs. Doyle's driveway, he and Beth walked to the front door as though ready to face an executioner.

A maid answered their knock, but Mrs. Doyle stood three feet behind her. "Hello, Mr. Preston, Miss Kirby. Come in, please."

"Good afternoon, ma'am. Is Mr. Doyle home?" Michael peered left and right.

"No, Lamar left town on business. I was about to have a cup of tea. Will you join me?"

"Sure," they both answered.

"We can talk privately in the living room." As the uniformed maid hurried to the kitchen, Mrs. Doyle led them to the art-filled room.

"We have prepared a report with the information you requested." Michael laid the manila folder on the coffee table.

Mrs. Doyle's pleasant smile vanished as she eyed the file. "Please tell me what you discovered before I look at any photographs."

"Why don't you get us started, Michael?" Beth asked when he looked her way.

He cleared his throat. "I'm sorry to have to tell you, ma'am, that Mr. Doyle has a second residence in Savannah, close to Forsyth Park. It's a condo or loft apartment in a converted mansion with rather expensive rent."

A slight flare of the nostrils was Mrs. Doyle's only reaction.

"A Miss Bonnie Mulroney lives at this address. Is that name familiar to you, ma'am?"

"I assure you, it is not. Continue, Mr. Preston."

"Expenses for this residence are paid from a checking account separate from your joint account. I have copies of Mr. Doyle's deposits and withdrawals for the past six months. Correspondence regarding this apartment is sent to his office, but your husband's name is on the lease, not Town and Country Insurance."

"Ah, here is our tea." Mrs. Doyle interrupted his narrative as the maid carried in a tray. After the girl disappeared down the hall, Mrs. Doyle busied herself with the tea ritual. *Cream? Sugar? Lemon?* "Please continue, Mr. Preston," she said, once everyone had their beverage.

"Mr. Doyle apparently met this young woman at a coffee shop near his office. The woman works thirty hours a week there. We observed them having lunch yesterday while Miss Mulroney was on her break."

"At the Cool Beans near Reynolds Square in broad daylight?" she asked.

"Yes, but there was nothing untoward in their behavior at lunch. They could have been family friends who'd accidentally run into each other."

Evelyn clutched her cup with both hands as she sipped her tea.

"Mr. Doyle returned to his office for the rest of the afternoon. When he left his office around five thirty, we followed him. He drove to a restaurant at the other end of Bull Street." Michael stole a glance at Beth, who didn't seem inclined to pick up the ball, so he continued. "Miss Mulroney was waiting at the restaurant when he arrived. They had drinks on the rooftop and then had dinner in the main dining room. Our photographs will show their relationship is not what you'd expect between casual friends, but at least their table was against the back wall with no diners on either side."

Mrs. Doyle turned very pale. "Are you talking about the bistro, Local Eleven Ten?" she asked, her tone icy.

"Yes, ma'am."

"Lamar took this…strumpet to a restaurant where our friends or his business associates could easily have been?"

Michael had never heard anyone use the word "strumpet" before. He'd only seen it in a book during a British literature class in college. "Yes, I'm sorry to say."

"Hopefully, your friends don't go there on Tuesdays," Beth interjected.

Mrs. Doyle looked at Beth as though she were a bug on the wall. "Continue, Mr. Preston."

"Dinner lasted more than two hours, after which Mr. Doyle drove Bonnie back to the apartment. We have photos of a passionate embrace on the front stoop."

With a shaking hand, Mrs. Doyle set her cup in its saucer. "Then Lamar must have headed home. I thought I heard him come in last night, but I'd fallen asleep in my chair watching something inane on TV."

"That's the only kind of shows they have anymore," Beth added.

Michael had been waiting for Beth to jump in and help. *And that's all she has to say?* She was staring at a Jackson Pollock painting as though the spatters held the secrets of the universe.

"No, ma'am," he said. "Mr. Doyle entered Miss Mulroney's apartment, where he remained for ninety minutes. Then he exited in a hurry. Miss Kirby and I followed him until he was on the Islands Expressway. We have no knowledge of what happened once he reached Tybee Island." Michael clamped his lips shut, knowing he sounded like a courtroom prosecutor.

Mrs. Doyle focused on the floor. When she lifted her chin, her eyes were moist and glassy. The woman seemed to have aged ten years in the last few minutes.

"Do you need a break, ma'am?" Beth asked. "Maybe we could go out on your deck for some fresh air."

"No, thank you. I'm fine," she said, straightening in her chair. "I hired you to do a job, and you've performed it quite efficiently. Perhaps a small part of me still believed this was all my imagination."

"That's certainly a normal reaction to a situation like this," Beth murmured.

"You've compiled a file for me?" Mrs. Doyle picked up the folder from the table and withdrew papers from it one at a time. She examined the hidden bank account printouts, utility statements, and rental agreement. When she perused the credit card statement, her expression changed from sorrow to sheer confusion. "What is this?"

Michael scooted forward on the couch. "Your husband gave Miss Mulroney an American Express card. She appears to spend quite a bit of money at Express, Claire's, and The Limited at the Oglethorpe Mall on Abercorn, plus she patronizes a few boutiques and nail salons on River Street."

"Express and The Limited? Why would she shop there when a Belk and Macy's are available in the same mall? Is she buying for other people? Let me see a picture of this woman." Mrs. Doyle spread the papers and photos across the table and then picked up a candid shot of the *strumpet* at the milk steamer. Bonnie wore her ruffled smock, a felt beret, and a stunning smile.

Their client broke into a fit of laughter.

Michael was flummoxed, while Beth arched her back like a cat. "All employees are required to wear that uniform, no matter what their age," she said.

"I'm not laughing at her attire. Goodness, I wore a cardboard crown while flipping burgers during high school, and a poodle skirt with roller skates to deliver milk shakes in college." She smiled patiently at Beth. "I'm amused by the *age* of my competition. What is she…twenty-one?"

"Twenty-four, according to her driver's license," Michael interjected.

Mrs. Doyle's focus remained on Beth. "I was afraid she would be someone in her thirties or early forties—a viable candidate to replace me. This"—she tapped a finger on Bonnie's image—"is nothing more than a midlife crisis, a passing fancy. Lamar would never divorce me and take *Bubbles* to our country club's Christmas party."

Michael looked at his partner. Beth seemed equally stunned by the client's change in attitude.

"Don't misunderstand me. This affair upsets me a great deal. I'm a Christian who takes the sacrament of marriage very seriously, and I thought my husband felt the same. But some men have feet of clay when they reach a certain age. This flirtation will pass for Lamar. Hopefully, he'll come to his senses and with counseling our marriage will be stronger than ever."

"You're going to let him off the hook? Just like that?" asked Beth shrilly. "Most women in your position would take these pictures to an attorney and file for divorce."

"Divorce the only man I've ever loved after one transgression? That would be an impulsive reaction from wounded pride. Have you ever been married, Miss Kirby?"

"No, but if I ever do walk down the aisle, it'll be for better or for worse until death do us part, with special emphasis on the 'forsaking all others' part." Beth crossed her arms.

"That's what I thought too, and basically I still do. I'm not condoning infidelity, but Lamar has never strayed before. People make mistakes in life. They say and do things they shouldn't. Are you saying we shouldn't forgive?"

"Only those who are repentant deserve forgiveness." Beth

pulled out the photo of Lamar and Bonnie locked in a passionate embrace. "Your husband doesn't look sorry to me."

Mrs. Doyle's composure faltered. "He may not be. In which case, my hopes for the future will come crashing down. But I'm willing to wait and see. God knows what's best for all parties concerned." With supreme dignity, she rose to her feet. "Thank you both for a job well done. I have what I need to confront Lamar. According to the dates on the credit card statements, this midlife crisis has gone on long enough. It's time for him to make a decision."

Michael tapped the papers into a neat pile. "You're welcome, ma'am. We'll be in town for a few days to do some sightseeing. Should you need the agency's help in any way, please don't hesitate to call. We're at your disposal twenty-four-seven."

Beth jumped up and followed him from the room. When they reached the front door, she pivoted on her heel. "I apologize, Mrs. Doyle, for what I said before. You do what's best for your family. I'm hardly an expert on love and marriage."

"Thank you, Miss Kirby. I know beneath that suit of armor beats a heart of gold. Your turn will come someday." She waved from the doorway as Beth beat a hasty retreat down the steps.

Michael waited until they reached the car to comment. "Can you believe her reaction? I sure didn't see that coming. And why didn't you help me explain what we found out? Discussing a private matter with an older lady embarrassed the heck out of me."

"Like you told me earlier—this is part of our job. Besides, you were doing so well, I simply let you continue. I'm the one who insulted the woman for having forgiveness in her heart. Talk about putting faith into action. Honestly, Michael, I was impressed with how you handled yourself."

"No kidding?"

"No kidding. You certainly didn't act uncomfortable." Beth shook her head.

"Hopefully, Mr. Doyle will come to his senses and get a second chance. Marriage is for better or for worse—I guess this is the 'for worse' part."

"Of course you would say that. You're a man."

"And I've heard you're a woman with a heart of gold beneath your steely exterior." Michael hooted. "Where did *that* come from?"

"Mrs. Doyle might not be a good judge of character, on any level. Now take me back to the hotel. I can't wait to jump in the pool and do my laps. Plus, it's taco night at the hotel."

Michael switched off the AC and rolled down the windows. The sea air might help him figure out two confusing women. Somehow he'd just impressed his partner during the most uncomfortable fifteen minutes of his life.

SIX

*F*ew other things annoyed Beth Kirby as much as being awakened in the middle of the night by the phone. Pleasant dreams didn't happen very often. She usually dreamed about drug-addled thugs chasing her down the street with butcher knives. Invariably, she would blunder into wet concrete, quicksand, or off the end of a cliff. Glancing at the clock, Beth burrowed her head under the pillow. *Almost four o'clock… Who would call at such an hour?* Throwing back the covers, she reached for her phone. "Hello?"

"Miss Kirby?" asked a scratchy voice. "This is Evelyn Doyle. I'm so sorry to wake you, but you said I could call anytime…"

Beth sat up, regaining full awareness. "Yes, ma'am. What can I do for you?"

There was a hesitation of several moments. "Is there any way you could come over?" she whispered. "I'm terrified and didn't know who to call."

Beth rubbed the top of her head, trying to clear the cobwebs. "What are you afraid of, Mrs. Doyle? Isn't your husband home yet?"

"He's not, but I didn't expect him to be. The agency has a three-day sales conference in Augusta."

Several possibilities ran through Beth's head. *Is she afraid to be alone?* Surely this wasn't the first time her husband had left on business. *Is she afraid to confront her husband with evidence of his infidelity?* Any courage bolstering could wait until tomorrow. "Please tell me what you're afraid of."

"Someone is trying to kill me," she whispered hoarsely.

Beth jumped out of bed and began to pace. "Is your security system turned on? Where's your maid?"

"My maid goes home every evening. My system is armed, both doors and windows, but electronics won't stop a bullet, will they? Someone shot at me when I was down at the beach."

"Did you call Tybee police or the Chatham County Sheriff's Department?"

"No. I-I don't want to make a report. What if I'm mistaken? The local police will think I'm a crazy woman. Could you please come over?"

"Of course. I'm on my way. In the meantime, lower those hurricane blinds and keep the phone handy. If you hear any more shots, call the police."

"Thank you, Miss Kirby. I'm grateful you would do this for me."

"No problem. Make sure the security guard at the gate knows I'm coming." Beth ended the call, pulled on some clothes, and retrieved her Glock from the wall safe. On her way to the elevator, she remembered she had no vehicle. She tried calling her partner without success. Michael finally answered his door the third time she knocked.

"What are you doing here, Kirby? Is the hotel on fire?" He checked the hallway in both directions.

"Sorry to bother you, but I need your car keys. I'm going out to Tybee Island."

He leaned his shoulder against the door frame. "You want to talk to Mrs. Doyle now?"

"She's in a panic. She thinks someone took a shot at her down at the beach." Beth stepped past him into the room and found his keys exactly where she thought they would be—with his wallet and phone on the nightstand. "It's probably nothing. Maybe just a car backfiring on the street. Go back to sleep. We'll talk in the morning." She headed for the door.

Michael blocked her path with a far bulkier frame than when he started with Price Investigations. "If you're going, I am too. Give me five minutes to get dressed."

Beth released an exasperated sigh. "This doesn't take two people. It's probably just nerves after the horrible news she received. The woman is scared, which is perfectly understandable."

"Did you forget you're supposed to be *training* me?"

"A partnership doesn't mean we're joined at the hip," she said. "Mrs. Doyle is facing a lonely future after spending forty years with someone she loves. You're a guy. You'd be no help."

"You don't *know* that it's nothing. I can check the yard and down by the dunes while you and the client discuss how creepy men are."

She tried to argue, but Michael pulled open the door. "Wait for me in the car, Kirby. If you leave without me, I'll report the Charger stolen. You can enjoy a *second* night in jail until the misunderstanding gets straightened out." He motioned her out with a flick of his hand.

Beth stomped down the hallway. As irritated as she was about not getting her way, she also felt a smidgen of pride. Michael's moxie proved his PI training was just about finished.

On the drive to the island, he made her repeat the conversation with Mrs. Doyle verbatim. Then he hypothesized possible explanations, from a drive-by shooting or a passing speedboat with engine trouble to teenagers setting off firecrackers.

"So you don't think her life is in danger?"

Michael glanced at her. "Who knows? I'm just making conversation until we can check out the evidence."

"What's wrong with the radio or simple peace and quiet?"

"I'm not good with quiet. I'm afraid people will think I'm dull and boring."

"Trust me. That should be the least of your worries."

Once they reached Mrs. Doyle, they both took her assertion seriously. The woman was weak with terror. While Michael went to get a glass of water, Beth helped her to a chair. "Tell us exactly what happened," she instructed.

"After you left, I drank a glass of wine to celebrate. I was so happy that Bonnie wasn't a woman Lamar would take seriously. Then I read for a while and went to bed. When I couldn't fall asleep, I went down to the beach. I have steps over the dunes to the water. Sometimes a long walk calms my nerves."

"Is it prudent to walk alone in the middle of the night?" Michael asked.

Mrs. Doyle sipped her water. "Everyone does it, and I've never been afraid. We have little crime on Tybee. But I hadn't gone very far when I heard a loud popping sound from the direction of the street. I looked back toward the house but saw nothing. Then I heard a second *crack* and felt something buzz past my head." She lifted a shaking hand to her ear. "I'm not stupid. Someone shot at me, twice."

"Did it sound like a rifle or a handgun?" Michael asked.

The woman blinked. "How on earth would I know that? I told you I didn't see anyone. I switched on the security lights with my remote control. I keep them off so they don't bother nesting turtles. The lights illuminated me but not whoever had the gun." Her voice trailed off as she ran out of breath.

"Take it easy, Mrs. Doyle." Beth placed a hand on her shoulder. "Tell us what happened next."

"I turned off the lights and dropped to the sand, hoping the dunes would block the view. I couldn't outrun a sand flea, so I just lay there, waiting for them to…to…shoot me at close range." She closed her eyes for a moment to gather herself. "I crouched on the wet sand for ten or fifteen minutes until my back started to spasm. I was in so much pain I didn't care if someone shot me. All the way back, I expected someone to finish me off, but nothing happened. When I got inside the house, I called you." She looked up at Beth.

"I'm glad you did, but your first call should've been to the police."

Mrs. Doyle shook her head stubbornly. "You're both investigators. Let's not involve the authorities until we have to."

Beth exchanged a look with her partner. "Michael, why don't you look around outside while I stay with Mrs. Doyle?"

"Good idea." Michael pulled out an LED flashlight. "Please turn off the security system, ma'am, and lift the hurricane shutters. I want to see how much of the home's interior is visible from the beach."

As soon as he went out, Beth got down to the heart of the matter. "Other than the current situation with Miss Mulroney, are you in a contentious relationship with anyone else? Maybe one of your neighbors on the island?"

"I'm not sure what it's like where you live, Miss Kirby, but people on Tybee don't shoot each other over loud music or grass getting too long." There wasn't a hint of amusement in Mrs. Doyle's statement.

Beth thought about a neighborhood brawl last summer over a dog barking too much, but at least only fists had been used and not guns. "That's a good point. What about your husband? Does he have any enemies at work that you are aware of?"

"Lamar is an insurance salesman for a well-respected firm, not an underworld mobster." She pulled a prescription bottle from the drawer and swallowed a pill with her last sip of water.

"Can you think of anyone who might harbor a grudge?"

"Honestly, Miss Kirby, I've thought about nothing else since it happened. I was hoping you would have some ideas."

Do you mean other than your fickle husband or his sleazy girl-friend? She said, "May I trouble you for a cup of coffee? Instant would be fine."

"I could microwave some from lunch." Mrs. Doyle pushed to her feet.

"That would be perfect."

As soon as she left, Beth checked the prescription bottle in the drawer. *Xanax.* Most likely uncertainty over the future was wreaking havoc on Mrs. Doyle's nerves. But even a single glass of wine could cause problems if someone was on sedatives. Beth slid the drawer shut and considered her options. Their client was paying their firm a lot of money. She was owed kindness in return, even if that meant sitting with her until another friend or one of her children could be located. The world would look like a different place in the morning. Michael could either stay or go back to the hotel and retrieve her later.

"Here's your coffee, dear. Plus I started a fresh pot in case Mr. Preston would like some."

"Speaking of Mr. Preston, there's something we need to discuss while he's still outside. I questioned one of Miss Mulroney's coworkers at the coffee shop and found out a scheme she could be plotting."

Evelyn lowered herself to the couch. "What kind of scheme?"

"She might be trying to get pregnant, hoping to snag support for her and her child. This is a new form of blackmail among unethical young women."

For the second time, Mrs. Doyle's reaction wasn't what Beth expected. She snorted derisively. "If that little hussy thinks she'll soak Lamar for big support checks, she has another thing coming."

"The courts will always put the needs of an innocent child first, no matter the mother's motivation." Beth shifted uncomfortably.

"As they should, but if that's Miss Mulroney's plan, it won't work. Lamar had a vasectomy years ago right after our son was born and the doctor advised me not to have more children. All we need to do is demand a DNA test so the child's true parent can bear the financial burden." Mrs. Doyle's expression hardened.

"All right then. One thing we don't have to worry about. Now we just have to determine the nature of the mysterious popping sound."

"It might not be your intention, but please stop patronizing me, Miss Kirby. I *know* what gunfire sounds like."

Beth was ready to assert that even she could confuse the backfire of a car with a shot from a gun, but at that moment her partner walked into the living room with a grim expression. "What did you find?" she asked.

"There's a spot in the yard where someone could have been hiding. Several stalks of pampas grass are trampled, and there are indentations in the mulch. Unfortunately, mulch doesn't retain shoe imprints like soft soil." Michael looked from her to the client.

Beth shrugged. "Neighborhood kids could've been playing hide-and-seek. We have no way of knowing it happened last night."

Evelyn shook her head. "My landscaper was here yesterday morning. He always weeds and rakes the landscaped beds. Besides, there are no young children running through the yards like hooligans. Tybee has several community playgrounds."

Unlike the neighborhood where I grew up. Beth lifted her gaze to Michael, her senses on red alert.

"There's more," he said. "Several feet away, I found a shell casing under a shrub. I forgot to bring gloves and an evidence bag, so I left it where it was." He turned a bright shade of pink.

"You shouldn't touch it even if wearing gloves. We're not law enforcement." Beth stood and set her empty cup on the table. "Speaking of whom, that's who we need to call."

"Absolutely not," Mrs. Doyle snapped. "I want Price Investigations to do their job, not the police. Why do you think I called you?"

"You called because you were scared and rightly so. But if Michael found evidence that someone is trying to kill you, we would be remiss—"

"Stop arguing with me. If you call the police, I'll tell them I made up the whole story. Then you can explain to Mr. Price why you were fired."

Speechless, Beth and Michael stared at each other. "What exactly do you want us to do?" she asked.

"Figure out who shot at me. Since I haven't annoyed anyone at Pilates or the garden club, it must have been that floozy. Find proof so that when I confront my husband, he'll be shocked out of his midlife stupor." Mrs. Doyle swayed unsteadily on her feet.

"All right, as long as you agree to leave the house for a few days. Even with the hurricane shutters closed, you shouldn't stay here alone."

"Where would I go?"

"To stay with one of your friends or maybe to your son's house."

Mrs. Doyle considered for less than a second. "There's not a single friend I could share this with. And as much as I would love to talk to my son again, Jamie was killed in Afghanistan a dozen years ago."

"We're so sorry, Mrs. Doyle," Michael interjected. "You have our deepest sympathy."

"Thank you, young man." Mrs. Doyle turned toward Beth. "But I will go to a hotel on the mainland."

"You'll leave today before nightfall? And you'll call me later with the location?" Beth asked.

"I promise." Mrs. Doyle forced a smile.

"Keep in mind, we're agreeing to investigate. You may still have to file a police report down the road. It depends on what we find out."

"I understand. Would either of you like fresh coffee?"

Michael started to accept, but Beth shook her head. "That's very kind, ma'am, but we should get to work. Lock everything up and turn on your security system again. We'll be in touch." She started for the door with Michael following at her heels.

"Try not to worry. We'll get 'em, Mrs. Doyle," he added, sounding like Wyatt Earp at the O.K. Corral.

Once outside, Beth rounded the house to the backyard. "Take out your flashlight. We'll need photos in case it rains and obliterates our crime scene."

But instead, Michael stopped and pointed at the water. "Wow, Beth. Look at that."

She halted midstride. "Now we know why people want to live at the beach."

The sun's corona, just below the waterline, streaked the sky with every shade of orange, pink, and purple. Soon the coast of Georgia would be flooded with blinding light, but for the next few minutes, dawn took their breath away.

"And why property values are so high," Michael whispered in reverential awe. "Could you imagine waking up to that every morning?"

"What's the big deal? I have a perfect view over the neighbor's fence of a race car up on cinder blocks." Not taking her eyes off the sky, Beth sat down on a bench. "We might as well wait for full light to take pictures."

"Will we take the shell casing with us?"

"That would be tampering with evidence." Beth offered her nastiest scowl. "The casing stays where it is."

"What if the gardener comes back or a chipmunk carts it off?"

Beth shrugged. "A chance we'll have to take. Now, who do *you* think tried to kill our client?"

"That's easy." Michael plopped down beside her. "The husband, of course. If Mrs. Doyle was out of the picture, he wouldn't lose half his net worth in a divorce settlement. Dollars to donuts, Doyle probably has an insurance policy on her as well."

Inhaling deeply, Beth filled her lungs with the salty sea air. "My money's on the strumpet. If Bonnie takes out the wife, Mr. Doyle would be free to marry her."

"Are we both talking about the same one-hundred-pound girl who makes lattes *in a beret*? No way would Bonnie drive out here to shoot somebody."

"So only large people wearing ball caps are killers?" Beth couldn't suppress a grin.

"You know what I mean. Consider the statistics in most homicides. They weigh heavily in favor of those you know over strangers."

Beth glanced sideways at him. "Here I thought you were the hopeless romantic. Anyway, the strumpet would qualify as a 'known' perpetrator."

"I might be a romantic, but this marriage has run aground. Big money makes people do terrible things."

"Okay, you check out Mr. Doyle's alibi. If he is in Augusta on business, someone there will vouch for him. I'll take a hard look at Miss Mulroney. Maybe one of her neighbors will talk to me if she plays her music too loud or doesn't clean out the lint filter in the dryer. I need to know how low her moral bar is set."

They silently watched until the sun broke free of the horizon. Then Beth jumped to her feet. "Show me where someone was hiding."

For a few minutes, she methodically photographed the crushed section of plant along with the shell casing from several angles, careful not to leave behind any hair or fibers. Squatting down, Beth pulled on latex gloves and lifted the shell high enough to determine the caliber. "Chalk up one for my suspect—the bullet came from a thirty-eight. That's a chick gun if I ever knew one." She carefully replaced the casing and got to her feet. "Let's get back to Savannah. We have our work cut out for us."

SEVEN

*M*ichael thought long and hard about everything he learned on Tybee, and everything his partner had said. On the one hand, Beth was right about him being a hopeless romantic. Once he fell in love with the right person, he planned to stay married for the rest of his life. "Till death do you part," and all that stuff. On the other hand, if a man dropped so low that he took up with a woman young enough to be his daughter, who knew what evil he was capable of?

What he couldn't understand was Mrs. Doyle's optimism for the future. She believed that given time and counseling, their marriage could be saved. *Nothing but a speed bump in the road of marriage.* Could she be that optimistic married to a man capable of murder? *How well do people in love really know each other?* Remembering his former fiancée, Rachel, and her amazing abilities at subterfuge curdled the protein shake he just drank.

Instead of trying to figure out human nature, Michael took a long, hot shower and put on a suit. An hour later he walked into the offices of Town and Country Insurance. "Good morning, I'm Michael Preston. I have an appointment with Mr. Doyle."

The receptionist, whose nameplate identified her as Violet

Frost, blinked her large brown eyes. "An appointment with Mr. Doyle? There must be some mistake."

"No mistake. I have an eleven o'clock with Lamar Doyle." He smiled politely and glanced at his gold watch, a gift from his grandmother. "We set this up last week to write new policies on my home, car, and boat."

The girl's expression turned anxious as she tapped her computer screen. "I'm truly sorry, Mr. Preston, but we'll have to reschedule."

Michael shot his cuffs with mild impatience. "Why would you have to do that? If Mr. Doyle is with someone else or running late, I'd be happy to wait." He gestured toward a comfortable-looking couch. "I can catch up on my email."

"That's very nice of you, sir, but Mr. Doyle isn't here. All of the agents in his department are in Augusta for a three-day seminar. He won't be back until tomorrow."

Michael straightened and opened his day planner on his phone. "This is quite bizarre. I remember he mentioned something about a conference, but he had changed his mind about attending."

Violet giggled like a child. "Oh no. Mr. Doyle would never skip these meetings. They're mandatory for every underagent on the team."

"What's an underagent?" Michael rubbed his chin.

Violet glanced around before whispering conspiratorially. "Agents whose sales figures and new client acquisitions don't allow them in the President's Gold Club. I'm sure Mr. Doyle will make it next year."

"Just the same, could you call the conference and verify? I hate to drive all the way back to Garden City when he could be on his way here now." He gave her a look that didn't encourage negotiation.

Violet glanced to the left where a burly man—presumably her

boss—was bent over a computer in his office. "Of course, sir. I would be happy to."

Michael leaned across her desk. "Find out if Mr. Doyle has been there the whole time. I want all the facts before I pursue this further."

Violet talked in low tones to a female on the other end. After a three- or four-question repartee, she hung up and offered a bright smile. "That was Mr. Reynard's assistant, Sarah."

"Who's Mr. Reynard?" asked Michael.

"He is Mr. Doyle's sales manager. Rachel confirmed that Mr. Doyle is there now and arrived yesterday. The seminar will conclude tomorrow around noon, and then the agents can come home."

"Thank you, Miss Frost."

"Shall we reschedule your appointment now?"

Michael tucked his phone into his pocket. "No, I don't think so. Why would I want to do business with a company that treats customers so poorly?"

"I'm sure it was just an oversight. Mr. Doyle is very nice and would never behave rudely. All of the other agents and assistants love him."

Spotting an opportunity, Michael pretended to mull the matter over. "I'll tell you what. We'll say no more about this for now. In fact, don't even tell Mr. Doyle that I stopped in. I'll wait for him to follow up with me. It was probably an innocent mistake."

"That's a great idea. Thanks, Mr. Preston. Again, I apologize for your inconvenience." Her phone rang, giving him a chance to exit gracefully.

Across the street in one of Savannah's famous squares, Michael sat on a stone wall and tried to figure out Lamar Doyle. His wife appeared to be in love with him. The office assistant liked him enough to shield his blunders from the boss. Apparently, he wasn't the one lurking in his flower bed, cracking off a few rounds when

Evelyn took her midnight stroll. Yet plenty didn't add up. How could Lamar afford a beach house when he sure wasn't on the fast track at Town and Country Insurance? If the money was Evelyn's, would she be so doggedly loyal?

With a sigh, Michael pushed off the wall and headed back to the hotel. He might be making strides with his PI training, but his comprehension of people—women in particular—couldn't fill a thimble.

～

Beth regretted not heading straight to the coffee shop when Michael left for Town and Country Insurance. But after a 4:00 a.m. wake-up call, laps in the pool followed by a hot shower sounded like heaven. Unfortunately, when she strolled through the door of Cool Beans, Miss Mulroney was nowhere in sight. Fortunately, her new career mentor was wiping tables with a linen cloth and a bottle of cleaner.

"Hi, Crystal. Remember me?" Beth offered a friendly smile.

Crystal cracked her gum. "Sure. You finish that application yet? If you don't get a move on, they'll hire somebody else."

"I'm having trouble coming up with three references. All I can think of is my mom."

"You think anybody ever checks those? Just pick two names out of the phone book."

"Good idea. I'll finish that application tomorrow or maybe on Saturday. Hey, is Bonnie workin' today?" Beth lowered her voice to a conspiratorial tone.

"She was here for the morning rush but left about an hour ago. How do you know her?"

"I'm tryin' to get to know all of you, in case I get a job here. Bonnie was real nice to me when I stopped in one day." Beth shuffled her feet.

Crystal tucked her rag into her belt. "She'll be in tomorrow at noon, but in the meantime, let me give you some advice. Don't worry about making friends. Go home and finish that application. Then call Mrs. Fletcher and ask for an interview. Once you get hired, you'll find we all stick up for each other." She offered a maternal pat on the arm.

"Thanks a lot," said Beth. She couldn't get out of there fast enough. At least her partner had walked to Doyle's office, leaving the car for her to use. If she had to walk to Bonnie's, it would have served her right.

Once at the Bull Street apartment, Beth determined in less than five minutes that Bonnie wasn't there either. No one answered the buzzer at the unit Lamar Doyle had leased. And when she gained access to the building, no one responded to her incessant knocks on the door. *Zero for two*, she thought.

Just as Beth concluded this would be a fruitless trip across town, she spotted someone in the back garden. "Excuse me, ma'am. Do you have time to answer a few questions?"

A woman clipping spent blooms from the roses peered up. "I'm capable of doing two things at once. Are you with the renters' association, the historical society, or the police?" Her drawl was slow and richly textured, almost melodic. Not at all how people sounded in Natchez.

"None of the above. I'm a private investigator, hired to check into one of the residents who lives here." Beth flashed her ID.

The woman dropped her clippers into the basket, her interest piqued. "Which resident would that be?"

"Miss Bonnie Mulroney in apartment 306."

Her expression left little question as to her opinion of Bonnie. "I'm not surprised someone is looking into that one's background."

"Could you be more specific?" Beth pushed her sunglasses to the top of her head.

"Look around. This is a nice neighborhood. People go to work, maybe out to dinner, and occasionally have a few friends over. Let's just say that girl only has late-night *gentlemen callers*."

Gentlemen callers? What century is this? "Are you saying Miss Mulroney might be a professional escort?" asked Beth.

"That's your job to determine." The woman picked up the clippers and savagely attacked a low-hanging bougainvillea branch. "But if that's what you conclude, you'll need to inform the association. That sort of behavior doesn't fly here."

"Would you say Miss Mulroney has a variety of…callers?" Beth pulled out her little notebook.

The rose clipper paused to reflect. "Two, I suppose. One is an older gentleman—well dressed, late fifties or early sixties. He drives a new BMW, or maybe it's a Lexus. I don't know cars very well."

Beth tamped down her irritation. People who didn't mind their own business were her pet peeve, but without busybodies, her job would be a lot harder. She pulled a snapshot from her tote bag. "Is this him?"

The woman took only a cursory glance. "Looks like him, but I don't make a habit of memorizing her visitors."

"What about the other frequent guest? Could you describe him?"

She huffed. "I wouldn't let that one through my front door. He's twenty-five, maybe thirty, long hair, scruffy beard." She rubbed the end of her chin.

"Do you mean a goatee?" Beth asked.

"I suppose so. And his clothes are always dirty."

Beth jotted prodigious notes. "What color hair does this thirty-year-old have?"

"I haven't a clue. He wears a ball cap. A dirty ball cap."

"Does he visit as often as the older gentleman? Maybe late at night?"

"Oh no. He's only been here two or three times, usually in the afternoon."

"Getting back to Miss Mulroney. Was she home last night?"

"No, I didn't hear a peep from her unit, and her car was gone all night. She drives a Honda in a horrible shade of yellow," she added helpfully.

Beth stopped writing and stared. *Either this woman is a stalker or someone Nate needs to hire.* "How would you be sure, Mrs...."

"Mrs. James. I live in 305, across the hall from Miss Mulroney, although I didn't know her name until today. My assigned parking spot is next to hers, and I can see both cars from my window. We've had trouble with teenagers stealing things from unlocked cars."

"Can you remember anything else?"

The neighbor pulled off her gloves to rub her neck. "Once when that creepy man came to visit, he parked his truck in front of the building. And when he left, mud dropped from the undercarriage all over the street. Ugh. Why would that girl spend time with him when the other man drives a Lexus?"

"There's no accounting for taste. Thank you, Mrs. James." Beth threw her notebook in her bag and started toward the gate.

"You won't repeat anything I said, will you? I wouldn't want to run into Scraggly Beard late at night."

Beth turned to face her. "I won't as long as our visit remains a secret as well."

Mrs. James gave a thumbs-up and whacked at dead flowers with new vigor. Beth returned to her car to resume her vigil, unsatisfied with what she'd learned. Was Mr. Scraggly Beard another paramour? If not, who was he, and where was Bonnie last night?

Four hours later, after Beth finished her novel and the newspaper, she fell asleep behind the wheel. A tap on the glass jarred her back to reality. She lowered the window to her partner's smiling face.

"What kind of surveillance is this?" asked Michael. He carried a large sack around to the passenger side and climbed in. "You were out like a light."

"I must have dozed off for five minutes. What's in the bag?"

"Dinner. Now stop destroying the ozone layer." He switched off the AC and rolled down the windows.

"How did you get here when I have your car?" Beth asked as she regained her full faculties.

"I took a bus. Where's Bonnie?" Michael pulled two chef salads from the bag.

Beth checked the assigned parking spot. No bright yellow Honda. "Still hasn't come home after her shift this morning, but I did have an interesting chat with her neighbor across the hall. Bonnie has two male visitors—Mr. Doyle and some creepy thirty-year-old with dirty hair. According to the busybody, Bonnie was gone all last night, which makes her a possible for the shooting on Tybee. How did you do?"

"Lamar is an impossible. He was in Augusta on business and will stay until tomorrow afternoon." He doused his salad with fat-free dressing. "When I got back from his office, I checked the databases for crime on Tybee. Mrs. Doyle was right—there's very little. No recent rash of break-ins, no serial killer stalking the dunes, shooting at late-night joggers. Local police write a lot of speeding and parking tickets and make a few underage-drinking arrests. That's about it. Aren't you going to eat?" He pointed at her untouched salad.

"I will back at the hotel. We might as well hang it up. I'm bushed and need to get out of this car." With a sigh, she started the ignition.

Michael turned it off. "Walk one block east and catch the bus to the riverfront. Go, Beth. I can watch for our chief suspect."

Beth offered an apologetic expression. "Don't take this wrong, but I want to be the one to question Mulroney. Since we're both females, I might make more headway with her."

He shrugged. "No offense taken. I'll sit for a few more hours to see if she returns and if she's alone. It's been a long day. I'll talk to you tomorrow."

Beth started to exit the vehicle with her salad and then turned back to him. "Thanks for relieving me and bringing supper. You're the best partner I ever had."

"Even better than Jack Lejeune?" Michael asked, fighting back a smirk as she got out and closed the door.

The memory of her old partner at the Natchez PD tightened Beth's already sore muscles. "After working with him, I'm lucky I'm not doing twenty to life. I mean it, Michael. Thanks for showing up tonight."

"In that case, I have a little gift for you. Your own set of car keys." He passed them through the open window to her.

"Thanks. I'll protect these with my life." It was funny how one honest statement could revitalize a person. Beth had walked halfway to the hotel before she remembered to wait at a bus stop. A breeze had picked up, cooling her skin and clearing her mind. Working with a man who transitioned from a hopeless trainee to her best friend rather quickly had certainly put a new spin on life.

~

The next morning Beth slept in and then swam laps in the pool. No sense in rushing back to the apartment. With Doyle out of town, Bonnie might have gone home or to see a girlfriend. According to Crystal, Bonnie's shift started at noon. That would be soon enough to keep an eye on Cool Beans. She left Michael alone until almost time to leave because she didn't know how late he'd staked out Bonnie's.

"Good morning," she said when he picked up the phone. "Did Miss Mulroney get home safely?"

"If she did, it wasn't to Bull Street. She must have another place to crash other than the luxury accommodations paid for by Lamar Doyle. I stayed past two o'clock."

"My opinion of the gold digger just dropped a notch, if that's even possible." Beth grabbed an apple from the bowl in the lobby, not in the mood for anything heavy. "I'm on my way to the coffee shop, hoping she doesn't skip her shift. Is it okay if I take the car?"

"Sure. But first I need to talk and you need to listen. Give me another five minutes on the phone."

"I have all the time in the world. What did you find out?"

"A Beretta Pico compact is registered to Lamar Doyle of Oleander Drive, Tybee Island. A thirty-eight-caliber Beretta. Same caliber of bullet we found under the bush."

Beth lowered herself to an upholstered chair. "Plenty of guns are thirty-eights—"

"Think about it, Beth. The husband is out of town for a conference. Mrs. Doyle just received confirmation of her worst fears. She's frightened, but not of a mysterious assassin hiding in her bushes. She's afraid that her husband won't come to his senses and dump the mistress."

"You think Evelyn staged this? She's sixty years old and has probably never fired a gun in her life." As soon as Beth spoke, Mrs. Doyle's words trailed through her head like a radio jingle: "*I know what gunfire sounds like.*"

"It doesn't take much to pull a trigger," Michael said. "Don't you find it odd that she didn't call the police? That would have been my mother's first choice once she reached the house. And when we offered to call them, Mrs. Doyle threw a fit. She said she would *make up a story* to keep from filing a report. That's pretty squirrelly in my book."

"Mine too, I'm afraid." Beth whistled through her teeth.

"She probably knows where her husband keeps the gun. She fired off a few shots into the water late at night when nobody was around. Then she called us. I just can't figure out what she aims to accomplish."

Beth ran a hand through her hair. "Attention. If Lamar hears about a possible attempt on his wife's life, he might take a hard look at the Latte Queen. This could be the kick in the pants he needs."

"Wow, women can be devious," Michael muttered. "Are we going to change our case report?"

"Desperate times call for desperate measures. And our report stands as is. We have no proof she staged the attempt. It's just a theory. Let's not forget who's paying a hefty fee for our services."

"What's our next step if we're no longer looking for a masked assassin?"

Beth smiled into the phone. *Nothing like enthusiasm for one's job.* "You let me relax last night. This morning is all yours. Why not try something crazy like eating a donut or watching TV? I still plan to see Miss Mulroney for a girl-to-girl chat."

"Why? We supplied the client with the proof she wanted. Mr. Doyle will be home after the conference. Isn't it up to them to work out their marital problems?"

Beth considered how much to tell, but keeping things from her partner hadn't worked well in the past. "It's time for Bonnie Mulroney to go away. Lamar doesn't need to choose between two women. I plan to convince the girl to consider community college or vocational training for a better future, and to give up manipulating married men."

Michael was speechless for a moment. "Didn't you tell me that our job was to remain objective and not influence the outcome? I could've sworn that was you, Kirby."

She rolled her eyes. "Okay, I'm about to break one of my rules.

But I want to improve Mrs. Doyle's chances, so Miss Mulroney and I need to come to an understanding. Just trust me on this."

"Just make sure your firearm stays locked in the safe."

Beth laughed as she ended the call, but her good mood was short in duration. Because she couldn't bear to face Mrs. Fletcher without a completed application or the gum-popping Crystal at the register, Beth had to sit across the street and watch Bonnie with binoculars for three and a half hours. The girl dutifully made cappuccinos and lattes wearing a smile along with her beret. Just as Beth started to jog in place to keep the blood flowing, she spotted Bonnie exiting a side entrance.

Apparently, some employees used an alley two storefronts away for a break room since smoking wasn't permitted anywhere near the shop's entrance. Bonnie lit up a cigarette just as Beth approached.

"Hi, Bonnie. Mind if I ask you a few questions?"

"You the chick getting friendly before she's even hired? Look, turn in the application and keep your fingers crossed. That's all I can tell you," the girl said dismissively as she exhaled a plume of smoke.

Beth snarled at a pimply-faced youth standing nearby. "Get lost. This is a private matter." The force behind her directive sent him quickly on his way. Then she moved until she was inches from Bonnie's face.

The girl didn't back down. "I take it you're not looking for advice."

"Nope, but I'll give you a little. Stay away from Lamar Doyle."

That caught Bonnie off guard, but annoyance quickly replaced her shock. "What business it that of yours? I *know* you're not his wife."

Beth feigned surprise. "Oh, so you *knew* that he's married? My mama has names for girls like you. How about if I whisper them in your ear?"

"How about if you just get lost?" This time Bonnie blew a plume of smoke into Beth's face.

Beth yanked the cigarette from her lips and tossed it toward the gutter. "Those will kill you if you're not careful."

"I'm calling the cops. You're harassing me!" Bonnie pulled out her phone.

"Go ahead. We'll sort this out at the station. Somebody took a shot at Lamar's wife early yesterday morning. And I'm the investigator hired to find out who it was, besides being Mrs. Doyle's close…personal…friend." Beth backed Bonnie up against the building.

"Leave me alone! I didn't shoot at anybody. I don't even own a gun." Bonnie pushed Beth's shoulders with both hands. Her behavior was brave, but a hitch in her voice gave her away.

"Sure, I'll leave you alone. Just as long as you leave Mr. Doyle alone. He's way too nice a guy for the likes of you. Oh, and by the way, your little plan of getting pregnant wouldn't have worked. So find another means of support. Why not go back to school? You're not too old." Beth headed for the street.

"I'm not planning on getting pregnant," she called when Beth was ten paces away. "Lamar loves me, and I'm going to be the new Mrs. Doyle."

Beth turned around as a dozen retorts crossed her mind. But seeing the girl's earnestness, she swallowed them down. "Take my advice and fall in love with someone your age. Life will be better for everyone." Beth stomped from the alley without a backward glance.

Funny how up until the end she had wanted to grab Bonnie's shoulders and shake vigorously. She hated the girl's low self-esteem and even lower ethical code. *But what does wanting to throttle someone say about my good Christian character?* It wasn't that she had no compassion for Bonnie, but one mistreated party per love triangle was enough.

Beth left the car where it was and spent the next two hours walking the city streets. Michael was right—the landscaped squares throughout the downtown area were gorgeous. What a lovely town. What a lovely day. With their case wrapping up— she hoped with a happily-ever-after ending—she looked forward to their mini-vacation.

When she returned to the hotel, Beth found Michael with his nose in a science fiction novel in one of the chaises on the roof. He tossed the book down when she approached.

"Where have you been? How long does it take to chat at Cool Beans with a twenty-four-year-old? I'm sure you two weren't catching up on old times."

"Sounds like you missed me. I'm touched." She dropped onto the opposite chaise lounge and laid her hand across her heart.

"I was worried, Beth. I thought you got arrested for doing something stupid."

"Will I ever live down one night in jail?" She scowled at him. "I don't have a violent nature, but I did have to wait for Bonnie's break time. After she and I came to an understanding about the future, I walked around town. You told me to enjoy the historic district while we're here, so I did. You were supposed to update the case file and our expense report."

"The paperwork is done, but next time check in with me." Michael's anger faded. "I have news on our case."

Beth reached for his water bottle. "The floor of the Home-wood rooftop utopia is all yours."

"Mrs. Doyle called about an hour ago. She was locked in the bathroom, whispering."

The hairs on Beth's neck stood on end. "Did someone take another shot at her?"

"No, she's fine. Quite joyous, in fact. She called her husband first thing this morning and asked him to come home. Lamar told his boss that his wife was sick and he needed to leave. He arrived around noon, and they've been talking ever since. When he ran out to the store, she decided to give us an update."

"Sounds like they might be able to work things out." Beth drained the last of the water.

"It's much better than that. Lamar said Bonnie was the biggest mistake of his life and swore he would never stray again. He agreed to go to marital counseling, and he's already called their minister for an appointment. He's willing to give going to church another try. Mrs. Doyle said he's stayed away since their son died." Michael laced his fingers behind his head. "Evelyn is so relieved, she's paying our expenses for another week, along with a generous bonus, and plans to give Nate a glowing report."

Beth scrunched the plastic bottle between her fingers. "That's it? Lamar gets caught red-handed, comes home with his tail between his legs, and she's willing to forgive and forget?"

"I'm sure Mr. Doyle was duly remorseful."

"If it were my husband, he'd have to crawl across hot coals on his belly."

Michael looked at her oddly. "Since neither of us has been married, let alone for forty years, we'll have to trust our client's judgment. At any rate, the case is closed and our work is done. I thought I'd hop on the sightseeing trolley that stops in front of the hotel. Care to join me?"

Beth shook her head. "No, thanks. I'm going to the gym to burn off calories on the machines. After that I'll be right here on the roof, either soaking in the pool or reading in a chaise. I thought I'd pick up a romance novel in the gift shop. There's so much I don't understand about love, I don't even know where to start. Later on we can split a pizza or nachos if you like."

"And go to Wild Adventures tomorrow?"

"Yep. A promise is a promise."

EIGHT

*A*s Saturdays go, yesterday had been the best one Michael had had in a long time. The weather had been sunny and breezy but not hot. And the crowds hadn't been too bad for a weekend. They had left the hotel by seven o'clock, arrived at the amusement park a little after nine thirty, and spent the next ten hours on the rides. He learned more about his partner during those hours than in the several months he'd known Elizabeth Kirby.

Beth ate hot dogs with mustard and relish, preferred iced tea over Coke, and doused her chips with vinegar instead of catsup. She loved roller coasters, except those that spiraled upside down in a corkscrew. Those left her rubber-legged and green around the gills for the next twenty minutes. She didn't mind getting wet, either from water rides or the occasional summer cloudburst, but humidity turned her wavy hair into a mane of long ringlets. All she'd needed was a pinafore to look like a children's book character, although Michael would never mention that in a million years. The one thing Beth didn't like was any kind of physical familiarity. Even an innocent hand on her shoulder made her nervous.

So it didn't matter how much fun they had at the amusement park or how well they got along as partners. It didn't matter that he loved her sense of humor, her smile, and the way she could fall asleep just about anywhere. Beth would always keep him at arm's length. If she ever found out his feelings toward her were no longer platonic, she'd be on the next Greyhound bus to Natchez.

When they'd gotten back to the hotel, Beth headed to her room with a new stuffed monkey and a bag of cotton candy. Michael went up to his room sunburned, mildly dehydrated, and absolutely certain he'd never know the joy or heartbreak of marriage. But he would rather spend his life as Beth's friend than live his life without her.

Sunday morning began with a disagreement. Although they both decided to attend church, they couldn't agree on where. "I'm going to New Covenant Church on Bull Street," he announced over coffee. "Their service should be the closest match to the evangelical I usually attend. Is that okay with you?"

"Why would you want the same old, same old?" Beth bit off a piece of muffin. "We both grew up in small towns and went to tiny churches painted white, where everyone knows everyone. I want a three-hundred-year-old cathedral with a bell tower, Tiffany stained glass windows, and flying buttresses."

"You don't even know what a 'buttress' is, flying or otherwise. Besides, Notre Dame is in Paris, not Savannah." Michael broke his whole-grain bagel in half.

"I'll know one when I see one. I googled historic churches and picked out Christ Church, also on Bull Street. It's described as the 'Mother Church of Georgia.' Afterward, I'll find out who throws the best Sunday brunch in town. Then I want to spend the rest of the day in Forsyth Park. The bellman said it's the best spot to people watch." Beth tossed the rest of her muffin in the trash. "Why don't I meet you here around noon?" Without waiting for his reply, she marched through the front entrance, her hair fanning across her shoulders, her skirt blowing in the breeze.

Michael watched her until she disappeared and then headed to his choice of services, which of course was held in a church with white clapboards and clear windows. Maybe he was plain toast in a designer cupcake world, but familiarity was reassuring, especially because his new career provided sufficient excitement.

After church he found a bench outside the hotel where he could read the newspaper and wait for his partner. His phone rang just as Beth walked up to him. "Michael Preston," he said without looking at the caller ID.

"Mr. Preston?" asked a familiar voice. "This is Evelyn Doyle."

Considering their investigation was done, her call caught him by surprise. "Yes, ma'am. How are you?"

"Is Miss Kirby with you? I tried calling her, but she didn't answer."

Michael gestured for Beth to move closer. "She's standing next to me. I'll put you on speaker."

"I've been taken to the Tybee Island police station. An officer said I could have an attorney present during questioning, but I didn't know if I should call our lawyer or just have you here. Both of you know what's going on better than Alfred Singleton."

Michael locked gazes with Beth, whose eyes were growing rounder by the moment. "Why do the police want to question you?" he asked.

"Because I'm the one who…who found…Lamar." She spoke in breathy gasps and then started weeping. "He's dead. My beloved husband is dead. What should I do, Mr. Preston?"

Glancing around at the passersby, Michael clicked the phone off speaker and angled it so Beth could hear as well. "Tell us what happened, Mrs. Doyle."

"I don't know. That's just it…I don't know how this happened." Horrible, wrenching sobs punctuated each of her sentences.

"What do you remember about Friday?" Beth asked, practically nose to nose with Michael.

"Lamar came home early from his seminar and we talked, just

like I told Mr. Preston. Then he went to see…that woman…to end things on Saturday."

"And when he returned from Miss Mulroney's, did you have an argument?" Beth prompted after Mrs. Doyle remained silent for several moments.

"Oh no. He hugged me and said it was over. I was so relieved. I didn't even want to hear the details."

"What happened next?" Michael elbowed Beth to one side.

"I asked Lamar if he wanted to stay in that night. I had asked the maid to fix us a light supper before she left. Lamar said yes, anything would be fine. He just wanted to be home." Mrs. Doyle's words broke into sobs. She struggled to continue. "We talked during dinner. Lamar…he promised to attend counseling with me. Then I…I walked the beach. I wanted to give thanks that the nightmare was finally…over. When I went to bed, Lamar said he would join me as soon as his television show ended."

Michael heard noise in the background. "The officer says I have to get off the phone," said Mrs. Doyle, sounding agitated. "Could one of you come for me? I must get home and start making funeral arrangements. There is…so…so much to do."

"Of course, but please finish telling us what happened," Beth insisted.

"When I woke up this morning, Lamar wasn't in bed. I assumed he'd gotten up early and gone down to the beach. He does that sometimes. He loves to watch the sun rise. I saw him in one of the chairs on the deck. At first I thought he was sleeping, but then I saw the blood. I shook him and called his name, but he was… he was gone." The rest of her words became unintelligible.

"Mrs. Doyle, this is very important." Beth pulled the phone from Michael's hand. "Have you been arrested?"

"No, I don't think so. But I have no way to get home." She sounded meek and almost childlike.

Michael wrestled his phone back. "The first thing we need to do is get ahold of Alfred Singleton. We'll call him for you. Don't answer any questions until Mr. Singleton gets to the Tybee Island police station. Do you understand?"

"And we'll come too, Mrs. Doyle," interjected Beth, hovering over his arm. "You'll see us either at the station or at home."

"Thank you, Mr. Preston, Miss Kirby. I am in your debt." The well-mannered, soft-spoken woman hung up, leaving the two partners thunderstruck on the sidewalk. Even though there wasn't a single cloud in the sky.

NINE

*B*eth had never had a very high opinion of lawyers, and Alfred Singleton did nothing to change her mind. Fortunately, his number was accessible through Google, and he picked up on the third ring. But that's where their luck ran out. As succinctly as possible, Beth explained who she was and the reason for interrupting his Sunday afternoon.

Singleton's response was less than professional: "Are you telling me Lamar is *dead*? I just saw him last week at the club."

"I assure you I wouldn't joke about something like that." Beth glanced at Michael, who rolled his eyes. In his car on their way to Tybee, he could hear every word the attorney said.

"And Evelyn asked you to call *me*? Who did you say you were again?" A hint of impatience shaded Singleton's question.

"Elizabeth Kirby of Price Investigations. My partner and I work for Mrs. Doyle in another capacity, but right now she needs you. She's being held at the Tybee Island police station."

"My expertise is tax law, with some experience in wills, trusts, and real estate acquisitions. I'm not a criminal lawyer. What has Mrs. Doyle been charged with?"

"I don't think anything yet, but she needs *her lawyer* to be present during questioning. If she needs a different type of lawyer down the road, you could arrange a replacement later."

"Do the police believe Evelyn had something to do with Lamar's death?"

"Look, Mr. Singleton, all questions will be answered in due time. Will you help her or not?" Beth's voice rose in intensity and volume.

"Very well. I'm on the other side of town, but I'll go there now."

"Thank you so much," Beth drawled sarcastically, but the man had already hung up.

"We just crossed the Wilmington River. Should I head to the station?" Michael asked.

"Let's check out the crime scene before Singleton springs her from jail. Just when we thought we had a few days of vacation..."

"Rude of Lamar to curtail our fun and games by getting shot."

"You know what I mean. Plus, I have a bad feeling about this."

"Someone wise once told me to let the evidence do the talking."

Beth rolled down the window as her bad feeling took root and began to grow. Although the security guard waved them into the complex with a friendly smile, whatever evidence might be in the Doyles' backyard was off-limits to them. The entire property had been cordoned off with yellow tape—a barrier they weren't allowed to cross. No matter how Beth pleaded or cajoled, their identification as Mississippi PIs carried no sway in Georgia. To kill time they listened to the radio and walked up and down the street as officers bustled around like ants. Finally, two more cops arrived in a late-model sedan. Beth knew by their suits and swagger that they were detectives. *Who said Tybee was just a little island?*

When the male detective headed to the police van, the thirty-something female marched straight to the Charger. "You two the PIs from Natchez?" she asked, extending her hand to Beth. "Detective Diane Rossi."

"I'm Beth Kirby, and this is Michael Preston. We're also friends of Mrs. Doyle."

Beth's description triggered a laugh as Rossi shook hands with Michael. "Yeah, I already know why Mrs. Doyle hired you. What I don't understand is why you're *here*." The question sounded straightforward, not accusatory.

Michael was quick to respond. "We're still on Mrs. Doyle's payroll for another week. So we'd like to find out who killed her husband."

A commotion erupted at the police barricade with the arrival of a television news van. The detective frowned at reporters pouring from the vehicle. "Sure doesn't take them long when the victim happens to be rich." She turned back to Beth and Michael. "Look, unlike many of my peers, I usually play nice with PIs as long as they follow the rules. But this is *my* case and *my* crime scene. I don't want you near that house until the tape is down. Then if you think you can help, have at it."

"Thanks, Detective," said Michael. "We offered assistance to both the Natchez PD and the FBI during our last investigation."

"Really? You don't mind if I verify that? And how come you didn't report shots fired here on Wednesday night?" Rossi aimed her question at Beth. "That certainly would have been *helpful*. Mrs. Doyle told you someone is trying to kill her, yet you don't alert law enforcement?"

"Our client was hysterical, distraught, and absolutely refused to let us call the police. She threatened to recant her story if we did. Because there were ongoing problems in the Doyle marriage, I figured it might have been a cry for attention."

"That she had shot the gun herself," Michael added.

"What gun would that be, Mr. Preston?"

Beth held up a hand. "We saw no gun, Detective. The sound could have been a car backfiring or kids playing with firecrackers.

Mrs. Doyle was down at the beach with a turbulent surf that night. When Mr. Doyle cut his business meeting short and came home Friday, Mrs. Doyle said they were able to resolve their differences."

"Their marital difficulties seem to be over now." The detective gestured toward the house.

"You can't possibly think Evelyn Doyle did this." Michael sounded like an afternoon talk show host. "She loved her husband."

"*Ahhh*, love. If my husband knew how many murders were committed in the name of love, he would be worried."

"What motive did she have?" asked Beth.

Detective Rossi scowled. "Please don't insult me. I know all about Lamar's affair with a twenty-four-year-old. That could make a wife trigger-happy."

"Mrs. Doyle's one desire was for them to reconcile." Beth crossed her arms.

"Maybe, but how come she didn't call the police when she first found him?" Rossi pulled out her notebook. "Mrs. Doyle said she woke up around nine this morning. The log shows the 9-1-1 call coming in at 10:16. That's approximately forty-five minutes. Then Mrs. Doyle took a shower before the paramedics arrived and washed her clothes. Who would do such things with her husband dead in an Adirondack chair?"

Beth did her best to hide her reaction. "I'll ask her that when I see her."

"Good idea. That information would be helpful. And be sure to stop at the station to turn over any evidence pertinent to the murder, unless you plan to interfere with an official investigation." Her smile didn't quite reach her eyes.

Beth surely did not, not after charges had been brought against her in their last case. "We'll make you a copy of our report, providing Mrs. Doyle grants permission. Where is our client, by the way?"

Rossi glanced at her watch. "Still being processed. She should be on her way home in a few hours. We're not charging her at this time, but she shouldn't venture too far from Savannah, if you catch my drift. And if you're really her friend? Tell her to hire a new lawyer. Singleton is the one who told us about Lamar's affair, not that we wouldn't have found out anyway."

When the detective turned to leave, Beth blocked her path. "Have you found the murder weapon yet?"

"If we did, Mrs. Doyle would be in a cell waiting for bail to be set for capital murder. When you see her, ask her where her husband's gun is—the one Lamar kept locked in his safe. That's something else we learned from Alfred Singleton." Rossi threw her head back and laughed. "If that lawyer keeps doing my job, I can put in for early retirement, and I'm not even forty." She ducked under the tape and headed for the front door.

"I could kick myself for mentioning the gun," Michael muttered once Rossi was beyond earshot.

Beth shrugged. "Don't beat yourself up. Thanks to her lawyer, they already knew about it. Or they would have soon found out the same way you did."

"What a mistake to call Alfred Singleton. An entry-level public defender would better serve Mrs. Doyle. If we don't get Singleton off the case, she will soon be doing twenty-five to life."

Beth climbed into the passenger seat without comment. Her silence didn't go unnoticed.

"What are you thinking, Beth? That Mrs. Doyle did it?"

She stared at the cops and news reporters milling around the Doyles' formerly pristine yard. "No way. She's totally incapable of such violence."

"Like Rossi said, Mrs. Doyle had plenty of motivation in that stack of eight-by-ten glossies. Maybe their conversation on Friday didn't go like she said it did. Maybe you and I were part of an elaborate smoke screen. And we fell for it hook, line, and sinker. Maybe if Mrs. Doyle couldn't have the man she loved, then nobody would."

Beth shook her head. "That's not love. That's jealousy, control, anger, and vindictiveness. Mrs. Doyle is a patron of local artists, donates to environmental charities, and grows prizewinning orchids in her little greenhouse. There is no way she could creep up and shoot her husband in cold blood. But something hasn't felt right since the night of the alleged shooting on the dunes. When I suggested a car had backfired, she said she knew what gunfire sounded like."

"So what? Everyone has heard gunfire on TV."

"Still, it's not something my mother would say."

"Then we'll put it on our list of things to ask her. Why don't we go somewhere and come back in a couple hours? I am starving." Michael turned the key, and his powerful engine roared to life.

"That will give Mrs. Doyle a chance to recover from her ordeal before we question her. I want to look into her background to see if there's anything else she's not telling us."

"We'll need to call Nate with a full update too. After the boss hears this story, he might want us off the case. I wonder if Mrs. Doyle's offer of expense-paid sightseeing still stands."

Beth turned to face him. "Right now I'm convinced she's innocent, but I want to make it crystal clear that I won't be part of any murder cover-up."

"On that succinct point, you and I are in complete agreement." As Michael drove slowly away, the crime scene faded from sight.

∽

Four hours later, after a lovely meal and walk on the beach, the partners returned to the Tybee beach house after verifying Mrs. Doyle was indeed in residence. The woman looked haggard when she opened the door, even though her incarceration was even shorter than Beth's recent jail stay had been.

"Good to see you, Beth, Michael. I hope it's all right if I call you by your first names now."

"Of course, but we're not sure how long we'll be on your case." Beth stepped across the threshold. "Since this is no longer a matter of spousal surveillance, the decision as to whether we can continue to work for you will be up to our boss."

"Goodness, I hope Mr. Price doesn't need you back in Natchez. If price is a problem, I can increase your fee considerably." Mrs. Doyle led them to the living room, her usual designer heels replaced by fuzzy slippers.

"Money isn't the issue, ma'am. As you mentioned, we're from Natchez. We're not only unfamiliar with the island, we're not even from this state."

She crooked a brow. "I can supply good maps if you're still getting lost."

Beth lowered herself to the love seat. "That's not it. To be effective, private investigators need to work with local law enforcement. That's especially true in a murder case. The Tybee Island police don't know us. A Savannah PI might better serve you— someone who has already gained their trust as a professional. We're fish out of water here."

The woman's bloodshot eyes filled with tears. "Please don't leave, Beth. I trust you and Michael. You're not only discreet, you see things as they are and are unafraid to speak your mind. I've had my head buried in the sand too long."

"Speaking of which," said Michael. "The first thing you should do is fire Mr. Singleton."

Couldn't that have waited until later? Beth glared at Michael.

Mrs. Doyle nodded. "I realized that when the police questioned me. I got the distinct impression Alfred thought I had… murdered Lamar." She gripped the arms of her chair. "How could he think that? Lamar and I have socialized with him and Sybil for years."

"Shows how much we really know our friends," said Beth. "If you like, we could contact the local bar association for a referral. They'll recommend an experienced criminal attorney to take over for Singleton."

"Thank you so much. I'm not sure what I would've done if you hadn't come back today. I'm so alone and so afraid I'll say or do something else stupid. Please don't go back to Mississippi. I beg you."

Unless Beth had been born yesterday, there was no faking the terror in the woman's voice. She locked gazes with her partner. Without exchanging a word, Beth knew where Michael stood. "If it's okay with our boss, we'll stay, at least until we're sure you're in capable hands."

Michael stepped into the bad-cop role. "But we have some questions you need to answer truthfully, Mrs. Doyle."

"Of course," she whispered, her chin trembling. "And I know what the first one is. On my honor as a Christian woman, I had nothing to do with my husband's death." She placed her hand over her heart.

Evelyn Doyle didn't so much as blink as Beth studied her. "Well, that's the most important one, but we have others."

Mrs. Doyle expelled a pent-up breath. "Ask what you like. I have nothing to hide."

"According to Chatham County gun registrations, your late husband owned a thirty-eight-caliber Beretta." Michael lifted his brows as though awaiting confirmation.

"I wouldn't know the caliber, but Lamar bought a gun for protection after he saw a frightening movie about home invasions. This stretch of beach is rather remote. Lamar kept the gun locked in the safe. But when he went out of town, I put it in a drawer in the bedside table."

"Do you know where that weapon is now?" Michael asked, glancing around the room as though it might suddenly materialize.

"I don't. After the police asked about a gun, I checked the drawer and the safe, and it's not anywhere. It's disappeared."

"On Wednesday, the night you heard shots on the beach, where was the gun then?" Beth asked.

Mrs. Doyle tightened her cardigan around her shoulders. "When I got back to the house, I checked the drawer, and it was right where I left it."

Beth jumped to her feet. "Had it been fired?"

"How on earth could I tell?"

"By counting the number of shots in the clip, sniffing the barrel, or checking for residue in the chamber—any number of ways."

"I have no idea. The gun looked normal, but I didn't pick it up. I've never fired the thing. To my knowledge, Lamar never had either."

"Not even at the firing range? Maybe in a class or a lesson?"

"No, never." Her complexion had grown waxy and pale and her speech labored. "I might have to lie down for a while. I'm not feeling well."

"I'll get you a glass of water, ma'am. We only have a few more questions." Michael left the room.

Beth considered how best to phrase her next question. "The detective is curious why you waited so long to call 9-1-1."

"Was it a long time?" Mrs. Doyle shrugged. "I remember seeing Lamar in the chair and thinking he was asleep. Then I saw the blood and thought he'd taken his own life. I threw my arms around him." With the scene replaying in her mind, Mrs. Doyle held out her arms and embraced the air. "I asked him how he could do such a thing. There was so much blood."

"What happened next, Mrs. Doyle?"

Her face contorted in anguish. "Lamar was so cold that I knew he was gone. Paramedics…EMTs…no one could help him now.

I just sat there, holding him and praying. I knew it would be the last chance I'd have."

Michael returned and handed her the glass. "Did you take a shower and change your clothes?"

"Of course I did," she said after a sip of water. "There was blood on my hands, on my face, even in my hair from holding him." Grimacing, she touched each offending area. "How could I ride in the ambulance with Lamar like that? All I could smell was blood, so I took a shower and put on clean clothes."

"Where are those clothes now?" asked Beth.

She paused a moment to consider. "The police took them from the washer and put them in a bag. I don't know where they are now."

"Did you wash them before or after you called 9-1-1?"

"I can't remember. What difference does it make, Beth?" Mrs. Doyle's voice turned shrill.

"If you look suspicious, the police won't search for the real killer," said Michael, almost as agitated as the client.

"All right, let me think. First, I took a quick shower." Mrs. Doyle ticked off tasks on her fingers. "Then I called the police and got dressed. Before they arrived, I started the washer so my maid wouldn't have to deal with set-in blood." She sighed with great weariness.

It was then that Beth realized their client wasn't quite *right*. "Did you take anything? Maybe some kind of medication?"

She stared blankly into space. "Only the Xanax prescribed by my doctor. I doubled the dosage since I felt a panic attack coming on."

"Before we leave, I'll call your doctor. You might be suffering a delayed shock reaction. Don't take any more pills until he or she examines you."

"Very well, if you think it best. I need to find his number for you." Mrs. Doyle staggered into the hallway for her purse.

Beth followed at her heels. "What about a close friend or family member? Someone really should be here with you."

The corners of Evelyn's mouth turned down. "All I have is my sister in Atlanta."

"Get me her number, and I'll make both calls."

"Thank you, Beth. I don't know what I'd do without you."

It took Mrs. Doyle five minutes to locate her address book. Afterward, she staggered into her bedroom, collapsed on the bed, and fell asleep almost instantly.

Beth drew the coverlet over her legs and turned off the lights. "Looks like we're in charge of tracking down the sister and finding her a new attorney," she said to Michael at the front door.

"You call her doctor and the sister. I'll try to find her a new lawyer." He followed her out, locking the door behind them. "Plus I need to talk to Nate before we get ourselves in deeper with Mrs. Doyle."

"How could we abandon her now? Evelyn Doyle might be the stupidest woman in the world, but I'm convinced she didn't do it."

"Then we'd better both hope Nate says yes."

TEN

On the way back from Tybee, Beth and Michael stopped at the City Market to sightsee. Walking through two blocks of shops, restaurants, and art galleries let them feel like tourists for a couple of hours before returning to the real world—made all the more real by a murder. When Beth headed to her room, Michael went to his for an overdue phone conversation with Nate Price. Michael had a hard time conveying the story once he dropped the bombshell on the boss.

"You're telling me our client's husband is dead?" Nate squawked.

"Yes. Mr. Doyle was shot sometime Saturday night."

"One day after Mrs. Doyle gave a glowing report about you two, along with a bonus and an extra week of expenses?"

"Correct. While Mrs. Doyle was sleeping and her husband was sitting on the deck, someone must have—"

"Was it a robbery? Some kind of home invasion?" Nate's impatience easily traveled three states and several hundred miles.

"I doubt it. There were no signs of forced entry, but we haven't seen the police report yet. The security system was turned off because the Doyles were home and awake."

"Do you suppose it was his girlfriend, Miss What's-her-name?

Didn't Mr. Doyle break off his affair in hopes of reconciling with his wife?"

"Yes, he did, but we haven't had a chance to—"

"Who are the police looking at, Preston? Don't tell me it's our client!"

"In that case, I don't know what to say."

Two or three moments passed while Nate processed the information. "Has Mrs. Doyle been arrested?"

Finally, Nate allowed Michael to explain the sequence of events while he listened without interruption. "What do you think? And what's Kirby's gut telling her?"

"For a change, Beth and I are in complete agreement. Mrs. Doyle behaved rather oddly because she's in shock. Plus she has a total buffoon for an attorney. But we don't think she's a murderer. I plan to call the bar association for a criminal defense referral."

"That's a relief." Nate's laugh held little amusement. "How do you want us to proceed?"

Nate didn't answer immediately. "Help Mrs. Doyle replace the lawyer. Then help her arrange the funeral if she has no one else, but don't interfere with the murder investigation. Let the police do their work. As far as I'm concerned, you're on vacation for the next week, along with a side assignment." This time his chuckle sounded genuine.

"What kind of assignment? Will I finally get to go undercover?" Michael reached for a tablet and pen.

"Not this time. We need to hire another PI in Savannah. I want you and Beth to interview prospective candidates."

"Which one of us is getting canned?"

"Neither. Thanks to Mrs. Baer—the lady I met in Mobile—we now have several new cases. The owner of a nail salon suspects her bookkeeper of embezzlement, a restaurateur wants to know who's stealing food from his kitchen, and a woman wants us to track down her long-lost cousin. Work keeps pouring in for Savannah, so unless you want to permanently relocate, Price Investigations needs a satellite office on the East Coast. Would you mind narrowing the field of applicants? If you and Beth can agree on a candidate, I'll hire him or her on a trial basis for a few weeks. Then I'll fly to Georgia for final approval."

"No problem," Michael answered without hesitation. "Beth and I would be happy to do it."

"Thanks. Maxine posted the job online a couple days ago, along with our minimum qualifications. I want an experienced investigator because Kirby won't be staying long enough to train someone from scratch."

Like me, he thought.

"Résumés will initially be reviewed on my end. Maxine will email the contact info of those who make it to the next step."

"This is happening fast, Nate. Shouldn't we get Beth in on this discussion? She's in her room."

"No time, Michael. Isabelle and I are on our way to an engagement party for my brother. Tomorrow I start a new case here in Natchez. Give Beth my best regards, and tell her to watch her email for those résumés."

Nate ended the call before Michael could ask any more questions, so he headed to Beth's room, where his inability to get a word in edgewise continued.

"We need to celebrate," Beth greeted as she opened her door. "Mrs. Doyle's sister, Charlotte Harper, said she'll come to Tybee Island tomorrow and will stay until this ordeal is over." Beth rubbed the back of her hand across her forehead. "Thank goodness. What do I know about arranging a funeral? I doubt if Mr. Doyle's body has been released yet."

"And I left a message on the legal referral help line. It shouldn't be long until someone returns my call."

"Good work," she said, and then she rattled on about funerals she'd attended.

While Beth reminisced, Michael scanned the room. Clothes, newspapers, magazines, and empty snack food bags were scattered everywhere. Beth's suitcase had been emptied onto the queen-size bed, leaving her the small half to sleep on. "Did someone ransack your room while we were on Tybee?"

"No, I just prefer an eclectic type of decor," she said after a quick perusal. "Anyway, since both of Mrs. Doyle's immediate needs are taken care of, we're free to pursue more important concerns."

"What's that? You need help finding your purse or maybe your Glock? I hope you plan to leave the maid a big tip." Michael remained by the door, uncomfortable invading Beth's privacy.

"*Nooo*," she drawled. "I know exactly where everything is. We need to find Lamar Doyle's killer."

"That's Detective Rossi's job, along with the Tybee Island Police Department."

Beth made a sour face. "Rossi has already made up her mind."

"Mrs. Doyle will soon have competent representation. And her sister will be here for moral support."

Beth closed the distance between them. "Neither one of those people will take the bull's-eye off her forehead. If Rossi has an easy target, she won't look for the real murderer. That's where you and I come in—her *private investigators*." She poked his shoulder with her finger.

Michael pushed away her hand. "Nate has other plans for us in addition to some R&R. Remember him? He's the boss." As succinctly as possible, he recounted his recent conversation.

Beth's nostrils flared with annoyance long before he finished. "Nate wants us to stay another *couple of weeks*, yet I don't have a say in the matter?"

"He was in a big hurry, but nothing's set in stone. What's wrong with the idea of interviewing potential employees?"

"I'm fine with that, but I have no intention of abandoning Mrs. Doyle. After we've taken the rich lady's money, now we're going to throw her to the wolves? No way! If you have doubts about her innocence, fine, you can abandon her. Since I don't, I'll work her case in my free time. Price Investigations doesn't own me twenty-four hours a day." She turned her back on him, something she'd never done before.

"Take it easy, partner. I'm with you." Michael poked her in the back.

"I feel sorry for her," Beth said softly over her shoulder. "She's all alone."

"Not anymore, she's not. Who do you want to look at next?"

Beth started pacing the room. "There's only one logical choice—the duplicitous Bonnie Mulroney of Bull Street. Maybe she retaliated after Lamar dumped her and ruined her chances for a bright and work-free future. Nothing says motive like a woman spurned." Beth dug her purse from the pile of debris and sprang toward the door. "And nothing spikes an appetite like a good lead. Let's go to dinner."

ELEVEN

After an invigorating four-mile run along the river, Beth decided to skip breakfast. Instead, she opted for a hot shower and then coffee and peanut butter crackers in her room. Even she'd grown tired of fried potatoes and cheesy grits after several days. Of course, no one had twisted her arm to choose hot food over low-fat yogurt and a hard-boiled egg. But when the scent of bacon and eggs wafted through the air, what was an American girl to do? At least she'd gotten enough exercise lately to counteract the calories. Today she hoped for a slower pace.

Beth opened her laptop to look at email. Surprised at the number of messages that had accumulated since she had last checked them, she deleted those from her favorite outfitter catalog, candle and scent shop, and tea purveyor and systematically whittled down her in-box to two dozen. Did anyone need to buy yoga pants or raspberry shower gel *every day*? She dashed off quick replies to her mother, Aunt Dorrie, and two girlfriends. Then she looked at the emails from the office assistant.

Maxine insisted on keeping Beth in the loop with local gossip: Their last client, Mrs. Dean, had decided to sell the family home and move to California with her daughter. Isabelle Price, Nate's wife, had several embarrassing bouts of morning sickness, one at a well-attended open house. Izzy planned to leave real estate for a few years after the baby was born, but if the nausea continued, her exit date would be sooner. Finally, Maxine got down to business and forwarded the five résumés of Savannah applicants that Nate liked best. Maxine put a little smiley face in the upper corner of her personal favorite.

Beth refilled her mug, stretched out her legs, and studied each résumé carefully. Each candidate possessed a different set of skills and educational background, yet every one of them had experience in some type of investigation. On paper, all five looked good, but most people stretched the truth when looking for a new job and locked away their skeletons in the attic. After Beth stacked the papers in order of personal preference, she called her partner.

"What's up?" she asked. "I'll tell you my news if you spill your guts first."

Michael snorted. "The productivity level of my morning will be hard to top, even for a type A personality like you. I got ahold of a real human being on the referral line. They gave me several criminal defense recommendations if our client doesn't qualify for a public defender. I assured the woman our client does not. Since then I researched the firms where each lawyer worked, and using a ten-factor algorithm, I narrowed them down to the perfect attorney for Mrs. Doyle."

Beth rolled her eyes skyward. "What did the algorithm produce for Mrs. Doyle? I'm picturing an aluminum capsule straight from *Back to the Future*. Suddenly, a door lifts up, and out walks a half-human, half-robotic lawyer."

"You do realize that… Oh, never mind. I found Mrs. Hilda Gwinn. She worked as a public defender for twenty years, winning several landmark cases, and is now a partner at a well-respected firm. She's fifty-seven, down-to-earth, and has tons of courtroom experience. I think the two ladies will get along fine."

"I hate to be the voice of doom, but will Hilda Gwinn take the case?"

"She has already agreed. When I described Mrs. Doyle's missteps thus far, she wasn't even surprised. She said people do all kinds of strange things while they're in shock. People only maintain their cool on TV shows. Mrs. Gwinn plans to meet her client this afternoon."

"Good work. Now we can cross 'find new lawyer' off our list. If you don't need the car, I'm on my way to Tybee Island to talk to Detective Rossi."

"Give me five minutes, and I'll go with you." From the background noise, Michael had already started moving around the room.

"No, I want you to review the résumés Nate emailed me because we must agree on the final candidate. While I'm gone, you can check references and make sure former employers have actually heard of them. I'll drop off printed copies at your room on my way out."

Beth knocked on his door five minutes later—not enough time to tidy up—yet Michael's room was neat as a pin. "Where's all your stuff?" she asked, handing him the résumés. "This room looks the same as the day we arrived."

"Clothes are either in the drawers or the closet, toiletries in the bathroom. My computer and briefcase are on the desk." Michael pawed through the papers. "Only five résumés?"

"So far those are Nate's favorites. I already narrowed it down to three. If you agree with my assessment, call the three candidates and set up interviews—the sooner the better."

"What's wrong with these?" Michael scanned the two rejects.

"Nothing, other than one lives in Swainsboro and one in Hinesville. Those are little towns just south of nowhere. Our Savannah office should have a Savannah resident for the same reasons we gave Mrs. Doyle."

"You must have forgotten where we live," he muttered. "But I suppose we must start somewhere. Are you sure you don't need me today? I'm curious what you plan to show Rossi that doesn't violate our client's confidentiality."

"The client-investigator privilege isn't protected like a doctor's or a lawyer's, so I must show the police any evidence that could have bearing on Lamar's murder, like the lovely photos of Bonnie."

"What if my work here doesn't take long?"

"Then feel free to relax. Maybe you could go for a carriage ride. You'll see me when you see me." Beth walked out the door before Michael could argue. As much as she enjoyed his company, she wanted to be alone when she talked to Rossi and when she checked on Mrs. Doyle.

～

Beth arrived at the police station three blocks from the beach around two o'clock. Detective Rossi had been in another part of the building but quickly joined her in the conference room. "Make yourself comfortable," she said. "Thanks for coming in today."

"We're happy to help find Mr. Doyle's killer." Beth settled on an upholstered chair.

"Speaking of whom, where is that handsome partner of yours?" Rossi asked with a grin. "I was hoping he'd talk more about that gun Mrs. Doyle fired."

"Like I told you, we saw no gun."

"Did you know a Beretta Pico compact is registered to Lamar Doyle? Although the autopsy isn't finished, I put in a rush order for the ballistics. Guess what I found out about the bullets that killed her husband?" Rossi leaned across the table toward Beth.

"I can't imagine."

"They're thirty-eights, just like the gun that's registered to Lamar Doyle."

"That's a common weapon, Detective. Probably lots of home-owners keep one handy."

"Not in Georgia, they don't. We love big guns. But let's not get off track when we have things to discuss." Rossi leaned back in her chair and interlocked her fingers. Like most cops, she had short fingernails. No acrylic manicures for women in this profession. "I'm rather troubled about that gun being missing. According to Mrs. Doyle's statement, Lamar's gun was kept in the wall safe in their bedroom. However, whenever hubby went out of town, Evelyn moved the gun to her nightstand drawer. Pity the poor cleaning lady who forgets something and comes back for it." Rossi clucked her tongue. "Since Mr. Doyle came home the day before, here's what I don't like: Evelyn doesn't know where the gun was Saturday night. Maybe in the drawer, maybe Lamar had locked it up. And now it seems to be missing."

Beth shifted uncomfortably. "Truly, they needed a class on firearm safety."

"According to Alfred Singleton, no one had the combination to the safe except for Lamar and Evelyn. I'm not sure why the attorney knew that, but that's what he told me." Rossi offered a smile.

"For the record, Singleton is no longer her lawyer. He was replaced today by someone with criminal experience."

"Probably a good idea since I believe Mrs. Doyle to be a criminal. As her friend, Beth, you might want to give her some advice. I will soon present evidence to the Chatham County DA. My guess is Evelyn will be offered a deal. Perhaps if she pleads guilty to a lesser offense, such as second-degree murder, she might avoid a lengthy sentence with no chance of parole. After all, it was a crime of passion."

Beth flinched as though someone pinched her. "Plead guilty to something she didn't do? I don't think so."

Rossi shrugged. "Just a suggestion. Who knows? In order to spare the state a costly trial, the DA might even consider a manslaughter charge. Maybe the couple fought that night; maybe Lamar threatened Evelyn's life. But if Mrs. Doyle sticks to her story, she might be the first blue-blooded former debutante on death row. I don't know about Mississippi, but Georgia still has the death penalty."

"Let's not get ahead of ourselves. You asked for anything pertinent to your case. This is what I have." Beth pulled a folder from her leather tote and laid it on the desk.

Rossi at least had the decency not to spread the photos across the surface. Lifting the stack, one by one she examined the proof of Lamar's lapse in judgment or conscience or common sense. Perhaps all of the above. With each candid shot, Diane Rossi's cool demeanor faded. She frowned at the last shot of Lamar and Bonnie embracing. "Yep," she concluded. "If the new lawyer seats a majority of women on the jury, I'd say manslaughter is a fair verdict. But then again, I'm married and the DA is both single and male."

Beth made no comment.

"Considering how much Xanax and how many sleeping pills she took that night, a good lawyer might even try a mental impairment defense."

"You ran a tox screen on my client?" Beth didn't hide her incredulity.

"Sure. Mrs. Doyle agreed to give us a blood sample, and her lawyer didn't object. Actually, that woman is lucky she didn't die in her sleep." Rossi waited for some sort of reaction that didn't come. "What else is in this folder?"

"Proof that Lamar was paying Miss Mulroney's bills and the name of Mrs. Doyle's pastor, Reverend White. Lamar called him

Friday night and requested marriage counseling. He hadn't been a churchgoing man lately, but apparently he was ready to turn over a new leaf. They made an appointment for Tuesday evening. Does that sound like someone on the verge of leaving his wife?"

"Not really, but since you've been forthright, I'll also share something. Apparently, you think this woman pulled the trigger because Mr. Doyle broke up with her. I went to see Bonnie Mulroney of 472 Bull Street this morning. She has an alibi for Saturday night. She was at a sleepover at a friend's house, a coworker from the coffee shop. I already talked to the girl. She swore Bonnie was there all night, even willing to testify in court." The detective closed the folder. "I do my job, Miss Kirby. I'm not trying to *hang* this on Mrs. Doyle."

"Would that helpful coworker be named Crystal? I met that little gold digger and wouldn't describe her as a credible witness."

"What reason would the girl have to lie to the police? What didn't you like about her? Violet-colored hair is commonplace among women her age."

"Her hair is fine. It's her ideas for a secure financial future that leave much to be desired, morally speaking."

"As Mrs. Doyle's PI, you should be less concerned with my potential witnesses and more worried about what we found in her bushes."

Beth felt Rossi's dark eyes bore through her forehead. It took everything she had to feign confusion. "Is that supposed to mean something to me, Detective?"

"We found a bullet in the backyard—another thirty-eight. I'm betting it was the shot Mrs. Doyle fired Wednesday night to back her story about a prowler. What do you want to bet it will match the ballistics of those taken from Mr. Doyle?"

"What does that prove?"

"As I said, only two people knew the combination to the wall safe—Lamar and Evelyn. With no other viable suspects, it'll be enough for a first-degree indictment once we match it to Lamar's Beretta."

"The gun you don't have."

Rossi smiled, almost as though the two women were old pals. "We'll find it. What with the showering and clothes washing, I'll bet that gun couldn't have gone far. We have techs with metal detectors combing the sand and divers checking underwater for a quarter mile in both directions. Mrs. Doyle wouldn't have pitched the gun into the surf farther from home than that. She wouldn't want members of the bridge club to see her."

Beth stood and slung her tote bag over her shoulder. "Such a waste of taxpayer money, but I understand you need to do a thorough job. Speaking of which, I'd like to check on my client. If her new lawyer doesn't take control, the state will have her railroaded into Emanuel Women's Facility by the weekend. Plus, Mrs. Doyle might need help with funeral arrangements until her sister arrives from Atlanta."

"The ME hasn't released the body yet. No one will be burying Mr. Doyle anytime soon." Rossi tucked the folder into a briefcase and rose to her feet. "Keep your cell phone on, Beth, in case I have more questions. And for the record, Emanuel is medium security. Evelyn will be headed to Arrendale with the rest of the murderers."

～

Beth left the Tybee Island police station with far less assurance than she had this morning. And that had nothing to do with Diane Rossi. Like the detective said, she was merely doing her job. The fact that Rossi had already questioned another suspect indicated she conducted a more thorough investigation than Beth's former partner in Natchez. No, Beth was troubled that Bonnie had a story lined up. Either she knew she needed an alibi, or the size 2 latte maker really was at a Saturday night sleepover.

Things don't look good for Mrs. Doyle.

During the ten-minute drive to her client's home, Beth was again amazed by the calming effect of the ocean. Just seeing a great expanse of water mitigated her anxiety. *Why worry about Arrendale State Prison when I can walk the pristine sands of Tybee today?* Someday before she died, Beth vowed to live somewhere with a view of water, even if it was from the window of a nursing home.

Mrs. Doyle opened the door wearing a pair of dark slacks and a long tunic. Her hair, which usually was in an elaborate upsweep, was held back by an enamel clip.

"How are you feeling today?" Beth asked. "I won't stay long, but I wanted to check on you."

"I'm much better thanks to you." Mrs. Doyle led the way to the kitchen. "My sister called. She should arrive sometime tonight. I will be so happy to see her. And you just missed Mrs. Gwinn. She agreed to take my case, and I have officially fired Alfred Singleton. Coffee?" She held up a carafe.

"Yes, ma'am." Beth climbed onto a tall stool. "This might mean the end of your friendship with Sybil Singleton."

Mrs. Doyle snorted. "No great loss there. I always found that woman arrogant and self-aggrandizing. I doubt she performed a single good deed without the press or at least an audience watching."

"My mom has a few friends like that too."

"Sybil's dinner parties were tiresome affairs of haute cuisine and social climbing, while Alfred peppered every conversation with political vitriol, no matter what the original topic." Beth couldn't think of an appropriate comment.

"I'm sorry, dear. You didn't need to hear that."

"No problem. I take it Alfred was more your husband's friend than yours."

"Yes, but enough about the Singletons. With Lamar gone, I'll soon discover who my true friends are." Her eyes filled with tears, but she blinked them back. "I'm very grateful you found Hilda Gwinn."

"You're welcome, but Michael was the one who found her." Sipping her coffee, Beth mustered her courage. "Mrs. Doyle, something is bothering me, and I want it cleared up now, with no surprises down the road."

"Ask me anything you want, Beth. You've proven worthy enough for my complete confidence. I need to prove worthy of yours."

Beth drew a breath. "The night that someone took a shot at you down on the beach…you said it wasn't a car backfiring because you knew what a gunshot sounded like. Yet you told me you never fired Lamar's gun, that neither of you had taken classes at the firing range. Then how do you know?"

Mrs. Doyle rubbed her knuckles one at a time. "I didn't grow up on Tybee Island in a house like this. For that matter, Lamar isn't from Tybee either. He grew up in a mansion on Broad Street in Charleston. One of those four-story pastel houses the tourists gape at from carriage rides." She smiled at Beth. "I grew up on a farm in Wilkes County, although I use the term 'farm' loosely. After my grandparents passed, my father never planted another crop, but he did love to hunt. My mother used to make stew from squirrels and rabbits that was quite good. My father was nice to my mother and us, but he had to be the laziest man on earth. He actually shot at deer from an upstairs window so he didn't have to stomp through the woods. That's how I know what gunfire sounds like." There was no condemnation in her voice, only a simple statement of facts.

"How did you meet Mr. Doyle?"

"At college. Both my sister and I met our husbands at the University of Georgia. After being kicked out of several private schools, Lamar finally found his niche at UGA. I graduated with a degree in art history, but Lamar wasn't much of a scholar. But then again, he knew one day he'd inherit from his rich father." She drained her cup. "And he did. By then we'd fallen in love and eloped, much to his mother's dismay. Lamar and his brother both worked for their father in Charleston. I didn't exactly fit in with Lamar's social life there, but I managed. After his dad passed, Lamar and I moved to Tybee Island. Unlike in Charleston, few people here know where I came from."

"Why should people care? You made something of yourself." Beth felt defensive for her new friend.

"The Charleston old guard judges every book by its cover. But I never really worried much about it. As long as I had Lamar and my art, I was a happy woman."

"Thanks for sharing that story with me," said Beth. "Michael will be the only person I ever tell, and I'll swear him to secrecy."

"What do I care who knows now?" Her smile was full of sadness. "Tell me about him."

Beth straightened her spine. "Michael? Not much to tell other than he's my partner."

"Nonsense. There is plenty more to tell. You just might not realize it yet."

"All this talk about young love has you imagining things." Beth refilled her cup for something to do. "We get along pretty well, but that's it."

"I know how partners can get along, and I know about good friends. But I sense there's something more. Wait and see. What you're capable of just might surprise you."

What I might be capable of? Doesn't Michael have a say in this? What is this woman talking about?

Questions ran through Beth's mind, but she didn't have the guts to ask any of them. "Thanks for clearing up the question about the gunfire. Now I'd better get back before my partner sends out the bloodhounds."

Mrs. Doyle pulled a Tupperware container from the refrigerator. "I had a feeling you might be by today, so I baked a German chocolate cake with cream cheese frosting. I made it, not my maid. I hope you and your partner enjoy it."

Beth accepted the cake with thanks and then was on her way. It took her ten minutes in the car with windows down before her head cleared enough to call Michael. "Hey, I just left Mrs. Doyle. What are you doin'?"

"I finished my workout and now I'm in the pool. After all, I am on vacation."

"Stay where you are. I'm hot, tired, and dying to get in the pool. What about your assignment?"

"Our first interview will be tomorrow at breakfast. Candidates two and three will be on Wednesday and Thursday. I take my job seriously, Miss Kirby. What do you think about free sliders in the Lodge tonight, along with Southern potato salad and coleslaw?"

"I say the price is right. Pencil me in, but save room for dessert. Our favorite client baked us a German chocolate cake that's calling my name from the backseat."

Despite Mrs. Doyle's generosity, Beth ended the call feeling mildly annoyed with her. *Why did she have to put ridiculous romantic notions in my head?* It was hard enough staying focused this far from home.

TWELVE

*M*ichael contemplated a grueling workout to compensate for the calories he consumed last night. After three Angus sliders and both side dishes, he devoured two pieces of chocolate cake. Although he didn't believe Mrs. Doyle baked the four-tier cake herself, Beth was willing to stake her life on it. For some inexplicable reason, his partner had taken a shine to Savannah's newest widow.

It was the last thing he would have expected when they accepted the case. What had she called them—Sleaze Incorporated? Michael knew that no middle-aged woman could fool Beth, so he had no trouble believing their client was innocent. Convincing their boss was a different matter. He didn't know Nate Price well enough to understand why he'd rallied around Reverend Dean's widow in their last case. Nate had wanted no stones left unturned as they searched for the killer. How was this any different? Mrs. Doyle hired them to determine the extent of her husband's duplicity. When Lamar turned up dead, wouldn't a client on Tybee Island deserve the same benefit of the doubt as one in Natchez? But knowing Beth's intuition, he would stick with his partner, even if they both ended up in the unemployment line.

Michael poured his third cup of coffee and stared out at the

Savannah River. A mist rose from the unusually calm surface, lending eeriness to the morning light. He knew he should *do* something. If he sat around mulling over the case, his thoughts would turn to Beth the way they always did. Last night they had overindulged in free food, shared a piece of chocolate cake, and played a silly board game under the stars. They had talked about old friends, high school flames, and their favorite movies. They laughed at themselves and each other and nothing at all, like very old, very good friends. It was too soon to tell, but that might have been the best night of his life. He loved being with Beth. That could be a problem. And sitting alone, reliving the night in his mind, wasn't doing him any good.

When his phone rang, Michael practically fell over the railing.

"Are you ready to grill the next potential member of Price Investigations within an inch of her life?" Beth seldom began a conversation with any form of identification.

"I'm as ready as I'll ever be. I have the standard set of interview questions Maxine emailed me." Michael retreated into his hotel room, closing the balcony doors behind him.

"Ha!" Beth howled. "I have a list of questions meant to thin the weak and hapless from the herd."

He grinned at the image. Beth was the type who bottle-fed abandoned birds until they were ready to leave the nest. He couldn't wait to see her promise put into action. "Ms. Hancock isn't meeting us until nine. It's only eight fifteen by my watch."

"Let's discuss our strategy in the Lodge and share our initial thoughts on the applicant."

"I'll be down in ten minutes."

He appeared on the first floor in eight minutes.

Beth was already in a front booth sipping iced tea. "Let's see the résumé of today's contestant." She practically ripped the top sheet from his hands.

"Easy, partner. We each have a copy." Michael tapped the sheets into a pile. "I contacted your favorite choice first. Ms. Hancock can set the bar, so to speak."

"Undergraduate degree in political science and finished two years of prelaw at Columbia," Beth read from the sheet. "Well educated, that's for sure. Received her investigative experience with the Georgia Department of Tax Enforcement. What do you suppose that means?"

"I imagine she tracked down people who didn't pay their state taxes, such as store owners or business employers who withheld the money from customers or employees but didn't fork it over."

"She hauled them off to debtors' prison?" Beth laughed behind the sheet.

"Those have been turned into shopping malls. Now tax agents issue threats and file liens against any real estate the debtor owns. Sooner or later, the state gets their money."

"Do you think she carried a gun? A forty-four magnum might prod folks into pulling out their checkbooks."

"I believe Ms. Hancock is headed this way, so add that question to your list." Michael clenched down on his back teeth, annoyed that the candidate had arrived thirty-five minutes early. Some might consider it a mark of good manners. At the moment, he considered it an invasion of privacy.

Beth stood to greet the applicant. "Are you Anita Hancock? I'm Beth Kirby of Price Investigations. Thanks for being punctual."

"I make it a point to be early instead of just on time. I can't stand people who are always late." Ms. Hancock offered a toothy smile.

While the two women shook hands, Michael had a chance to assess her appearance: fortyish, tasteful hair and makeup, dark suit with white blouse, high heels. Conservative except for a rather short skirt.

"How do you do?" he greeted, also rising to his feet. "I'm Michael Preston. We spoke on the phone."

"I'm doing just fine ever since I saw your ad online. Finally, I thought, something I can sink my teeth into and leave the government work doldrums behind." She widened her smile in his direction.

"Why don't you sit there, Ms. Hancock?" Pointing at his vacated seat, Michael pulled a chair to the end of the booth. "It'll be easier for a three-way conversation."

"Anita, please. Ms. Hancock makes me feel old." She slipped into the booth. "And I assure you, Mike, I'm far from being that."

"Coffee, Anita?" asked Beth, filling the extra mug. "May I ask why you didn't finish law school? The world always needs more lawyers, considering how litigious society has become."

Anita wrapped her fingers around the mug. "Do you have any idea how boring law school is? Obsessing over ancient court cases that might be useful in the future. I thought my eyes would permanently cross. I had to get out or go mad. Don't believe what you see on TV—law school is *filled* with geeks who love memorizing useless trivia." She mimed a yawn.

Michael tamped down a frisson of irritation. His ex-fiancée had described accountants—his former profession—with the exact same words. "Did you find tax enforcement work more interesting?" He struggled to keep his voice even.

"You bet I did. I loved tracking down white-collar thieves. They thought that just because they went to work in a suit and tie, they could avoid paying what they owed. We're not the IRS, willing to settle for partial back taxes as long as you promise not to cheat again. If you collect sales tax on purchases, you'd better turn over every dime, or I'll make your life a living nightmare."

Oddly, a few legitimate reasons for being late with payments sprang to Michael's mind, but instead he asked a more pertinent question. "Why do you wish to change careers if you find the work satisfying?"

"Ever been a government employee, Mike? Stacks of paperwork, endless mumbo-jumbo meetings, plus all that backstabbing and hand kissing. Ugh. That's why I steered clear of the police academy. Bring down one bad guy, and you'll be filling out forms at your desk for weeks."

Beth laughed, mainly to take control. "I doubt you carried a weapon in your last job, but we sometimes do in ours. Are you licensed to carry in this state?"

"You bet I am, sister. Fully trained and certified. I usually pack a Sig Sauer."

Beth glanced at Michael before answering. "A Glock is my weapon of choice, but let's get back to—"

"How 'bout you, Mike?" asked Anita, apparently not ready for the topic to change.

"I have a new Smith and Wesson I'm becoming proficient with," he murmured.

"Where are you *really* from? Most Mississippi guys owned a gun before they owned their first car."

Michael locked gazes with the applicant. "That's funny. None of my friends had a gun rack in their truck or an arsenal in the basement to fit your image of Southern manhood. I suppose it's in the company you keep."

"I suppose so." Anita forced a laugh, finally aware she was standing on thin ice.

He glanced down at her résumé. "I'm curious as to what special skills you have."

"I'm a self-starter, accustomed to hard work and long days. I'm willing to travel and can be flexible with my schedule. I have no husband or kids tying me down."

He shook his head. "Let me be more specific. Beth is adept with surveillance and interrogation, while my accounting background helps us follow the money trail to the suspects. What specific talents will you bring to the team?"

She hesitated a few seconds. "I hold a black belt in mixed

martial arts. I could do the heavy lifting, so to speak." Her big, toothy smile reappeared.

He leaned back in his chair. "You do realize, Ms. Hancock, that we're a reputable private investigation firm, not the real-life counterpart of *Dog the Bounty Hunter.*"

"All righty, then," interrupted his partner. "Thanks so much for coming in, Anita. We have a few more candidates to interview, and then we'll let you know."

"Thank you, Beth. It was a pleasure to meet you." Candidate number one extended her hand solely to Michael's partner and left quickly.

He held his breath until the woman went out the door. "Good grief! *She* was your first choice?" He covered his face with his hands.

"Anita sounded better on paper than in person. Looks like we'll have to see who's behind door number two." Beth glanced at her watch. "While you vet the other applicants, I'm going to the coffee shop for a chat with Crystal."

"Do you remember what Nate said about letting the police do their job?"

"I do, but aren't we still on Mrs. Doyle's payroll? Now that we did what the boss wanted, I want to see what Bonnie's alibi has to say. I'll be back in time for the free food. What surprises will we discover tonight?" She gave his arm a squeeze as she headed for the door.

With Beth's touch, Michael completely forgot his next argument. Instead, he watched her leave, feeling an entirely different set of emotions than those he experienced with Ms. Hancock.

Thirteen

*B*eth chuckled all the way to Cool Beans. *Could a job interview have gone any worse than that?* As soon as Ms. Hancock called her partner "Mike" not once but three times, Beth knew Anita's future at Price Investigations was doomed. But honestly, why would a tax compliance officer think PIs had exciting, action-packed lifestyles? So much of their time was spent searching databases, combing through files for overlooked details, or surveilling people who did *nothing* for hours. Although Beth enjoyed her current job, work for her wasn't as intense as it had been when she was a detective on the Natchez police force. But working with a partner she trusted made up for any dearth of excitement.

Beth spent so much time reliving the interview that she arrived at the coffee shop without a plan. Fortunately, her target, Crystal, was manning the pastry oven, while the ethically impaired Bonnie was nowhere in sight. For someone suddenly without a sugar daddy, the girl took many days off. Beth considered nursing a caramel latte in the corner until Crystal took her break, but her cover as a hopeful new employee had been played to death.

Without a better idea, Beth settled on a park bench across the street with mini binoculars and a paperback book. Long before the Victorian-era debutante caught the duke's eye, Beth spotted Crystal heading to the alley for her smoke break. *The hopeful heiress will have to wait.*

Beth sprinted across the street. "If it isn't my old friend Crystal Callahan. How you been?" she asked sweetly.

"What do *you* want? And don't give me that baloney about looking for a job. You're some kind of cop, aren't you?" Crystal glared down her nose, her superior height courtesy of six-inch platform shoes.

"I knew I couldn't fool a smart girl like you for long." Beth arched up on her tiptoes until they were nose to nose. "Actually, I would love to work at a fun place like this…so many chances to meet cool men. Too bad I already have a job—finding out who killed my friend's husband. You remember Lamar Doyle, don't you? He was supposed to set your pal Bonnie up for life."

Crystal almost fell off her shoes trying to move away. "Look, I'll tell you the same thing I told that lady cop yesterday. I have no idea who killed Mr. Doyle and neither does Bonnie." She spat out the words. "Go look for your killer someplace else. After we closed the shop, Bonnie came home with me Saturday night. And she stayed there *all night.*"

Beth studied the girl's defensive posture—crossed arms, jutting chin, squinting eyes. *This young egg won't crack the old-fashioned way with intimidation.* So Beth tried a softer, gentler approach.

"Look, could you cut me some slack here? Mrs. Doyle employed me to find out details. I won't get paid unless I come back with the same story you told that detective. If Bonnie didn't do it, fine with me. I just want to fill out my report."

"What do I care if you get paid? You've been nothing but a pain in my neck." Crystal lit another cigarette, even though she just stubbed out the last one.

Beth smiled slyly. "Because the sooner I report back it wasn't your gal pal, the sooner the cops will look someplace else."

Crystal considered that in a haze of blue smoke. "I just told you what I know."

Beth pulled out her notebook and pen. "From the top, everything you said to Detective Rossi. Then I'm outta here."

Crystal sighed heavily but began talking. "We first had to clean the displays. Then Bonnie came to my house for a sleepover. We left here around nine thirty. I had my car here that day."

"Did you set this up ahead of time or spur of the moment?"

"Spur of the moment," Crystal said after a brief hesitation.

"What about her stuff like a nightgown or toothbrush?"

"Stop interrupting me! And who wears nightgowns anymore other than old grannies?" As punishment, Crystal blew smoke into Beth's face. "I gave her a T-shirt to sleep in, and maybe she used my toothbrush. I don't know."

Yuck, Beth thought, but wisely she stayed silent.

"Like I said, we were at my place all night, watching movies and playing video games. Then I went to bed, and Bonnie slept on the couch. I don't know what time that was. In the morning, I took a shower and went to work. Bonnie had the day off. I don't know what time she left or where she went." Crystal punctuated her story with a glare.

Beth jotted notes prodigiously. "Okay, where do you live—in a house or an apartment? Do you have other roommates?"

"I live with my grandmother, but it's like having my own place." She recited the address while picking at her cuticle.

Beth stopped writing. "How so? I live with my mom and dad, and it's *nothing* like having my own place."

"My bedroom and bathroom are in the back of the house, with a separate entrance off the porch. My grandma watches TV in the front room. I come and go as I please." Crystal's expression was nothing but smug.

"Huh, I gotta work on that when I go home. What about food? Did you guys send out for pizza that night?"

"Nope. We had chips and Coke. We didn't get very hungry."

"Can you think of *anyone* who might have seen Bonnie at your place Saturday night?"

Crystal checked the time on her phone. "Look, you wanted what I told the other cop, and that's what you got. Sorry if it didn't meet your expectations, but I gotta get back to work." She pushed away from the wall.

"Just one more question, I promise."

Crystal offered a disgusted eye roll. "*What?*"

"Have you seen her since you left for work Sunday morning?"

"No. Bonnie's taking some time off. I don't know when she'll be back. You know, she's sad about losing Lamar." She headed for the street with Beth at her heels.

"So she didn't stop over or call in order to synchronize your stories?"

"I haven't talked to her."

"Then how do you know she's sad about Mr. Doyle dying? He wasn't dead the last time you two talked."

Crystal stopped on a dime. "I want you to get away from me, or I'll tell that lady detective you're harassing me."

Beth lifted her hands and stepped back. "Just trying to help you out since you gave me good advice on the job application."

"Yeah? Well, here's a little more advice…"

Beth tucked her notebook in her purse. "I'm all ears, Crystal."

The young woman's grin brightened her rather bland features. "Get your own place to live. You are *way* too old to live with your parents."

Beth burst out laughing. *Ain't that the honest-to-goodness truth.*

⤳

Back at the hotel, Beth spotted her partner in the lobby. Michael sat reading the paper while tourists and businesspeople milled around him noisily. "What are you doing here? This place is a zoo."

He folded the paper in half. "I was waiting for you. I wanted to catch you before you went to your room." In his cotton shirt and chinos, Michael looked cool, casual, and handsome.

"Couldn't wait to hear my news? Well, let me say that Miss Cappuccino shouldn't count on a stage career. Her rehearsed delivery of Bonnie's lies wasn't very believable. I'm sure Detective Rossi saw right through her performance. Just the same, I'd like you to delve into Crystal Callahan's background. Maybe we'll learn something to help pry out the truth." She tore the sheet with Grandma's address from her notebook.

"Consider it done, but Bonnie's alibi isn't why I've been watching for you."

Beth perched on the arm of a chair. "Discover some skeletons in our applicants' closets?"

"I found out George Faraday's former career as a CSI tech was a bit of a stretch. He did work in a medical lab, but mainly in prep and cleanup work, not analyzing data as potential evidence."

"People love to spin straw into gold. We'll see if he comes clean tomorrow." Beth pulled off the tight band holding her ponytail. "Ready to hit the free food? I'm hoping for buffalo wings on Tuesdays."

Michael stretched to his full six feet two and smiled. "*That's* why I was waiting for you. What do you say we skip the freebies tonight and go to dinner in one of Savannah's best restaurants? Seafood, steak, whatever you have a taste for." He seemed to look at her oddly.

"You mean burn through some of the expense money we've been hoarding?"

He shrugged. "Either that or let me buy dinner. Real people do spend their own money even while on assignment."

Beth scratched her scalp, which had started to itch. "This sounds very much like a date."

"It could be, or it could be two partners burning through our expense stipend. That's up to you," he added softly.

"Nothing like springing this on me when I had free sliders and slaw on the mind. Now you dangle fancy cuisine in front of a starving woman?" She jumped to her feet and started to pace, oblivious to a cluster of nearby children. "Let's go someplace snazzy, and we'll both order whatever we want. Price will be no object. Then, at the end of the night, *I'll* decide whether you or Mrs. Doyle picks up the tab." She stopped in front of him. "I suppose capris and sneakers aren't going to cut it."

Michael appraised her outfit far longer than necessary. "How about a dress and heels if I put on my funeral-and-wedding suit?"

Beth threw her hands in the air. "Fine, but we're eating Italian at some place with white tablecloths and real espresso. I'll meet you at the car in two hours, and don't call me in the meantime. I need that long to pull this rabbit out of my hat."

During the next ninety minutes, Beth showered and dressed in a long, sleeveless silk dress. Then she carefully applied makeup to the best of her ability, which truly wasn't saying much. She used pressed powder to even out her skin tone, a bronzer to simulate a tan for cheeks that only freckled, and navy mascara to highlight her blue eyes. At least that's why her friend Jacklyn told her to buy it. But the seldom-used eye shadow palette had her baffled. *Which shadow is supposed to go under the brow and which into the crease above my eyes?* With a sigh, Beth selected the prettiest of the four shades and dusted it over both lids, leaving her time to stare into her mirror and wonder what she was doing.

It wasn't that she didn't like Michael, because she did. A lot.

He was no longer the nerdy, pocket-protector-wearing number cruncher, thanks to his high-protein diet, weight training, and a better haircut. Although she was glad to see the old buzz cut go, she had never agreed with his personal appraisal. And there was plenty about the old Michael she hoped he wouldn't lose. Learning to defend himself and how to handle firearms were necessary in their line of work, but she appreciated his compassion and self-deprecating sense of humor. How many men listened when others talked and treated everyone respectfully, whether their behavior warranted it or not?

Truth was, she really *liked* Michael, but was simple fondness a solid foundation for romance? She felt none of the stomach-wrenching, breath-snatching, heart-pounding excitement that she had with Chief McNeil, her former boss at Natchez PD. Where was all that fiery passion now?

She knew she would never forgive herself if she didn't try. Michael would survive if they simply remained work pals. He would meet someone else and live happily ever after. But she would always wonder what she missed. Beth took a final look in the mirror, whispered a prayer, and inhaled a deep breath.

Downstairs, Michael was leaning against his car, talking on the phone. He looked fit and handsome in a tan sport coat, dark slacks, and Italian loafers. "You're in luck," he said after he ended the call. "We have reservations at Belford's in the City Market. They assured me their tablecloths are white and their espresso machine works. They also have a good selection of steak and seafood." He swept open the car door. "You look nice by the way. And so *tall* in those heels." He winked at her.

"Are you mocking me, Preston? That's never a good idea."

"I'm merely stating the obvious as a conversational icebreaker."

"Let's stick to sports or the weather until something clever comes to mind. And remember, we're no longer in the eighth grade." As he backed from the parking space, she caught a whiff of aftershave. Oddly, she never had noticed the spicy scent before.

"Let's see…" Michael tried to look serious. "The weather is lovely and I have no idea what's going on in sports, so let's bring each other up to date on the case. Anything else you'd like to share from your interrogation of Bonnie's alibi?"

While Michael wove through Savannah traffic, Beth recounted several details from the conversation, including Crystal's slipup about Bonnie's melancholia, even though they hadn't spoken since Saturday night.

Michael was grinning by the time she finished. "Doubtlessly, a seasoned veteran like Rossi can smell a fishy story a block away, just like you. She's probably ferreting out where Mulroney really was Saturday night as we speak." He pulled into the valet queue at a very fancy restaurant. "We're here, Cinderella."

"I hope the Charger won't turn into a pumpkin at midnight. I can't walk far in these shoes." When the attendant opened her door, Beth climbed out as gracefully as possible. *How do those red carpet stars manage long dresses and high heels from a low center of gravity?*

Michael gave his name to the hostess, and they were shown to a table next to a fountain in the courtyard. "Or would you prefer something indoors, Beth?" he asked, pulling out her chair.

Michael always had impeccable manners, but tonight his attention was practically solicitous. "No, this is lovely." She accepted a menu from the waiter and made her selection without gasping at the prices. After Michael had given him their order— Caesar salad for two, linguini with clam sauce for her, veal marsala with angel hair pasta for him—Beth steered the conversation back to comfortable ground. "Tell me more about the other two applicants."

"I believe George Faraday vastly stretched the truth when he described his former position. But I don't want to influence your opinion before tomorrow's breakfast appointment."

"Fair enough, since he was my second favorite choice. Let's hope he works out better than Ms. Hancock." Beth nibbled at a bread stick.

"And I discovered something else interesting while you were gone, something that had been gnawing at me since I visited Town and Country Insurance. The assistant had so low an opinion of Doyle's performance that she felt sorry for the guy. I learned today that he made only thirty-three thousand dollars last year in commissions while Mrs. Doyle had no income whatsoever."

Beth reached for a second bread stick, wishing she'd eaten more lunch. "So what? Evelyn already told us her husband inherited the big bucks from his father. It's probably invested to throw off a stream of income."

"True, but why would the largest insurance agency in the state keep a nonperforming slug like Doyle on the payroll?"

"Didn't you say he only received commissions, instead of a regular nine-to-five paycheck?"

"Yes, but a sales manager's bonus is tied to performance—namely, the dollars generated by the agents under his supervision. Why not hire someone ambitious, someone hungry enough to set the world on fire? The better the agents perform, the better the boss looks."

Beth set down the rest of her bread as the Caesar salad was served with great fanfare. "I see your point," she said, after the culinary performance was complete. "He's worked there for a while, right? Maybe Doyle and his boss were friends."

"That's not the impression I got from the woman I spoke with. I smell something fishy at Town and Country Insurance. Call it my own gut instinct. I intend to find out why Mr. Reynard didn't replace the weakest link on his team."

She nodded and dug into the best Caesar salad of her life, followed by an entrée that should be in every Italian cookbook in the world. Michael ordered a bottle of the house's *best* sparkling cider, and they discussed everything from their happiest childhood memory to what each considered their dream vacation if price were no object. The food was sublime, the conversation easy, and Beth laughed more than she ever had before.

Then, without warning, the waiter laid the bill on Michael's side of the table. It commanded their attention as though neither had ever seen one before. Michael's hand hovered above the leather folder like a magician performing a trick. "The moment of decision has arrived. What'll it be—the stash of cash advanced by Nate or my personal platinum MasterCard?"

"You have a platinum card?" she asked, wide eyed. "That must be the difference between someone with an accounting degree and someone who never balances her checkbook."

He leaned toward her, his smile fading. "No more jokes. It's a simple question, Beth. Was this just dinner between work partners or the first of what I hope are many dates? I'm a big boy. I can handle the answer. But it's time to make up your mind." He settled back and thrummed his fingers on the leather sleeve.

Beth shifted as a blast of air-conditioning hit her neck. She knew what she should say based on her last experience. She also knew that every magazine warned against work relationships—too much friction after the breakup. And her dear mother's words rang in her ears like a radio jingle: "*Don't you ever learn, Betsy?*"

Maybe one day she would.

But that day wouldn't be today.

"Slap down the personal platinum, Preston. This meal is on you."

Michael laughed at her string of *p* words. "Does this mean I made the cut?"

Beth shook her index finger. "Look, I think we get along well in a yin-and-yang kind of way, whatever that means. So we should probably date and see if our toes start tingling. But don't count on any mushy good-night kisses in the elevator. That is *waaay* down the road."

Michael scrubbed his hands down his face. It was a gesture she'd seen her father make many times. "That's the last thing on my mind, Kirby. What I really want is dessert, so stand up and catch the waiter's attention. Put those five-inch heels to good use."

FOURTEEN

*M*ichael had been far too keyed up to sleep when he returned to his hotel room last night. Not only had dinner gone better than he dared to hope, but the food had been pretty good too. At least that's what Beth told him. He must have eaten some of the one-hundred-twenty-dollar meal, because his plate was empty except for a smear of marsala sauce. He was so happy she let him pay, he wouldn't have cared if the bill had been five hundred dollars. One thing he did remember was how good Beth had looked in that long dress with her wavy hair fanning across her shoulders. Even though they had worked together for weeks, he still couldn't take his eyes off her. If it hadn't been for the car's warning signal, he would have backed into a concrete pillar.

Michael had paced his room for an hour, then tossed and turned for two more before he fell into a fitful sleep. Now as he waited for candidate number two to arrive in the Lodge, fog filled every nook and cranny of his brain, until the appearance of his partner broke through the haze like a ray of sun.

"How ya feeling today?" Beth slipped into the booth. "Still stuffed to the gills but poorer in the pocketbook?"

"Will the letter *p* be your favorite for two days in a row? And where is that cool dress from yesterday?" He pointed at her over-sized shirt. "I was hoping you would sleep in it and come straight here."

"What kind of impression would that make? I'm the senior investigator, and so far Nate hasn't sent any more potential applicants. I believe our next victim is headed this way. Let's hope he's a winner."

Michael swiveled around to see a sixtysomething man with thick gray hair, a full beard, and deep creases around his mouth and across his forehead. Here was a Southerner who didn't believe in high SPF factors or sunglasses. "Mr. Faraday? Hi, I'm Michael Preston, and this is Elizabeth Kirby. Thanks for your interest in Price Investigations." This time when Michael pulled over a chair, it was intended for the interviewee. He remained across from Beth. "Please have a seat."

Surprisingly, Faraday turned the chair around backward, straddling it like a cop in a 1940s film noir. "So you're not Nate Price?" he asked Michael. "I was hoping to meet the boss right off the bat."

"Mr. Price is in Natchez at our home office. But because there is so much work here, thanks to referrals, he wants to hire a permanent Savannah-based investigator. While Miss Kirby and I are on assignment, we'll hire someone on a trial basis. If he or she proves a good fit, Nate will fly out to meet them. I take it you're from Chatham County."

"All my life, born and raised. I'm curious about your current case. It must be something pretty juicy to come all the way from the Mississippi River." Crossing his arms over the back of the chair, Faraday leaned in Beth's direction. "Care to fill me in?"

"We're not at liberty to discuss ongoing investigations," she drawled. "But we are interested in you. Tell us more about your previous experience. Did you work in a local forensic lab or the Georgia Bureau of Investigation?"

"I worked in the lab at St. Joseph's Hospital here in Savannah, but occasionally we got work from the Chatham County Coroner's Office, like prepping slides and whatnot. I'm interested in hands-on investigating, like stakeouts, surveillance, and undercover work." Faraday's smile stretched across his craggy face. "I have some great ideas that could make your agency lots of dough."

Michael tried not to laugh. "I'm game. Let's hear one."

"I set myself up online as the owner of a national chain of bridal salons. I supply wedding parties with everything from designer shoes, bridal gowns, handbags, luggage, jewelry—all that overpriced stuff that women buy just because of a designer's name. The fine print on my ad stipulates I'm only interested in high-end merchandise at *deeply discounted* prices." Smirking, Faraday peered from one to the other. "That should draw the counterfeiters and knockoff manufacturers out of the woodwork. We compile a list of the counterfeiters and sell it to companies like Coach or Louis Vuitton for a fat commission."

"That sounds a lot like entrapment," Beth said, frowning.

"No, it's not because we ain't cops. We're investigators, offering a service to manufacturers." His irritated tone stretched the boundaries of polite conversation expected in an interview.

"Interesting idea, but right now we have more than enough cases to keep us busy." Michael pulled out the man's résumé. "Getting back on target, I see you went to the University of Georgia. Did you graduate with a degree?"

"Nah. I didn't want to get in too deep with college loans, so I left and went to work in store security."

"Yes, that's why I chose you for an interview." Beth took the sheet from Michael's hand. "Ah. Here it is...surveillance and loss-prevention experience. Could you elaborate on your position?"

"I worked the security desk at a department store in West Palm Beach. I helped the store clerks keep track of merchandise in the fitting rooms. You have no idea how many times six garments go in but only four come back out on hangers. And you can't believe which ones are pulling this stunt."

"Young, naive college girls?" Michael asked.

"That's what I would have guessed too!" Faraday punctuated the air with his fist. "But usually it was middle-aged gals—every one of them looking like they could easily afford the clothes hidden beneath their coats."

"Dishonesty has no upper age limit," mused Beth. "How did you catch them—strip-search women in the center aisle?" Her tone clearly indicated sarcasm, which was lost on candidate number two.

"No, that wasn't allowed. All we could do was call the police and wait for a lady cop to confirm the theft." Faraday huffed with disappointment. "I suggested to management we monitor *everything* that happens in those fitting rooms. The thousands saved in loss prevention would pay for those hidden cameras in no time at all."

Beth tucked the résumé back into the folder. "Another great suggestion promptly ignored. Oh, those pesky privacy laws getting in the way again."

This time Faraday picked up on Beth's mockery. "A store is private property. If a person doesn't like the rules, they can shop elsewhere."

"Management probably feared that's what ladies would do if word got around." Beth's sweet drawl returned.

"Funny how criminals these days have far more rights than law-abiding folks." After Faraday delivered this summation to Beth, he scooted the chair around to face Michael directly. "If you got the time, Mr. Preston, I'd like to share another lucrative idea I have for the agency."

Michael didn't know if he was more flabbergasted or intrigued by the man's effrontery. Curiosity won out. "By all means. I'm interested in how you would make money for Price Investigations."

Beth's eyes turned as round as an owl's as Faraday turned his back on her.

"I've done my homework on PIs. I've wanted to get into the business since I was a kid. I know that messy divorces are an agency's bread and butter. I'm willing to bet that's what you're in town for." Faraday offered a smile that was the epitome of smarmy.

Michael was afraid his partner's head might explode.

"I thought I had made it quite clear that we won't discuss ongoing cases—" Beth began.

"Let me finish," Faraday interrupted. "Mr. Preston wanted to hear my ideas. He's the one in charge until Mr. Price comes to town."

Despite the entertainment factor, Michael couldn't tolerate the man's rudeness. "Wait a minute, Mr. Faraday…"

Beth held up her hand like a crossing guard. "No. I absolutely must hear the rest of this." Her tone of voice, along with the applicant's, was attracting attention from the surrounding patrons.

Faraday continued to address Michael. "It doesn't matter which case brought you to Savannah. Bundles of money can be made outside those chic clubs along the river. First I create a database of every mover and shaker in the city, those with society connections and deep pockets. Then I find a good vantage point across from one of those clubs, maybe from another building or even up a tree. Then I photograph any well-dressed gentleman leaving with a woman who might not be his wife. I have a sixth sense about that kind of thing. With a good telephoto lens, I could make the agency a great deal of money."

Michael shoved the folder away. "The woman might be his daughter or granddaughter or a myriad of other logical relationships. Even if the older man was dating a younger woman, how is that our business?"

"Hear me out. I contact the guy using an email address that

can't be traced to the agency. Pretending to be a journalist, I ask for permission to use pictures I took in an article about nightlife in Old Savannah." Faraday chuckled, pleased with himself. "If the man has nothing to hide, he can either agree or disagree, but he'll never hear from us again. If he was up to no good, he might be willing to pay to make sure those photos never see the light of day."

Michael felt himself tense. "Listen to me very carefully, Mr. Faraday. What you're suggesting is called blackmail, which is not only illegal but the lowest form of income generation in the world."

"If those men have nothing to hide—"

"I'm not finished!" Michael snapped. "Not only am I *revolted* by your ideas, but if I ever get wind of you putting this scheme into practice, I'll give your fiction-filled résumé to law enforcement. They'll be eager to track you down for a chat."

Faraday stood, almost knocking over the chair. "And I thought you were the logical member of the team."

Beth rose regally to her feet. "Since we don't need a professional Peeping Tom, I think we're done. If you hurry, you can still catch the bus to Sleazyville." Honey dripped from her words. "And just for the record, *I'm* the senior investigator here. Maybe you should rethink the sexist pig routine before your next job interview." With her hands balled into fists, Beth glared until Faraday vanished from sight. Then she slumped down and dropped her face into her hands. Odd sounds emanated from beneath her mass of hair.

Michael patted the top of her head. "There, there. Don't cry. We still have candidate number three to look forward to."

Beth lifted a streaky face. She had laughed herself hysterical. "Does *everyone* lie on job applications? I only fudged a few pounds off my weight."

Michael reflected a moment. "I might make myself taller, but that's because I don't own a tape measure. Are you going to be all right, Kirby? For a moment there, I thought you might strangle Faraday with your bare hands."

"I am going up to call Nate and give him the blow-by-blow before I forget a single detail. He was first to vet Mr. Faraday. Nate needs to provide more viable candidates, or you and I will be stuck here until Christmas."

Michael left a generous tip on the table and followed Beth into the lobby. "After you update the boss, what else is on your agenda for today, Ms. Senior Investigator?"

"I've been thinking about what you told me last night. You could be on to something. Plenty of guys work even though they don't need the money. Doyle might have liked the camaraderie of an office and enjoyed hawking insurance as a hobby, but what's the incentive for his boss to have him around? I'm heading to Town and Country to see if the guy will talk to me. If you give me your notes, you can goof off for a few hours."

"The boss's name is Joseph Reynard, but if you're going, so am I. The agency assistant is already eating out of my hand."

Beth hooted. "As helpful as that could be, you don't have to do this. We both know what Nate said. For some reason, he wants to leave Mrs. Doyle swinging in the breeze, at the mercy of a defense lawyer who might not be any better than the last."

Michael pressed the button for the elevator. "I don't think it's that. He just has faith that the Tybee Island police will do their job. As out-of-towners without contacts on the force, we're at a disadvantage."

"I understand, but as I said before, it's none of Nate's business if I want to help a friend in my spare time. You don't need to get in trouble on my account." Beth stepped into the elevator and pressed the button.

Michael blocked the door open with his foot. "Let's get something straight. You're not tracking down Doyle's killer without me, partner. While you talk to Nate, I'll call that assistant and sweet-talk my way into an appointment with Reynard. Then I'll review my notes on Town and Country on my laptop. Come downstairs whenever you're ready." He withdrew his foot.

As the elevator closed, Beth met his gaze with her luminous blue eyes. "I was hoping you'd say that."

Michael strolled to his favorite couch in the lobby, his mood significantly improved since Faraday had left. As much as Nate wanted them to hire another investigator as soon as possible, there were worse fates than staying in charming Savannah until Christmas.

FIFTEEN

*T*here ought to be a limit to how many times a person was allowed to say, "You've got to be kidding me," within a fifteen-minute period. Because Nate Price sounded like a mynah bird by the time Beth finished describing Faraday's interview.

"I assure you, boss, the quality of the applicants you sent us is no laughing matter."

"Sorry about that, Beth. I'll have Maxine contact a Savannah headhunter to see if they have any experienced investigators looking for work. Let's have them do the initial screening since résumés can't be trusted for accuracy. Did that guy really want to spy on women in store fitting rooms?" Nate's skepticism rivaled his contempt.

"Yes, but let's change the subject. I want to forget I ever met nasty George. He's the reason some folks have low opinions of PIs."

"Agreed. I'll never bring him up again, but I must tell Isabelle. She thinks that stalker back in Memphis was one of a kind." Nate made a *tsk* sound with his tongue. "Take the rest of the day off, Beth. You earned it. Go do something fun like parasailing or hang gliding."

"You know I hate heights. Let me pick my own pastime."

"How are you and Michael getting along? I notice you haven't referred to him as 'Wonder Boy' or 'Mikey' in a long time, to my supreme joy."

"And you never will again. We're getting along fine—nothing for you to worry about. Give that headhunter my personal cell number and have them call anytime, twenty-four-seven. I want to move this interview process along in a positive direction."

"Will do. Stay in touch. And make sure you have fun in Savannah. That's part of the reason you're there."

After Nate ended the call, Beth stared out the window for several minutes. *Wonder Boy?* It had been awhile since she had such little respect for her partner. Michael had made great strides in his quest to reinvent himself. His new buff physique had bolstered his self-image, but Beth hadn't found him unappealing before. His new confidence and assertiveness on the job, even under pressure, were amazing. Michael hadn't stammered or blushed in ages. These days, if she had to pick a moniker, it would probably be *Wonder Man*, but she wasn't ready to tell Nate they were dating. Too much could go wrong as they got to know each other.

Beth took out her makeup bag for the second time in two days and dabbed on blush and lipstick. If she was to meet the manager of the largest insurance agency in Georgia, she should look her best. Or at least that's what she told herself.

Michael shut his computer the moment she reached the lobby. "Are we still on the payroll?"

"We are. Nate felt so bad about Faraday's résumé that he ordered us to take the afternoon off. We are free to do whatever we like."

"Then we're free to take our chances at Town and Country Insurance."

"I take it the conversation didn't go well with the assistant." Beth tucked her hair behind one ear.

"It went…adequately." Michael shoved his laptop in his bag.

"She assured me Reynard would be in the office this afternoon, but he was booked solid with meetings and appointments. If we want to wait, she will try to squeeze us in."

Beth walked through the revolving doors into hot afternoon sunshine. Although the time of year was officially declared autumn, the blast of humidity begged to differ with the calendar. "Looks like we'll spend an otherwise perfect day in an office waiting room. Last chance to change your mind." She paused on the sidewalk as passersby skirted around them.

Michael checked his watch and pulled out his map of the historic area. "Let's leave the car and walk instead. That way the air-conditioning will feel good once we get there. And with a small detour, we can see two squares we might have otherwise missed—Chippewa and Orleans."

"Fine by me," she said when Michael set out at a brisk pace. The squares were shady city parks with moss-draped oaks, brick pathways, fountains, benches, and statues honoring Revolutionary War heroes. Each one unique, each one soothing to the soul. Residents brought their dogs or kids or came alone to eat their lunch, read, meditate, or simply watch the world hurry by.

Beth matched Michael's stride, grateful she'd opted for flats instead of last night's heels. She was also grateful that his pace precluded conversation. Both of them needed time to adjust to the change in their relationship. Once they reached the insurance office, Beth took a seat in the waiting area—chilly, as anticipated—while Michael approached the reception desk.

"Hi, Miss Frost. Remember me? Michael Preston." His smile would dazzle the comatose.

"Of course I remember. You had an appointment with Mr. Doyle that he didn't keep. But can I ask why you want to speak with Mr. Reynard?" The girl spoke so softly Beth had to crane her neck to hear. "Mr. Doyle unfortunately has passed away, but

I can easily set you up with another agent. Mr. Reynard is our sales manager."

Michael cocked his head as though contemplating what kind of yarn to spin. Much to Beth's surprise, he opted for the truth.

"I'll be honest with you. I did want an appointment with Mr. Doyle that day, but it wasn't to purchase insurance. I'm a private investigator hired by his wife. Right now my job is to look into his untimely death. I have a few questions for his immediate supervisor that won't take very long."

Beth held her breath to see how the truth would be received.

The girl blinked several times and tapped her screen. "Know what, Mr. Preston?" Violet whispered conspiratorially. "I liked Lamar. He brought in candy and donuts and jugs of apple cider. And he called me 'Miss Frost' like you just did, instead of 'honey' or 'sweetie.' I am sorry that he's dead."

"Sounds like some people might not have been," said Beth. She'd crept close enough to listen but couldn't stay out of the conversation.

"Who's *she*?" Violet asked suspiciously.

"This is Miss Kirby. She's in training at our firm." Michael dragged her by her elbow to his side.

"Oh, I see." Violet dismissed Beth after a quick perusal and refocused on her monitor. "If I make Mr. Reynard's one thirty wait a few minutes, I can squeeze you in then. For now, please be seated."

"Thank you very much, Miss Frost." Michael all but bowed from the waist.

Beth followed him back to the upholstered chairs. "Your charm seems to have won another heart," she said from behind a magazine.

"I can't seem to help myself." Michael picked up a copy of *Southern Living*. "Do you think it's the new aftershave?"

"I have no idea, but I'd like to read that when you're done." Beth dropped her copy of *People* back on the stack.

Miss Frost, however, gave them less than fifteen minutes of reading time. "If you'll follow me, Mr. Preston, Miss Kirby, Mr. Reynard will see you now."

Michael offered a second dazzling smile, while Beth nodded her appreciation.

The office manager was far less cordial. "Mr. Preston, Miss Kirby, what's this all about? I was told it's of utmost importance. I hope that's true, because I have a full slate this afternoon."

Beth's initial appraisal of him offered her little optimism. Reynard's face was taut and his posture stiff as he blocked their path to the cushy chairs. "We appreciate you making time for us, sir," she said.

"And we promise to be brief," added Michael. "We're looking into the death of Lamar Doyle, and that's why time is of the essence."

"I don't understand. I thought the police were investigating."

"They are, but Evelyn Doyle hired us to make sure no stone goes unturned."

"We just have a few questions." Beth threw in her two cents' worth of persuasion.

"Of course I'll help if I can. Please have a seat." Reynard walked back to his desk. "My wife served on a church committee with Mrs. Doyle. She's a fine lady. How is she doing?"

"As well as can be expected, considering someone killed her husband." Beth's assessment was devoid of emotion.

Reynard froze. "Has Lamar's death been ruled a homicide? I thought he'd taken his own life."

Michael and Beth exchanged glances, but Beth was first to react. "Why would you assume such a thing?"

"Lamar rushed home during a mandatory meeting because

there was some kind of family crisis. And we heard it happened while he was alone after his wife had gone to bed. Perhaps I jumped to an erroneous conclusion."

"We're getting ahead of ourselves," said Michael. "No official ruling has been made yet on the cause of death. Our questions today have more to do with Mr. Doyle's situation at work, in order to provide clarification for Mrs. Doyle."

"Such as?" A muscle in Reynard's neck jumped.

Michael opened his folder of notes. "Primarily, I was shocked by Mr. Doyle's income last year. And from what I understand, he hasn't been doing much better lately either."

"If you're privy to Lamar's finances, then you know he didn't need to work to maintain his lavish lifestyle. Of course, I would have appreciated a bit more effort." Reynard's lips pulled into a thin line.

"That's exactly what I'm getting at. I hope this isn't too intrusive, but I'm curious why you kept Mr. Doyle around." Michael crossed one leg over the other.

"Wouldn't his sales figures bring down the average for your entire team?" asked Beth. "Doyle made your franchise look bad."

Her question produced a smile. "Selling insurance isn't like major league baseball, Miss Kirby. His personal batting average didn't affect the rest of us. But Lamar had taken up space here long enough. I told him if his sales figures and new client acquisitions didn't improve, this would be his last quarter at Town and Country. That's one reason I might have jumped to a wrong conclusion."

"How did he take the news?" she asked.

Reynard sighed wearily. "Same as always. Like rain off a duck's back. Lamar promised to work harder and went about his day as usual."

Michael leaned forward in his chair. "Was that how he took the news he was needed at home? Like rain off a duck's back?"

Reynard considered his answer carefully. "No, Lamar was definitely worried something was wrong with Evelyn. Otherwise he wouldn't have left, in light of my recent ultimatum."

Beth tapped her toe. "You would fire someone who needed to tend a sick wife?"

"No, Miss Kirby," said Reynard, his patience slipping. "Although quarterly meetings are crucial, I gave Lamar a full quarter to improve his numbers."

"Okay, but it still sounds as if you didn't like him."

"How dare you judge me? The truth is that I put up with Lamar's total disregard for company protocols far too long because we had mutual friends at the country club." Reynard tossed his pen across the desk. "People in sales must be assertive. Yet he would only close the deal if the client practically begged for a policy. If someone was the least bit hesitant, he wouldn't even bother with a follow-up call. How could such an agent mentor the new people we just hired? I need agents who can close the sale, not drink coffee in somebody's kitchen. Those days are gone."

"More's the pity. That's why I don't own life insurance," she said, offering him a megawatt smile.

"And with that I'm afraid your allotment of borrowed minutes is up."

Michael scrambled to his feet and tucked his folder into his bag. "We're grateful for your time. We'll see ourselves out." He helped Beth to her feet as though she were eighty years old, but halfway to the door he stopped. "One more question, sir. Did Town and Country have a life insurance policy on Mr. Doyle, and if so, who was the beneficiary?"

"Now see here, young man—"

"It's a simple question, and the answer will soon be public record. We would like to facilitate matters for Mrs. Doyle."

A muscle jumped in Reynard's neck. "He had the standard

term life policy for one million, same as every employee, with the payout split between Evelyn and the company."

"Five hundred *K* would go far to make up for Lamar's shortfall in commissions," Beth murmured softly.

Reynard's chin snapped up. "What's the matter with you? I told you Lamar and I used to be friends."

"Money can wreak havoc even on besties. I was wondering if you have an alibi for the night Mr. Doyle died."

A flush crept up Reynard's neck into his face. "If I need an alibi, I'll provide it for the Savannah or Tybee Island police, not for two obnoxious gumshoes from out of town." He added a contemptuous inflection on the last three words. "Now get out of my office before I call security. And if you ever come back, I'll have you arrested for trespassing." He stabbed the air with a finger aimed at Beth's chest.

"No problem. This place is colder than a tomb." Beth skipped out the door with Michael breathing hard down her neck.

Once they reached the street, he blew out his breath in a sound close to a growl. "Why on earth did you bait Reynard until he blew his stack and kicked us out? You're the *senior investigator*, and that's not how you trained me." Michael lifted his hands as though in supplication.

"Because I realized the good PI–bad PI gig was working for us. You usually get them talking, and then I incite them to let something slip. If we confuse the person in the hot seat, they can't anticipate or second-guess us."

"So that was all part of your plan?" He screwed his face into a scowl.

"Absolutely. Was there any doubt?"

"Right from 'hello.' You might let me know what you're up to next time." Obviously irritated with her, Michael started back toward the hotel.

Beth had to run to keep up. "What's your hurry? Are you mad at me?"

"Not mad. Just eager to get to my computer. While you were launching your next salvo, I watched for Reynard's reactions. The beneficiary question made him nervous. I want to see if it's *his* name and not the agency listed as co-beneficiary."

"Good idea. I'll call candidate number three and get that particular show on the road... Should I meet you at the pool later?" Beth gulped air in between sentences.

"Sure, but don't bother waiting for me. If anyone needs some extra head-soaking time, it's you, Kirby."

Sixteen

*A*ny hotel guests present on the rooftop yesterday never would have guessed they were dating. Michael swam his laps while Beth read a paperback book stretched out on a chaise. Then she did her laps while he watched CNN Sports on the outdoor TV. For supper they picked at the assortment of free appetizers, augmented with a take-out pizza. They chatted about college football, an excursion to Fort Pulaski, and the case, as well as Beth's success in lining up the third candidate for tomorrow morning. They had heard nothing from Nate's headhunter. At eight o'clock, Beth grabbed a fistful of celery sticks and went to her room, leaving Michael the rest of the pizza. There had been no warm embrace, no poignant farewell, and no peck on the cheek. Michael abandoned the pizza to the seagulls and headed to his room for a night of bad TV, his hopes for tender, romantic conversation squashed.

The next morning, the professional appearance of their next applicant was a pleasant surprise. "Miss Webb?" Michael asked when a young woman dressed in a white blouse and navy suit approached their usual spot in the breakfast area.

"Yes, I'm Kaitlyn Webb. You must be Michael Preston and Elizabeth Kirby. What a pleasure to meet you both! Thanks so much for giving me an interview." She spoke with proper diction and grammar and shook hands with a firm grip, which earned her high marks. Then she waited to be invited to sit. More high marks.

"Please have a seat," Michael said, but he deferred to his partner for the first question.

"As our classified ad suggested, Price Investigations is looking for someone with surveillance experience," said Beth. "What previous work experience qualifies you in this regard?"

And please don't say you put up spy-cams to keep tabs on neighborhood pets, Michael thought, drumming his fingers on the table.

But Miss Webb was apparently prepared to back up her résumé. "My current position is with the Georgia Industrial Commission, a branch of Workers' Compensation. Although I started with the Florida Bureau, I transferred here on assignment and have since relocated. I use old-fashioned surveillance, besides monitoring social media, to verify that those applying for permanent disability are truly unable to work."

Michael threw out his first question. "What if they were injured and can't work at their present job, such as lineman for the phone or electric company?"

"For that sort of injury, we allow a certain period of disability and compensate for any permanent impairment suffered on the job. This is known as *partial* disability. Then if a worker can no longer string high tension lines, for instance, the utility company will find them a desk position. Permanent *total* disability means that person can't function in *any* job, not even answering telephones in an office. The legal definition is quite rigid and specific."

"So that man or woman shouldn't be painting the house or scuba diving with buddies while on vacation," suggested Michael.

"Exactly. My job is to verify claims for permanent total disability. We don't want to deny benefits to anyone entitled, but unfortunately people try to scam the system, which hurts employers and employees alike." Kaitlyn tried to make equal eye contact with both interviewers.

"Yes, some people do try to get something for nothing," said Beth. "But I hope you understand PI work is often tedious and usually a far cry from the secret-agent lifestyle portrayed in the movies."

"Or the action-packed manhunts of *Dog the Bounty Hunter.*" Michael couldn't rid himself of the memory of Anita Hancock and her quest to beat bad guys to a pulp.

Kaitlyn's expression brightened. "I certainly hope so. I took the job with the Industrial Commission because I wanted to work behind the scenes, investigating in a nonconfrontational way. I've never had aspirations of becoming a police officer or a federal marshal."

Michael glanced back at her résumé. "Our boss, Nate Price, expects his investigators to be weapons trained and licensed for concealed carry. Would you have a problem with that?"

"Not at all. I'll complete whatever training the agency requires. I've taken gun safety classes and have fired a handgun before. My parents keep a gun at home under lock and key."

Michael asked the question foremost on his mind. "Have you lived in Savannah long enough to establish any relationships with local police?"

"No. I'm afraid our paths have yet to cross, either profession-ally or personally." Kaitlyn punctuated her sentence with a smile.

"The personal part is a good thing," added Beth. "Settling a long string of parking tickets can derail a gal's budget."

"That brings back memories of my days at Florida State. I was so afraid the dean would withhold my diploma until I paid the city of Tallahassee that I borrowed the money from my grand-mother interest-free. But I paid her back in full."

"We appreciate people who handle their finances responsibly," said Beth.

"So you're a former Seminole fan?" asked Michael, chopping the air with an imaginary hatchet.

Kaitlyn's eyes grew round. "You won't hold that against me, will you?"

Michael laughed. "Of course not. I've outgrown my rabid Bulldog days. But I am curious how long you've lived"—Michael quickly scanned her résumé—"on Fifth Street."

"Not very long. Less than a year." Kaitlyn's lower lip began to quiver.

The ambiguity of her answer struck an odd chord. "Could you be more specific? And is this a house or an apartment?"

"Four weeks, and I would describe it as a long-term rental." For some unknown reason, Kaitlyn flashed a pleading look at Beth.

"I'm sure we don't need to belabor semantics," Beth murmured.

"All right. We'll call it an apartment." Michael made a notation on the sheet.

"Actually, it's a motel you rent by the week, but I want more than anything to stay in Savannah. I love it here."

Michael shifted in his chair. "The ad posted by Price Investigations was quite specific—we're looking for a local resident who's familiar with the area. I don't feel that staying in a motel for four weeks qualifies."

"I didn't lie on my résumé, Mr. Preston. I consider my move to Savannah to be permanent even if my address is only temporary. This is my new home. As far as finding my way around, thanks to GPS in my car and Google Maps on my phone, I don't see that as a problem."

"Just for the record, where exactly did you live previously?"

Kaitlyn's grip on her purse tightened as she delivered a one-word answer. "Florida."

Florida—a state that stretched from Key West to the Florida-Georgia line with millions of people, yet Kaitlyn offered no further details. Michael exhaled, dismayed by her secrecy.

Beth, however, left little doubt as to whose side she was on. "I love the fact you've worked surveillance here for the past month."

Michael wasn't so convinced. "Have you ever dealt with law enforcement in a professional capacity?"

The question should have been fairly straightforward, but Miss Webb contemplated for half a minute. "No, not really," she finally said. "But according to my most recent evaluation, I have great people skills."

"May we contact the supervisor who made that assessment?"

"Of course. She's listed as one of my references, Vicky Stephens."

"That's her phone number there." Beth tapped the spot on Miss Webb's résumé.

Michael bumped Beth's knee under the table. "I understand you're on assignment. *If* you were our successful applicant, the position we offer has a trial period. Our boss would make any permanent hiring decisions. What if we or you decided we weren't a good fit?"

"I would take a three-month leave of absence from my current employer."

"*If* you were our successful applicant, when could you start?" He emphasized a level of uncertainty.

"I'd like to give the Industrial Commission a week to replace me, but if you needed me sooner, I could moonlight every evening. I'm able to survive on very little sleep. *If* I'm the successful applicant, of course."

"That is very accommodating of you." Beth reached for her hand and shook vigorously.

Michael kept his enthusiasm in check as he extended his hand. "Thank you for coming in today, Miss Webb. We're considering several candidates, and we would need to verify your references. But you'll hear from one of us within the next few days."

Kaitlyn shook his hand, straightened her spine, and squared her shoulders. "I know I shouldn't say this, but I must. If you hire me, I'll work harder than any other trainee to prove you made the right choice for the company. Thank you for your time, Mr. Preston, Miss Kirby." She bobbed her head and then hurried toward the door.

"Wow. I've never seen anyone so eager to please," Beth said.

"Or someone so desperate to change jobs."

"You didn't like her?"

"I liked her just fine, but I don't trust her. And I'm not sure why."

"You have a bug up your nose because she's not a native. Can't we give her a chance? After all, it's on a trial basis. Nate has the final say-so."

Michael studied the face of the woman he was falling in love with. Beth's blue gaze bored through his skin, his chest muscles, and his rib cage to reach his heart. He hoped she would never ask him to rob a bank, because he was almost incapable of telling her no.

"Let's wait a couple days to see if that headhunter comes up with any viable candidates. After all, Nate has gone to the trouble of hiring one."

"All right. Two days and then we hire Miss Webb." In the middle of the Homewood's breakfast area, Beth threw her arms around him and gave him a hug.

Michael was both thrilled and mortified by the gesture. Feeling heat rush to his face, he said sternly, "Control yourself, Miss Kirby. We're in a public place."

She snickered with amusement. "We're both single adults in a town where no one knows us. You don't think Nate sent Maxine to spy on us, do you?"

"I don't, but I expect all women with a crush on me to maintain a sense of decorum."

Beth tapped her temple as she pondered. "Let's see...that

would be Maxine, my Aunt Dorrie, the assistant over at Calvary Baptist, and me. Have I left anyone out?"

Michael bit the inside of his cheek. "No. I think that's probably everyone."

"Okay, then I'll use Aunt Dorrie as my example because I know her best. But just so we're clear, she pulled all kinds of pranks on Pete Kirby before he proposed, including throwing his car keys into Lake Concordia and burning all his old issues of *Field and Stream*. Just thought I should mention that." Beth checked the display on her cell phone. "Looks like I missed a call from Mrs. Doyle. I'm going somewhere private to call her back. Where do you plan to be?"

"I'll be in my room trying to dig up something on Joseph Reynard."

Beth headed for the door with a spring in her step. "All right, I'll call you if this is something important."

If he were the same man as he was a year ago, Michael would have been worried about Beth's choice of mentors. But because he recycled old magazines and had four extra sets of keys to the Charger, Aunt Dorrie was no threat to him. He whistled a tune all the way to his room as though he hadn't a care in the world.

SEVENTEEN

*M*ichael had barely reached his room when his phone rang. His heart rate spiked when he spotted Beth's name on caller ID. "Did you miss me already? What's up?"

"Not quite yet. Mrs. Doyle wants me to meet her sister from Atlanta and talk to her new attorney. Care to join me on a trip to Tybee, or would you rather remain at the hotel?"

"Considering the Doyle residence would be a likely place to find out how Lamar felt about his boss, I'll join you. While you pump the lawyer for an update, I'll snoop into Mr. Doyle's personal emails."

"If Evelyn gives you permission. Right now she trusts us, and I don't want that to change."

"I'll be a model of good behavior, but their home computer could hold the break we're looking for."

"We sure could use one of those right now. I'll meet you downstairs."

Beth needn't have worried about how Michael would be received. Mrs. Doyle practically bowled them over as they climbed the front steps. "Beth, Michael. Thanks so much for coming to see me. Charlotte and Mrs. Gwinn practically have me under house arrest, or I would have driven to the city." She wrapped her thin arms around Beth and hugged, the reserve demonstrated in previous visits gone.

Michael used the time to digest the woman's appearance. Grief often diminished appetite and disrupted sleep, but Mrs. Doyle looked ten years older and ten pounds thinner in a period of a week.

When she finally released Beth, she extended a hand to him. "Thank you for coming as well, Mr. Preston. Let's talk in the library. It's cozier than the living room on windy days like this."

He and Beth exchanged glances on their way to a room with three walls of floor-to-ceiling books, mostly leather-bound classics and literary novels, and a fourth wall of glass overlooking the ocean. Today the wind churned the waves into frothy whitecaps.

Seated in a high-back chair was a younger, rounder version of Mrs. Doyle. "Miss Kirby? I'm Charlotte Harper. We spoke on the phone. I can't thank you enough for calling me. Evelyn would have waited until the last minute."

As Beth greeted her, Michael locked gazes with the other stranger in the room. "How do you do, ma'am? Michael Preston from Price Investigations. We're here to provide any assistance Mrs. Doyle might need."

"Hilda Gwinn," the woman said, nodding. "A pleasure to meet you both. And Evelyn most likely will need investigative help. She refuses to acknowledge the uphill battle we face."

"If that's the case, I'm glad someone with your courtroom experience agreed to represent her," Michael murmured.

Mrs. Doyle's sigh of relief precluded further comments. "I'm just glad the ME released Lamar's body to the funeral home. I can't believe he's been lying on a slab in a drawer instead of on his way to his just reward."

"The spirit leaves the body upon death," Charlotte instructed. "For better or for worse, Lamar's soul has been set free."

"Not until Reverend White gives him a proper Christian send-off." Evelyn reached for Beth's hand. "We can bury Lamar on Saturday, and we've made the arrangements except for the luncheon menu. Please tell me you and Michael will be there."

"Of course we will, ma'am." Beth squeezed the woman's fingers.

Michael spoke quietly to the lawyer. "If Mr. Doyle's body has been released, then the medical examiner must have issued his findings."

Mrs. Gwinn nodded with a frown. "His death has officially been ruled a homicide, hence my concern for Evelyn."

The widow shook her head. "They can't possibly think I killed Lamar. Anyone who knows me knows that I loved him."

"Unfortunately, that rules out most people on Tybee Island," said Charlotte. "Few people know you since you weren't as... sociable as your husband. Only your family knows what a kind person you are."

"What about the Tybee Island Flower Club?" Beth demanded. "You mentioned you were a member."

Charlotte didn't let her sister answer. "If *active* means forwarding pictures of your plants but skipping the meetings and luncheons, then Evelyn fits the description."

"My sister has always considered me a recluse. Can you guess which one of us was the homecoming queen?" Evelyn asked, smiling at her sibling.

"You can't simply assure the police of your innocence and expect them to believe you." Charlotte wrung her hands in her lap. "I can't believe how insulated from reality Lamar has kept you all these years. He doted on you endlessly. I should have visited here more, instead of you coming to Atlanta to go shopping. This could be my fault."

Beth jumped in to prevent another teary episode. "Nonsense. Most of life's challenges can't be avoided. You're here now, Mrs. Harper, and that's important."

"I will help give Lamar the send-off he deserves." Charlotte dabbed at her eyes. "He was a very devoted husband."

"In the meantime, I'd like to pursue a lead on another suspect." Michael directed his words at Mrs. Doyle. "But I need permission to look at your husband's personal emails."

"Of course you may. Lamar's laptop is in his office down the hall. His email address and password are written on the box of staples in the drawer. Lamar always feared growing forgetful in old age." Evelyn's voice cracked with emotion. "Look at anything you want. No one needs to protect Lamar's secrets anymore."

The attorney stood. "I'll accompany you to the office, Mr. Preston."

Michael didn't know if the lawyer didn't trust him or was simply curious about Lamar's correspondence.

Hilda clarified her motivation once they were halfway down the hall. "I wanted to talk to you privately about the case. Although Mrs. Doyle refuses to acknowledge the seriousness of the situation, the police are building a strong case against her." She motioned him into the office and closed the door behind them. "Let's talk about what the police know. First, they know about Lamar's affair, and that he'd been supporting this young woman for a while. They're aware Evelyn sent the maid home early so she and Lamar would be alone that night. Lamar was shot with the same caliber gun that he owned—a gun that was either kept in Evelyn's bedside table or locked in the safe. A safe that only he and Evelyn knew the combination to."

"Unless Lamar wrote it on the bottom of a box of paper clips," Michael interjected.

The lawyer's gray eyes warmed. "True, but unless we find proof of that, the police will stick to cold, hard facts, such as that the security cameras at the guard booth showed no one coming into the complex who can't be accounted for. And the fact that Evelyn showered and washed her clothes after finding him dead. Who does that sort of thing?"

Michael settled into the chair at the desk. "Mrs. Doyle gave a legitimate reason to Detective Rossi. And I'll bet there's a way to reach this house without driving past the security guard. Or maybe someone who belongs on Oleander Drive harbored a grudge against Doyle." He opened the laptop.

Hilda's smile was slow in coming. "I like the fact you and Beth are fond of Evelyn. For what it's worth, I not only like her, but I also think she's innocent. However, thinking it and proving it aren't the same." She gestured toward the computer. "I'll leave you to your snooping because time is of the essence. The only reason our client isn't behind bars is because the police didn't find the murder weapon or GSR on her hands. But rest assured, they're racking up overtime looking for that gun. I believe Tybee Island detectives will do their job, but sooner or later the DA will pressure them to put *someone* behind bars and close the case. Let's make sure that someone isn't Evelyn."

Michael found Doyle's email address and password exactly in the high-security spot described by his wife. Although the man regularly dumped his trash, his Sent folder contained the original emails at the bottom of Lamar's replies. Michael almost fell asleep reading an assortment of messages that featured such topics as "What time are we meeting for golf?" and "I won't be at the club Saturday because we have a wedding in Hilton Head." Abandoning the sent email, Michael checked folders Lamar had created for a variety of reasons: school board business, warranties for major appliances, correspondence regarding a trip planned to Spain and Greece. In the folder labeled "Golf courses along the Gulf Coast" were emails pertaining to Bonnie Mulroney. Apparently, Bonnie had been in an ongoing battle with the building association. She'd been given an eviction warning because of her loud music and disrespect for assigned parking spots. Doyle had been the woman's champion, her advocate in a world where Bonnie had a difficult time fitting in.

Who will fight your battles now, Miss Mulroney?

When Michael opened a folder labeled "March Madness," he hit the mother lode. Instead of Doyle's brackets for past NCAA basketball tournaments, he found a string of email between Doyle and the sales manager at Town and Country Insurance. In each case, the email contained the sentiments from both men, in some cases a back-and-forth exchange with half a dozen responses. In short order, Michael drew three conclusions. First, there was no love lost between Lamar Doyle and Joseph Reynard. Second, Doyle had discovered that his boss had attained his superior sales figures using duplicitous measures, and when confronted, Reynard had reacted with a level of hostility unacceptable at most places of employment. Third, Michael realized he could be looking at motive for murder.

He copied the folder and sent it to his email address, Beth's phone, and Maxine in Natchez for safekeeping. Then he printed hard copies for the case file. On his way down the hall, Hilda intercepted his path. The lawyer had been watching for him from the library doorway.

"Find anything useful, Mr. Preston?"

"Michael, please. I think I have, but I want to check it out before I get your hopes up."

"I'm an optimistic sort of woman. Just don't do anything illegal tracking down your lead."

"I'll do my best," he said as they rejoined the others. "Are you about ready?" he asked Beth.

She extracted herself from a conversation about Saturday's funeral. "I am." To the sisters she said, "You have the situation under control here. Michael and I will be at the church on Saturday. Call me if you need us for any reason before then." She gave both women hugs, yet it was still ten minutes before the PIs were able to leave the residence.

"Mrs. Doyle is growing quite attached to you." Michael waited until they were inside his car to state the obvious.

"I know, but I can't bring myself to discourage her. Her sister is nice enough, but Evelyn needs a little coddling right now." Beth pulled sunglasses from her purse.

Michael chuckled. "If there's ever been a woman up to the challenge of having two mothers, it's you, Kirby."

"Very funny. I take it by your gleeful mood that you discovered something helpful on Doyle's computer. Either that or you're thinking about a late lunch at the beach."

"No time to eat. We're on our way downtown to see Joseph Reynard. I found out what Doyle had on his boss."

"Didn't that creepy guy threaten to have us arrested? Unlike you, I've been to the slammer and didn't like it—bad food, no Internet connection, and friends who promise to stay in touch but never do."

"Trust me, Kirby. Nobody's going to jail but Reynard."

"You really think he could have murdered Doyle? Motive is one thing, but what about opportunity? No one who didn't belong in the development showed up on the security tape."

"I haven't dotted every *i*, but Reynard could have been an invited guest at a neighborhood party."

"How did he get his hands on the gun?" Beth crossed her arms.

"If Doyle wrote the password to his laptop on a box of staples, he could have left personal information in his office. Or he might have given his boss the combination so that important documents could be accessed in case of emergency."

Beth remained quiet for a long while.

"What are you thinking? That I'm crazy?"

"Nope. Cases have been cracked from far thinner leads than

this. I say full speed ahead to Slimeball Insurance. If nothing else, we can beat a confession out of the guy."

Michael tamped down a surge of exhilaration. "I'm so glad I can finally tell when you're teasing."

"Ha! That's what you think." Beth lowered the window and turned so he couldn't see her face. "I intend to keep you guessing forever."

⁓

When the distinguished Joseph Reynard exited his office at five fifteen, Michael and Beth were waiting under a shady tree.

"Good afternoon, Mr. Reynard. Could we talk to you for a few minutes?" Michael's cordiality belied the tension of their previous encounter.

When the sales manager determined the source of the sound, his complexion flushed to a dark hue. "I made myself perfectly clear yesterday. Get off Town and Country property before I call the police." Reynard held up his cell phone as a warning.

"Actually, this strip of land belongs to the fine city of Savannah." Michael pointed at the narrow tree lawn. "So we'll stay right where we are."

"Stay all night for all I care." Reynard dug his keys from a pocket and unlocked the door.

"We were just curious why Lamar Doyle wanted to discuss policy pushing with you." Being smaller than Michael, Beth had to stand on her tiptoes and shout to be heard. But her efforts didn't go to waste.

Reynard jumped out of the vehicle as though he'd encountered a swarm of hornets. "Keep your voice down. You have no idea what you're talking about." He scanned the parking lot for a potential audience.

"Are you inviting us onto your property to discuss this like adults?" Beth asked loudly.

"Fine. I'll talk to you." But instead of remaining between parked cars, Reynard led them into the alley to a choice spot next to the Dumpster.

"Couldn't you pick a less malodorous location?" Beth asked, pinching her nostrils.

"We won't be here long. I need to pick up my son at school in twenty minutes. What questions do you think you have about policy pushing?" He dropped his voice to a whisper.

Michael cleared his throat. "Coming from an accounting background, I have a decent understanding of the concept. You encourage your agents to sell policies to people who can't afford them in the long run in order to collect the commission. One minor budgetary setback and people are forced to let the policy lapse, wasting whatever money they've paid in thus far. According to his emails, Doyle felt that's what you were doing at Town and Country. And he wasn't very happy about it."

"If you hacked into our corporate database, I'll have you arrested, Preston. We have laws that protect privacy in this country." Reynard puffed out his chest as though he'd scored a goal.

"Actually, I found the thread of emails between you and Mr. Doyle on his home computer, sent from a personal account—an account I've been given full access to. So *I'm* not the one who's broken the law here." Michael's inference didn't go unnoticed.

Reynard took a step back, narrowly missing the Dumpster. "Policy pushing isn't illegal. I own the company, so technically I haven't broken any laws."

"Ah, therein lies the rub, as that famous British guy once said." Beth closed the space between them, cutting off a possible escape route. "Your inclusion of the word *technically* leads me to believe what you did wouldn't impress the folks who own the name you paid a lot of money to use."

Michael closed in from the other side. "Correct us if we're wrong, but isn't your agency a franchise of a major corporation? Agents are required to maintain a certain persistency rate during a two-year period. If too many customers let their policies lapse during that period, the agent's rate plummets and he or she could be fired. But *you* would still keep your five percent commission on each policy that agent wrote."

Reynard twisted the ring on his left hand. "Agents have no way of knowing who will or won't maintain premiums on policies."

Michael smiled. "Lamar also found proof you'd been writing policies for certain friends and relatives."

"A sales manager can write all the policies he wants."

"Yes, but many of those pals have college-aged children with expensive cars parked on campus. You indicated those cars were kept in their parents' suburban garages in areas with substantially lower rates of theft. If there's ever a claim, the adjuster could refuse to pay the policy amount if deception was involved."

Beth clucked her tongue. "National brands don't like agents with shady ethics tainting their image. They might revoke your franchise and put you out of business. That spells motive in my book."

"You'd better have proof of your allegations," sputtered Reynard. "Or I'll sue your fly-by-night PI firm for defamation of character."

Michael couldn't stop smiling. "Doyle had proof. That's why he wanted a meeting with you on Monday. He wanted to give you a chance to make this right. If you refused, he planned to go to the Georgia Department of Insurance. But someone killed him before that meeting could take place." His expression changed to one that reflected contempt.

Beth moved in for the final thrust. "And the proof Mr. Doyle had? We have it now. And we're turning it over to the Tybee Island police. Anything you want to say before they haul you away in handcuffs?"

"The next words I say will be to my attorney." Reynard pushed her out of the way and strode to his car.

"That's probably a wise choice," called Michael.

"And we're not 'fly-by-night,' buster," Beth hollered. "We drove here in a high-performance Charger, which is a much cooler car than your boring sedan."

Michael covered his face with his hands.

"What's wrong?" Beth asked as Reynard drove away. "I didn't like the way he defamed our agency."

"Not a thing." Michael slipped an arm around her waist. "You said something nice about my car and you *didn't* shoot Reynard in the leg. I'm happy as a clam."

For the first time, Beth didn't shrug off his touch. "Yeah, but don't think for a minute that winging him didn't cross my mind."

EIGHTEEN

*I*t was almost six thirty when Beth walked through the doors of Homewood Riverfront Suites. She was tired, but at least she was no longer hungry. She and Michael had a huge early dinner at a restaurant on West Bay mainly frequented by local residents and business travelers, not tourists. The restaurant described their menu as Southern cooking—a bizarre definition, to be sure. It certainly wasn't the Creole/Cajun dishes of New Orleans, or the rich delta cuisine of barbecue and corn bread of her hometown. Instead of French fries, sautéed greens, and pinto beans, this place offered shrimp corn dogs, chargrilled oysters, and Brunswick stew. But it was all good, and she'd eaten more than her share.

Beth was pleased with how things turned out on Tybee Island. She liked Charlotte Harper. Although the woman badgered Evelyn a bit, the two sisters obviously truly loved each other. And she liked Hilda Gwinn. She was smart, professional, and experienced. The fact she'd cornered Michael not once but twice went a long way toward showing that she wanted this case to have a happy ending. The Price Investigations master plan included finding the real murderer of Lamar Doyle. But if she and Michael failed, Hilda had enough courtroom experience to blow holes in the flimsy, circumstantial evidence against Mrs. Doyle.

When Michael dropped her off in front of the hotel, he drove away to find a car wash and a health food store. He was running low on nutritional supplements, and he couldn't stand his beloved Charger to be dirty a minute longer. Beth thought they shouldn't spend every evening together now that they were officially dating. Didn't absence make the heart grow fonder? After her past disaster with the chief of police in Natchez, she needed to slow things down. Not because she was unsure of her feelings for Michael, but because she didn't want to make a fool of herself. After deciding to call her mother, paint her toenails and fingernails, catch up on email, and then head to the rooftop for a late-night swim, Beth wasn't thrilled when someone called her name. As she scanned the crowd in the lobby, her gaze landed on a familiar face.

Kaitlyn Webb stood in the doorway of the Lodge. "Could I speak to you for a minute, Miss Kirby?"

"Of course. What a *surprise* finding you here." Swallowing her disappointment, Beth followed Kaitlyn to a high-top table.

"I intend to fully explain, but first can I buy you something to drink?" Kaitlyn patted the empty seat next to hers, her green eyes sparkling in the reflected light.

"You can't buy a drink here. Snacks and libations are free during the social hour for guests, but I don't imbibe. I'm going to get a glass of iced tea."

"I usually don't either, except for a glass of wine at the holidays. This is just sparkling water with a wedge of lime." Kaitlyn lifted the frosty glass.

"That sounded good, so I got the same," Beth said when she returned with her drink. She climbed up on the stool. "Since you're not staying here, you must have been waiting for Michael and me. He's running errands tonight. I have no idea what time he'll be back."

Kaitlyn picked up her glass and took a sip. "Actually, I'd hoped to talk to you alone."

"Why? Michael and I are partners. We'll make the hiring decision together."

"I understand, but I wanted to explain a few things to you. Then you could either relay the information to Mr. Preston or tell me I have no chance of getting hired at Price Investigations. And I will slink away quietly." Kaitlyn stared at the lime bobbing around in her drink.

"Aren't you two girls eating? Would you like a bowl of mixed nuts?" asked the Lodge attendant, looking at Kaitlyn. "You're probably getting hungry by now."

"Yes, that would be nice," said Kaitlyn.

"No, thanks," answered Beth at the same moment.

"I mean, no, thank you," Kaitlyn sputtered.

"Please give us the nuts," Beth said to the confused woman. Then she turned to Kaitlyn. "Look, I just ate a huge meal ten minutes ago. If you're hungry, snack. But *please* get what you came for off your chest."

"I must seem like a crazy person." Kaitlyn laughed nervously. "Truth is I didn't come across well during this morning's interview. If there's any way I can rectify the poor impression I made, I want to do so." She poured some nuts onto her cocktail napkin. "I would work harder with more dedication than anyone for your agency."

Beth nodded sagely. "Michael's concern is that the ad specified a Savannah resident, and you appear to be a recent transplant. If the Georgia Industrial Commission terminates your assignment, wouldn't you be sent back to Florida?"

"No. I was overjoyed when my boss found me this out-of-town assignment. She knows I have no intention of returning to the Panhandle. When the IC no longer needs me, I'll find a job someplace else. But I fell in love with Savannah the moment I arrived. I want to plant my roots here. I wasn't lying about that."

Beth sipped her drink but didn't take her eyes off Kaitlyn. "It sounds like you're running from something…or someone."

"I suppose I am, but I promise you it's nothing illegal or unethical or immoral. It's mainly bad memories." She popped a few almonds in her mouth.

"Could you be more specific than that?" Unable to stop herself, Beth reached for a Brazil nut from the napkin.

A tortured expression filled Kaitlyn's face. "I'm afraid not, but I can assure you it has nothing to do with my ability to work."

Beth didn't like the woman's bizarre cloak-and-dagger act. Anybody looking for a PI job should be up front about who they were. Yet something about the fact that Kaitlyn had apparently staked out the lobby for hours made Beth reluctant to send her away. She poured a handful of nuts to help her think. Kaitlyn did the same. They both sat crunching while the TV ran the local news and the crowd grew louder by the moment.

"Did you ever want to go away and make a fresh start?" Kaitlyn finally asked. "I've wanted to do that for a long time but have been too afraid. When my boss suggested this transfer, I saw my chance. I'll never be that frightened, pathetic woman again, no matter where I end up working. Please give me a chance, and I promise you won't be sorry."

Beth wiped her salty fingers on the napkin. "I believe you. If I'm able to convince my partner, the position is yours on a trial basis."

Kaitlyn's green eyes filled with tears. "Look at me, crying like a teenager."

"Hey, I cry during commercials for the Humane Society. It's a woman thing." Beth eyed the empty nut bowl. "You want me to take you for a real meal?"

"No. You should get back to whatever you had planned for the evening. I'll wait for your call as I was originally instructed. However this ends, I appreciate you and Mr. Preston making the time for me. And I wish your agency the best of luck." Kaitlyn laid a five-dollar tip next to her napkin and pushed in her stool.

Beth watched her go with her mind firmly made up. Two hours later, after talking to her mom and doing her nails, she sent Michael a text: "Can you meet me on the roof? There's something we must discuss or I won't be able to sleep."

Michael soon materialized beside her on the outdoor sofa. "What's up, Kirby? Did you decide you couldn't spend another minute without me?"

"Yes and no. Kaitlyn stopped me in the lobby after you dropped me off. She wanted to talk."

He made a face. "Kaitlyn Webb? I'm thinking you're ready to propose, and you asked me here to discuss a *job applicant*? What don't you understand about downtime?"

"Kaitlyn had been waiting for a while, so I talked to her. After hearing why she was so evasive about her past, I can't possibly think about romance." Beth pulled out her hair clip and fluffed her wavy mane.

"All right. Let's hear the story." Michael's face softened.

"I suspect she might have been abused by a spouse."

Michael grew serious. "Did she actually say that? She described her marital status as single on her résumé."

"Maybe she's divorced or maybe she's running away from a boyfriend, but I got the distinct impression she's leaving a bad relationship behind. I'm good at reading facial expressions and body language."

"More of Beth Kirby's gut instincts? You read entire paragraphs between the lines of everything Kaitlyn says. You know how famous Florida is for drug smuggling. She could be on the lam from the DEA."

"For crying out loud, how can you slander an entire state based on old reruns of *Miami Vice*? I've seen what you have stored on your DVR."

Michael winked. "That Crockett and Tubbs—they knew how to bring bad guys to justice. And they dressed cool too."

"Getting back to Kaitlyn, it would be easy to check for any outstanding arrest warrants. I think she's a nice person looking to make a fresh start in life—the same choice you made not long ago, and one I made too. Nate hired you even without an ounce of investigative experience, and he hired me despite my bad blood with Natchez PD."

"To be precise, Nate hired me for my forensic accounting expertise and hired you because you were a crack shot with fire-arms. Although the opportunity to shoot aluminum cans off a fence rail has yet to present itself." The lines around Michael's eyes deepened with his smile.

Beth balled her fingers into a fist and shook it before his nose. "Nate hired me for my ability to incapacitate cretins—a skill I'm fully prepared to demonstrate right now."

"Considering how often you threaten me, how could we hire someone who might have been abused?" Michael crossed his arms over his chest. "Your bullying tactics will scare her."

"I will be on my best behavior for at least six months. Think of the plus side: Kaitlyn is smart, motivated, trained in firearms, and experienced with long stretches of uneventful surveillance. Please, Michael? Let's hire her on a trial basis. Then we can tell Nate to forget about the headhunter and give us some of those small cases he has piling up. Kaitlyn can handle them while we find Doyle's killer. Working a case will prove she can do the job."

Michael burst out laughing. "Fine. I'd already come to the same conclusion before you opened your mouth. I just wanted to hear you fight her battle."

Beth dropped her chin to her chest. "And you wonder why I threaten you with bodily harm," she muttered.

Michael wrapped his arm around her shoulder. "You'll change your tune once you see how many pounds I can bench press now. You'll start calling me *Mister* Preston."

NINETEEN

Saturday morning dawned sunny and clear. If weather counted in such matters, it was a perfect day for a funeral. Because the memorial service wasn't until one o'clock, Michael had a little time to relax. He'd spent most of yesterday reviewing the new cases Nate had sent him. Luckily, none of the referral work contained any measure of urgency. The boss wasn't thrilled with the news they wouldn't need the headhunter's applicants. Price Investigations had already paid the employment agency two hundred dollars up front. Of course, résumés filled Michael's email in-box all morning, now that they were no longer needed.

But Nate, being a nice guy, respected their judgment and agreed to hire Kaitlyn Webb on a trial basis. He would fly to Savannah with Isabelle next month to meet the new investigator and hopefully sign a contract. With her own career in real estate, Isabelle wasn't involved in agency decisions, especially as she was expecting their first baby. But who could blame her for wanting to visit Savannah, a city whose beauty lived up to its reputation?

While Michael had been prioritizing new cases, Beth had contacted the three candidates for the position. The two unsuccessful applicants weren't surprised by the news. Both had to have been aware that their interviews hadn't gone well. And Kaitlyn Webb? She was so grateful for the chance, Beth didn't think she'd ever get off the phone. Kaitlyn planned to ask her supervisor at the Industrial Commission for a leave of absence. If they denied the leave, she would give her one-week notice. In the meantime, Kaitlyn would work for them a few hours each evening starting on Monday.

With the hiring decision made, Michael and Beth had only another week or two in Savannah. Sunday would mark two full weeks, and as eager as he was to see the muddy Mississippi River, they both wanted to do more sightseeing before returning to Natchez. Michael sent the file of applications back to the headhunter and spent his morning at tourist websites. Time waited for no man—especially not one in love.

Promptly at eleven, Beth phoned his room. "What's wrong with you, Preston?" she demanded. "I sent you two SOS texts that you ignored."

"Is the hotel on fire? Because it's too early to leave for Tybee Island." Michael smiled, even though she couldn't see him.

"I want to stop by Mrs. Doyle's in case she needs help. Please tell me you're ready to go." Beth sounded close to tears.

"Why are you so nervous? Her sister is with her."

"Yes, but they're older women who might be emotionally overwhelmed. I don't want anything to go wrong."

Michael considered pointing out that sixty wasn't old, and that Mrs. Doyle had a funeral director, a minister, the women's guild, and a professional caterer helping her, but then reconsidered. "I'll meet you in the lobby in five minutes."

Beth stepped off the elevator wearing a dark sleeveless dress, high heels, and a penitent expression. "Sorry if I barked at you on the phone. Apparently, I'm the one who's overwhelmed." She wrapped her hand around his elbow. "This day has to go smoothly."

"Mrs. Doyle and Mrs. Harper have had more experience with funerals than us. Everything will be fine." He savored the touch of her fingers all the way to the car.

"Is this dress okay? It's not too short, is it? Should I have bought a hat? I think women are supposed to wear hats to funerals, but all I own are baseball caps."

"Your dress is fine and a hat is unnecessary. Please try to relax, Beth." Michael turned on the AC full blast.

She leaned back on the headrest. "Okay, then talk to me. What are your thoughts about Reynard? You think he's a killer?"

Michael considered his reply carefully. "I want to see where the evidence takes us on Reynard. It's Lamar Doyle I'm having a hard time figuring out."

"What do you mean?"

"From all accounts, he was devoted to his wife. So why the affair with Bonnie?"

"People make mistakes. Men especially have weak moments." She pulled her sunglasses down to glance his way. "I'm not excusing him. I'm just saying that humans sometimes veer from the right path."

"It's not only the affair I don't get. How could he be so happy-go-lucky at work? The guy made so little money, he was at the bottom of the rankings among agents."

Beth swiveled to face him. "Why should someone work hard if they don't need the money? Doyle apparently loved kibitzing around the coffeemaker and meeting new people on sales calls. I see nothing wrong with that."

"Maybe not for women, but men are hardwired to compete. It's not normal to be content in last place. Most men would strive to improve their sales figures and reach the President's Gold Club, even if advancement and year-end bonuses weren't necessary. Doyle should have tried harder to prove he was just as good as the other agents."

"If you really believe that, maybe my mother was right all along."

"Okay, what sage advice would Rita Kirby dispense on the subject?" Michael asked as he accelerated around a slow-moving truck during a break in the traffic.

"That men aren't playing with a full deck of cards."

"Please be serious, Beth."

She patted his arm. "Not all men are competitive. You are, and that's okay. It's how *you're* hardwired, but Doyle wasn't like that. Maybe the people in his office wouldn't have loved him so much if he were competitive. He knew the other agents needed money more than he did. Lamar Doyle won by simply refusing to play the game."

Momentarily flummoxed, Michael said the first thing that popped into his head. "Joe Reynard certainly didn't love him."

"No, he didn't. And we need to find out just how deep Reynard's resentment went."

Michael switched on the radio to give him time to process everything Beth said. He probably needed much longer than the drive to Tybee Island. At least when they arrived at the beach house, the funeral director had the situation under control. A waiting limousine would take family members to the church, including Charlotte Harper's husband and children, who had arrived late last night. An assortment of flowers had been delivered to the church, where the casket would remain open for viewing for one hour. Following the service, mourners would then be served lunch at the community center. Lamar Doyle's mortal remains would travel to Bonaventure Cemetery in Savannah for a private interment later on. Beth approached the widow, who stood like a statue in head-to-toe black. "Everything seems to be ready, Mrs. Doyle. How are you holding up?"

Evelyn reached out to clasp Beth's hand. "Much better now.

Will you please ride in the limo with us? There's plenty of room. For some reason, I feel safe when you're around."

Beth shot Michael an unreadable look. "Of course. I'm here for whatever you need."

Funny how Beth made Evelyn feel secure when no one else did, but Michael didn't mind. This would give him a chance to watch the crowd. Didn't murderers love to attend their victim's funeral? If that were true, he soon had a list of potential suspects. Half the island jammed the Chapel by the Sea Baptist on Butler Street, along with several Town and Country employees, including Violet Frost and Joseph Reynard.

As Michael entered the church, he locked gazes with his recent adversary long enough to learn that absence hadn't made Reynard's heart grow fonder. Beth sat in the front row next to Mrs. Doyle, while the Harper clan filled the rest of the pew. Michael found a good vantage point where he soon learned Reynard wasn't the only suspect in attendance.

The infamous other woman entered the church after the casket had been closed. Bonnie and her cohort Crystal Callahan sat in a pew on the left side, a position that allowed Bonnie to shoot dagger looks at Mrs. Doyle while Reverend White read Scripture and delivered a poignant homily. Then several insurance agents gave tearful eulogies about their friend Lamar. As the saying went, there wasn't a dry eye in the house.

A man identified as a brother of the deceased delivered the final tribute. For someone Evelyn had never mentioned before, Curtis Doyle had nothing but kind words for his late sibling. Although Michael noted that every reminiscence was from childhood or their teenage years.

Throughout the forty-five-minute funeral, Evelyn Doyle bobbed like driftwood in choppy seas, clinging to Beth or her sister as though they were life rings. Several times he thought she might fall to the floor. Her grief was genuine and almost palpable, erasing any doubt as to her innocence in his mind.

After the benediction, Michael followed the crowd down the center aisle, most still dabbing their eyes. When he reached the main foyer, the female Tybee Island detective stepped out from behind a potted plant.

"Ah, perfect timing," said Rossi. "One of the two people I wanted to see."

"Hello, Detective. A pleasure to see you again," Michael said as they walked from the church into blinding afternoon sunshine.

"Likewise, I'm sure. Could we chat in the shade a spell?" Rossi pointed at a weather-beaten palm tree that provided a little protection.

Beth squeezed in beside Rossi. "There were still seats toward the front. Why did you stand in the back the entire time?"

"It's much easier to gauge people's reactions when they don't know they're being watched. I was hoping for a balcony, like in the big Savannah cathedrals. I love balconies, lofts, crow's nests—anyplace I can spy on the world."

"Thanks for the tip." Beth lifted the hair off her neck with one hand.

"In exchange, maybe you can explain why you ambushed Joseph Reynard when he left his office."

"We didn't exactly—"

Rossi dismissed the denial with a wave of her hand. "Joseph Reynard's attorney called this morning. Before I drank my first cup of coffee, I listened to a tirade about stalking and verbal intimidation in the alley. Are you going to deny this?"

"No," Michael conceded, "but we stayed on the tree lawn until Reynard *invited* us onto Town and Country property."

Rossi shook her head. "You Mississippians really know how to make friends on the East Coast." Rossi directed her statement at him.

"I'll admit we could be more selective regarding those we admit to our inner circle."

A dimple deepened in Rossi's cheek. "Maybe I wouldn't like Reynard either, but it makes no difference if the vampire invites you in."

Beth held up a hand. "You have that backwards. The victim must invite the vampire in, and in your analogy—"

"Never mind," Rossi interrupted. "The law says you can't harass people in public. Reynard is threatening to file charges. And he plans to sue Price Investigations for defamation of character if you release any documents to the press. His lawyer insists everything in the emails Lamar collected can be explained. Now, I believe one of you has evidence to give me?" She peered from one to the other.

"Yes, ma'am, we do. But I didn't bring the file to Mr. Doyle's funeral. The papers are locked in my hotel room safe."

"Drop the file off at the station later, but give me the gist of it now."

Beth took over the explanation. "We have evidence that Doyle caught his boss in shady dealings within the agency. Reynard encouraged his agents to sell policies beyond the client's ability to pay for in the long run. That way he got his cut of the commission and looked great in his quarterly reports to the parent corporation. He also had clients lie about where cars were being garaged in the under-twenty-five bracket."

"High-handed and unethical to be sure, but Reynard's attorney assured me none of his client's actions were illegal. Not that an attorney has never been known to lie." The corners of her mouth lifted in a smile.

"Maybe the evidence won't land Reynard in jail, but it's still important to the case. We think Reynard would stop at nothing to hang on to his franchise agreement. What we have is motivation for murder."

"I do like your enthusiasm, Kirby. Ever consider joining the police force? If you score high enough, you might be able to skip the academy and go straight to the department exam. Assuming, of course, you don't have ghosts lurking in your own closet."

"No, thanks. I'm content working as a PI with Michael as my partner." Beth bobbed her head in his direction.

Rossi pulled her sunglasses down with one finger as she studied him. "And I can see why."

"Do you two not see me standing here?" Michael felt a flush rise up his neck. "Getting back to the file on Joseph Reynard, I would like to wait until Monday to drop it off. Miss Kirby and I plan to leave town for the weekend."

"I don't have a problem with that, especially since Reynard has an alibi for the night Mr. Doyle died." Rossi spoke quietly as several mourners passed on the way to their cars. "He was at a wedding in Savannah, a high-society shindig. That means photographs and videos of the event will be available. It'll be easy enough to verify."

Beth huffed out her breath. "Weddings don't continue all night. He still could have driven out to Tybee."

"My wedding sure didn't," Rossi agreed. "But apparently a select group had booked rooms at the hotel, including Mr. and Mrs. Reynard. The lawyer said they didn't leave until after brunch on Sunday. Again, easily verified."

Michael felt sweat run down inside his collar. "Are you coming to the luncheon at the community center, Detective? We can continue this conversation later in air-conditioning."

Rossi clicked open her car door. "Nope. Luncheons are for family and friends. I've seen what I came for. Drop that file off on Monday, but I doubt your so-called evidence has anything to do with Doyle's murder." She focused on Evelyn as Charlotte helped her inside the limousine. "And whatever your weekend plans, make sure you stay away from Reynard. That guy really doesn't like you two. Don't worry. I'll check out his alibi. That's my job."

Beth rode in the limousine while Michael drove to the community center alone, lost in his thoughts, but Beth was waiting for him on the walkway.

"Where's Mrs. Doyle?" he asked.

"She's already inside with some church ladies. She sent me to find you so you wouldn't eat lunch alone."

"Sweet of her to worry, but I'm fine."

Beth took his hand as they climbed the steps. "Looks like the creepy sales manager is off the hook if his alibi holds."

"He's not our problem if he didn't kill Lamar." Michael pulled open the massive door. "Why don't we eat a sandwich and then make sure Mrs. Doyle is okay. If she no longer needs you, we can go to the hotel to pack."

"*Pack?*" Beth halted halfway across the threshold. "I thought the line about leaving town was a ruse because you didn't want to fight traffic twice in the same day."

Michael pulled her to the side. "Rossi ruined my surprise. I booked us one night in Charleston at a hotel in the heart of the action. Charleston is the cultural capital of the South."

"Why are we going there? We haven't finished seeing Savannah yet."

"We can take a horse-drawn carriage ride, walk the battery, and dine at Magnolias or the Chop House. Tomorrow we'll take the ferry to Fort Sumter to see where the first shots of the Civil War were fired."

Beth placed her hands on her hips. "Other than Civil War stuff, we can do those things here in Savannah. We should finish checking out this town first."

"If we stay here, you'll find something *urgent* to do on the case. You can't help yourself. We'll see the rest of Savannah during the week and see the city named by *Foder's* as one of the best vacation destinations in the world. Who knows when we'll be back to the East Coast?"

Beth considered less than a moment. "That makes sense, but no funny stuff. We just started dating."

"Relax. I booked two rooms at a cost easily covered by our expense money. If there's enough time, could we take a plantation tour? I've always wanted to do that."

"Sure. We can visit a wide variety of interesting tourist traps if they fit our budget. I, for one, would love to dine lavishly on Low-Country cuisine."

"I have no clue what kind of food that is. What if I don't like it?"

"Then I suggest you eat something from the sandwich trays." Beth pointed at the buffet set up along the wall. "I'm going to spend time with Mrs. Doyle before we leave for Charleston." Beth snaked her way through the mourners, soon disappearing from sight.

Instead of heading toward the food for a snack, Michael wandered the room and observed the crowd. Detective Rossi had been smart to watch from the back. People might let their true selves show if they thought no one was looking.

Doyle's former boss didn't come to the luncheon.

Neither did Bonnie. Apparently, being odd-woman-out had its limits. Mainly those in attendance were neighbors from Oleander Drive and Doyle's coworkers, business associates, and fellow country club members. As Michael observed the behavior of those remaining, he had to agree with Charlotte's assessment: Evelyn didn't have many friends on Tybee Island, but at least two of her known enemies had already gone back to the city.

TWENTY

*O*n the drive up the coast from Savannah to Charleston, Beth made several new realizations. First, these historic cities on the East Coast had been settled and were still populated by far wealthier people than the towns along the Mississippi River. Sure, Natchez had many gorgeous, stately mansions built by antebellum planters and postwar titans of commerce. And several of its upscale restaurants stayed in business year after year. But after touring the historic downtown area south of Broad Street, between Bay and Battery, Beth thought it looked as if *everyone* who lived here for the last three hundred years was loaded. Reservations were needed at Charleston's four- and five-star restaurants seven days of the week.

Michael not only had reserved a table at Magnolias but had arranged for a private carriage ride with a guide who knew an amazing amount of history. His fanciful ghost stories and tales of broken hearts during wartime entertained them for more than an hour. Then they walked the Battery, making up their own stories about the people who lived in the pastel mansions. When Beth finally fell into bed that night, she dreamed of dashing sea captains and brave Confederate generals—and all of them looked uncannily like Michael.

By Sunday morning, Beth had come to her second realization: She enjoyed being with Michael and might really be falling for the guy—a fact that scared her socks off. This wasn't the same heart-racing, gut-fluttering excitement she had felt with her former boss, a man she'd developed an unhealthy crush on. This was the simple desire to spend the rest of her life with him, along with the knowledge that without him she would never rise to her full potential. And she'd be absolutely miserable in the meantime.

Beth jumped when a knock jarred her from her woolgathering. She yanked open her door to find Michael with his hair still damp and his cotton shirt clinging to his chest.

"Are you packed and ready?" he asked.

"We don't have to go back already, do we?" Beth tried not to whine but failed.

"Not until this evening, but we need to check out. We can hit the Grace Episcopal Church on Wentworth—a huge Gothic cathedral, the kind you love. Then we'll hit a Sunday brunch and catch the ferry boat out to Sumter." He picked up her suitcase and headed for the elevator.

"Instead of going to the fort, why don't we get hitched and buy a house after lunch? I remember that pink mansion on South Battery with four wrought iron balconies is for sale."

Michael tripped over an imaginary hump in the carpeting. "Don't tease me like that. It's not nice. You know you'll want your friends and family present when we walk down the aisle. Besides, we can't afford to fly everyone to Charleston for a destination wedding."

"What about our expense money?"

"Not enough left, so let's get moving." Michael almost dragged her into the elevator.

After church and during brunch there was no more talk about elopements or weddings, but Beth noticed Michael watching her slyly. He also spilled his coffee, dropped his fork, and knocked over the little pitcher of cream during the meal. Much to his dismay, they missed the last tourist boat to Sumter, so after a final spin around town, they hit the coastal road south to Savannah.

"I didn't want to bring up the case while on our getaway, but I didn't tell you about my conversation with Mrs. Doyle," said Beth, keeping her focus on the incredible scenery.

Michael turned down the radio. "Now is a perfect time to shed your burdens."

"Evelyn asked me to remain on her payroll. She wants you too, but I said our boss has new work for us. More accurately, she begged me not to leave."

"Sounds like her sister convinced her that innocent people sometimes go to jail."

"Yep. Since there are no other suspects, Evelyn could be in trouble. She asked me to come for lunch tomorrow before her sister returns to Atlanta."

"Are you going to run this by Nate? I have to call him later to see if he agrees with my prioritizing of the new cases."

"We won't have to. Evelyn is calling Nate sometime today. How could he turn her down?"

"And Kaitlyn? She starts work tomorrow."

"I'll be at the appointment with you when we discuss the case. I won't abandon you. Set the meeting up for around six."

"It's not me I'm worried about." Michael swigged his bottle of water.

"I know." Beth sighed and shook her head. "I'm praying Kaitlyn needs little supervision."

"What have you told her about us? Or told Nate, for that matter."

"Nothing yet, but I'll cross that mountain soon." Beth turned away from the scenery. "I had a nice time in Charleston. I had a nice time with you," she added softly.

"Me too, Beth. Let's just hope the other shoe never drops."

"What shoe? What are you talking about?" Beth felt her mouth go dry.

"When you discover I have three ex-wives and eleven children that I support. Or I find out you binge eat from the neighbor's refrigerator when you're sleepwalking." Michael kept his features bland as he watched the road.

"Ha-ha. Did you finally pick up my wry sense of humor? Stop it right now."

An amusing game of "What's the weirdest thing you ever did on a date?" kept them busy for the rest of the drive. When Michael parked the Charger in Homewood's private lot, Beth felt a rare spike of nerves.

"Okay, then. Thanks again for a great time. I'll touch base with you before I head to Mrs. Doyle's tomorrow. I can use Uber if you need the car." She reached for the door handle.

"Wait, there's one more thing."

When she turned to face him, Michael did the unimaginable. He kissed her squarely on her mouth—not too long or too short, and certainly not sloppy. As Goldilocks would say, it was just right.

"Wow, I didn't see that coming." She blinked several times, as though waking from a long sleep.

"Don't go crazy on me, Beth. It was just one little kiss." Michael climbed out of the car, grabbed both suitcases from the trunk, and strolled toward the entrance.

She just sat in the car, struck by a fit of paralysis. *Just one little kiss? Yeah, just like the Grand Canyon is a little river valley and Niagara just another waterfall.*

⁓

On Monday morning, Beth discussed the particulars of Kaitlyn's employment with Nate Price. Then she swam laps and followed up with a grueling workout in the fitness room. Perhaps sore muscles would keep her mind off the rest of her life. One short weekend with a nice man and one little kiss had pulled the rug from beneath her feet. How could a dedicated professional investigator turn into wife material? Her culinary repertoire included ramen noodles, oatmeal, and spaghetti with sauce from a jar. *Do men expect women to cook like Rachael Ray, decorate like Martha Stewart, and dance like J.Lo? How many tin cans can those gals shoot off a fence rail?*

Michael, however, wasn't the least bit discombobulated when she picked up the file on Joseph Reynard. Because she would have the car, she would deliver the file to Detective Rossi on her way to lunch. Michael planned to run, have breakfast, and then do paperwork until their evening meeting with Kaitlyn. His parting words were reminders to roll up the windows and lock the doors on the Charger, even while parked in Mrs. Doyle's driveway. Cloudbursts happened without warning, and car thieves were everywhere these days. So if Michael could be lackadaisical about an escalation in their relationship, so could she.

I am a crazy woman. Beth burst into hysterical laughter as she turned onto the road to Tybee Island. And that simple acknowledgment gave her a sense of peace.

Mrs. Doyle's luncheon on the expansive deck overlooking the Atlantic Ocean provided the distraction she needed. Although the maid would serve the food, Evelyn and Charlotte had helped her cook the meal.

"Do you like mulligatawny soup and Caprese salad?" asked Charlotte. "Harriett made the soup, but I baked the baguettes and Evelyn made the Caprese."

Before Beth could answer, Mrs. Doyle threw out a second

query. "I hope this isn't too morbid, but I brought home the African orchids someone had sent to the church. They were too pretty to toss on a grave."

"I've never heard of mulligatawny," Beth said to Charlotte. "But since I eat anything, I'm sure it'll be delicious." And to her hostess, she said, "It's sinful to waste, so enjoy the flowers as long as they last."

With that the three women sat down at a table right out of a magazine—crisp linens, sparkling crystal and china, gleaming silver, and, of course, the arrangement of orchids that probably cost a week's salary. With the sound of crashing waves in the background and a soft breeze cooling their skin, Beth couldn't imagine a prettier place to dine.

The entrée with a strange name turned out to be a chicken soup with celery and apples, served cold. Caprese salad was just tomatoes and fresh mozzarella. And even she knew what a baguette was. But before she scraped the bottom of her bowl, Beth decided it was time for honest conversation.

"I appreciate the delicious meal, but I know you asked me here for a reason."

Evelyn exchanged glances with Charlotte and cleared her throat. "My sister feels that for you to find who killed Lamar, you need to know why many on the island don't like me."

"Why would you say that after so many people came to the funeral?"

"They showed up because everyone loved Lamar. Me, they merely tolerated. Charlotte is right—I never tried very hard to fit in, to break through the invisible barrier. I was happy at home with my hobbies. As long as Lamar loved me, I didn't need lots of friends or snobby country club folks. The women at my church accepted me—I suppose they had to—but I didn't fit in anywhere else."

Beth glanced from sister to sister. "I don't understand. I've seen your bank account. You were every bit as rich, if not richer, than any of them. Why would they be snobby to you?"

Charlotte reached for her sister's hand. "You're doing well, my dear. Tell Beth the rest."

Evelyn pushed away her plate. "Lamar came from very old money, like most of the residents on this lovely island. Money isn't money. Oftentimes it's where it came from and how long it's been in your family. As I told you, Lamar and I met in college. Charlotte and I had always been good students—Mama saw to that. We were there on full academic scholarships, or we wouldn't have been there at all. I was the girl who loved cafeteria food and cleaned my plate every time."

Charlotte took over as Evelyn's composure crumpled. "We were dirt poor, living in the mountains on my grandparents' farm. But 'farm' is a euphemism for a tumbledown shack where no crops were ever planted. We survived on federal subsidies that my dad went through like water and whatever game he hunted. Mama earned what she could by selling honey to health food stores and taking handouts from people at church."

"We won't bore you with unnecessary details, but going to college was a dream come true for both of us." Evelyn squeezed Charlotte's fingers. "Charlotte met her husband, and I found Lamar. Life has turned out well for us."

"Nobody should care where someone was born—" Beth began.

"I'm afraid society people care a great deal, dear. Lamar often spoke first and thought later when we were first married. He told several friends in Charleston how proud he was of how far I'd come from my humble roots. Unfortunately, he also told Alfred Singleton, who was from Savannah." Evelyn paused to let the significance sink in. "Alfred felt it was his duty to spread the word to his acquaintances on Tybee Island when we moved here. Even after we had been married for forty years, some women were still waiting for Lamar to come to his senses." Evelyn released a bitter laugh.

"You don't need friends like that," said Beth. "Good thing I didn't know this yesterday, or some of those big-hatted shrews might have accidentally fallen into the koi pond."

This time Mrs. Doyle's laughter was genuine. "You are a fireball, Beth. If anyone can get to the bottom of this, it'll be you. Just don't expect any of yesterday's mourners to help you."

"At least your husband got a nice send-off. Those eulogies touched my heart, especially the one from his brother." Beth scooted back as the maid cleared the table.

Charlotte uttered a dismissive huff. "What a shock that was. Who would have figured Curtis to have a one-hundred-eighty-degree change of heart?"

"Control yourself, sister," Evelyn admonished. "Beth doesn't need you to air the Doyle family dirty laundry."

"Yes, I do. I need to hear everything. A person never knows what could be useful."

"Very well. Do you want to do the honors since you got this ball rolling?" Evelyn asked Charlotte while motioning for the maid to serve coffee and dessert.

Charlotte blushed but jumped into the story nevertheless. "When John Doyle passed, his will didn't divide the estate evenly between his sons, Lamar and Curtis. Their mother had died long ago. John had been on his third wife, who inherited the house and a few hundred thousand."

"That must have made her happy."

Evelyn shrugged. "Perhaps, but Lamar's father had made a fortune with his import business. Both sons were already married at the time, and although his father didn't care much for me, he'd had a major falling out with Curtis."

"How unevenly did Dad divide the estate?"

"Lamar inherited everything. John Doyle cut his younger son out altogether."

"Yeow! That had to sting."

"It did. Curtis blamed Lamar and accused him of poisoning their dad against him. Lamar wanted to make things right, so he sent his brother a check for half the estate."

"Which Curtis promptly tore up and mailed back the pieces," Charlotte added. "That man should have been on medication under a doctor's care."

Beth's gaze shifted between the sisters. "How long ago was this?"

Evelyn pondered for a moment. "I'll bet it's been fifteen years since their falling out."

"So why the change of heart now?"

"That's a very good question," Charlotte said. "I was shocked when that loose cannon stood up during the service and approached the pulpit. I held my breath the entire time he talked."

"They hadn't spoken to each other the entire time?" Beth asked.

Evelyn grimaced as though suddenly hit with indigestion. "That's what everyone thinks, but it's not exactly true." She inhaled a deep breath. "Curtis's silence lasted a few years, and then he called Lamar. He was in deep financial trouble—his home in foreclosure, his wages garnished, his credit cards canceled. When Curtis asked for money, Lamar gave it to him." Evelyn locked eyes with her astonished sister. Apparently, this was all news to Charlotte. "Curtis didn't want his family to suffer because of his rash act. He allowed them to continue spending money as though he still had a generous salary at the import company. I'm afraid their debt spiraled out of control."

"Was this bailout a onetime occurrence?" Beth asked.

"No. Lamar bailed him out three times, as far as I know."

"Why, that little varmint!" Charlotte's opinion of Curtis seemed to have dropped lower. "Pretending to be the poor, mistreated son while letting Lamar secretly bankroll him."

Evelyn patted her sister's hand. "Easy, Charlotte. Curtis never received his full share of the estate, not even after the third bailout."

"Let's hope he learned his lesson, because that gravy train has run off the rails."

"No, not exactly," Evelyn said softly. "Lamar named Curtis a one-third beneficiary of his estate, the other two-thirds going to me. Curtis is to receive the share that would have gone to our son."

Charlotte covered her mouth with her hand, momentarily speechless.

"If the younger brother still hadn't learned how to handle money, then he had a motive for murder." Beth watched both women for their reactions.

Charlotte's lip furled. "I would say anything is possible, since he's probably gone through every dime Lamar gave him."

Evelyn shook her head dismissively. "I don't believe Curtis is capable of murder. The man has no focus and no initiative, but there isn't a ruthless or cruel bone in his body. That's why John Doyle disinherited him. Curtis wasn't cut out for the cutthroat import world."

"If you don't mind, Mrs. Doyle, I'd like to look into Curtis and any other disgruntled Doyles you can think of."

"I don't mind at all. I'll get whatever photographs and information I have, but I hope everything I just told you will remain confidential. Curtis begged Lamar years ago to keep all this secret, and my husband agreed. There's no reason the family shame should come out now." Evelyn looked from Charlotte to Beth, waiting, until they both nodded in agreement.

"Now that that's settled, I want you to start calling me Evelyn.

I feel we're more than client and employer now. You said we were friends." The woman's eyes lit with hope.

"Absolutely we are, Evelyn."

"Good, so we'll have no more talk about sad subjects. Why don't I share some fond memories of Lamar?"

Picking up her fork, Beth cut into her key lime pie. "I am so ready for some happy stories."

There would be time to fixate on her brand-new murder suspect later.

TWENTY-ONE

For someone who only recently started believing in miracles, Kaitlyn Webb experienced a minor one firsthand thirty minutes before quitting time. She'd been watching a man for five days now on behalf of the Industrial Commission of Georgia. He claimed he had hurt his back on the loading docks at the freight terminal. Millions of tons of freight manufactured in the United States were loaded into containers at the port of Savannah and would make their way across the sea to the United Kingdom, other parts of Europe, and the Near East. Those containers would be emptied and then refilled with foreign goods destined for American consumers. The shipping industry employed thousands of people who safely performed their tasks without injury. However, accidents did happen, and when they did, injured employees were entitled to benefits while they were unable to work. And if their disabilities were total and permanent, the benefits should last for their lifetimes.

Every now and then a worker tried to defraud the system by inventing an injury or exaggerating the severity. Kendall Blankenship applied for permanent total disability after falling from a loading platform twenty feet onto the vessel below. However, no one witnessed the fall, which Kendall neglected to report to his supervisor. Only that evening, long after his shift ended, did Blankenship seek medical attention for his back. However, his wife took him to a clinic in the next county instead of choosing the emergency room six blocks from their home. All very suspicious. Kendall claimed he didn't want to jeopardize his standing with the boss until he realized the severity of the injury much later. His wife claimed the hospital nearby didn't accept their insurance, and she feared an exorbitant bill they wouldn't be able to pay. Both assertions could be valid. It wasn't Kaitlyn's job to determine fact from fiction. An independent doctor paid for by the Industrial Commission would examine the patient several times before issuing a report. Evidence would be presented at trial by attorneys for both the defendant and the state. Kaitlyn was to watch Blankenship for any activity not in keeping with the designation "permanently unable to work at any job." Thus far the claimant's activities outside the home provided nothing useful in the state's case. Blankenship arrived at his son's soccer game in a motorized wheelchair, driven there by his wife in a leased van with an electric lift.

About the time Kaitlyn decided to pull the plug on today's spy games, she got the break she needed to wrap up the Blankenship case in her final week on the job. Following his son's victory and a pizza celebration on the sidelines, Kendall waited while his wife struggled to raise the chair into the van using the controls on the electric lift. For ten minutes, she repeatedly pressed the control button and then banged on the gears with a wrench. Next, she manually tried to crank up the chair containing her husband, all to no avail. All the other parents and team members had dispersed, giving the Blankenships a false assumption they were alone at the soccer field. But hidden in the trees, Kaitlyn watched with amazement as Kendall uttered a foul word, pushed himself up, and stood. He grabbed the tool from his wife's hand and ratcheted up the lift with the chair inside. Then he walked around the van and climbed in, unaided by his wife. Maybe Blankenship would never jog or work the docks again, but the man could indeed walk and function in a less strenuous type of career. And Kaitlyn had the video proof on her camera.

She returned to her apartment with just enough time to shower and meet her new coworkers at Price Investigations. At 6:00, Kaitlyn walked into Panera Bread dressed in cotton slacks, a long white tunic, and espadrilles. She hoped a second miracle would take place today—this one not so minor. She would get the fresh start she'd been praying for ever since someone taught her how to pray.

Beth and Michael arrived at the entrance at precisely the same moment—a good sign if ever there was one—and they both looked happy to see her.

"Good evening, Miss Webb," said Michael.

"Hey, Kaitlyn." Beth greeted their new employee with a big smile. "Let's grab a quiet table in the back. Should we order before we get down to business?"

"Absolutely. You picked one of my favorite places. I can't decide which of the combos to have."

"Sorry, Kaitlyn, something came up that requires Beth and me to eat later. But you should go ahead now so you'll be ready for your assignment."

"Okay, then," said Kaitlyn, stepping up to the counter. She noticed Beth flashing him a confused expression.

For a while they talked about national news, pro sports, and the lovely weather while she ate soup and a sandwich. Michael seemed reserved, as though he'd learned his manners and intended to use them. Beth was friendlier and more open, yet when they started discussing the role of a PI, Beth's confidence spoke volumes as to how well she performed her job. The partners were as different as sugar and salt, yet their regard for each other was almost palpable.

Are they dating? So not my business. But curious was a woman's natural state.

"Ready to get down to specifics?" Beth drew a sheet of notes from her purse.

"Ready, willing, and able," Kaitlyn said, stacking her plates out of the way.

"I spoke with Nate this morning. You will be paid with a 1099 as an independent contractor during your trial period. That means you will be responsible for your taxes and health insurance. After the trial period, you'll be placed on the payroll with our mediocre hospitalization plan, two weeks paid vacation, and five days sick time. Our company benefits might be a disappointment after working for a government agency."

"Good benefits aren't everything. I like the job description. Mr. Price sounds very nice. And I know I'll like working with you two." Kaitlyn hoped her last declaration didn't sound juvenile.

"Likewise," said Beth, mitigating her discomfort.

"We can sure use you in Savannah," said Michael. "Thanks to client referrals, new cases keep piling up. Right now they are small. Nothing you can't handle alone when Beth and I return to Natchez." He looked her in the eye.

"Oh, I understand I'll be working by myself here. That suits me fine since I'm a loner by nature. That's also why I'm happy to leave the commission. Too many energy-draining days spent inside the office. I'm not much for gossip or office politics. And I have little...personal life to share with the other women."

"In that case, you'll like Price Investigations," said Beth. "We only have one gossip, Maxine, but she has a heart of gold."

"Every so often you'll be asked to come to Natchez for a company meeting or Christmas party." Michael resumed the narrative. "We have another agent who works in New Orleans—Nicki Galen—who happens to be Nate's cousin."

"Offices in three states? This company is on the move." Kaitlyn smiled.

"That we are," said Beth. "But if Nate lands a major case here, Michael or I or both of us will come back to help you. Flexibility is the key to a small agency like ours, and it's a requirement for the newest hire." Beth paused for the point to be made. "Nate and his wife are expecting their first child. Nicki and her husband are new parents. Neither partner wants to travel much. Michael and I will usually be manning the home office. That means you would be the investigator who would travel from place to place…wherever out-of-town work is."

"I understand completely." Kaitlyn gazed from one to the other. "This is exactly what I'm looking for. I'll remain in Savannah for as long as necessary. But if the work dries up, I'll go wherever I'm needed. I have a valid passport, all my possessions fit into the trunk of my car, and I didn't replace my dog after she died at the ripe old age of thirteen."

Beth folded her hands on top of the notes. "I know I said Maxine was the nosy one, but I must ask. Do you have a husband, serious boyfriend, or children who might impede your flexibility?"

Kaitlyn's back stiffened. With the job of her dreams at stake, she had to phrase her answer carefully. "I have no kids and no romantic relationship that will interfere with my career again." She slowly released the breath she'd been holding.

Beth let two or three moments spin out before she spoke. "Well, with that out of the way, welcome aboard. Michael will explain your first case."

"To get your feet wet, you'll be working undercover." A smile spread across his tanned face. "What do you know about sushi, sashimi, and upscale Japanese and vegetarian cuisine?"

"Not much, other than I love hummus with veggies and pita."

"Same here, but a restaurateur in the business district needs someone to spy on his employees. He does a lucrative lunch trade, mostly takeout and delivery with a few sidewalk tables. He and his wife leave around four o'clock, but the deli stays open until eight. The amount of food disappearing doesn't jibe with the amount of sales. We're not talking the price of bagels and cream cheese. This is gourmet-quality imported eel, squid, bluefin tuna, and yellow-tail amberjack, besides local red snapper, scallops, and mackerel."

"I'm curious why he doesn't install a camera to tape what goes on. I don't want to cut our throat, but wouldn't that be cheaper than hiring a PI?"

Michael nodded. "I asked the same thing. The people working for Mr. Tanaka are family members and children of close friends. If he installs a closed-circuit monitor, his kids would be highly offended. He wants to find out what's going on without ruffling anyone's feathers."

Kaitlyn finished the last of her iced tea. "Sounds interesting. What's the plan?"

"The deli is closed on Sundays and Monday evening. Mrs. Tanaka will meet you tonight to train you in making sushi rolls, one of their specialties. She will then tell her kids that her hands are bothering her, so she hired someone to make rolls for a week or two."

"My chef skills don't extend past mac-and-cheese and burgers on the grill."

"Not a problem. As long as the smell of raw fish doesn't bother you—and you're willing to wear a hairnet, which she will pro-vide—Mrs. Tanaka will teach you everything you need to know."

"My father used to take my brother and me fishing. He taught me to clean and debone the fish. I'll be fine."

Beth consulted her notes. "This assignment should last five or six days. If you can gain the trust of those working your shift, they might resume whatever activity is costing the Tanakas an extra grand per month."

"A thousand dollars a month in lost food?" Kaitlyn sputtered.

"Like I said, this is exotic cuisine purchased by professional stockbrokers, bankers, and dot-com entrepreneurs with plenty of disposable income."

"And to think I just ate turkey on whole wheat."

"Me? I prefer an Italian sub on multigrain," said Beth. "Under no circumstances are you to confront the misbehaving workers. You will report to Mr. Tanaka privately, and he will handle the matter however he sees fit. Any questions?"

Kaitlyn could only think of one. "May I call you tonight, Beth, after my first sushi-making session?"

"That's a great idea. Let's touch base every night this week when you finish work. Questions might come up on the job that would come under standard policy."

"Standard policy?" asked Michael, his serious demeanor slipping a notch. "Is there a company handbook I was never given?"

Beth elbowed him in the ribs. "We weren't sure you would last this long. I'll have Maxine put two of them in the mail."

Kaitlyn opened her mouth to ask a question, but she clamped it shut just as quickly. She would figure out the exact nature of their relationship later. For now, the case they gave her sounded like fun, and she always wanted to learn to cook something fancy. She was also thrilled to work with interesting people her own age. And most of all, she was grateful she wouldn't have to return to Florida.

Who knows what the future will hold? Kaitlyn didn't like starting a new career under a veil of deception. Eventually, if they hired her as a permanent member of the team, she would tell them every last secret. But for now she shook hands, thanked them from the bottom of her heart, and headed toward Tanaka's Culinary Creations with a surprising amount of energy. Considering she had two jobs this week, Kaitlyn would sleep better each night than she had in ages.

TWENTY-TWO

I thought that went well," Michael said as he and Beth watched Kaitlyn leave for her first assignment as a Price Investigations employee.

"I agree, but why wouldn't you let me have soup and a salad? I love the food here." Beth hooked her purse over her shoulder.

"Me too, but I have plans for us for dinner." Michael pointed her in the direction of the door.

"Don't tell me more free snacks at the hotel. What's the Monday night special? We'll run that place out of business if we're not careful."

"Nope. We shall dine under the stars with the sound of waves to serenade us. We're on our way to Tybee Island."

Beth halted in the center of the sidewalk, causing several passersby to divert around her. "Did you accept an invitation from Mrs. Doyle? Talk about wearing out our welcome. I just had lunch with her and Charlotte—"

Michael pulled her from the flow of pedestrians. "We are not going to Mrs. Doyle's. On such an auspicious occasion, we're going to eat at Marlin Monroe's Surfside Grill. According to the tour books, it's the only restaurant right on the beach, but we still haven't tried it." He headed toward his car, hoping Beth would follow.

She didn't disappoint. "What occasion, Preston? This is just another run-of the-mill Monday."

Michael waited to reply until she was inside the vehicle with her seat belt fastened. "Not according to our home office. Maxine informed me that today is your birthday. She said if I ordered flowers, she would give me ten bucks when we got back. Now that I have twenty, maybe I can find a florist called Day-Old Roses or Peonies for Pennies. "

Beth smiled. "You two are the last of the big-time spenders. But Maxine should have kept my personal information personal. That woman breaks a different workplace law every month."

"Maybe you're jealous because she has a crush on me."

Beth rolled her eyes. "I happen to know Maxine adores her husband. And that man is bigger than a woolly mammoth, so you'd better watch your step."

Michael reached for her hand. "Relax. I already told Maxine I'm off-limits." He kissed the back of her fingers.

"While we were still in Natchez? That would've been a little premature."

"A man needs to be optimistic."

Extracting her hand from his, Beth watched the passing scenery—a view she'd seen many times now. "I don't know why people make such a fuss over birthdays. Everyone has one each year. It's just another day. Whenever I go to Applebee's, it's always somebody's birthday. Complete strangers are supposed to join in the singing. You'd better not pull that on me."

"Tell me why you don't like birthdays. It's certainly not because you're old—Maxine said you turned twenty-eight today. Did Stan and Rita forget your big day one year, scarring you forever?"

"Hardly. Mom and Dad always made the usual fuss. But

something during Lamar Doyle's funeral made me realize how unpredictable life is. Unpredictable and frighteningly brief." Beth glanced in his direction. "Those two had a good marriage. Yes, Lamar made a mistake, but he wanted to make amends. Then somebody killed him before he had a chance to straighten things out, probably for no good reason. And if I don't figure out who, Evelyn will go to prison for a crime she didn't commit."

"That's why you and I will stay until we get to the bottom of this." Michael braked to a sudden stop as traffic slowed. "But for the rest of tonight, you're going to relax and enjoy your special day. Your biggest concern will be which dressing to put on your salad."

"Is that even possible for me?" Beth cocked an eyebrow.

"I will make sure of it. Find us a radio station with oldies. Maybe if we sing loudly and badly, we'll get in a carefree mood."

Beth followed his instructions, but the first two tunes about cheating paramours failed to do the trick. When the third song turned out to be Jackie Wilson, his half-baked idea actually took hold. " 'Higher and Higher' was my parents' favorite song when they were dating," she exclaimed and turned up the volume to full blast.

"Hey, I even know the words to this one." Michael joined in, adding his best harmony to the chorus.

"You should see those two when that song comes on the radio. Even after all these years, they dance around the kitchen like teenagers." Beth shook her head.

"It brings back fond memories of their youth."

"Or indicates early-onset dementia."

"That's not funny, Beth." Michael turned into the parking garage for Marlin Monroe's Surfside Grill.

"No, I suppose not, considering how prevalent that disease is. I always make stupid jokes when I'm nervous. Hey, you want your jacket? It might cool off later."

Before he could answer, she grabbed his jacket off the backseat and exposed the wrapped gift underneath. "Don't tell me you bought me a present! Ten bucks' worth of flowers would've been more than enough." She began to shake the box.

Michael pulled it from her grasp and tossed it in the back. "We'll leave the present for now because I haven't made up my mind who to give it to." He climbed from the car.

Beth's expression turned smug. "I think I know who it'll be."

"Time will tell." Michael slipped his arm around her waist as they took the steps to the pool area between the resort and the restaurant.

For the second time, Beth shrugged from his touch. "Why don't you put our name in for a table?" Then she headed toward the beach instead of Marlin's main entrance.

"What are those?" she asked when Michael caught up to her. She pointed at several birds flying low over the water.

He shielded his eyes for a better view. "Pelicans, fishing for their supper. Dinner for us hopefully won't be as much work."

Beth stood by the rail for several minutes, watching the seabirds.

"Are you ready to go in?" He glanced at his watch. "Our table should be ready."

But Beth remained stationary with arms crossed. "I hope this place isn't too fancy." With a small sigh, she headed slowly toward the building.

"Trust me, it's not." Michael opened the back door and waved her through.

As though headed to the gallows, Beth shuffled to the hostess station. "If I know you," she whispered as they waited to be seated, "you bribed someone for the best table in the house."

Michael neither agreed nor disagreed as he tried to swallow his irritation.

Soon the hostess led them to an outdoor umbrella table with

a perfect view of the ocean and the pool area. "How's this, folks?" she asked.

"If you don't like this table, Beth, we could request seats near the kitchen or close to a fish-cleaning station."

The confused hostess looked from him to Beth and back again.

"This will be fine," Beth said politely. "Although we might get wet if it starts to rain," she said to him. "That sky is turning ominous."

"Let's hope for the best." Michael handed her a menu and buried his nose in his. "What sounds good to you?"

Beth peeked around the tall menu. "I think the ribs and fries or maybe the ribeye with a baked potato."

"You did notice we're on an island, didn't you? I thought you liked seafood." Michael's mood was eroding to match his companion's.

"I do. What are you having?" She stuck her nose back in the menu.

"I decided on the flounder. It's served with a pecan-peach chutney, jalapeño cheddar grits, and collard greens. Mm-mmm." Michael rubbed his stomach.

"Okay, I'll have the fish tacos with the Baja red rice, although we are far from any *baja*." She slapped her menu down on the table. "Do you even know what *chutney* is?"

"It'll be chopped peaches and pecans. Now why don't you tell me what's wrong?" Michael slapped his menu atop hers with equal force. "Is it the restaurant? The weather? Or is it me? We're not leaving until you answer me. I don't care what *day* it is. You don't like birthdays anyway."

Beth grabbed a fistful of hair on both sides of her head. "I can't explain it, but the moment I realized you were turning this into an occasion, I got nervous." She dropped her chin but didn't let go of her hair.

"Nervous about what? Ever since you agreed to give us a try, you have fought me at every turn in the road. If you changed your mind about us dating, then just say so."

"I haven't changed my mind about you, but I'm not good with dating." Beth released the death grip on her curls. "I'm not polished like your former fiancée. I brought only stupid stuff to wear because I packed in ten minutes. Most women would have agonized for hours and had a manicure and pedicure before leaving." Beth held up one hand. "I put this nail polish on a few days ago, and it shows. I might be good at my job, but I'm a total washout as a classy girlfriend."

"First of all, I like your skirt and top. Frankly, I can't tell the difference between designer fashions and Walmart. Manicures and pedicures are things women do for themselves or each other, not to impress their dates. I don't care what your nails look like."

Unfortunately, the server chose that moment to deliver their drinks. In the time it took to set down two glasses, Beth's eyes filled with tears and Michael lost his momentum. He softened his tone. "I wanted you to enjoy yourself and have fun on your birthday. But if you can't relax, we'll go back to just being partners. That's worked for us so far. Maybe we shouldn't rock the boat."

Beth picked up her iced tea with a shaky hand. "It sounds like you're breaking up with me. I hope that's not the case, because I would like another chance."

Michael studied her face for any hint of deception but saw none. "All right, tell me how we should proceed."

She inhaled a deep breath. "Let's order our fish tacos and chutney flounder and start over."

"Even though the closest baja is three thousand miles away?"

A smile lifted one corner of her mouth. "Even though."

"What if it starts raining?"

"We'll huddle close under the umbrella. Or we can grab our plates and run inside. Other than my hair turning crazy curly, we'll be fine."

"Your hair is already crazy curly." Michael couldn't help himself.

Beth wiggled her eyebrows. "Then I have nothing left to worry about."

Michael signaled the server, who had been patiently waiting for their order. The food turned out to be delicious, and the chutney was exactly as he predicted. But unfortunately, he forgot to cancel arrangements made earlier in the day. Not long after they finished dinner, several employees appeared with a slab of ice cream cake containing a lit mini-sparkler. The trio of servers broke into an off-key but energetic version of "Happy Birthday."

Michael leaned close to her ear. "Sorry. I forgot to head them off at the pass."

Beth smiled at the cheerful teenagers. "Don't be silly," she whispered. "A girl needs to be the center of attention on her birthday." When they finished singing, Beth thanked them for their efforts and picked up a spoon. "Don't just sit there, Preston. Help me eat this."

"No, thanks. I prefer to watch you eat. I'm in training, remember?"

Beth cut off a corner for a taste. "I would say your training is complete. Nothing about you needs improvement."

"That's the nicest thing you've ever said to me."

She seemed to have trouble swallowing her mouthful of ice cream. "If that's true, I need to mend my ways. And a birthday is the perfect time to start."

For several minutes, Michael sat back and watched Beth enjoy her ice cream. Then he picked up his spoon. Clouds thickened over the water while the warm breeze changed to a strong wind. In the distance, lightning lit up the sky and thunder rumbled, announcing the imminent storm. But the mini-tempest in their new romance was over. Michael refused to think too far into the future. He had learned his lesson with Rachel. Maybe things would work out with Beth and maybe they wouldn't, but he refused to plan more than a few days into the future. He wasn't making that mistake again.

When they left Marlin Monroe's, rain was just beginning to hit the windshield. "We made it just in time," Beth said, ducking into his car.

Michael started the engine and switched on the AC. Then he reached for the wrapped box in the backseat and handed it to her. "Why don't you open this before we drive back to Savannah in a monsoon?"

She sank lower in her seat. "Are you sure that's for me? I wasn't exactly Miss Cordiality tonight."

"I'm sure." He bumped her with his elbow.

"In that case…" Within seconds, she had ripped off the paper and opened the box. "It's a purse! A Dooney and Bourke purse," she added with almost reverential awe.

"Do you like it? I hope it's not too big or too small or the wrong color. Maxine helped me pick it out on the Internet, but my mom said buying a purse for a woman was a horrible idea."

"Not to disagree with Margo Preston, but I *love* it." Beth lifted the purse from the box. "I can't believe you remembered that I wanted one."

"The website said you could exchange it for something different if—"

Beth stopped his ramblings with a kiss on his cheek. "It's perfect. Thank you very much."

"If it's so perfect, why are you crying?"

"Maybe because I'm a year older." She wiped away her tears. "Or because it's the best birthday present I ever got."

Michael turned onto the beach road that would take them back to Savannah. Considering that Beth must have received many other gifts during the last twenty-eight years, he settled back and smiled, despite a storm raging all across the tiny island.

TWENTY-THREE

*B*eth awoke to the sweet fragrance of magnolia, crepe myrtle, and roses. And those were just the flowers she could easily identify. When she'd returned to her room last night, the hotel bellman knocked on her door within five minutes. The man walked in with an arrangement of flowers more in keeping with a major event than a non-milestone birthday. *These couldn't possibly be for me.* The bouquet had to cost Michael a fortune, not twenty dollars from Peonies for Pennies.

Michael. No matter how she tallied the score, she truly didn't deserve a boyfriend like him. Dinner on the shore, the purse straight from her wish list, and now a botanical cornucopia? It wasn't the expenditure—money didn't mean that much to her. It was his ability to make her feel special, whether on the anniversary of her birth or an ordinary Tuesday. If it was the last thing she did, she would learn how to reciprocate his thoughtfulness. If he could learn to shoot straight at long last, she could learn how to be a girlfriend.

Beth had just finished her floor exercises when her phone rang. She was hoping for her partner, but Tybee Island Police popped up on the caller ID. "Beth Kirby," she said sweetly into the mouthpiece.

"Diane Rossi, Tybee Police. I got a message that you wanted to talk to me. What's up, Miss Kirby?"

"Thanks for returning my call, Detective. I have new information on the Doyle homicide. I'm sure you noticed the man who delivered a rather poignant eulogy at Lamar's funeral."

"Yeah, Curtis Doyle. Not a dry eye in the house when the younger brother sat down."

"Are you aware that younger brother has a strong motive for murder? When his father cut him out of the will, Curtis lost out on his share of a substantial estate—ten or twelve million dollars." Beth tried not to sound gleeful over her news.

"I wouldn't be earning my huge paycheck if I didn't check out all family members and close friends. We're well aware Curtis irritated John Doyle so thoroughly he didn't get a dime in the will. But that was twelve years ago. Homicidal rage should have kicked in well before now. Why wait this long? And anybody listening to Curtis wouldn't describe him as a loose cannon, ready to explode."

Beth didn't have an easy answer to the detective's logic. Not without betraying the confidence Evelyn had placed in her. Was it better to keep a dark family secret at her expense? If Detective Rossi didn't come up with a reasonable possibility, eventually the DA would formally charge the one suspect they already had. For several moments, Beth pondered the conundrum of whether to remain loyal to Evelyn—a woman who needed friends she could trust—or to get the woman absolved of a murder she didn't commit.

Rossi terminated her woolgathering. "If that's all you wanted to talk about, I need to appear in court soon."

Beth made a hasty decision. "There is one more thing, Detective. It wasn't the bequest of John Doyle that has me worried. Are you aware of the contents of Lamar's will?" she asked, already knowing the answer.

"Nope. It hasn't been filed in probate court yet."

"Curtis was named as a beneficiary of one-third of Lamar's estate, with the other two-thirds going to his widow, Evelyn. Curtis will receive the share that would have gone to their son, who was killed in Afghanistan. Mrs. Doyle indicated Curtis managed money like an eight-year-old. He was always in foreclosure, with a horrible credit rating and garnished wages."

"That's true for half of the American population."

"Yes, but most people won't inherit millions should one of their siblings meet with an untimely death."

"Maybe that's why Curtis had such nice things to say even though they hadn't seen each other in years," said Rossi, no longer sounding in a big hurry.

Beth bit the inside of her mouth. "The two actually had occasional contact. Lamar had bailed out his brother several times, but for some reason Curtis didn't want his family to know. And he didn't want them to know he was one of Lamar's beneficiaries."

"My, my. Mrs. Doyle has really taken you under her wing."

"Yes, and that's why I'm not happy about spilling the beans. Please keep everything I told you in confidence."

Rossi clucked her tongue. "I'm not the type to call the *Savannah Post* gossip page, if there still is such a thing. Besides, the moment the will is filed in probate court, it becomes public record. The world will soon know the ne'er-do-well brother is a rich man."

"The whole thing sounds fishy to me. If your husband was heir to a fortune, wouldn't he tell you?"

"Sure, if he knew what was good for him." Rossi chuckled on the other end. "All right, Beth, I'll look into Curtis Doyle. But right now I need to get to the courthouse and testify, or a bad guy could walk if I don't. I wasn't making that up."

"Will you keep me in the loop, Detective?"

"Yes, if your lead turns into something concrete. Otherwise, my conversation with Mr. Spendthrift will remain confidential.

I'm not the gossipy type, remember?" Rossi clicked off, leaving Beth oddly disconcerted.

What if I'm wrong? What if Curtis isn't on the brink of destitution? Or what if he has a solid alibi for the night Lamar died? She would have betrayed Evelyn's trust for no reason.

Beth headed to the shower, hoping soap and hot water would wash away remorse. But a second phone call postponed any absolution.

"Good morning, sunshine. Did I wake you?" Michael asked.

"Not at all. I was just about to thank you for the flowers. Twenty bucks goes much further at Savannah florists than those back home. Your extravagance is much appreciated."

"I've been saving money for a long time, and I don't want to anymore. Live life to the fullest—that's what I always say. Or maybe I just read it on a billboard."

His humor lifted Beth's spirits. "Where are you? Could we meet for breakfast? There's something about the case I want to discuss."

"Sure, but I'm over by Fort Pulaski on a training run. Give me an hour to get back and twenty minutes for a shower. How about ten thirty in the Lodge?"

Beth's heart sank. The last thing she needed was to sit around brooding for ninety minutes. "No, I'll grab something now and then follow a new lead. We'll talk this afternoon. In the meantime, why don't you look into Curtis Doyle's background?"

"As you wish. You know where the car is parked, and you have a set of keys. Just don't solve the Doyle murder without me." Michael ended the call, his laughter ringing in Beth's ears as she considered her next move.

The more she thought about her conversation with Detective Rossi, the more she wanted to talk to Curtis first. He might open up to one of his sister-in-law's friends, but if Tybee Island police showed up flashing badges, Curtis would call his attorney faster than a jackrabbit. After all, just like Lamar's boss, Curtis could afford the best these days, leaving Evelyn still in the bull's-eye.

The long-lost brother wasn't hard to find. Curtis had signed the funeral guest book with his complete address down to his zip code, along with his cell phone number. He certainly didn't want to make it hard for the executor to deliver his share of the inheritance. Thanks to the photocopy Beth had made of the guest book, she punched the address into GPS and headed out of town. The drive would give her plenty of time to contemplate her job performance lately.

What happened to Nate Price's ace detective—the one entrusted with Michael's training not long ago? If she didn't get her head on straight, she would be the one needing supervision when they returned to Natchez. *Is this why dating coworkers is a bad idea?* Falling for Christopher McNeil had ruined her career on the police force, but Chris hadn't been in love with her. Only time would tell what Michael's true feelings were.

Beth arrived in Jessup long before she could sort out her relationship issues. The GPS directed her to a medium-sized colonial on a suburban lot. The house might be a comfortable place to raise a family, but it couldn't compare to Lamar's beach house. Her subject was in the front yard, sparing Beth the effort of knocking on the door. Curtis Doyle wielded an electric hedge trimmer along the privet hedge, dragging a heavy extension cord behind him. With his thick safety goggles and ear protectors, he remained oblivious to her approach.

"Mr. Doyle?" Beth said, tapping him on the arm.

Curtis spun the trimmer in a wild arc. "Good grief, young lady! You could have lost a finger."

"Sorry about that. I'm Beth Kirby, a friend of Evelyn's. Could I have a word with you?"

Curtis turned off the trimmer and set it down in the grass.

"I remember you from the funeral." Stripping off his gloves, he extended a hand. With his goggles pushed up his forehead, Curtis looked like a four-eyed creature from outer space.

Beth shook halfheartedly. "Since her husband's passing, I'm working on Evelyn's behalf on several matters. Of course, her attorney will handle Lamar's estate, but I would like to ask you a few questions."

"What can I help you with?"

"Some questions will be rather personal since Evelyn allowed me access to family history."

Curtis glanced back at the house. "Ask what you like, but be quick about it."

"You shared some lovely memories of your brother, so I'm curious why you were estranged for a number of years."

"If you are in Evelyn's confidence, then you know the reason."

"Losing your share of the Doyle fortune must have been hard to take."

Curtis wiped sweat from his brow with his sleeve. "It was. I blamed Lamar for turning Dad against me, but eventually I had to face the truth."

"What truth is that?" Beth asked, stepping into the shade of the hedge.

"That Dad was right—I couldn't handle the responsibility he'd given me. I wasn't cut out for the family business. Neither was Lamar, for that matter. But my brother bowed out more gracefully than I did."

"Care to elaborate?"

"I can't imagine how any of this is cogent to Evelyn's tying up loose ends." Curtis stepped behind an overgrown bougainvillea bush to be out of sight from the living room window.

"Humor me, please, if you don't mind."

Curtis swept his safety glasses from his head. "My grandfather started a shipping corporation that my father built into one of the largest in the world. I'm sure you've seen those colorful containers piled high on the Savannah River."

Beth nodded to keep him talking.

"Those containers contain American-made goods bound for Europe, the Near East, and South America. They will be refilled with French wines, Swiss chocolates, English wool—world trade at its best. Even during recessions, people can't seem to live without coffee."

"So what was the problem? As the boss's sons, you and Lamar probably had cherry-picked positions."

Curtis issued a bitter laugh. "That's how it works at other corporations, but not at ours. My father was a tyrant. He drove his employees hard and his sons harder. He said he was bound and determined to turn his *sissy college boys* into men. Dad had insisted we go to college, and then he held it against us." He shook his head. "We were paid commissions only on freight we contracted. So in order to earn a decent wage, I had to work seven days a week, ten-hour days, never sitting down to a meal or attending church with my family or seeing my son play soccer. Lamar took a leave of absence after his son was killed and signed up for insurance classes at the community college. He never came back to the docks."

"Your father couldn't have been too happy about that."

"He wasn't, but he wrote it off to grief over Jamie's death." Curtis looked at his watch. "Look, Miss Kirby, my shift at the lumberyard starts in an hour. I still need to take a shower."

"Please tell me the rest," she said softly. "What happened between you and your father?"

Curtis focused on children playing across the street. "One day I witnessed him berating a female employee and I became unhinged. The woman didn't understand a new procedure, and that madman humiliated her in front of everyone. I called him a sadistic bully whose cruelty masked his own ineptness, along with a few other profane adjectives."

"And he fired you."

"Oh, yeah. Right then and there. Unfortunately, my family had grown accustomed to a seventy-hour paycheck. I found another job, but I only made half the salary. With so much lost time to make up for, I insisted my wife buy whatever she wanted on the credit cards. The kids were already in private schools, and we continued to give them whatever they wanted. Problem is, kids never stop changing their minds as to what they want."

"That's why you asked Lamar to bail you out." Beth made sure her voice contained no recrimination.

Curtis nodded. "I begged him not to say anything. I was afraid my wife would be ashamed of me. Finally, when I could no longer look myself in the mirror, I told Amy how close we were to financial meltdown. She'd suspected something was wrong but was afraid to ask."

Beth took a step closer. "What did you do?"

"We sold our big house and bought this one. We put the kids in public school and started to live on what I earned. It wasn't easy, but we made the adjustment. Now I have a real family and work I enjoy. My wife actually likes having me around. Imagine that." Curtis began wrapping up his extension cord.

"You never told Amy about Lamar bailing you out three times." Beth took a chance, but it paid off.

"Not until Evelyn called to say Lamar was dead. I was so ashamed." His gray eyes clouded with moisture. "I told Amy on the way to Savannah."

"Your family's situation is about to change, isn't it, Mr. Doyle?"

"And you think that pleases me?" His tone grew shrill. "If I didn't have three kids to put through college, I would refuse Lamar's legacy. But I won't be selfish." He picked up his gloves and trimmer and marched away. "Now you must excuse me."

But he didn't get halfway to the garage before a sedan with

Chatham County plates pulled into the driveway. "What now?"
he demanded.

"Uh-oh," Beth murmured as Detective Rossi and two uniformed officers stepped from the car. "That woman is with the
Tybee Island Police Department. Just tell the truth, Mr. Doyle,
and you'll be all right."

Curtis's head snapped around. "Is *that* what this is about—
you think I had something to do with Lamar's death? I loved my
brother and owed him more than I could ever repay."

Beth didn't know which angry face to look at—the one in
front of her or the one headed her way. "Um…good afternoon,
Detective. I thought you had to appear in court."

"The defense lawyer requested a continuance." Rossi placed
her hands on her hips. "You had better have a good reason for
being here, Kirby, or I might think you're interfering in a police
investigation."

"No, ma'am. I was just checking on Curtis on behalf of Mrs.
Doyle." Beth walked backward to her car, while Curtis headed in
the opposite direction into the garage.

"Curtis Doyle, would you come with us, please? We'd like to
ask you a few questions in regard to your brother's murder."

"You tell Evelyn she's got this wrong!" Curtis addressed Beth
instead of the three officers closing in around him. "I didn't want
Lamar's money. My life was just fine without it."

Beth was speechless. All the way back to Savannah, she tried to
figure out if Curtis just delivered an Oscar-worthy performance
or if she just muddied up already murky water. When she reached
the parking lot for the Homewood Riverfront Suites, she was no
closer to an answer than when she left.

TWENTY-FOUR

*M*ichael glanced at his watch and then at the clock on his nightstand, just in case one of them was wrong about it being three o'clock. He hadn't heard from Beth in hours, despite having called and left a message on her voice mail and then sending two texts.

The longer he waited, the more annoyed he became.

Since when did partners not tell each other what leads they were following? She could have run into a psychopathic killer, crossed paths with one of the rejected job applicants, or gotten a flat tire. A simple phone call would stop the continuous loop of horror scenes running through his mind.

He already knew more about Curtis Doyle than anyone other than his wife—and he probably knew a few tidbits even Amy Doyle wasn't aware of. Michael bounced his stress ball off the wall just as someone knocked on his door.

"Are you in there, partner? It's me." A contrite voice permeated the reinforced steel.

"Me who?" he demanded.

"Beth. Please open up. I come bearing snacks."

When Michael yanked open the door, she marched in with

two overflowing grocery bags. "By all means, make yourself comfortable." He pointed at the couch.

"I brought chips, pretzels, salsa, Snapple, Coke, and Dr Pepper." Beth dumped the contents across the coffee table.

"I've already eaten, but I am curious about today's adventure. Which lead were you following?" He settled in the room's sole upholstered chair.

Beth grabbed a stack of napkins from the counter and ripped open the barbecue potato chips. She took a liberal handful from the bag. "I drove to Jessup, a town ninety minutes from here, to visit Curtis Doyle. I would have asked you to join me, but you were training for your he-man competition."

Michael laced his fingers behind his head. "If time was of the essence, I could have come straight back and been ready within an hour. Even when I'm training, I still answer the phone and read my texts." He let his words hang in the air.

Beth swallowed a mouthful of chips. "You're right. I should have called or sent a message. Truth is, I wanted to sort things out before I talked to anyone else." She reached for another handful.

"Why don't you start at the beginning?" Michael opened a Coke, trying to relax.

"I called Detective Rossi this morning with the information I learned from Evelyn."

"Before you even shared it with me?" His attempt at relaxation was short lived.

"Yes. I wanted to point Rossi in the right direction. But as soon as I did, I got a bad feeling about the whole idea." Beth reached for the chips bag while still chewing her last batch.

Michael pulled the bag from her hand. "What's going on here? You never power-munch like this."

"I'm drowning my sorrows in potatoes. This is what people do who don't drink—they overindulge in junk food until they founder." Beth dropped her chin. "I plan to eat myself sick."

Michael placed a hand on her shoulder. "Tell me the story from the beginning. Then maybe I can help you."

Beth took a swig of Coke and launched into a tale that included conversations with Evelyn Doyle, Detective Rossi, and Curtis Doyle in the front yard of his home. Michael had a hard time keeping the three conversations separate. Beth's tale ended with Doyle being hauled away in a Tybee Island patrol car while insisting Evelyn had it wrong—he never would have hurt Lamar in a million years.

"Except it wasn't Mrs. Doyle who thought Curtis was a murderer," Michael said when Beth finally finished her tale.

"No, it was me," she wailed. "And now I'm not so sure. I should have waited until we had a chance to look into Curtis."

"Wasn't that the busywork you gave me to do?" It was a rhetorical question, but Beth answered it anyway.

"It wasn't busywork. I wanted to know, but then I let the situation careen out of control. I'm obsessed with getting Evelyn off the hook for murder." She pressed her fingertips to her eyelids. "I'm supposed to be the veteran detective, yet I've been acting like a brand-new rookie."

"Hey, I wanted to point that out, and you beat me to the punch." Michael hoped his teasing would lighten the mood.

"Give me that bag of chips. This is one train wreck I won't be crawling away from. At least you won't have to worry about dating your partner when Nate gets done with me."

Michael pulled three chips from the bag and placed them on her napkin. "This is all you get, Kirby. I'm staging an intervention. After you eat, we'll figure out what to do."

One by one she chewed and swallowed. Then she wiped her hands and mouth and sighed. "Don't you get it? Evelyn trusted me with an intimate family secret that I promptly shared with Rossi. I'm so ashamed of myself. Tell me what you found out."

"I discovered Curtis's years of money mismanagement, including the world's lowest credit score. Every credit card they ever had was maxed out and canceled. Then on three occasions a mysterious influx of cash saved the family's cable TV and the daughter's ballet lessons, not to mention the roof over their heads. No record that the money came from Lamar. I would be shocked if the IRS wasn't watching Curtis for possible money laundering."

"Lamar promised to keep quiet. Hard to imagine Amy Doyle was that naive about finances, but I guess some women don't want to take responsibility."

"That would never be you, Beth."

"Nope. I prefer to remain oblivious in other ways." When she met his gaze, her eyes were filled with pain. "I should have consulted you long before this, but what should I do now? What if it turns out Curtis had nothing to do with his brother's murder? I'll have betrayed Evelyn's trust for no good reason."

"You have to tell her the truth."

"I know, but not yet. First, I need to figure out where Curtis was the night Lamar died."

Michael recapped his drink and rose to his feet. "I'll leave you to your figuring and the rest of the snacks, if you still need them."

"Where are you going?"

"Nate called me about a small case that should only take one or two days."

"What kind of case? Do you want me to come with you?" Beth sounded like a frightened child.

"One of Mrs. Baer's elderly friends lost her poodle. It dug a hole under the backyard fence and escaped five days ago. The poor woman is upset because none of the local shelters have found him, so she hired Price Investigations."

"To track down a lost dog?"

"I shall go valiantly wherever the boss sends me." Michael bit back his smile. "I already called the lady's vet. Unbeknownst to her, the dog was chipped at the original shelter where it came from. When the vet scanned the databases, he found the dog on Hilton Head."

"The dog walked all that way?"

"Not quite. Some couple picked him up along the highway and took him to their vet to be checked out." Michael finished the rest of his drink. "I'm on my way there to pick up Harold and return him to our client. This might be the shortest case in the history of Price Investigations. While I'm gone, you can follow up with our protégé."

"You still trust me to train Kaitlyn?"

"Of course I do. One mistake doesn't make you a bad PI."

"Thanks, Michael. I'll have my phone handy in case you need advice with Harold." Beth leaned her head back and stared at the ceiling. "Who knew you had dog whispering in your long list of talents?"

Michael closed the door behind him. It seemed as though Beth forgot she was in *his* room. But after her ordeal in Jessup, Michael saw no reason to tell her.

TWENTY-FIVE

*K*aitlyn couldn't wait to finish her report on the Blankenship investigation for the Industrial Commission. With her eyewitness account and videotaped evidence, the case would be sent for review by her supervisor and then passed to their legal team. Industrial Commission lawyers would show the evidence to Mr. Blankenship's lawyer and ask if they still wished to proceed with the petition for permanent total disability. If Blankenship decided to go ahead and a court of law found him ineligible, the State of Georgia could file fraud charges. That rarely happened in cases of such blatant falsified complaints. Once the attorney pointed out the available options, such as a partial disability award, along with job retraining provided by the Bureau of Worker's Compensation, the claimant usually made the right decision.

Kaitlyn spent the last hour of her workday on the phone with her former boss in Florida. Vicky Stephens wasn't just the woman responsible for her transfer to the Georgia bureau, she was her mentor, confidant, and friend—something Kaitlyn had few of. It took quite a bit of convincing before Vicky agreed that working as an independent PI was a good idea.

"Savannah is too close to Pensacola, Kaitlyn. It would be better to keep moving around. And a small firm will make your past their business, especially with partners close to your age."

Kaitlyn quickly put her friend's concerns to rest. A professional PI would have the best shot at covering her tracks in the digital world of nonexistent privacy. At the moment, however, it wasn't the subterfuge with Michael and Beth she had to worry about. She first had to convince the Tanaka siblings she was fully trained after four scant hours of sushi making.

Kaitlyn walked into Tanaka's Culinary Creations at ten till four for her second day of undercover work. The two twenty-somethings behind the counter peered at her with thinly veiled disdain.

Their mother greeted her warmly. "Hi, Kate. Okay that I call you that?" Mrs. Tanaka handed her a starched white tunic on a hanger. The required dress code was black, loose-flowing slacks and a black T-shirt. A white tunic would be provided at the start of each shift to maintain a professional appearance among all employees.

"Hi, Mrs. Tanaka. Yes, Kate is fine." Kaitlyn grinned enthusiastically at her new coworkers.

"This is my son, Jason, and my daughter, Amy." Mrs. Tanaka hooked her thumb over her shoulder. To them she said, "This is Kate. You be nice to her or I'll take a stick to you." Mama Tanaka moved toward the door.

"Look, Mom, if your wrist hurts that bad, I'll be happy to make the rolls for tomorrow." Amy dropped her voice, but it was still easily heard by Kaitlyn. "There's no need to hire somebody else. Cousin Joan will also help out if she doesn't have night classes."

Mrs. Tanaka turned on one high heel. "I already told you, Amy, that Kaitlyn is my yoga friend's daughter. She just moved here and ran out of money. She needs a job."

"Does she even know how to make Asian food?" Amy arched a brow as her gaze landed on Kaitlyn.

"Yes. I taught her what she needs to know yesterday." Mrs. Tanaka pivoted toward her son. "You have anything to say? Now's the time!"

Jason held up his hands in surrender. "Nope. I'm good, Ma."

The bell over the entrance jingled, signaling customers. "Good. Then everybody get to work." Mrs. Tanaka marched out the door to her husband's car, which stood idling by the curb.

Amy rolled her eyes the moment her mother left the building.

"I'll go wash and start the sushi rolls." Kaitlyn carried her tunic into the restroom. On her way back to the kitchen, Amy blocked her path.

"I'm sorry. You're probably thinking I'm a total jerk, but my mother has made lots of bad employment decisions. The last person she hired stayed only one day. Then the man cleaned out the cash register on his way out."

"I promise to keep my fingers out of the till." Kaitlyn's tone turned frosty.

"I didn't mean to impugn your integrity, but it usually works out better when Dad makes the business decisions."

"No offense taken. Now if you'll let me get past," Kaitlyn murmured.

Amy stepped to the side with a sheepish expression. "I'll be waiting tables and handling phone orders. Jason runs the cash register and updates the computer during our slow periods. Just holler if you need anything."

"You can count on it." Kaitlyn tightened the belt on her tunic. *"My yoga friend's daughter"?* She vaguely remembered the story Mrs. Tanaka had concocted during yesterday's training session. Kaitlyn hadn't planned on an elaborate ruse to explain her presence. Couldn't Mrs. Tanaka hire whom she wanted without consulting her children? She would have a hard enough time as a culinary master without dealing with surly employees, unhappy because she took work from Cousin Joan.

She'd taken explicit notes about the *maki* sushi rolls she would be making—those with *nori*, which was roasted seaweed, on the outside and the vinegared rice and other ingredients on the inside. Mrs. Tanaka had her practice rolling thin rolls, *hosomaki*, which contained one ingredient, such as raw crab or fish, and medium rolls, called *chumaki*, containing two ingredients, such as cucumber and pickled plum or eel. When Mrs. Tanaka mentioned "toro and scallion" was a two-ingredient local favorite, Kaitlyn made the mistake of asking what "toro" was.

"Chopped tuna belly," answered Mrs. Tanaka without batting an eyelash.

Kaitlyn didn't inquire about the origin of ingredients from that point on. Mrs. Tanaka would continue to make the thick rolls, called *futomaki*, those containing four or five ingredients, along with the Western-style rolls, such as California, dragon, rainbow, and caterpillar, which were often rolled inside out. And the Tanakas would continue to make the exotic types, often done the traditional Japanese way with fermented rice.

Kaitlyn placed today's fresh seafood on clean sheets of parchment paper and started chopping the cucumbers, scallions, and other vegetables. Mr. Tanaka had already made the rice in a large batch in the steamer. In keeping with the health-consciousness of their patrons, the Tanakas used organic brown rice instead of traditional white short-grain. Kaitlyn then laid out five sheets of *nori* she would cut into strips, a bowl of vinegared water for hand dipping, soy sauce, wasabi, and pickled ginger.

Once she had all her kitchen tools, she whispered a prayer and started cutting, scooping, and rolling on a bamboo mat. After her eighth or ninth roll, her shoulders relaxed and her back straightened. As her mentor explained, it was all in the wrist action, but nimble fingers helped too. With New Age music on the satellite radio station and no one interrupting her concentration, Kaitlyn started to unwind. *This could be an easy assignment after all.*

A large rectangular window separated the prep kitchen from the public area of refrigerated displays, soft drink coolers, counter seating, and tables. Customers were able to see what went on behind the glass, while Kaitlyn could watch Jason sitting at his cash register and Amy flitting around like a hummingbird between the tables inside and out. The supper crowd was far lighter than at lunch, yet the courtyard remained full for the next two hours. Jason also rang up the take-out orders.

Around six thirty, Amy trudged into the kitchen with a tote filled with dirty dishes. "How's it going? Run into any problems?" She flashed a smile as she loaded plates and cups into the commercial dishwasher.

"None that I'm aware of." Kaitlyn made eye contact only briefly. "We won't know until tomorrow when customers try rolls made by a half-German, half-Dutch wannabe."

Amy finished loading, washed her hands, and walked over to inspect. "Well, they sure look good—exactly the same as my mother's. How many did you do?"

Kaitlyn didn't answer until she finished cutting her current roll into pieces. "Close to eighty. I was afraid to count until the end of my shift."

"Don't worry about the number. If you don't meet quota, my aunt can make more when she gets here tomorrow. She starts work at eight and leaves at one." Amy pulled up a tall stool.

"I still have another hour and a half in my shift." Kaitlyn focused on the calamari.

"Tuesday is usually our slow night, so Jason and I close up early."

Kaitlyn lifted her chin and frowned. "Don't you still have customers outside?"

"Nope. They're all gone. I closed up the courtyard. This isn't like a suburban or mall restaurant. We cater to businesspeople in town from nine to five. They might grab something after work or to take home, but by seven o'clock we're usually deader than a doornail."

"It's odd, then, that your mom hired me to work until eight." Kaitlyn continued rolling sushi as though her life depended on it.

Amy dragged her stool to the worktable. "Look, Kate, you and I got off on the wrong foot. Jason and I have recently been trying to coax our parents into the current century. I'm afraid you landed in my crosshairs, and I apologize for that."

Kaitlyn placed a perfectly rolled creation with wasabi and tuna on a tray. "Seems to me that if this is your parents' restaurant, they should be able to run things their way."

"Absolutely, especially since I'm just taking a break between undergrad and graduate classes, and Jason is waiting to hear if he got into law school." Amy popped an oyster that had fallen to the side into her mouth. "But my parents don't realize how incredibly well they have done. They have saved and invested for years, not only in the restaurant, but with several different financial planners. They don't need to work *at all*, let alone this hard."

Kaitlyn cocked her head to the side. Considering her parents died long ago, she had little background to call upon, but that didn't stop her from forming an opinion. "From what I hear, if people enjoy the work, they should keep working even if they don't need the money."

"Jason and I don't want them to retire. We just want them to ease up on their *extreme austerity* program."

"If you need a raise, why don't you just ask for one?"

Amy shook her head. "I don't need more than minimum wage. As long as Jason and I are in school, our parents pay all our bills. This isn't about us."

With a shrug, Kaitlyn shifted her weight between hips. "If it's just the same to you, I'd rather not get pulled into a family feud, especially since I have no idea what you're talking about."

Amy got to her feet as Jason carried another load of dishes into the kitchen. "Not much foot traffic on the street," he said. "We might as well shut down early. I turned off the outdoor lights so people know we're closed."

With a nod to her brother, Amy pushed the stool back to the other station. "You keep rolling, Kate, while Jason and I clean up. I'm sorry if I upset you. I just needed to vent a little steam."

"No problem." Kaitlyn tried to sound earnest.

"We love our parents, but sometimes it's tough work for people of their generation." Amy carried the dish tote back into the restaurant.

Maybe because you're spoiled rotten, Kaitlyn thought.

For the next twenty minutes, she rolled sushi. At seven o'clock, the Tanaka siblings escorted her out the door with the assurance she'd be paid for her full shift. *After all, I've fallen on hard times and can't pay my bills.*

As Kaitlyn left Tanaka's Culinary Creations, she couldn't help noticing the siblings drove very nice hybrid sports cars that, although fuel efficient, hadn't been purchased from minimum-wage paychecks. Something was going on, just as Mrs. Tanaka thought, but she wouldn't discover what that was rolling sushi in the kitchen.

By tomorrow she would have a battle plan to help her client stop the silver-spoon crybabies in their tracks.

TWENTY-SIX

*H*aving left all the snacks in Michael's room, Beth wandered around hers with nothing to do. She planned to leave a message on Kaitlyn's voice mail, but their new hire picked up the phone on the first ring.

"Kaitlyn Webb," she said. The loud music in the background suddenly ceased.

"Hi, this is Beth Kirby. Did you get fired already? I thought your shift at Culinary Creations ended at eight." Beth laughed so there would be no doubt that she was teasing.

"It's only a matter of time," said Kaitlyn. "The brother and sister shut the place an hour early and sent me home. I'm going to pull over so we can talk. I don't have Bluetooth."

Beth waited a few moments. "Give me your first impression. Are they about to clean out the cash register and head for the border?"

"Jason Tanaka mans the register and updates the computer software. If he's skimming money, you'll need a forensic accountant with access to the books. I've only been taught to roll sushi."

"It's food that's disappearing, not money. Notice any musclemen carrying crates of seafood to a truck in the alley?"

Kaitlyn chuckled. "Not yet, but those two spoiled brats are up to something. They threw a fit about Mrs. Tanaka hiring me, as though she's not entitled to run her restaurant how she sees fit."

"Hmm, sounds like battle lines have been drawn." As they talked, Beth walked around her room putting things away.

"You got that right. Jason and Amy think I'm in league with Mama Tanaka, so building trust will take more time than Mr. Price has for this case. Tomorrow I'll come up with an excuse to leave early and then double back and spy on them. If they're selling smoked salmon on the corner, I'll catch them red-handed."

Beth grinned at the woman's enthusiasm. "Sounds like you have this slippery eel by the tail. How about joining me for supper tonight? We can share case notes. Privacy laws don't apply inside the agency."

Kaitlyn answered without hesitation. "Absolutely, as long as it's not raw meat or seafood. Where should I meet you?"

Beth quickly concocted a plan. "Would you mind picking me up at my hotel? We can buy supper at the City Market and eat while surveilling suspect number one in our murder investigation."

"Perfect! I'll get to observe an ace investigator in action."

Beth's stomach tightened. After her latest misstep, she didn't feel much like anyone's idea of an "ace," but she wanted to encourage Kaitlyn any way she could. Beth described the valet area and headed downstairs to the lobby to wait.

Forty minutes later, with take-out boxes in hand, Beth and Kaitlyn parked under a moss-shrouded oak in front of Cool Beans. Kaitlyn's old Mustang wouldn't draw the kind of attention Michael's flashy Charger would.

"Wow, I can't believe people drink coffee this late in the day." Kaitlyn pulled the lid off her plastic tub of chef salad.

"Plenty of stockbrokers and investment bankers work and live in the area. When dealing with world financial markets, morning and evening is a matter of perspective. I believe the woman serving up vanilla lattes and cappuccinos murdered my client's husband in cold blood." Beth glanced at Kaitlyn's salad as she poured dressing over her lettuce, cucumbers, ham, cheese, and croutons. "What? No anchovies?"

"Please, no more fish jokes until I crack this case." Kaitlyn winked and popped a cherry tomato in her mouth. "Tell me about the murder and what we hope to see here."

In between bites of salad, Beth delivered an abbreviated version of the Doyle homicide, including the fact that their client was the police's chief suspect. "Rest assured, our agency would never help anyone get away with murder. I'm absolutely positive Evelyn didn't kill her husband."

Kaitlyn studied the employees milling behind the counter. "I take it her husband's mistress has an alibi for the night of the murder."

"One that my gut tells me is bogus. The alibi for Lamar's boss turned out to be ironclad. Lamar's brother has money problems and stands to inherit from the estate, but is he a murderer? I no longer think so. So I'm back to Bonnie Mulroney. Maybe she was blackmailing Lamar, and when he said 'no more,' she lost her temper."

"A woman scorned. Isn't that the oldest motive in the world?" Kaitlyn speared a pile of sliced ham and cheese. "But how did she get into a house with a high-tech security system? Finding the gun she used sure would come in handy. Then there is that pesky alibi Bonnie has for Saturday night."

Beth peered out the window through light rain. "A minor technicality, since I don't believe a word Crystal said. Or maybe I just don't trust people with purple hair."

"I'm dyin' to get a look at these two. Let's go inside. I'm sure they sell decaf."

"Both women know me, but you can have a look-see." Beth handed her a ten-dollar bill. "Your drink will be on Price Investigations, but make sure you get a receipt. Our Natchez bookkeeper is a stickler about such things. Look for a skinny blonde with a ponytail—that's Bonnie. Crystal has black hair with purple streaks."

Kaitlyn snatched the bill and jumped out. She soon returned with a caramel-swirled concoction covered with whipped cream. "Here's what I learned. First, Crystal can't make change without help from the cash register." She held up two fingers. "Second, Bonnie smiles at every male patron but avoids eye contact with women." Up popped a third finger. "And charging almost six bucks for this should be a second-degree misdemeanor." Kaitlyn placed the change in the console and took a noisy slurp of her drink.

Beth took an even noisier slurp of iced tea. "Something tells me you're going to fit in well with us, Miss Webb."

"I hope so, although I never would do that in front of Mr. Preston. Is it okay if I call him Michael?"

"He would like that better than Bob or Frank or Mike, for that matter."

Kaitlyn covered her mouth with her hand. "Good to know. I asked because I don't want to overstep any boundaries. He seems more formal than you."

"He is, but he's also very nice. I'm the one who should be worried about overstepping," Beth added softly.

"Where is he tonight? Unless that's none of my business. In which case, just say so." Kaitlyn pivoted toward her on the seat.

"Relax. We don't have anything top-secret planned until the weekend. Tonight Michael is in South Carolina. Some rich lady hired us to find her missing poodle. Michael tracked him down with help from his microchip."

"Someone hired a PI to find a dog?" Kaitlyn shoved her empty cup into the trash bag.

"Yep. The boss picks the cases, and we go wherever we're sent."

Beth switched on the AC to clear the windows. "A vet in Hilton Head found the dog, but he won't release the dog to Michael without the owner's signature. Our client doesn't know how to scan and email a document, so tomorrow she will fax her permission from the senior citizen center." Beth picked the olives and garbanzo beans from soggy lettuce. "Poor Michael has to spend the night alone at a luxury resort. As long as the client sends the fax, Michael and Harold will be back in Savannah tomorrow." Beth crunched her container and added it to the bag.

Silence settled over the small car for several minutes while rain pelted the windshield. "Would you mind if I ask another none-of-my-business question?" Kaitlyn asked.

Beth nodded, already knowing what it would be.

"Are you and Michael dating? Again, feel free to—"

"Yes. What was the dead giveaway? The 'all alone at a luxurious resort' part?"

"No, I got a hunch during the interview. The two of you kept *looking* at one another."

"And I thought we were so clever," Beth murmured. "For the record, Michael would be *alone* even if he were here. We just started going out, and so far I keep messing up every chance I get."

Kaitlyn peered silently through a clear patch in the condensation.

"What's wrong? Too much information?" Beth asked. "Sorry about that."

"Not at all. I'm the one who stuck my nose into your business. But this is the time when the coworker steps up and offers advice, whether sought after or not."

"Feel free to speak your mind. I'm open to suggestions."

"Maybe you just need time to adjust. The longer people are single, the more set in their ways they become. It's human nature to be annoyed by someone's idiosyncrasies but not see your own."

"Are you saying not everyone has expired food in the fridge and owns three pairs of rubber muck boots?" Beth feigned a look of shock.

"I don't even own one pair, and my fridge only has a bottle of catsup."

Both burst out laughing. When Beth finally sobered, she rolled down the window, oblivious to the rain. "Then it's hopeless. Either people get married at nineteen or they're destined to be alone forever."

"I wouldn't throw in the towel quite yet. Relationships take time to develop. At least, that's what they say on the talk shows. My last boyfriend was during high school, and we broke up at the prom. I had lots of male friends in college, but none of them fell asleep dreaming about me. I'm afraid I can't give much advice on relationships."

Something niggled in the back of Beth's brain, but before she could put her finger on it, Bonnie exited the building's side door. "Romantic guidance will have to wait. My favorite suspect just exited the building. Let's see where Bonnie goes after work."

Kaitlyn started the engine and turned the defroster on high. She waited until Bonnie's yellow Honda pulled into traffic and followed at a distance of two car lengths. She didn't weave in and out or tail too closely, yet she managed to keep their suspect in sight.

"Well done," Beth said at the traffic light. "Someone's had a few lessons in clandestine driving."

Kaitlyn smiled. "My mentor at the bureau taught me well."

Beth would have asked more about her former mentor, but Bonnie turned into the parking lot of a familiar three-story brick-and-stone building on Bull Street. "Well, I'll be a monkey's aunt," she muttered.

"Wow, nice digs. Your suspect lives *here*?" Kaitlyn gawked at the ivy-covered facade.

"This is the swanky love nest provided by my client's late husband. You, too, could live here for around three grand a month."

"How can Bonnie afford this place working in a coffee shop? I didn't even see a tip jar. Mr. Doyle can't still be paying the rent."

"That question is at the top of my list," said Beth.

Bonnie stepped out of her car, took two more puffs on her cigarette, threw it down on the pavement, and climbed the steps to the building.

Kaitlyn clucked her tongue. "Doesn't she know what those things do to your lungs?"

"I forgot to mention the part about her not being smart." When Beth was certain Bonnie was inside the apartment, she climbed out of the Mustang. "Let's go talk to the super who lives in the basement. I want to know why Bonnie still lives here. Maybe the girl has already found a replacement sugar daddy."

Unfortunately, fifteen minutes later the two PIs drove away without an answer. The superintendent either wasn't home or didn't want to answer the door. Beth left a note along with twenty bucks and her phone number.

"Where to now?" Kaitlyn still sounded bubbly despite her long day.

"Back to my hotel. Price Investigations is officially closed for the night. I need a hot shower and a good night's sleep. Thanks for your help, but this PI has had enough surprises for one day."

"Call me anytime. This was much more fun than sushi rolling."

TWENTY-SEVEN

Hilton Head, South Carolina

*M*ichael had no idea how a man could feel so out of sorts at such a luxurious resort. Any activity one could want was available—world-class golf, tennis, deep-sea fishing, sailing, spa facilities, beautiful beaches, and an array of restaurants. Everything was right here—except for a cheap place to sleep. So he pulled out his personal American Express card and paid three hundred dollars for one night. He would deduct a normal night's lodging from their expense allowance, but Nate shouldn't have to foot this kind of bill.

I should have driven back to the mainland. This wasn't the kind of place you stayed at while working a case. Rich people like the Doyles vacationed here along with their extended families, plus a few budget-savvy honeymooners. Seeing those couples strolling hand in hand made him feel lonely. How he wished Beth were here. They could have had dinner on the terrace and walked the beach in the moonlight. More likely, they would have talked about the case until their eyelids drooped and then padded off to their separate rooms. But that would have been fine too.

Because after one little kiss, he couldn't stop thinking about her.

At first light, Michael ran the beach, worked with weights for thirty minutes, and took a hot shower. After a light breakfast, he arrived at the vet's with a newspaper and cup of coffee. Dr. Rhoden's assistant greeted him, and the good doctor arrived a few minutes later. There was a slight delay due to the wording of the release, but they worked through that, and then Harold, an overly styled French poodle, was sprung from incarceration. At least the vet provided a cardboard carrier so Harold wouldn't be loose inside the Charger.

With Harold whimpering mournfully on the backseat, Michael headed back to the Homewood Riverfront Suites and Beth. For the first time, he felt a pang of sorrow at the thought of leaving Georgia. Natchez, on the banks of the Mississippi River, was home. But something about this eighteenth-century city had latched onto his heart. He would miss the beautiful landscaped squares once Nate summoned them back. And he had a feeling Beth felt the same way.

Hilton Head was just a stone's throw from Savannah if you were a seabird, but the distance by car was close to an hour. Michael turned up the radio to drown out Harold's whining and settled back for the scenic drive. But long before he reached the open road, his phone rang. A quick glance at the screen told him it wasn't the love of his life.

"Good morning, Detective Rossi. What can I do for you?"

The detective's chuckle sounded wry. "I'm glad I chose to call you, Mr. Preston, instead of your partner. I would have answered that question from Miss Kirby far less politely than how my mama taught me to talk."

"I take it this involves Mr. Doyle's younger brother."

"You're right about that. On Kirby's hunch, we brought Mr. Doyle to the station for questioning, and what a waste of time that turned out to be."

"Curtis Doyle has a long history of bad money management. Lamar kept the roof over his head and the utilities turned on more than once. As a one-third beneficiary of Lamar's estate, he stood to inherit plenty. Maybe Curtis got tired of waiting for nature to take its course."

"Is that how they do things in Mississippi?" Her rhetorical question dripped with scorn. "You get a wild hunch and then ruin a person's life with unfounded accusations?"

"No, ma'am." Michael provided the only acceptable answer.

"If your hotheaded partner would have looked deeper into Curtis's finances, she would have seen he straightened out his money troubles years ago. He hadn't asked Lamar for any more help because he hasn't needed to." She whooshed out a breath. "In fact, Curtis considered money the root of his family's troubles and preferred life without it."

"People will say all kinds of things to cover their tracks." Michael felt the urge to defend his partner, even though Beth's actions had been undeniably rash.

"Oh, you don't believe he had a change of heart? Then maybe you'd like cold, hard facts instead. Such as there's no evidence Curtis visited Oleander Lane during the past month. And several witnesses can place him at his son's soccer game in Jessup Saturday night. Even with several million dollars at stake, the guy can't be in two places at the same time."

"Miss Kirby only wanted to eliminate Mr. Doyle as a suspect—"

"Is *that* what Miss Kirby wanted? You tell your partner I'm the detective in charge of this case, not her. What she did was close to interference in a police matter. And she also messed up that guy's life unnecessarily. Curtis was humiliated in front of his neighbors. And he has some uncomfortable explaining to do at the next soccer game. There are some things that should stay buried in the past."

"Beth and I apologize for any unpleasantness we caused—"

"Oh, you didn't cause me any unpleasantness. Trust me. If you cross the line, I'll just throw you both in jail. And it'll be a long drive for your Mississippi pals to come visit. Beth owes Curtis an apology, but I would advise strongly against it. If she shows up at his house again, he'll take out a restraining order against her. So tell her to back off."

"I'll tell her, and thanks for the update on the Doyle homicide—"

"I'm not finished yet. Wait until you hear what I found out about your client, Mrs. Doyle…"

When she was finished, Michael was rendered speechless.

"For the record, I don't have a problem with you, Mr. Preston. In fact, we could probably work a few cases together if you were planning to stick around." Rossi chuckled merrily. "But since you aren't, when are you heading west?"

Michal smiled at Harold in the rearview mirror. "Probably in another week. We still have a little more sightseeing to do."

"Fine, but you know what they say about screen doors on your way out." With that, she ended the call.

He pulled over to the side of the road, filled Harold's bowl from his water bottle, and punched in Beth's number.

"Good morning, stranger," she said cheerily. "Do you miss me already?"

"More than you know. I'm on my way with a poodle who won't stop whining."

"Poor thing. He probably misses his mommy."

"Or his hairdresser. Why would someone put bows in Harold's fur?"

"I don't think gender matters with poodles. They all get bows. When will you get back?"

"After I take Harold home. Then you and I need to talk, Beth. I just got off the phone with Diane Rossi."

"Oh dear. This can't be good."

"The police questioned Curtis and then released him. Apparently, he has a solid alibi for the night his brother died. He was at his son's soccer game. Half the town of Jessup saw him there.

And what's more, his finances have been in order for several years. He's furious that you embarrassed him in front of the neighbors and tore the scab off an old family wound. He doesn't want you to come near him."

"No problem. I already ruled him out as a suspect."

"Curtis isn't the only one angry," he added. "Rossi wants you off her case."

Beth hesitated before she replied. "I'm really sorry I dug up the past for Curtis. I'm sorry I eroded our relationship with Rossi. And I truly regret betraying Evelyn's confidence. While you're returning Harold, I'm headed to the island to confess my sins to our client. I'll call you when I'm done so we can meet for coffee or something to eat or a thorough browbeating—your choice."

"Sounds good. Just don't get arrested for anything on Tybee. Considering Rossi's mood, posting bail would seriously crimp our expense account."

TWENTY-EIGHT

*B*eth showered, dressed, and arranged for an Uber driver in record-breaking time. But she waited until she was halfway to Tybee Island before she called Evelyn to make sure she would be home. *Perhaps I could hide in the bushes if she is out running errands.* Considering the nature of her visit, Beth wanted to circumvent any offers of hospitality, such as, *Will you stay for lunch? We could have lobster salad on the deck.*

Evelyn greeted her at the front door wearing a navy silk dress, heels, and a friendly smile. "Where is Michael today? And who was that who dropped you off?"

"The man's name is José. Michael is on a case in South Carolina."

"Are you dating this José? I was under the impression—"

"No, ma'am. José is an Uber driver. I'm still dating Michael, much to his dismay." Beth's smile was a bit wobbly as she stepped into the cool foyer.

"It sounds like we need some girl talk." Evelyn hooked her arm through Beth's elbow. "Let's go to the living room. I know you enjoy the view."

Beth let the woman drag her to the white leather sofa facing the water. "I'm not here to talk about my dating debacles, although they could certainly fill a few hours. I'm here to explain my recent lapse in judgment and ask for your forgiveness."

"Oh, Beth, nothing can be as dire as all that," Evelyn said soothingly as she accepted a mug of coffee from her maid.

Beth did the same and then launched into the woeful tale about her trip to Jessup. "What's more, according to Detective Rossi, Curtis has an alibi for that night. And he's cleaned up his bad money-management habits."

"I told you he simply wasn't capable of murder." Evelyn's statement contained not one ounce of resentment.

"Yes, you did, but that much money can change a person's nature. Still, I should have done my homework before I rushed into action. Now I've made trouble for Lamar's brother, and what's worse, I betrayed your confidence."

Evelyn cocked her head as though confused.

"You asked me to keep the information under my hat, and I didn't. I didn't even warn you about what I planned to do. Maybe I'm not cut out for PI work."

"Nonsense. You were just doing your job, which is trying to catch my husband's killer. And that's more important to me than keeping an old secret from years ago. If Curtis had a change of heart about his father's will and no longer resents Lamar, he should be glad someone wants to find the person who murdered his brother."

"He didn't act very *glad* when I saw him."

"He might be after he calms down. No one wants their shameful past hung out to dry, especially if it implies motive for murder."

"As much as I regret my behavior toward Curtis, it's your pardon I seek." Beth lifted her gaze to meet Evelyn's.

"You already have it. Now, what has caused friction between you and your handsome partner?" She arched one eyebrow.

"That's something else I'm not cut out for—having a partner, at least not one I'm romantically involved with. Let's just say my jumping to conclusions about Curtis added to friction already in progress." Beth released a sigh far too weary for midmorning. "I'm not talented enough to make a work relationship work."

Evelyn's laughter sounded like crystal wind chimes. "Nobody is savvy enough at first. It'll take extra effort, but I wouldn't give up just yet—not on the romance or the work partnership. Couples in the movies make it look easy. Experience tells us something much different. I can only say it's worth it in the end." A hitch in her voice revealed that tears were close to the surface.

Beth crossed the space between them and took hold of her hand. "You make me miss my mom. When I get back to Natchez, I'm going to be extra nice to her for a full week."

"Mothers and daughters—often a challenge but always a blessing." Her smile erased several years from her face. "Can you stay for lunch?"

Beth rose to her feet. "Thank you, but no. Michael wants a powwow as soon as he returns from Hilton Head. Considering the thin ice already beneath my feet, I shouldn't keep him waiting."

"All right, but I've just figured out what your penance shall be."

Beth blinked with surprise.

"Instead of a week, you must be extra patient with your mother for a full month. And regarding Michael? You must be nice to him for a solid year with no thoughts of walking away from a relationship with him during that time. If I have to hire a Natchez PI to make sure you stick to my terms, I will." Evelyn winked impishly.

"Save your money. Toeing those two particular lines will be easy."

The Uber driver appeared five minutes after she called for the return trip to Savannah. Beth kissed Evelyn's cheek on her way out and greeted José as if they were long-lost friends. But her lighthearted good mood proved short lived.

"Beth Kirby," she said to the unknown caller when her phone rang.

"Are you the private investigator who slipped a twenty-dollar bill and this number under my door?" The cool voice sounded a thousand miles away instead of on Bull Street, in the heart of the historic section.

"Yes, ma'am. Thanks for returning my call. I'm investigating the death of Lamar Doyle, your former tenant."

"What does his death have to do with me? My job is to collect the rent and make sure people park where they're supposed to." Distrust inched into the conversation.

"Yes, and that's why I'm calling. I'm curious as to why Miss Mulroney is still living in Mr. Doyle's apartment."

"Why shouldn't she be? The rent has been paid."

Beth phrased her next question carefully. "Are you saying Mr. Doyle paid the rent before he died?"

"Well, I don't believe in ghosts, Ms. Kirby. Just like you did, he—or someone—slipped an envelope under my door while I was out. The note said 'For the rent of Miss Bonnie Mulroney in number 306.' There was a check for the full amount of the rent for six months."

"Did you happen to scan or photocopy the check?" Beth asked.

"What difference would that make? The rent is paid, so the girl gets to stay. Why are you making trouble for her?"

"I don't care if Bonnie lives there rent-free forever. I just want to know who signed that check."

The superintendent sighed. Then she said, "Please hold for a moment."

While Beth waited, she noticed José watching her in the rear-view mirror, his expression a mixture of curiosity and apprehension. "I'm a secret agent working deep undercover," she said, covering the mouthpiece with her hand.

"Like Emma Peel?"

It took her a moment to make the connection. "Exactly like Mrs. Peel."

"Ha!" José's hoot was a dead giveaway he wasn't buying the story.

"Okay, I found the photocopy in the file." The building super's exclamation pulled Beth's attention back to the conversation. "Looks like Evelyn Doyle signed the check on the twenty-fifth of September. Is that it?" Apparently it was, because the superintendent clicked off without waiting for confirmation.

Beth didn't care. She was already digging her datebook from her purse. September 25 was the day that Lamar broke up with Bonnie and recommitted himself to his marriage. *So why on earth would Evelyn pay the rent for six months?*

Beth slouched down in the seat and closed her eyes. She had some thinking to do before her meeting with Michael. He would want to know why. *She* wanted to know why. But considering she'd just shored up Evelyn's faith in her, she couldn't call her and ask. Just as they passed the Welcome to Savannah sign, a text from the very person she'd been fretting over dinged for attention.

Michael: Where are you?

Beth: I'm with a handsome Uber driver name José. We just reached city limits.

Michael: Ask your Latin paramour to drop you off at Johnson Square. Your luncheon waits under an oak tree by the fountain. Wear a flower in your hair. We'll have ten full minutes to be alone before Kaitlyn arrives.

Feeling warm and tingly all over, Beth sent an emoji of a dancing fish with a top hat as her response and gave the new directions to José.

When she climbed from José's vehicle minutes later, Michael was checking his messages at a park bench. As usual, he looked cool, calm, and collected in the shade.

He glanced up as she approached. "How did José handle the news of your breakup?"

"He might never get over me." Beth plunked down her purse on the bench. "What are you hiding, Preston?"

Michael produced a bouquet of flowers from behind his back. "I thought you could use these after your visit to Mrs. Doyle."

"How did you find time to buy flowers after delivering Harold to his rightful owner?" She pressed them to her nose and inhaled.

Michael pointed at a vendor selling identical bouquets fifty feet away. "I hope you don't think less of my gesture." When he plucked one of the blossoms to tuck behind her ear, his fingers brushed her cheek tenderly.

"Not in the least, thank you." Beth stretched up and kissed his cheek. As an afterthought, she planted a second kiss on his lips.

"Wow, the flowers *were* a good idea." His dark tan deepened with his blush. "Let's sit down. I want to finish relaying my conversation with Rossi. We can eat later after Kaitlyn joins us."

"Sure." Beth plopped onto the park bench. "But first I need to bare my soul about the meeting with Evelyn."

"Why don't you tell me tonight while our trainee is at the restaurant?" Michael perched on the wall of the fountain.

"No, please let me go first. I can't believe how nice Evelyn treated me." Beth launched into a highly animated recap of their conversation. Although she'd tried to be brief, Kaitlyn was strolling up the flagstone path by the time she finished.

"Good afternoon, fellow private investigators," Kaitlyn crowed. "I'm so glad you texted me, Michael. Turns out there wasn't much to do at the bureau, so they released me early. And I love picnics," she added, eyeing the bag of Subway sandwiches.

"Pull up a bench. We have to finish our employee meeting before we chow down." Beth peered up at Michael. "Tell us about your conversation with Rossi." Looking at Kaitlyn, she said, "Rossi is the Tybee detective assigned to the Doyle homicide."

Michael looked from one woman to the other. "Maybe we

should hold off until later, since the Doyle case is before Kaitlyn started."

"Want me to walk around the block a few times?" Kaitlyn asked after a few silent moments. "I understand about wanting to protect a client's privacy."

Beth shook her head. "No, you're one of us now. Besides, staying on the right side of enforcement is paramount. If I'm in trouble with Rossi—and I have a feeling I am—then we'll both benefit by hearing this. I won't let pride stand in the way of a good teaching moment." She winked at Michael.

He didn't wink back. Instead, he looked stricken but nevertheless resumed the narrative. "I told you that Curtis had been released for lack of evidence and an airtight alibi, but I didn't tell you what else Detective Rossi was mad about."

Beth felt a nervous twinge grip her stomach. "Why not? We both had time to chat."

"Because I knew you were on your way to Mrs. Doyle's to apologize, and the rest of Rossi's revelation had to do with her. It's not good news for your new best friend."

Overhead the sun slipped behind a cloud, depriving them of its much-needed warmth on the cool day. A breeze lifted goose bumps on Beth's arms, while the sound of children at play inexplicably ceased. It was as though the universe sensed a new tilt of the earth's axis. "Wouldn't it have been helpful if you'd told me?" Beth asked. "Then I could have straightened out any misunderstanding on the part of the Tybee Island police."

Michael fixed her with his honey-brown eyes. "If I'd told you, and you tipped off Evelyn, then Rossi could have arrested you for interfering with police business or obstruction of justice. We need to let Rossi do her job."

Beth's twinge exploded into the sensation of impending doom as memories of their last case returned with a vengeance. "What did Rossi tell you about Evelyn?" In her peripheral vision, Beth saw Kaitlyn's eyes turn round as saucers.

Michael rubbed the back of his neck. "Mrs. Doyle was told to leave Tybee Island Thursday night, the evening after someone shot at her on the beach." He turned to Kaitlyn. "How much has Beth told you about the case?"

Beth answered for their newest team member. "Pretty much everything, so you can speak plainly. Of course Evelyn left the island. We told her not to stay in the house alone, and she agreed to go to a hotel."

Michael kept his tone soft and nonconfrontational. "But Mrs. Doyle didn't go to a hotel like she promised. She went straight to the Bull Street address, knowing Lamar wouldn't be there. He was in Augusta at a sales conference." Michael aimed this explanation at Kaitlyn. "Evelyn went to see Bonnie right after telling us someone was trying to kill her. She's on the security camera leaving the island and then on traffic cameras on Bull Street, including the one across the street from Lamar's apartment. Later that night, she was photographed returning to her development on Tybee Island."

Beth blinked like an owl. "I'm sure she had her reasons for not going to a hotel—"

"I'm sure she did, but we can't ask until Rossi has a chance to check her and Bonnie's phone records."

Kaitlyn took this opportunity to wedge a question in sideways. "Do the police think they planned the murder together?"

"Rossi needs to rule out that possibility."

"That's ridiculous!" Beth declared.

Michael's smile was bittersweet. "I don't disagree, Beth, but we must let the police do their job."

"I can't ask Evelyn about this? She's our client. We can't just throw her to the wolves."

"Mrs. Doyle has an attorney to protect her legal rights in case she's arrested. If she isn't, then we can talk to her. Keep in mind that she lied about going to a hotel."

"She didn't exactly lie," murmured Beth.

Michael lifted her chin with one finger, which was a very bold gesture in front of Kaitlyn. "Don't split hairs. Mrs. Doyle had plenty of chances to explain why she went to see Bonnie, but she chose not to."

Kaitlyn leaned forward. "Did you ever find out who's paying Bonnie's rent now that Mr. Doyle passed away?"

As much as she loved the woman's enthusiasm, Beth wished that particular question could have waited for later. "Yes. Evelyn's signature is on a check that paid for six months of rent."

"When were you planning on telling me this?" Michael crossed his arms over his polo shirt.

Beth made eye contact with him. "Right now, at our meeting. The building superintendent called on my way back from Tybee. I'm not keeping secrets from you, partner. Not anymore."

Kaitlyn mitigated the uncomfortable moment. "I know Mrs. Doyle is our client, but is there any chance she and Bonnie are in this together? I mean, why would she pay six months of rent for the woman running around with her husband?"

Beth took the lead on answering the question. "I have no idea, but Evelyn is a good woman who understands Christian kindness and forgiveness."

She shrugged. "I just started going to church, so I'm fairly new at this. But logic tells me there should be a limit on that kind of charity."

Beth crossed her arms to match Michael's stance. "I know without a shadow of a doubt that she loved her husband and wouldn't hurt a fly."

"Conjecture and gut feelings won't help us now." Michael slicked a hand through his hair. "After the police have had a chance to do their job, Beth and I will get to the bottom of this.

In the meantime, this meeting is adjourned. Let's eat. Before you know it, Kaitlyn, it'll be time for your shift at Tanaka's Culinary Creations."

A shiver ran from Beth's scalp to her toes. "Good idea, because I'm starved." That wasn't true, though. Her appetite had disappeared with the news of Evelyn's shenanigans. "Who had a tuna on nine-grain with hot peppers?" she asked, pulling sandwiches from the bag.

"Definitely *not* me." Kaitlyn passed the sub and chips to Michael. "I had the turkey on Italian bread, all the veggies, with light mustard."

Once everyone had the correct sandwich, Beth pulled the last sandwich from the bag. Even though it had been prepared exactly how she liked it, each bite stuck in her throat when she swallowed.

Evelyn, an accomplice to murder. How could anyone possibly think that?

TWENTY-NINE

*K*aitlyn hardly tasted her sandwich at the meeting in the park. So many sparks were flying between Michael and Beth that it was a miracle the Spanish moss didn't catch fire and burn down Johnson Square. Had it always been like that between those two? They both must fall into bed at night utterly exhausted from all the dancing around each other's feelings. *Poor Beth.* No wonder she had been seeking advice from someone she barely knew. She was floundering in her new romance. *Unfortunately, I know even less about forming positive human relationships than you.*

And poor Michael. At least the guy seemed to be logical, quick thinking, and most of all, patient. Kaitlyn arrived at three conclusions while they cleaned up the trash. First, Michael didn't share Beth's certainty that Mrs. Doyle was innocent. Second, he would do everything in his power to keep Beth from running afoul of the law. And third, he was just as madly in love with her as she was with him—and almost as clueless.

Kaitlyn had gotten so caught up in their drama that she arrived at Tanaka's Culinary Creations without formulating a plan of attack. She parked on the street and assessed the restaurant with her field glasses. Patrons lingered over late lunches or cups of herbal tea at three tables. Walk-ins would be sparse at this hour. Kaitlyn locked her car and walked around to the courtyard, where only one table had occupants—an elderly couple sharing an order of sushi rolls. If their smiles were any indication, they were enjoying her handiwork.

Entering the restaurant through the service door, Kaitlyn ran headlong into Jason, who had bags of trash in both hands.

"K-Kaitlyn," he sputtered. "What are you doing here?"

"Your mother asked me to work every night this week so that her hand can heal. Once the freezer is stocked, she'll cut back my hours. Didn't she tell you?" Kaitlyn peered up at him.

"Yeah, she told me, but I didn't think you knew about this entrance." Jason squeezed past her on his way to the alley.

"Every public establishment needs two points of access to meet the fire code." She sounded like a schoolteacher, but her lesson was lost on the young man. Jason had already disappeared around the privacy fence.

Inside the back door were employee restrooms, a time clock mounted to the wall, and a dozen employee storage cubicles. None of them had locks, so theft between employees apparently wasn't an issue. Of course, she was the only nonfamily member working here. Kaitlyn tucked her purse into her assigned compartment and entered the kitchen, where Amy stirred a simmering pot on the stove. A heady fragrance of basil, parsley, celery, and onion filled the air.

"Hi, Amy. Something sure smells good."

"A good, hardy soup for our first chilly day," she said over her shoulder. "I see you've returned for day number two."

"Yep. The rent and utility bill won't pay themselves." Kaitlyn smiled at the porcelain-skinned, raven-haired girl.

Amy dragged the pot from the burner with mitts and turned to face her. "About those bills… I've been asking around. One of my friends works for the Savannah Historical Society. They need a front desk clerk to fill in for six months while a woman has back surgery. It's easy work. All you have to do is pass out brochures, sign people up for various tours, and make sure teachers keep their students in line around the displays."

Kaitlyn dawdled as she scrubbed her hands and arms at the sink to give her time to think. If Amy had conned one of her pals into creating a job for her, the brother-sister team definitely had something to hide. "You think if I can roll sushi, I must be good at crowd control?" She reached for a paper towel to dry her hands.

Amy's chuckle sounded forced. "Look, I'm talking about a good job that will last longer than this one. You would work in a beautiful, air-conditioned mansion and not go home with clothes smelling like smoked trout. Did I mention the salary will be twice what my mother pays you?"

How could anyone turn down such an attractive offer? "That was incredibly nice of you!" Kaitlyn produced an expression to reflect her appreciation. "Especially since I got the impression you didn't like me too much yesterday. Then you turn around and go to bat for me today."

"I like you fine. We just got off on the wrong foot."

"Good. I'm glad that's straightened out." Kaitlyn spritzed her prep counter with nontoxic sanitizer and polished until the surface shone.

Her soup forgotten, Amy took a step closer. "Will you call my friend about the job?"

"I don't think so, but thanks anyway." Kaitlyn's smile was worthy of a pageant contestant.

"Please don't be offended, but a Japanese deli isn't a good fit for you. If our clients see a non-Asian making our famous sushi rolls, they might think our cuisine isn't authentic."

"Good point." Kaitlyn glanced up briefly. "From now on I'll work with my back to the window. That way my ethnic heritage will remain a deep, dark secret." She rewashed her hands, pulled a tunic over her head, and headed to the refrigerator for ingredients.

Amy marched around the table until she stood face-to-face with Kaitlyn, her arms akimbo. "May I ask why you don't want the job at the Historical Society? If you're behind on your bills, doubling your salary would catch you up faster."

Kaitlyn dumped an armload of plastic tubs on the stainless steel counter. "That is the honest truth, but I…I have personal reasons for not wanting a front desk position, especially if it involves dealing with tourists, frazzled teachers, and hordes of kids with more energy than common sense."

Amy remained rooted in place as though her expensive running shoes were glued to the floor. "That sounds suspiciously like you're on the lam or something. If you expect my family to trust you, don't we have a right to know the answer?"

The girl doesn't know how close she is to the truth.

Kaitlyn shrugged her shoulders. "It's nothing like that. I have a mild case of agoraphobia. Crowds make me nervous, as in clinical anxiety. My shrink told me I've come a long way since having full-blown panic attacks whenever too many people enter the room. The doctor has even weaned me off meds except in emergencies." She sucked in a deep breath before continuing. "That's why I'm trying a temporary job in a restaurant. I'll be fine as long as I stay in the kitchen and deal with only one or two people at a time. Right now I couldn't do what you do." She hooked her thumb toward the dining room. "Maybe someday, but it won't be soon."

Suddenly, the door swung wide and Jason's head appeared. "What's going on, Amy?" he demanded. "We have customers out here who want their checks before Christmas."

"I'm on my way," she snapped as the door swung shut. "Okay, fine. You can keep making sushi rolls for as long as my mom needs you. And don't worry about keeping your back to the window. That doesn't sound very politically correct the more I think about it." Amy picked up her check pad and pen.

"What will you tell your friend?" Kaitlyn called.

"What?" Amy held the door open with her backside.

"At the Historical Society."

"Don't worry about them. Some brave soul is bound to be looking for a job."

Kaitlyn smiled at both her Oscar-worthy performance as a phobia sufferer and her own intuition. She knew right off the bat that the job had been fabricated to get rid of her. Although the position probably wouldn't last more than a couple weeks, it was still a kinder gesture than inventing a lie to Mrs. Tanaka so she would be fired.

For the next two hours, Kaitlyn created dozens of *hosomaki* and *chumaki* sushi rolls—each one a culinary masterpiece, at least in her own mind. Amy served customers, refilled condiment containers, wiped out the refrigerated displays, and chatted with her brother at the counter. While the siblings huddled over cups of coffee, Kaitlyn examined the stockpot, still bubbling away on the stove. It was full of beef soup with brown rice, barley, and every vegetable that grew in American gardens across the South. There wasn't anything exotic or gourmet or even Asian about it. There also wasn't anything like it on the menu, including the list of daily specials.

As the afternoon turned to evening, Amy and Jason grew more distant and secretive. Once, Kaitlyn caught Jason watching her through the window, and Amy avoided eye contact each time she entered the kitchen.

Had she truly been agoraphobic, this would be a perfect job, because she'd become practically invisible at the prep counter.

Around seven o'clock Jason entered the kitchen and went to work at an area of counter as far from her as possible. With nimble fingers, he lined up slices of whole-wheat bread and then topped each slice with sliced ham and Swiss cheese. Before he'd finished his first row, Kaitlyn scrubbed the last sushi residue from her hands.

"Can I help with those?" she asked, joining him at the counter.

The question made him flinch. "No, thanks, Kate. You keep making Mom's rolls."

"I finished my quota for the day. And we'll need the fresh fish delivery to start tomorrow's. If those are for the take-out cooler, I'd be happy to help." She reached for the second loaf of bread.

Jason pushed the bag beyond her reach. "No, they're for a card game with my frat brothers. Tonight we're playing at my apartment." He cleared his throat. "Mom doesn't mind providing the food, but she would blow her stack if I let you help me on the time clock."

"Is there something else I can do? Maybe you can show me how to steam the rice."

"You'd never get the correct consistency or the sourness right. Besides, Dad loves to do the rice himself," said a voice from behind them. Amy had crept silently into the kitchen. "Uniformity is his pride and joy."

A shiver ran up Kaitlyn's spine. *When were we transported into a scary movie set?* "Okay, tell me what I can help you with. I'm used to working hard for my paycheck, and I still have another hour to go."

Amy took hold of Kaitlyn's arms and spoke to her as if she were a child. "We're all set for tomorrow, Kate. Wouldn't you like to get home and put your feet up an hour early?"

"Of course I would, but I don't want to get into trouble with your mother…"

"Jason and I aren't the type to make things difficult for people who work for a living. Either take off or stick around twiddling your thumbs, but we're just about done for the night." Amy gave the mysterious pot another stir and turned off the burner.

"If you're sure it's okay, I would love to take a hot bath and hit the sack early. See ya tomorrow." Kaitlyn pulled off her tunic, threw it in the laundry bag, and strode to her storage cubicle.

There was no need to be coming down with a cold or to invent an excuse to leave early. These two spoiled brats made it easy for her.

She jumped in her car and drove away just as the Open sign in the front window was switched to Closed. After one trip around the block, Kaitlyn parked two storefronts down and waited. With her field glasses, she watched the restaurant for thirty minutes and observed nothing out of the ordinary. Lights in the main dining room were off, and no one entered or exited the front door. Tucking her hair into a ball cap, Kaitlyn donned an oversized black sweatshirt that almost reached her knees. With daylight fading, she meandered down the street, turned the corner, and found the back entrance to the alley.

Feeling more foolish than surreptitious, Kaitlyn crept down the alley behind two law offices, one upscale hair salon, and a real estate office. She passed ripe-smelling Dumpsters, several bicycles chained to posts, and one reclusive tabby cat along the way. Just as she neared the delivery entrance to Tanaka Culinary Creations, the sound of voices broke the quiet solitude of the alley. Kaitlyn could hear people but saw nothing. A ten-foot fence, completely covered with kudzu vines, protected the privacy of courtyard diners at Tanaka's. The only way in was a solid metal gate used by deliverypersons during business hours—a gate that would be locked at this hour.

Seeing two people approach from the other direction, Kaitlyn ducked behind a panel of electric meters and held her breath. But instead of walking past her, a shabbily dressed man and heavyset woman pushed open the gate to the courtyard. Before it swung shut behind them, Kaitlyn caught a glimpse of patrons clustered around the patio tables.

Is this what Amy and Jason are doing—running their parents' restaurant after hours and keeping the money for themselves? No wonder profits were off by a grand each month.

With mounting indignation, Kaitlyn plucked at the kudzu to

create a peephole into their clandestine activities. She would take photos to show Mrs. Tanaka exactly the kind of kids she had coddled and pampered for years. But Kaitlyn's expanding window into their world did nothing to mitigate her confusion. Instead of the Tanakas' usual dressed-for-success lunchtime clientele, an odd assortment of people sat at the tables, perched on overturned milk crates, or leaned against the fence. Men, women, teenagers, and even one young mother with a baby talked and laughed as they dined on soup and sandwiches and whatever gourmet cuisine hadn't sold from the take-out coolers. Music played from unseen speakers, adding a convivial mood. Amy and Jason moved through the crowd like hosts at a society cocktail party. They topped off plastic cups with lemonade, encouraged diners to refill their soup bowls, and tucked sandwiches and containers of cold seafood salad into battered backpacks and frayed coat pockets.

One aspect about these partygoers was clear to Kaitlyn from first glance. Without a shadow of a doubt, every one of these guests was homeless. Amy and Jason, the spoiled, living-large college kids, weren't stealing food from their frugal parents to sell from a food wagon across town. They were running their own version of a soup kitchen from seven to eight o'clock from the back alley. Now how exactly would she explain this to her client, the hardworking, penny-pinching Mrs. Tanaka?

THIRTY

It had been a long time since Michael had had such a sleepless night. After their impromptu meeting in Johnson Square, he and Beth had returned to the hotel, pretending that everything was hunky-dory. Yet nothing was right between them. While he went for a five-mile run, Beth chose to work out in the fitness room. When he cut the run short and showed up dressed to pump iron, Beth was on her way to the pool. Then when he casually meandered to the rooftop, his partner was nowhere in sight. So he bought a take-out dinner and ate it in his room in front of the TV. Miserable and alone—the way he'd been before they met, and probably how he would be for the rest of his life.

He no more believed Mrs. Doyle was a murderer than Beth did, but aggravating the Tybee Island police wouldn't do them any good. And it would make life that much harder for Kaitlyn once they went home. His insistence that they sit on their thumbs waiting for Rossi didn't demonstrate much faith in their client. Evelyn was still their client, whether or not she continued her arrangement with Price Investigations. And Beth was his partner as well as his girlfriend. He needed to support her, no matter what.

Pulling himself out of bed, Michael showered and punched her number on his phone. He had no desire to exercise or go to breakfast or spend more time on email. He needed to hear her voice and clear the air between them. But before the call went to voice mail, a ding indicated an incoming text: "If that's you calling me, Preston, I suggest you open your door."

When Michael complied, Beth marched into his room carrying two steaming cups of coffee and a large white sack. "I hope you haven't had breakfast yet. Can we sit out on your balcony? My mother would frown on me being in a gentleman's hotel room, but I don't think balconies count."

He opened the sliding door. "I'm surprised you still consider me a gentleman after yesterday. I regret embarrassing you in front of Kaitlyn."

She shook her head. "I wasn't that embarrassed. Besides, you wanted to wait. I was the one who insisted we discuss the case in front of her." She handed him a coffee and a wrapped sandwich. "Egg whites on a whole-grain bagel with low-fat cheese."

"Thanks, but just for the record, I'm getting tired of healthy food."

"I saw that one coming awhile ago." A dimple appeared in her cheek. "I honestly didn't know about Bonnie's rent until mere minutes before I saw you."

Michael took a bite of dry bagel. "I believe you, Beth."

"Now that we're dating, honesty should always be our policy."

He opened the sandwich to eat the egg open-faced. "Sounds like another Rita Kirby maxim."

"Nope. That happens to be my new motto." When Beth unwrapped her breakfast, the scent of bacon and melted cheese filled the air. "So that brings up my second reason to visit you."

"Tell me what's on your mind."

"I was on the phone with Evelyn earlier. She was crying, almost hysterical. Detective Rossi had just left her place after questioning her for a full hour. Since Rossi had done so without an attorney being present and no one had Mirandized her, the police must not be planning to arrest her. But she was upset nevertheless."

"We knew this was coming." Michael rewrapped his tasteless sandwich.

Beth fixed her attention on a freight hauler sitting low in the water. "Do you think if one of those ships sinks, the top few layers of containers would still be above water?"

"I have no idea how deep the Savannah River is, but I do know there's something else you want to say." Michael put a hand on her shoulder. "Spit it out, Beth."

"I know I agreed to let the Tybee Island police do their job, but I can't abandon my friend. With her sister back in Atlanta, Evelyn has no one but me." Beth pushed to her feet. "I wanted to tell you to your face that I'm going out to see her."

"How are you planning to get there?"

Her expression indicated that she hadn't thought that far ahead. "I guess I'll call Uber. Might as well spend the expense money on something other than food."

Michael picked up her forgotten sandwich. "Absolutely not. As your boyfriend, I forbid you to spend another minute with that Latin Casanova."

"José is at least fifty years old and harmless as a dove. So you'll have to shoot me to stop me."

"Gunplay won't be necessary, because I'm going with you." Michael took a huge bite of eggs, bacon, and cheddar inside a buttery croissant. "Just as soon as I finish eating your breakfast."

"What about Rossi?"

"What about her? We simply want to hear our client's side of the story. That doesn't sound like interference or obstruction to me."

Grabbing her coffee, Beth pulled open the sliding glass door. "Are we going to tell Nate?"

"Of course we are." Michael followed her through his room, grabbing his jacket from the back of a chair. "It just won't be today and probably not tomorrow either. He will receive a full update in our weekend report. This is only Thursday."

Inside the elevator, Beth bumped him with her shoulder. "Why the change of heart? I could have sworn you wanted to stay far away from Evelyn."

"You're my partner. If you have complete faith in her, I'm in this with you until the bitter end. Did the Karate Kid turn his back on Mr. Miyagi?"

"Who's Mr. Miyagi?" She fluttered her eyelashes.

"We'll save that movie for some rainy Saturday in January." When the elevator opened, they stepped into a lobby filled with tourists. "In the meantime, let me take the lead with Mrs. Doyle. It'll be good practice for me."

⌒

Once they reached Evelyn's, no one answered the door despite several hard knocks.

"This can't be good," Beth muttered. "Evelyn, it's me, Beth. Please let us in so we can talk."

"Want me to go around to the water side?" he asked, stepping back to watch for movement through the filmy curtains.

"You check the deck while I go down to the—"

Before Beth could finish, the massive oak panel swung wide. "Mrs. Doyle didn't think you would come," the maid said. "It's been nearly an hour."

"Traffic was heavy," Michael explained as they stepped past the maid into the foyer.

"Would you like me to tell Mrs. Doyle you're here?"

"No, thank you," said Beth. "We can find her on our own. And this conversation needs to be private."

Michael cast the woman a stern look to preempt any argument before they headed down the hall.

As expected, they found her in the expansive living room sitting in a leather recliner with her feet beneath her. An afghan covered her legs and a book was open in her lap. But she wasn't reading. She was staring at the turbulent surf beneath a gray and ominous sky. The view through the expanse of windows perfectly matched the somber mood in the room.

Evelyn startled when Michael cleared his throat. "Beth, Michael, I was lost in a daydream and didn't hear you come in."

"We got here as soon as we could," Beth said consolingly as she went to her friend. "How are you doing?"

"I'm better now that the lady detective is gone. Why can't she find Lamar's killer without bringing up hurtful subjects that are none of anyone's business?" She peered up at them with moist, red-rimmed eyes. Any makeup she might have put on that morning was gone. Her skin looked as thin as tissue paper, and she had dark smudges beneath her eyes.

"Until Detective Rossi has every bit of pertinent information, she will keep coming back." Beth took hold of her hand. "That's why you should have been up front with us from the beginning."

The woman flinched. "I don't know what you mean."

Beth dragged an ottoman closer to Evelyn's chair. "I think you do. Michael is going to ask you some questions. You must tell us what you told Rossi and anything you might have left out. Then if you wish to fire us, you can, and your secrets will not leave this room."

Two large tears ran down her sallow cheeks. "Why are you being like this, Beth? I thought we were friends."

Michael crouched down on his haunches to be closer to eye level with the older woman. "She is, Evelyn. We both are. That's why we need to know why you went to see Bonnie Mulroney two days before Lamar died. You agreed to go to a hotel, but instead you drove straight to the individual who might have shot at you on the beach."

"Because I'm a foolish old woman. I thought if Bonnie met me, if I became a real, flesh-and-blood person, she would realize what she was doing was wrong." Evelyn dropped her head into her hands. "So I drove to the address in the historical section that was on the report you gave me."

"You knew Lamar wouldn't be there," Beth prompted. "He was already in Augusta."

"Yes. It was a perfect opportunity for some girl talk."

"Miss Mulroney knew who you were?" Michael asked.

"Not at first. She thought I was collecting money for charity." Evelyn's laugh sounded brittle as she tightened her grip on the chair. "When I introduced myself, Bonnie turned pale as milk but then soon recovered. She said I had no business there because this was her apartment, hers and Lamar's. She said I was his past and she was his future. She told me I needed to accept it."

"That had to be awful," Beth murmured. "But the horror could have been avoided."

Michael wanted the conversation to remain on track. "Didn't you consider the possibility of Bonnie being the one who shot at you?"

Evelyn looked him in the eye. "Yes, at first. But I'd spent hours that day considering how to live the rest of my life. If someone wanted to kill me because I still loved Lamar, then so be it. I went to that apartment to fight for my husband—not with fists and hair pulling, but like a civilized, God-fearing woman."

"What happened next?" he prodded.

"I told her that despite what my husband might have promised, he would never leave me. I said it would be better for everyone if she went home and reunited with family and friends her own age."

"How did she react?" Beth asked, casting Michael a sideways glance.

The woman's face crumpled. "Bonnie was stomping around the apartment as though she were crazy. "Go back *home*? Oh, do you mean that dump I shared with Lenny so he can smack me around some more?" Evelyn's voice became high-pitched and shrill, as though mimicking the younger woman. "Nothing I ever do is good enough for Lenny Mulroney—not the way I cook or clean the house or launder his filthy clothes."

For several moments, the living room went deathly quiet. Then Mrs. Doyle resumed the narrative in her own voice. "All of a sudden Bonnie stopped ranting and raving. She calmly told me that Lamar loved her and that they were starting a new life together. Then she picked up a vase to admire, handling it very carefully as though it were a rare artifact from the Ming Dynasty. She said she would be a fool to leave all *this* behind." Evelyn pulled a tissue from her pocket and blew her nose. "I felt so sorry for her. That vase was probably just a cheap knockoff, but Bonnie didn't know the difference."

"Is that when you left the apartment?" Michael asked, mildly annoyed by her arrogance.

"No, that's when I pulled out a check for twenty thousand dollars so she wouldn't have to return to that horrible Lenny. I told her to go back to school and maybe earn a degree or train for a better-paying career. She could make a new life for herself."

Beth sucked in a lungful of air. "You tried to bribe her to go away?"

Mrs. Doyle nodded affirmatively. "I know it was shameful. That's why I didn't want to tell you, but I didn't want to lose my husband. If the temptation was no longer around, Lamar would come to his senses that much faster."

"Bonnie could have been the one trying to kill you!"

She shook her silvery head. "That's something else I decided after you two left. If someone truly wanted me dead, I would be. How hard is it to shoot a person on a wide-open beach? If they had been trying to scare me off, twenty thousand dollars might convince them to go instead." Mrs. Doyle ran a hand through her tangled hair, a far cry from her usual elegant coiffure. "Are we finished? I really need to lie down for a while."

"Almost, Evelyn." Beth laid a hand on her arm. "Tell us how Bonnie reacted to that much money."

"The girl tore the check into little pieces and dropped them into the trash can. She said she was never going back to Lenny and would stay right there in her dream home. She told me to call my lawyer and prepare for the inevitable." With a weary sigh, Evelyn struggled to her feet.

Beth jumped up to support one arm. "Did you tell this to Lamar when he came home early from his conference?"

"Of course I did. After I confronted him and showed him your report, he broke down and wept. He said he knew what he was doing was wrong, but he didn't know how to stop. Bonnie was very manipulative, but he also felt sorry for her. He knew she came from an abusive household. That's when I told him I went to see her."

"And you were ready to forgive him? Just like that?" Beth asked.

"You're very young, my dear. By the time you're my age, you learn that people make mistakes, including those you love. But if they are remorseful, they deserve to be forgiven."

"I'm starting to figure that one out," Beth said with a weak smile.

Evelyn patted her arm and shuffled down the hallway to the bedrooms.

"Did you tell your husband about offering a check for twenty grand?" Michael called.

She halted and looked back over her shoulder. "Yes. I wanted Lamar to know I had no ill feelings toward Bonnie. I told him I had given her landlord a check for her rent and I'd given her a check to use as she saw fit. But she ripped it up. That's why when he went to see her on Saturday he took an envelope of cash for her fresh start. Ripping up a check was very dramatic, but no one would rip up two hundred one-hundred-dollar bills. Now if you'll let yourselves out, I must take an aspirin and lie down."

Michael and Beth stared at each other. Then they walked out of the house—a designer showplace that grew more formidable each time they visited.

Beth clung to his arm on the way to the car, as though she were suddenly weak-kneed. "That little viper took twenty thousand dollars and then killed the guy? How depraved is that?"

Michael slipped his arm around her waist. "Murderers aren't known for their ethical code. Who is this Lenny Mulroney? If Bonnie already had a husband, why was she eager to marry Lamar?"

"Maybe Lenny is her ex or her about-to-be ex-husband." Beth buckled her seat belt. "Time to pay Miss…or perhaps Mrs. Mulroney…another visit."

"You let me take care of Bonnie while you go talk to Kaitlyn." Michael started the engine and drove down Oleander Drive well above the speed limit.

"Our Kaitlyn?"

"One and the same. I noticed a few things in her résumé that aren't adding up. Hey, don't look at me like that. The boss told me to check her background thoroughly. If Nate decides to hire her permanently, he doesn't want any surprises down the road."

Beth rubbed the back of her neck. "What kind of things?"

"Like the fact that Kaitlyn Webb didn't exist until a couple years ago."

"You've got to be kidding. There's no record of her working at the Florida Bureau of Worker's Compensation?"

"Oh, she worked there all right, for a little more than a year. Her one and only professional reference, Mrs. Stephens, really is a supervisor at the Florida bureau. But I found no record of her at

Florida State, supposedly her alma mater. Several Kaitlyn Webbs live in Florida, but none of them seem to be the one who works for us. My guess is she is on the run from something or someone."

"And it's not an abusive husband or boyfriend like I thought originally."

Michael tightened his grip on the steering wheel.

"With everything happening so fast, I honestly forgot about this until now. Two days ago when we followed Bonnie back to Lamar's apartment, Kaitlyn said she couldn't give me advice because she had little relationship experience. Her last boyfriend had been during high school."

Michael scratched his head. "Why were you seeking romance advice from someone we just met?"

Beth blushed from the neckline of her blouse to her hairline. "You're missing the point. Kaitlyn's not starting over after a bad breakup. So much for my gut instinct."

"No, I caught the point, but if we could digress for a moment... Tell me what had you so upset that you were asking a total stranger about relationships." Michael reached for her hand.

Beth didn't pull away from his touch, but she did turn her focus out the window. "Because I'm not very good at this. And I don't want to mess up because I might be in love with you."

Michael switched off the radio. "*What?* I didn't quite catch that."

Beth swiveled around. "You heard me, Preston. In case this turns out to be the real thing, I don't want you giving up on me too soon."

Michael fought the impulse to burst out laughing. This was about the oddest way to find out his dream just might come true. "Let me ask you a couple questions. When I couldn't shoot and hit the barn, let alone a can on a fence rail, did I give up?"

"Um...no?"

"In my early attempts to get into shape, did I give up when five push-ups made me pant like a dog?"

"No, and I believe you're up to at least seven now." Beth covered her giggles with her hand.

Michael bumped her with his shoulder. "I can do fifty without breaking a sweat. And what about the time we decided to run that 5K race along the river?"

"Okay, okay. I get it that you're not a quitter, but maybe romance isn't the same thing as running a marathon."

He let her "maybe" hang in the air awhile. "Haven't you been listening to Evelyn, your new best friend? Love is *exactly* like a long-distance race. Now it's up to you to decide whether or not this is love."

"Give me until this case wraps up. I should have my mind made up by then."

Michael smiled. After what they had learned today, that could be in no time at all.

THIRTY-ONE

*K*aitlyn punched in Mrs. Tanaka's cell number at 4:00 p.m., the exact time when the owners of Tanaka's Culinary Creations usually left for the day. "Hello, Mrs. Tanaka. This is Kaitlyn Webb."

"Good afternoon, Miss Webb. I gather you either have news for us or decided you've rolled enough sushi to last a lifetime and you quit." The woman's laughter sounded a little forced.

"Both of the above, ma'am. Could we meet to talk? I would prefer discussing the case in person."

"Of course. Why don't you come by our house? Would within the hour be too soon? Eric and I are attending the grand opening of a new art gallery tonight."

"An hour would be just fine. See you then." Kaitlyn ended the call, checked her watch, and slipped on running shoes. If she walked fast, she could reach the Tanakas' magnificent home from her modest rental unit before they had to leave. And walking would give her a chance to figure out what she would say.

When she had accepted the assignment, Kaitlyn assumed the Tanakas were just like any other hardworking, self-made American entrepreneurs who also happened to be parents. They struggled and sacrificed for years to build a successful business. From their efforts came expensive private schools, prestigious colleges, fancy cars, and luxury family vacations. Kaitlyn had also assumed Amy and Jason were like all other overindulged, pampered rich kids—disrespectful and ungrateful for everything they were handed.

Funny how so many preconceived notions a person formed were incorrect.

Amy and Jason had been handed just about everything in life, but they weren't ungrateful. Neither were they disrespectful, at least no more so than any other independent twentysomethings. Amy and Jason had strong social consciences for the disenfranchised of the world—something they hadn't inherited from their parents. Weren't those who had so much obligated to share with those who had little or nothing at all? It wouldn't be easy for the elder Tanakas to open up their doors and give away the lifeblood of their business. Kaitlyn could hear her grandfather's favorite maxim still ringing in her ears: *"If we can pull ourselves up by our bootstraps, why can't everyone?"* She had a feeling Mr. and Mrs. Tanaka might share that conviction.

No matter how Kaitlyn tried to see both sides, there was only one correct conclusion: Mrs. Tanaka had hired Price Investigations to find out what was going on in her restaurant when she wasn't there. She had an obligation to provide that information and file a case report with Nate. What Mrs. Tanaka did with the information was her business.

Mrs. Tanaka greeted her at the door wearing a long evening suit and crystal-studded high heels. "Come in, Miss Webb. Let's talk in the sunroom while my husband finishes dressing. I have no idea why men take longer than women to get ready." Her diamond earrings sparkled as she walked. "First of all, did either of my children figure out what you were up to?" she asked, not waiting until they sat down.

"I don't think so. They believed my story about needing a job and found my sushi rolls at least adequate."

"They were more than adequate. I sampled one. It was delicious." Mrs. Tanaka patted the sofa beside her. "Did Amy take you in her confidence? That girl makes friends easily, with little discretion as to the class of people they hail from."

Kaitlyn sat, wondering if she should be offended by the comment. "No, I don't think either one of them trusted me, but it wasn't hard to see something was going on after the restaurant closed."

"Did they close early?" she asked, frowning.

"Yes. Jason shooed out the last dawdlers and turned off the sign by seven." Kaitlyn noticed a painting on the wall from a Dutch master—one that would likely fetch seven figures if it was authentic.

Mrs. Tanaka sniffed with indignation. "That explains why profits have been down, but not why so much food has disappeared."

"It wasn't hard to figure out even without gaining their trust."

But before Kaitlyn could elaborate, Mrs. Tanaka interrupted. "My son is selling food out of his dorm room on campus, isn't he? Or Amy has rented one of those tacky food trucks and is selling sushi rolls and lunch on the beach on Tybee. That girl always had a devious streak."

"My little darling?" asked Eric Tanaka as he entered the sunroom. "Nonsense. If anything, Amy is passing food out to bums who live under a bridge somewhere." He shot the cuffs of his impeccably tailored tuxedo.

Both Tanakas looked to her to confirm their suppositions.

"Your husband is closer to the truth." Kaitlyn focused on Mrs. Tanaka. "Last night they again encouraged me to leave early, so I drove around the block and parked where I wouldn't be spotted. I came in behind the restaurant from the alley."

"Are you saying you walked down an alley alone at night?" Mrs. Tanaka looked aghast.

"I did, but I'm licensed to carry a firearm, so I wasn't exactly helpless. Anyway, I saw no one except an elderly couple heading for the back entrance of Tanaka's Culinary Creations."

"There is no back entrance," she snapped, annoyed. "People who want a patio table must enter through the front doors."

"I understand, Mrs. Tanaka, but I watched the couple sit down at one of the umbrella tables to eat."

Mr. Tanaka stroked his silvery goatee as though deep in thought, while Mrs. Tanaka turned the color of poppies. "My son and daughter are selling food off the books right on the premises? How could they cut our throats like this?"

"Actually, they're not *selling* anything. They're giving away the day-old food from the coolers to the homeless. Word must have spread though their community, because no one showed up for a free meal except for people who really needed one. At least that's what I saw last night."

"They're giving away imported bluefin *otoro* and *chutoro* and *hamachi* yellowtail that costs us fifty-eight dollars per pound for *free?*" she squawked.

"Maybe Amy and Jason see this as a better use for it than throwing it in the Dumpster."

Mrs. Tanaka's nostrils flared. "It would never go into the Dumpster. I could have cooked up that raw food the next day. It would've been perfectly fine in a stir-fry or baked into casseroles for my family or my sister's family."

"I'm only reporting what I saw. Your children aren't financially benefiting from the food they are giving away."

"But we've lost a thousand dollars each month from their ridiculous soup kitchen."

"Actually, Amy cooked a big pot of soup right after you left, and Jason made ham and Swiss cheese sandwiches. They probably knew you had noticed all the exotic seafood disappearing, so they added less expensive items to the menu. Or maybe the clientele doesn't care for eel and squid."

"I'm not amused, Miss Webb. Tanaka's isn't licensed to run a soup kitchen in the backyard. What if the Board of Health found out?"

"It's legal to serve food at a party, right? Maybe Jason and Amy invited those people as guests."

Suddenly, Mrs. Tanaka's eyes bugged out. "What if one of those…homeless people has a food allergy? Tanaka's could end up getting sued by a bum." Her indignation grew by leaps and bounds.

Mr. Tanaka lifted both palms to end the discussion. "All this conjecture is getting us nowhere. Right now, Iris and I have an event to attend. We appreciate your hard work, Miss Webb, but we'll take it from here. We'll pay your salary for the rest of the week, plus include a generous bonus when we pay Mr. Price's fee. You did exactly what we wanted."

Kaitlyn scrambled to her feet. "I prefer you keep my wages and the bonus as reimbursement for the lost food. Although Amy and Jason shouldn't have gone behind your backs, I believe their hearts are in the right place." She headed toward the door as fast as her feet would move.

"Hold up there, young lady," Mr. Tanaka demanded. "I won't have you believing my wife and I have no compassion. We'll speak to our children and our lawyers to hammer out a solution that's legal, ethical, and protects us against lawsuits."

Kaitlyn glanced at Mrs. Tanaka's face. She was equally surprised by his suggestion. "You don't owe me any explanation, sir. I just couldn't help sticking in my two cents' worth."

"I've never known a woman *without* an opinion, Miss Webb.

You shall receive your full pay and bonus. What you do with it once in your possession is your business. Thank you again." Mr. Tanaka bowed in her direction.

Kaitlyn left their lovely home feeling on top of the world. She'd solved Nate's case quickly and efficiently and felt confident harmony would be restored to the family. As she started back home at a leisurely stroll, she fully intended to enjoy the brisk autumn evening. But her serenity lasted less than ten minutes. Kaitlyn's phone rang. She nearly didn't answer when she didn't recognize the number, but to her relief she heard the sweet voice of her mentor at the Florida bureau and best friend in the world.

"Hi, Kate. It's Vicky."

"What's up, girl? Did you get another phone? I didn't recognize this number."

"That's because this phone is a burner. Probably a huge overreaction, but someone slipped up today at work…concerning you."

The blood chilled in her veins. "Slipped up how?"

"A new trainee in payroll got a call from a Mr. Mardones in Human Resources. He wanted to know which office Kathryn Weller transferred to. Unfortunately, the trainee tracked down the information and told him the Savannah, Georgia, office."

"I take it there's no Mr. Mardones in Human Resources." Kaitlyn swallowed hard, her mouth dry.

"Correct. I know it's of little consolation, but the trainee has been reprimanded. One more mistake like that and she's out."

"You're right. It's of very little consolation." Kaitlyn picked up her pace, suddenly feeling vulnerable on the street.

"At least the trainee hadn't divulged your new name yet. Only the city where you're working."

"That buys me some time, but I won't be able to stop looking over my shoulder now. It's a shame, because this beautiful old town has grown on me."

"I'm truly sorry." Vicky exhaled noisily into the phone. "If there's anything I can do, just say the word. Money, job references in another city. You name it."

"I like working for Price Investigations. I can't...I won't pick up and leave again. I can't keep running from this."

"Think it over carefully. You can't stand up to these men, Kate. They've had a lifetime of experience at nastiness."

"I'll think about it, and thanks for the call. You still rock as far as best friends go."

Vicky's laughter held no humor. "Now that I've introduced you to church, are you still attending?"

"I tried the Baptist church near my apartment, but I won't go back. Those folks sing at the top of their lungs and clap their hands. You know I don't like loud displays. I don't even like fireworks."

Her chuckle sounded genuine. "That sounds like *my* kind of church, but you should try a different one. You're going to need more than a new employer and a friend in Pensacola to get through what's coming."

Kaitlyn mumbled that she would and ended the call as tears filled her eyes. She couldn't think straight, let alone figure out how to advance her spiritual rebirth. All she was capable of was getting back to her apartment without looking over her shoulder a dozen times. When she reached her front stoop, Beth was waiting for her.

"Wow, you weren't joking about living in Nowhereville," Beth said, dabbing sweat from her face.

"Did you *walk* here? Where's Michael?"

"I ran, jogged, walked, and then staggered, in that order. Michael's on another errand. I'm here to talk to you. I'm hoping that when we finish, you'll drive me back to my hotel."

"Wanna come in or talk out here?" Kaitlyn asked, mildly ashamed of her shabby furnishings. "How about a bottle of water?"

Beth smiled up at her. "Out here is good, and water would be great."

Kaitlyn went inside and came back out a minute later carrying two bottles of water. She sat down, sighed, and said, "I have a feeling I know why you're here."

Beth drank deeply. "When you heard Michael was a forensic accountant, you knew he would check everything you put down on your résumé."

Nodding, she focused on a woman feeding pigeons across the street. "Yep. I had a feeling it was only a matter of time, but I *really* like working with you. So I couldn't pull the plug and run."

"What are you running from? We know it's not the law. There are no arrest warrants out for Kaitlyn Webb. But there's not much of anything for that name before a couple of years ago."

Kaitlyn turned to face her. "I've done nothing illegal, I promise. And I really did work for the Florida Bureau of Worker's Compensation. It's my personal life that's messed up. So I changed my name, and my boss helped me find a new job. I'm trying to make a fresh start."

"If it were my call, I'd say we were fine and dandy. I hate nosy people." Beth took another drink. "But I'm not the boss. Nate has a right to know who you really are. Trust me. He's a stand-up guy. If there's any way he can help you, he will. We all will *after* you tell us the truth."

Kaitlyn smiled sadly. "The truth isn't very enlightening. When I was eight years old, I accidentally witnessed a crime. It was a robbery gone bad, and several people lost their lives. My brother, Liam, was sentenced to twenty-five years to life for his part in their deaths. Unfortunately, his accomplices went free because he refused to name them."

"I'm guessing he received a stiffer sentence because of his loyalty."

"Yes, but it wasn't due to misplaced loyalty. My brother felt he had no choice. His accomplices were part of an organized crime syndicate. Our parents had recently died. They'd left little to provide security for me. My brother feared if he fingered them, they would retaliate against my aunt and uncle and me."

"You actually witnessed your brother committing a crime?"

"According to the police report, yes, but whatever I saw I blocked out long ago. I'm not protecting any murderous thugs. My shrink called these protective repressed memories."

"And the bad guys want to make sure they stay repressed."

Kaitlyn nodded. "I'm surprised they didn't just kill me. Every now and then they let me know they are still watching. For their previous reminder, they kidnapped my little dog. Peaches was almost dead from dehydration when they finally told me where to find her."

Beth crunched the plastic bottle in her hand. "They can't be allowed to get away with intimidation. We live in a—"

"No, Beth. I appreciate your concern, but this is my business. My aunt, uncle, and cousins still live in Pensacola. Any one of them could become their next target. Funny thing is, I couldn't put them behind bars if I wanted to. I simply can't remember what happened that night." Kaitlyn slapped her palms on her thighs.

"There are doctors who—"

"No. I can live with getting fired, but I can't live with my relatives in jeopardy."

"I will tell Michael and Nate but no one else. The decision will be Nate's, but he'll hear my opinion on the matter." Beth locked gazes with her. "Call me if you ever decide to go after these thugs with guns blazing. I'm a crack shot. I never miss."

Kaitlyn looked away, not wanting Beth to see how her offer had touched a chord. "I'll keep it in mind. Tell Michael to look into Kathryn and Liam Weller of Pensacola for my background, but please keep that info private. Now let's get you back before your handsome boyfriend starts to worry."

"Actually, I changed my mind. Could I please borrow your car for a few hours? I still have one more errand to run. I want to see if a certain someone still wants to provide a flimsy alibi. I'll replace any gas I use."

"I don't mind at all." Kaitlyn dropped the keys into Beth's palm and handed her the second bottle of water.

"Thanks, and like I said, don't lose hope. As bosses go, Nate Price is one of the best."

Kaitlyn waved as Beth drove away. They barely knew each other, yet Beth had volunteered to enter a gun battle with her.

What are the chances of getting a second amazing boss like Vicky Stephens? Nobody is that lucky.

Thirty-Two

*M*ichael was having a hard time being a patient man. He didn't mind waiting for Beth to meet him for breakfast or pick something off a menu or even return his phone calls, but waiting in an alley for Bonnie to take her break was driving him crazy. What if she finally decided to give up smoking and no longer needed to walk down three storefronts to the designated zone? He would have waited in the cool, damp air for nothing.

Turning up the collar on his trench coat, Michael shifted his position on the fire escape steps, trying to get circulation back in his legs. Just about the time he considered throwing in the towel, Bonnie rounded the cardboard compactor and pulled out her pack. She lit up her first cigarette even before he could stretch the kinks from his spine. He quietly approached his target.

"How's it goin', Bonnie?" he asked, opting for a casual approach.

She peered through heavily made-up lashes. "Do I know you?"

Michael closed the distance in a few strides. "Let's just say we have a mutual friend."

Bonnie let her gaze travel from his Italian loafers up to his recently cut hair. "I doubt that. I don't have any friends who dress like you." She dragged so hard on the cigarette, Michael could almost see minutes being crossed off her life.

"How about Mrs. Evelyn Doyle? We have her in common."

"What's she to you? You her son or something?"

"Actually, Mr. and Mrs. Doyle's only son was killed in Afghanistan. I'm surprised Lamar never mentioned that to you."

His verbal arrow hit its mark. Bonnie cringed, visibly shrinking in her Cool Beans uniform. "We had other things to talk about."

"Yeah, I bet you did." Michael moved close enough to tower over the girl. "I work for Mrs. Doyle. And what I want to know is how come you turned down *her* generous offer of twenty thousand bucks but had no trouble taking it from Mr. Doyle two days later? Like most married couples, they shared the same bank account."

Bonnie's face looked as if it might burst into flames. "I don't know where you got your information from, but I didn't take twenty *K* from either one of them." Stretching up on tiptoes, she jabbed a finger in his face. "Yeah, he offered it on Saturday to make his wife happy. She was pressuring him to break up with me. It wasn't Lamar's idea. I told him I didn't want any money. I loved him, and I was willing to wait for them to get divorced." She dug into her pocket for her cigarettes.

"Hadn't you noticed the age difference between you two? Was Lamar some kind of father figure to you?"

"Don't be ridiculous. I had a daddy, and he was nothing like Lamar. Lamar treated me with respect. I planned to work my butt off being a good wife." Bonnie blew a stream of blue smoke in his face.

Michael could feel his own days being crossed off. "If all you wanted was to get married, why did you take the money?"

"You're crazy! I turned down that stupid check from his wife. I slapped Lamar's face and told him he would never be happy until he stood up to Evelyn." She exhaled again in his direction.

Michael yanked the cigarette from her lips and tossed it into the gutter. "Then what happened?"

"I don't know!" she snapped. "I was upset. I walked out of that fancy apartment and told Lamar not to call until he came to his senses. Then his wife killed him before he could think matters through."

"And the twenty *K* in cash?"

"Is something wrong with your hearing, or are you just plain stupid?" Bonnie shouted, heedless of the attention they were attracting in the alley.

"Lamar left the envelope of money on the kitchen table." Michael kept his voice down. "You must have found it when you came home from your tantrum."

Bonnie shook her head as if waking from a nightmare. "I have no idea what you're talking about. But I need to get back to work." She staggered down the alley as though drunk.

"Wait, Bonnie." Michael tried to follow her.

"No!" she screamed, putting up a hand. "I don't know what happened to that lady's money, and I'm done talking to you. Either stay away from me or I'm calling the cops."

~

At the end of the street, Beth pulled into a parking space and drank her entire second bottle of water. Her head was swimming, partly from fatigue but mostly from Kaitlyn's bombshell. *Or should I say Kathryn's bombshell? The woman is on the run from Florida mobsters because she witnessed a crime she can't even remember? And her sole sibling is doing twenty-five to life for murder?* Good grief. Michael said Beth had a made-for-television imagination, but even she couldn't have guessed anything like this.

Tonight when she said her prayers, she would make sure to pray for Nate to be in an exceptionally good mood when he received the news. After some of his cousin Nicki's shenanigans in New Orleans and some of hers in Natchez, Nate might not want a third high-maintenance investigator on the payroll, but Beth sure hoped he did. Because from the first time she met Kaitlyn, she liked her. Even if they had to take on the Florida mob to keep her alive.

Right now, however, she had a murder to solve. Beth punched Crystal's address into the car's GPS. If Bonnie took twenty thousand dollars from the Doyles, ostensibly to start a new life, maybe some of it ended up in Crystal's pocket. After all, if your best friend was providing an alibi for the night your lover was murdered, wouldn't you want to share some of your newfound wealth? If Crystal suddenly retracted her statement, Bonnie would have both motive and means. Beth wanted to see how much silence cost these days.

For the next thirty minutes, she inched through congested city streets and crawled along behind a school bus with no opportunity to pass. Traffic didn't improve until she reached the outskirts of Savannah, five minutes from Crystal's ramshackle farmhouse. But as Beth drove down the rutted lane, it wasn't local residents returning home after work who clogged her path. Four police cars, with blue and red lights spinning, sat along the road or cockeyed on the lawn. The crime tech van pulled into the driveway just as Beth parked across the street.

If she were smart, she would have hightailed it out of there, because one of the police vehicles belonged to none other than Diane Rossi of the Tybee Island Police Department. But after pondering a few moments, Beth decided tomorrow would be a better day to turn over a new leaf.

"Hi, Detective Rossi," she called as she approached. "Don't look now, but we're on the mainland. Not a single seagull or sandy beach in sight."

"If my memory serves, Miss Kirby, you're from Natchez, Mississippi. So you have real nerve asking what *I'm* doing here."

"That's an excellent point." Beth grinned. "Let's call it a draw. Mind sharing what's going on?"

Rossi said something to the uniformed officer on her left, and he wandered off. Then she focused her attention on Beth. "This is called an active investigation at a crime scene. I am police and you are not, so no, we won't call this a draw. Didn't I make it sufficiently clear to your partner you're not to interfere in police business?"

"Yes, ma'am, you did." Beth looked appropriately penitent. "But how could I interfere in something I'm clueless about? I'm here to question Miss Callahan about twenty thousand dollars of Mrs. Doyle's money. I would like to know if any of it ended up in her pocket. What's the ambulance for? Did something happen to Crystal's grandmother?"

With an exaggerated sigh, Rossi pressed her clipboard to her chest. "I'm afraid you're too late to ask Miss Callahan any questions. If she took someone's money, she won't be using it in the hereafter. Someone shot her in the head."

Beth felt her gut tighten. She'd met Crystal in the coffee shop and in the alley down the block. The girl had acted haughty and bold in her six-inch platform shoes and violet-streaked hair. But the idea of someone so young dying made Beth sick to her stomach. She staggered back a step.

Rossi reached out and grabbed her arm. "You all right, Kirby?"

"I…I knew the girl. I mean, not well, but she gave me pointers on getting a job at Cool Beans. It's a long story." Beth looked the detective in the eye. "Tell me what happened…please. I promise not to cross the crime scene tape or mess up your investigation."

Rossi pulled her several feet away from the milling lab techs. "We don't know much yet. Crystal lived in the back of the house. She came and went pretty much on her own. Her mother is dead and her dad's in jail. Her grandmother lives in the front four rooms, but the woman is almost deaf and walks with a cane. She and Crystal ate one or two meals a week together, but Grandma was asleep in her recliner when the police arrived. She never heard the sirens, let alone any shots."

"The grandmother didn't find the body?"

"Nope. The next-door neighbor saw Crystal's cat out in the yard, which isn't supposed to happen. The cat never goes outside because it's declawed. So the neighbor caught the cat and brought it home as a favor to the Callahans. She found the back door wide open and Crystal lying facedown on the living room rug. The neighbor called 9-1-1."

Beth gazed up at the gabled two-story house. It had a certain charm, despite needing a fresh coat of paint and the bushes trimmed. It was the kind of gingerbread house that storybook characters lived in. But Crystal and her deaf grandmother wouldn't have a happy ending.

She refocused on Rossi. "No forced entry?"

"Nope. Looks like she let the killer in. And nothing was ransacked, either."

"Sounds like Crystal knew her killer."

"That's my take on this too. Crystal opened the back door; they chitchatted, and then she went into the living room. She must not have felt threatened or she wouldn't have turned her back on him...or her. Two shots, close range, from maybe four or five feet. We'll know more later, but that's all *you're* going to know, which is probably more than you should. I trust you can find your way to your car."

"Was she shot with a small-caliber gun—like a thirty-eight?"

"Like I said, we'll know more later." Rossi's features hardened. "By the way, there was no big pile of cash scattered around the room, so Mrs. Doyle won't be getting her money back anytime soon."

"Do you realize what this means? Crystal was Bonnie Mulroney's alibi for the night Lamar Doyle died—an alibi I thought was totally phony."

"It's so like you to put two and two together and end up with seven." Rossi shook her head. "Most likely, whatever this is"—she hooked her thumb toward the house—"it has nothing to do with the Doyle homicide. Probably a lovers' quarrel that ended badly for Crystal."

"If that was really what you thought, Detective, you wouldn't have shown up. Savannah Homicide could have handled a run-of-the-mill shooting. You and I both know this is connected. We just don't know how."

With her retort delivered, and before Detective Rossi had her hauled off the Callahan property in handcuffs, Beth jumped into the Mustang and drove away. She hoped Kaitlyn didn't want her car for a pizza run, because Beth needed to make one more stop. She planned to clear up what happened to Mrs. Doyle's money, and maybe a whole lot more.

Thirty-Three

*B*onnie Mulroney had never seen three hours pass so slowly in her life. Twenty thousand dollars had been in an envelope on her table? Lamar had apparently left it lying around like a few bucks for the babysitter.

Ever since that Preston guy dropped his little bombshell, all she could think about was one thing: Who came into her apartment after she left in a huff? Because that person was the lowest form of life on the planet. What would she have done with that kind of cash? Buy a pair of shoes that didn't hurt her feet? Get her hair cut at one of those fancy salons by the river? Maybe get new tires for her Honda?

The entire time Bonnie ran the cash register at Cool Beans, made lattes and iced coffees, and wiped down tables, she mulled over the list of people with keys to her apartment. *Could Lamar have changed his mind and come back for the money?* Not likely. The man had never been anything but generous toward her. *That building superintendent has a key to everyone's unit.* But lately the woman had been cutting her some slack. So why would she barge in now when they were starting to get along?

When Bonnie pulled off her smock and punched out for the day, she knew of only one person who could have stolen her money. Lenny Mulroney. That man had taken her keys one day with the trumped-up story of making a copy of her car key just in case she ever locked herself out of her Honda. He probably made copies of *all* her keys, because that was the kind of sly conniver he was. The first thing she would do if she got her money back was move far away from her brother.

This hadn't been a good day to save on parking and ride the dot to work. Now she had to ride a crowded bus all the way up Price and then walk five blocks to Bull Street while planning what she would say to Lenny.

Once she was inside her apartment, Bonnie peered around the decorated rooms. All Lamar had had to do was call a number and people showed up with furniture, bedding, stuff for the kitchen, and even pictures for the walls. Was that what it was like to be rich? Was that how her life would have been? Just pick up the phone and anything she needed would be sent right over? But instead, in six months Cinderella's gilded carriage would turn back into a pumpkin. Bonnie picked up her favorite vase and threw it at the wall, where it shattered into pieces. Nothing would ever be the same again. She needed to get her money back from Lenny. Then she would have a chance. She and Crystal could find jobs someplace else—maybe Charleston or Myrtle Beach. And she would forget this nightmare with the Doyles ever happened.

Bonnie changed clothes, loaded the beer Lamar had left in the refrigerator into a cooler, and locked the door behind her. If she hurried, she could get inside her former home before Lenny returned from work. She would make sure no sharp objects were lying around during their discussion. Along the way, traffic moved slowly enough for her to view the subtle change in the neighborhood. Funny thing about old buildings. The Bull Street apartment was in the historic section of town, where real estate cost big bucks and neighborhood associations made sure each blade of grass never surpassed a certain height. Nothing was historic or preserved in the neighborhood Lenny lived in. Clapboard shot-guns on narrow lots had peeling paint, tin roofs, and yards with more weeds than grass. Home, sweet home.

Bonnie parked in the gravel driveway and slipped inside. According to her watch, she had exactly thirty-five minutes to pack up whatever she still wanted from this place. Because when she was forced to leave Bull Street, she'd rather die than come back here.

~ᔓ~

When Beth circled the block of the Bull Street apartment and spotted Bonnie's car, she whispered a prayer of gratitude. It was parked in its assigned spot, cockeyed as usual. Bonnie must be upstairs, maybe packing for a quick getaway. She was someone Crystal would have let inside and turned her back on without a second thought.

Could this skinny little blonde be a murderer of not one but two people? Hard to imagine, but murderers came in all shapes and sizes.

Beth unsnapped her seat belt, but before she could climb from the vehicle, Bonnie emerged from the front entrance of Lamar's former love nest. She ran down the steps and jumped into her car. Considering that she almost sideswiped a Lincoln as she peeled out, the girl was in a big hurry. Beth followed her down Wheaton Street onto Bonaventure Road at a discreet distance. Fortunately, the car's shade of neon yellow made the Honda easy to keep in sight.

Soon neat rows of brick mansions behind wrought iron fences or manicured hedgerows gave way to small, unkempt homes interspersed between commercial establishments of various types and condition. The buildings might not be as old, but the neighborhood lacked the charm of the historic section. Some homes were well cared for, while others reflected either poverty or elderly residents unable to do maintenance.

Bonnie turned into the driveway of a white, two-story house with green shutters and stopped. At least it had been white once upon a time. Now most of the paint had peeled away, leaving bare wood rapidly deteriorating. Two shingles were missing, while a third hung precariously from a single nail. In one upstairs window, tattered lace curtains fluttered in the breeze, the screen long gone.

Beth pressed the button to lower her window and slouched low as she drove past. Bonnie wouldn't recognize the Mustang, but she certainly knew *her* and wouldn't be happy to see her. With a cigarette clenched between her teeth, Bonnie sprinted up the concrete steps into the house, letting the screen door slam behind her. Beth drove to the end of the narrow street and turned around. Anywhere she parked along the street would make her highly visible as she approached the house.

A small church stood at the end of the block. Beth parked Kaitlyn's car under a mercury vapor security light, locked the doors, and assessed the area. The sidewalk offered no more protection than the street, but a set of train tracks ran behind the homes on Bonnie's side of the street. Climbing over a chain-link fence, Beth started down the tracks. A scant three feet separated the tracks from steep embankments on either side. She hoped these tracks weren't as busy as those running behind her mother's house in Natchez.

Beth counted houses as she crept along the tracks and hopped the fence at what she believed to be the Mulroney backyard. Peeling paint, green shutters, and lace curtains flapping in the breeze told her she counted correctly. At least no vicious watchdog prowled the property on guard duty. When Beth saw a child's rusty swing set, a sandbox full of water instead of sand, and a bicycle chained to a post, she felt a pang of pity. *Does Bonnie have a child from a previous relationship? Is that why she longed for the stability and financial security of Lamar Doyle?*

In the distance, Beth heard a train whistle, doubtlessly on the same tracks she just walked. She picked her way through tall weeds to a metal storage shed filled with gardening implements and cast-off housewares, most of them broken. From this vantage point, Beth had a clear view of the side and back doors, along with the driveway in front of the shed. She didn't have long to ponder her next move.

A rusty pickup truck with knobby tires—tires that had to be worth more than the truck—pulled into the drive and screeched to a stop. The man who climbed from the driver's side made Beth glad she was carrying her weapon. He was tall, with sinewy muscles beneath his T-shirt, and biceps that stretched his sleeves to the limit. He had stringy blond hair halfway down his back, a scraggly goatee, and a pockmarked complexion. When Beth noticed clumps of dried mud on the bumper and wheels, the words of Mrs. Johnson, the nosy neighbor on Bull Street, came drifting back. *"I wouldn't want to run into Scraggly Beard late at night."* Was this Bonnie's current or ex-husband—Lenny Mulroney? If so, he was quite a step down on the socioeconomic ladder from Lamar Doyle. Although Miss Mulroney's ethical code left much to be desired, she was at least well groomed and reasonably attractive.

The man pulled off his ball cap, tossed it into the cab, and slicked a hand through his hair. But before he took two steps, Bonnie bounded out the side door, reaching him in four or five strides.

"I've been waitin' to talk to you." She didn't look happy as she lit up a cigarette.

"I figured there must be a good reason why you'd come back," snarled Scraggly Beard. "Now that you got that rich man's place to live in." He lifted a soft-sided cooler from the back of the truck.

"Yeah, well, that rich man also gave me twenty thousand bucks. Me, Lenny, not you!" Bonnie crossed her arms over her chest, her fingers bunching into fists.

"Is that so? Then what are you doing here? If he gave you that kind of money, you shouldn't need to borrow ten bucks from me."

"You know very well why I'm here. Somebody stole that envelope of cash from my kitchen table. And I know that somebody was *you!*" Although almost a foot shorter, Bonnie arched up on tiptoes and jabbed a finger into his chest.

Lenny knocked away her hand. "Keep your voice down, you little fool. You want the whole neighborhood crawlin' through our windows tonight, trying to rob us?"

"I don't care who hears me! I know you copied my house key when you copied the key to my Honda. I want that money so I can get out of town."

In plain view of passing cars or anyone out for an evening stroll, Lenny picked Bonnie up by the shoulders and shook her like a rag doll. "After all I've done for you, you want to make a fresh start *away from me?*" He apparently didn't care who overheard them now.

From where Beth watched, hidden by an overgrown forsythia bush, she felt a pang of pity for Bonnie. *How on earth did she get mixed up with this loser?* As much as the two charmers probably deserved each other, she hated to see a man intimidating a woman. Yet at the moment, Beth needed to withhold compassion long enough to find Lamar Doyle's killer.

"All those years I put food on the table, a roof over your head, and bought the clothes on your back!" Lenny shouted. "So any cash that comes your way rightfully belongs to me!" He gave Bonnie another rough shake.

Possible motives swam through Beth's brain. *Did Bonnie and Lenny plan the murder together? Had they been blackmailing Lamar and then become incensed when he confessed his sins to Evelyn?*

When Lenny released her shoulders, Bonnie staggered back but quickly regained her footing and just as quickly changed her attitude. "You're right about us not talking about this out here," she said, soft as a cat's purr. "Are you hungry? Let's go inside and I'll fix you something good to eat."

"What's your idea of 'something good'? Macaroni and cheese out of a box?" Nevertheless, Lenny's ugly scowl softened as he stomped up the steps. "How come you never invited me to dinner at that rich old man's fancy apartment?"

Bonnie's reply was lost to Beth as the pair entered the house, the screen door slamming behind them. She turned off her phone so any signals for incoming texts or new emails wouldn't draw attention to her. Ducking low, she crept around the shed and zigzagged between obstacles to the bushes behind the house. From the gingham-patterned curtains, she surmised her new position was beneath the kitchen window.

"Would you like a beer?" Bonnie's question drifted through the open window. "I brought the Amstel Lamar had in the refrigerator."

"Nothing but the best for your old boyfriend." The sound of an aluminum can popping open punctuated Lenny's comment.

Beth balanced on a rock so she wouldn't miss any of their conversation.

"I see your point, Lenny," Bonnie cooed. "Half the twenty K should be yours for all you've done for me. But I want to make a fresh start in a new town with the other half."

"A fresh start away from me?"

"Wouldn't you like to finally get your sister off your back? You could be footloose and fancy-free for the first time since Mom and Pops died."

Sister? The Mulroneys are siblings and not spouses? Beth almost fell off her rock.

"If I wanted to ditch the responsibility, I would have long

ago." Judging by the telltale sound, Lenny opened a second beer. "You're the one with stars in your eyes about becoming a fancy lady in a big house out on Tybee Island."

"But somebody made sure that never happened, didn't they?" Bonnie's temper reappeared with a vengeance. "Once Lamar and I were together, he would have set you up in your own landscape business, but you never could be patient."

"Yeah, right. If you thought the guy would welcome me with open arms, how come you never invited me over for dinner? Then we could have met face-to-face."

"I told you, I just started watching Rachael Ray!" she shouted. "I would have once I learned how to cook, but you never trusted me to do anything right."

"That's because you never have. Your whole life, Bonnie, has just been one disaster after another."

Beth reached down to touch her gun in her ankle holster. If Lenny kept this up, she'd be tempted to wing him based on his cruel nature alone. Somehow, knowing Lenny was Bonnie's brother and not Bonnie's spouse softened her opinion of the poor girl.

"Meeting Lamar at Cool Beans wasn't a major disaster," she said stubbornly. "That man was in love with me. He told me so."

"No, Lamar was in love with his wife. You, he was just using." Lenny spoke with equal conviction.

"He loved Evelyn once, but not anymore. Lamar was ready to make big changes in his life."

"You…are…such…a…fool."

Beth had never heard such conviction or so much venom in five little words before. Unfortunately, Lenny wasn't finished berating his sister.

"You're always so eager to believe whatever people tell you. If a man told you to jump off a bridge, you would probably do it. You're pathetic."

Unable to resist, Beth stretched up to peek into the room but stayed hidden behind the checkered curtain. Lenny stood with his feet splayed, towering over Bonnie. With his hands balled into fists, he looked like a boxer ready to spring into action.

Bonnie, although at a disadvantage size-wise, looked as mad as a proverbial wet hen. "You're just jealous because no one ever felt that way about you!" she shouted.

Fearing for Bonnie's safety, Beth silently drew her weapon from its holster.

But instead of lashing out, Lenny sauntered across the linoleum floor and extracted his third beer from the fridge. "If Lamar loved you so much, why would he offer you twenty *K* to crawl back under whatever rock you came from?"

"His wife made him give me the money. Evelyn already tried to bribe me two days before with a check. I ripped that check into little pieces right under her nose and dropped them in the trash." Bonnie stood hipshot with her arms crossed—the classic posture of a belligerent child in the middle of a tantrum.

But Lenny wasn't a loving parent. He was a frightening bully who was rapidly getting drunk. He grabbed Bonnie's arm and pushed her down in a chair. "It's time you woke up, little sister. When you came here Saturday night after your lovers' quarrel, I'd never seen you so upset. I planned to rearrange Lamar's face for making you cry. But when I got to the apartment, he was already gone. He'd hightailed it back to his cushy life on Tybee Island." Lenny paused for another long pull of beer. "I found the envelope of cash, along with a note saying he was sorry if he made promises. He said he loved his wife, and they both hoped you could use the money to make a new life for yourself. Maybe you could go back to school or enroll in college or get some vocational training." Lenny paused to inhale, as though preparing to deliver his final salvo. "Lamar wasn't coming to his senses. He was kissing you off!" Lenny roared loud enough to rattle the glass in the window frame.

Beth released a pent-up breath and peeked at Bonnie. Sobbing hysterically, the girl had curled into a ball on the chair. "What did you do, Lenny?" she asked in between hiccups. "And I'm not talking about the money. I know you took that."

There was a long moment of silence. Then Lenny spoke in a chillingly calm voice. "I made Lamar Doyle pay for disrespecting my sister."

Beth swayed on the rock, momentarily unbalanced. She had followed Bonnie hoping to find proof of her guilt but instead heard the confession of a murderous brother. *Perhaps being an only child was a blessing after all.*

"You killed him? You killed the only man I ever loved?" Bonnie whimpered like a wounded animal.

"You were in love with the idea of being a rich man's wife, not Lamar Doyle." Lenny took another drink.

"I was so scared when you didn't come home that night." Bonnie struggled to her feet, moving as though underwater. "When I heard Lamar was dead, I was sure you'd done it."

"What changed your mind?" Lenny sounded as though he was merely curious.

She took a few steps toward him. "I told myself that was impossible. You didn't even know where Lamar and Evelyn lived."

"That's how stupid you are. Thanks to the Internet, you can find out where anyone in the world lives. Just in case you can't put two and two together, I copied Lamar's house key when I copied the apartment's." Lenny tipped up the can and drained the contents. "Frankly, I couldn't believe how easy it was. The code to their security system was written on a piece of paper in your purse. You never could remember numbers." He shook his head. "With his wife sawing logs like a lumberjack in the bedroom, and Lamar asleep in the deck chair, it was done and over with fast. That woman was so zonked out on sleeping pills she never heard the shot. It's the only reason she's still alive."

Bonnie closed the distance between them and pounded on his chest with her fists. "How could you shoot someone you didn't even know?"

Lenny pushed her away effortlessly. "That's where you're wrong, little sister. As a landscaper, I've known men like Lamar Doyle my whole life. You can be trimming hedges two feet away, and they'll walk by like they don't even see you. Not so much as a 'How ya doing?'"

Bonnie marched back undeterred. "Lamar wasn't like that. He was nice to everyone. My friends at Cool Beans, his assistant at work, and every single waitress when we went out to dinner."

Lenny grabbed both of her arms and shook her viciously. "Do you ever listen to yourself? Every single person you mentioned is *female*. Lamar was nice only to women because he was a womanizer."

"That's just your dirty mind," she shouted, struggling against his grip. "You want me to stick around cooking your food and washing your clothes. I'm someone to slap around after a hard day of cutting people's grass." Unable to break free, Bonnie opted for a passive-aggressive approach—she spit on his shirt.

Lenny released her arm and slapped her across the face. Bonnie fell over the chair, landing in a heap next to the stove. "Someday you'll thank me." He glared down at her without pity. "After you realize that old guy made a fool out of you."

Beth had seen enough. She jumped from her rock and stumbled away from the overgrown shrubs. "Freeze!" she shouted, bursting through the back door. "Lenny Mulroney, you're under arrest for the murder of Lamar Doyle."

Unfortunately, in the time it took Beth to get out of the bushes, Bonnie had launched herself at her brother. The two siblings were locked in hand-to-hand combat when Beth entered the kitchen, but both stopped to gape at her.

"Who are you?" Lenny demanded, adding an expletive for emphasis. "You ain't no cop!"

Bonnie blinked. "She's that nosy PI who works for Mrs. Doyle. Beth Somebody-or-other. Will you never stop harassing me?"

"I will as soon as the police have your brother in custody. Step away from your sister, Mulroney." Beth aimed her weapon at a spot between his eyes.

Apparently, brotherly love had its limits. Lenny pulled his sister in front of him like a shield and extracted a small-caliber handgun from under the back of his dirty shirt. "Put the gun down, PI. You don't want to kill an innocent woman, do you?"

Bonnie's eyes turned round as saucers. "Please don't shoot me. I'm sorry I said those things about Mrs. Doyle."

Beth stared into the cold eyes of a hate-filled man. With Bonnie between them, she had no clear shot. "Look, nobody has to get hurt. All I want to do is walk out of here with your sister." She aimed well to the left of Lenny's head.

"Then put your gun on the table and get out. Bonnie's not going anywhere."

"Okay, you win." Beth slowly placed her Glock on the table. But before she could plan her next move, Mulroney shoved his sister into her. Beth quickly regained her balance, but Lenny had already grabbed her gun. With two weapons aimed at her chest, there was little Beth could say or do.

Bonnie, however, had plenty to say. "What's the *matter* with you, Lenny?" she screamed, stomping her foot. "That crazy chick could have shot me."

"Nah, I knew she wouldn't. And you know I'd never hurt you." Lenny pulled his sister into a loose embrace and kissed the top of her head. Equally as unexpected, Lenny then handed Bonnie the Glock. "Keep this pointed at the nosy PI until I can tie her up. We don't want any more surprises until we're ready to leave."

Even though she was an only child, Beth felt this kind of

behavior between siblings couldn't *possibly* be normal. She lifted her hands in surrender and stepped toward the door. "Look, all I want to do is go back to my hotel and mind my own business."

Lenny sprang at her with the sure-footedness of a leopard. He slapped her hard across the face—twice as hard as the blow he delivered to Bonnie. "Do you think I'm stupid?" he asked in a soft, controlled voice. "You just heard me confess to killing Doyle. You ain't going anywhere until we're long gone."

With stars swimming before her eyes, Beth couldn't focus. She tasted blood from where her teeth cut her mouth or tongue, the coppery bitterness roiling her stomach. If Mulroney could deliver that kind of force open-palmed, she hoped never to connect with his fist. Ridiculously, her father's motto that nice boys should never hit girls ran through her head, but wisely Beth kept her mouth shut.

"There should be rope under the sink." Lenny dragged Beth roughly across the room, pulled a chair up to a chest freezer, and slammed her into it. Her head bounced against the freezer, adding to the existing dull ache. "Keep the gun on her, Bonnie!"

Unfortunately, little sis was quick to comply. Beth wasn't sure how often Bonnie had handled a weapon, but Glocks didn't have a safety. "Please be careful with that. I'm not planning any great escapes."

"Bet you're sorry you stuck your nose in my business now, huh?" Bonnie asked. But at least the girl took her finger away from the trigger.

"You're not kidding." Beth tried to smile, but her lips hurt.

In a moment, Lenny was back with a length of rope. None too gently he tied her wrists together, tied her to the chair, and then tied the chair to the freezer handle. *Not a man who does things halfway.* As he bent over her, Beth caught the scents of fresh-mown grass, stale perspiration, and something harder to pin down—fear or maybe desperation.

"I'm going upstairs to pack my stuff, because we're never coming back to this dump again," he said to his sister. "You keep an eye on her so she doesn't slip those ropes like Houdini."

"Where are we going?" Bonnie's tone contained zero enthusiasm for the idea.

"I don't know. Maybe Miami or the Keys. I heard Key West is nice. Plenty of old folks in Florida need their yard work done. Some of them are bound to be getting forgetful and won't notice when their jewelry goes missing."

"Are we taking Beth with us?" Bonnie asked as Lenny loaded the remaining beers and sodas into the cooler.

"Sure we are. Everyone has a pet PI on a leash down in Miami." Lenny cast a withering glare in her direction.

"Look, Lenny, I've never killed anybody, and I'm not eager to start now." Despite being half his size, Bonnie spoke with conviction.

Beth expected the madman to lash out as he had earlier. But instead, he walked to where Bonnie was perched on the counter and placed a gentle hand on her shoulder. "I know how you hate blood. Right now I haven't worked out the details, but you need to trust me to do what's best for us. Haven't I always taken good care of you?" He lifted Bonnie's chin with one finger.

"Yes," she answered, sounding small and childlike.

For the second time, Beth felt nothing but pity for a girl who apparently had no other family except this abusive tyrant.

"Okay, then give me a few minutes, and you'll get that fresh start you want." Lenny turned on a heel and strode from the room.

When Beth heard his heavy work boots stomping up the steps, she knew she only had a short amount of time. "You have to untie me. Your brother plans to kill me. And that's not something you want on your conscience for the rest of your life."

Bonnie's blue eyes were glassy with moisture. "I know that's what he plans to do, but I don't have much choice." A tear ran down her cheek.

"Of course you do! I'll get us both away from here. Then my friends and I will protect you." Beth wasn't sure how Michael, Kaitlyn, and Nate would feel about this idea, but she would cross that bridge downstream.

Bonnie bit down on her trembling lower lip. "No, Beth. I've tried getting away before, but Lenny always finds me and drags me home. So you and I are going to do exactly what he says." She lifted the Glock and leveled it at Beth's forehead, curtailing conversation.

THIRTY-FOUR

For a short while, Beth listened to Lenny moving around the room overhead. One thing about steel-toed work boots— it was hard to be stealthy in them. "What's this about Lenny not letting you leave him?" Beth asked. "He's your brother, not your jailer."

"You know nothing about us. When our ma died, not one of my relatives wanted to take us in. So much for *family*. We were thrown into the foster system, but as soon as Lenny turned eighteen, he petitioned the court and got me out. He had a good job back then."

"Well, he did the right thing. But he's not doing right anymore."

Bonnie rolled her eyes. "You don't know what he's got planned. He might tie you up and leave you in the country somewhere. All we need to do is get out of Georgia."

Beth chose a new, risky angle to pursue. "You were planning to make a fresh start with Crystal. You two were going to find jobs and a new place to live in a different town. Unless Lenny really is keeping you a prisoner."

"He would let me share a place with her as long as I don't move in with some man. Lenny kinda likes Crystal. He could always come visit us." She shrugged. "I sure could use that money now."

"Crystal won't be moving anywhere." Beth spoke very softly. Bonnie's chin jerked up. "You don't even know her!"

"Yes, I do. She helped me fill out a job application at Cool Beans. She had the coolest streaks in her hair. When I stopped by her grandma's today looking for you, the police were all over the place." Beth glanced at the doorway, not wishing any surprise interruptions. "Your friend is dead. I'm sorry."

Jumping off the counter, Bonnie loomed over her. "You're lying!" she hissed.

"I would never make up such a thing. Why would I? Crystal opened the door to someone she knew. Then when she turned her back, that so-called friend shot her. Where was your brother this afternoon?" she whispered just loud enough to be heard.

Bonnie bent down until they were face-to-face. "You...are... crazy! Why would he do such a thing? I told you he likes her."

"I have no idea. But if it were me going on the lam with Lenny, I would ask him."

Two or three seconds spun out—the lull before a coming storm—then a voice floated from the kitchen doorway. "Ask me what?" He dropped a duffel bag and a second suitcase on the floor.

Bonnie reacted before Beth had a chance to concoct a plausible story. "This crazy PI thinks you're going to kill her. I said you don't need to. You know how to live so far under the radar no one ever finds you wherever you go. None of those bill collectors ever tracked us down here." She offered Lenny a dazzling smile and stretched up to tuck a lock of stringy hair behind his ear.

Lenny shook her hand off. "Yeah, yeah. You ready to go? I see you already packed before I got home."

"A girl has to be prepared." Bonnie grabbed the handle of her suitcase.

Lenny focused his cold eyes on Beth. "You're coming with us, Miss Busybody." He withdrew a long hunting knife from a sheath beneath his shirt and grabbed one of the ropes.

"Too bad Bonnie didn't empty out Lamar's safe before she left the apartment," Beth blurted out. "A little extra traveling money wouldn't hurt. Even twenty thousand only goes so far these days."

Lenny stopped sawing at the knot. "What's she talkin' about, Bonnie?"

"More crazy stuff. She's just trying to buy more time."

Lenny inserted the blade between Beth's wrist and the rope. The back of the blade cut into her skin.

"I *am* trying to buy time, but I'm not lying about money in the safe. Lots of it. Evelyn Doyle told me to retrieve it when you weren't around. She had a feeling you didn't know about Lamar's stash." Beth smiled sweetly at the girl.

"Another lie! You could have gotten it today instead of following me here."

"True, but when I arrived at the apartment and then saw you peeling out of the lot, I wanted to know where you were going in such a hurry. I knew I could get the money another time. Lamar didn't trust banks, so he had safes installed in his home and in his office. According to a note Evelyn found, Lamar also had one installed in the apartment. He didn't want that money left rotting in the wall if something ever happened to him." Beth tried to blow her bangs out of her eyes. The safes on Bull Street and in his Town and Country office were pure fabrications. *Perhaps if I get out of this alive, I can start writing fiction in my spare time.*

"Lamar never told me about any safe." Bonnie balled her hands and kicked the leg of Beth's chair.

"You two hadn't been going together that long," said Beth, hoping not to encounter one of Bonnie's fists.

The explanation seemed to make sense to Lenny. "Where is this safe?" he asked.

"Behind the fake Renoir in the living room. It has a combination lock. Lamar used the date of his son's birthday, 1-2-0-8-8-8."

"There ain't no safe," Bonnie insisted.

"Did you ever look behind the pictures?"

"Well…no," she whined. "But Lamar would have told me and not Evelyn about it."

He stared at the floor for a few moments before seeming to come to a decision. He looked at his sister and snarled, "You just keep the gun pointed at her. If she gets away while I'm gone, I'm coming after you, Bonnie. And you won't be smiling when I get done." Then he turned to Beth with an evil glint in his eye. "What exactly is a fake Renoir?"

"It's a painting of a lady with a red hat sitting with a little girl. The girl's wearing a hat too." It was the only painting Beth remembered from her art history class in college.

"If you're lying, that will be the last lie you ever tell." Lenny slipped his knife into its sheaf and the gun into his waistband and went out the door. In another moment, the engine of his truck roared to life and gravel spun in the driveway. Beth heard his muffler for a long time. *Maybe some of that tire money could have been spent on an exhaust system.*

Bonnie leaned over Beth and shook her head. "It wasn't smart to send Lenny on a wild-goose chase. He can get to the apartment and be back within forty minutes. You have no idea what Lenny's like when he's mad."

"I needed to buy us some time." Beth opted for the truth.

"I knew there was no safe!" Bonnie shook a finger in Beth's face. "There isn't even a painting close to what you described. What makes you so sure I won't call him on his cell?" She pulled out her phone with a smug expression.

"Just hear me out. Right now you haven't killed anybody yet, unlike your brother. But if you leave with him, you'll be an accomplice to murder. That carries the same penalty as if you'd pulled the trigger. But if you cut my ropes, I'll help you start over someplace far away. Lenny won't be getting out of jail anytime soon."

Her young face contorted. "I'm already going to jail if we get caught. No judge in the world will believe I had nothing to do with Lamar's death. I'm the stupid person who told Lenny where Mrs. Doyle kept the gun."

"How on earth did you know?"

She shrugged. "Lamar told me. He invited me to his fancy beach house twice while Mrs. Doyle was out of town visiting her sister. He wanted me waiting when he came home from work. He told me she kept the gun in her nightstand when he was out of town, so I'd better not come on the wrong night or Evelyn might shoot me as an intruder. Lamar thought that was funny."

"And you told your brother about the gun?"

Bonnie rubbed her eyes. "I didn't mean to, but Lenny didn't believe that I'd ever been on Tybee Island. He said I wasn't classy enough for Lamar to invite to his house. But Lamar wasn't like that. I told Lenny about the gun to prove I'd been there. Then he found the paper in my purse with their security code. I never thought he'd go there and shoot at Mrs. Doyle." Her tears started up anew.

Beth gaped. "Lenny tried to kill Evelyn?"

Bonnie shook her head vigorously. "He missed on purpose. Lenny wanted to scare her into giving Lamar a divorce so he would be free to marry me. Lenny thought he was doing me a favor."

"When he realized that wasn't going to happen, he killed Lamar."

"Lenny loves me in his own way."

"I can see that," Beth conceded. "You didn't go to Crystal's after you stormed out of the apartment. You came here."

She nodded mutely. "I thought our fight would blow over, so I didn't want to tell Crystal. She was so happy that I found a nice man."

It was hard for Beth to understand how two women could celebrate a ruined marriage, but this wasn't the time for a lesson in morality.

"I thought for once Lenny would just be nice, but he started yelling about how stupid I was, telling me I was nothing but trash, no better than him." She dissolved into a fit of sobbing. "I begged Crystal to lie about my whereabouts because I knew no one would believe me."

"And she did. That could be what got your friend killed."

Bonnie grabbed her stomach as though she might be sick.

"There's still time to save yourself. Your brother is going to jail for murdering two people. Turn on the TV. Channel 4 usually has local news. Please, do this for yourself as well as me."

Bonnie locked gazes with her. Then she walked into the living room where a television droned.

For an interminable amount of time, Beth watched the clock and prayed for either deliverance or forgiveness. When Bonnie shuffled back into the kitchen, every bit of blood had drained from her face.

"The reporters kept calling her the Callahan woman and said drugs haven't been ruled out as a motive in her death. She wasn't 'the Callahan woman'! Her name was Crystal, and Crystal never touched drugs in her life. She was the best friend I ever had." Bonnie laid the gun on the counter and started sawing at Beth's ropes with a kitchen knife.

Beth felt the first seeds of hope stirring when they heard Lenny's loud truck roar up the driveway and come to a squealing, gravel-scattering stop. Both women froze as a pair of heavy boots stomped up the steps.

"*What do you think you're doing?*" The slam of the screen door punctuated his angry question as Lenny pushed his sister away from Beth with one hand.

"I don't want any part of killing this lady," Bonnie said from the floor.

"Oh, really? Because this *lady* just sent me down a rabbit hole. I couldn't get close to that safe. Your building is crawling with police."

"It doesn't matter, Lenny, because there ain't no safe. She lied to buy more time."

He didn't take the news well. He slapped Beth across the face, cutting short her joy over duping him. "Still feeling smug now?" Then he turned toward his sister with only slightly less venom. "That still doesn't explain why you were helping her."

Bonnie picked herself up and bravely confronted her brother. "Because you killed Crystal. I *know* it was you. There aren't too many people she would let into the house and turn her back on."

"Shut up, Bonnie. You don't know what you're talking about."

"Your boss called here looking for you. He said you left the job early today without any kind of explanation. Lenny…" Her voice broke. "Crystal was my best friend in the whole world."

A horrible flush darkened his face. "*Your best friend,*" he sneered. "Want to know what your best friend was doing behind your back?" He wasted no time with guessing games. "Blackmail! Crystal demanded five hundred bucks to fix the transmission on her old clunker, so I gave it to her. Then she started thinking I must be made of money, because she demanded a thousand bucks this morning. She told me to bring it over today or she'd tell the cops you weren't with her that night. Crystal thought that was a fair trade for her silence." The evil glint in Lenny's eye reappeared. "What do you think about your best friend now?"

Bonnie planted her feet. "I think she didn't deserve to die."

"Tough luck for her. People die all the time."

Bonnie lunged at her brother. But it didn't take much of a shove to send a hundred-pound woman across the room.

Beth thought this was a good time to keep her mouth shut.

THIRTY-FIVE

*M*ichael was sick of checking his watch and pacing the floor. He was even sicker of calling Beth and getting her voice mail immediately. *Why on earth would she turn off her phone? Even if she didn't want to be interrupted, why couldn't she turn the phone to vibrate?*

The last thing he wanted to do was call Kaitlyn without knowing how her meeting with Beth had gone. By now she would have figured out that he was the one snooping into her background. Although that was standard procedure when hiring a new PI, it might make for uncomfortable conversation.

After another trip down to the ice machine and back, Michael punched in Kaitlyn's number. "Hello, Miss Webb? Michael Preston. Beth was supposed to talk to you today about some questions we had on your résumé."

She hesitated only for a second. "Yes, she jogged all the way here and was waiting when I got back from talking to the Tanakas. I explained to her that—"

He didn't have time for this. "I don't mean to be rude, but that's not why I'm calling. I'm sure Beth will fill me in on the meeting when I see her. Trouble is, I expected her back hours ago and she's still not here."

"Have you tried calling her?"

Michael bit down on his back molars. "Yes, about a hundred times. The calls go straight to voice mail. I've never known her to turn off her phone. Did Beth call Uber in order to get back? I doubt she would want to jog in both directions." For one horrible instant, he pictured some sociopathic Uber driver kidnapping Beth and holding her captive in some remote hideout miles away.

"No. Beth borrowed my car for a few hours. She said she had an errand to run and would return it later. Goodness, I fell asleep on the couch and didn't realize what time it is. She should have returned the car long ago."

Michael closed his eyes as a bad feeling washed over him. "Please try to remember your conversation with her and tell me *everything* she said."

Kaitlyn remained silent so long Michael thought the call had been disconnected, but then she said, "Beth told me she had one more errand to run, and that she wanted to see if a certain someone still wanted to provide a flimsy alibi. Those were her exact words."

"Anything else? This is very important."

"Only that she would replace any gas she used. What's going on, Michael? I don't care if Price Investigations fires me tomorrow. Beth and I really clicked. Please let me help you."

Michael needed all the help he could get. "The person who provided a flimsy alibi for our murder suspect was Crystal Callahan. She worked with Bonnie Mulroney, but Beth never believed Bonnie was with her that night."

"So that's who Beth went to see. Let's start by—"

He didn't let her finish. "Crystal was shot tonight, murdered by someone she apparently knew. Knowing Beth, if she found that out when she went there, she probably went straight to Bonnie's."

"Should I meet you there? Beth showed me where the apartment on Bull Street is."

"No. To save time, I'll call the Savannah police and let them check out the apartment. Beth could be in trouble. Then I'll call the Tybee Island detective in charge of the Doyle homicide. Although they have no jurisdiction in a Savannah murder, I have a feeling the two crimes are connected."

"Tell me how I can help."

With Beth's life at stake, Michael squashed any misgivings about Kaitlyn's background. He didn't care if the woman was on the run for Swiss bank fraud as long as she helped him find Beth. "How are you with searching databases, hacking into them if necessary?"

"I might not be as good as you, but I can hold my own. Just tell me what you need me to do."

"Bonnie lived with a Lenny Mulroney before she moved into Lamar's apartment. I'm assuming he's her husband or ex-husband. If the police don't find Bonnie or Beth at the Bull Street address, this Lenny is the only lead I have. If we both work at this, we should find this guy in half the time. Call me the moment you know anything, and I'll do the same." Michael spelled the surname and ended the call, buoyed by having an angle to pursue.

But sixty minutes later, he was no closer to finding either Beth or Bonnie. The Savannah police agreed to check out the Bull Street residence in possible connection to the Callahan homicide. When the building's superintendent allowed them into the apartment, the only thing they found was pieces of a vase that had been smashed against the wall.

Michael pinned his hopes on his call to the Tybee Island police. "Detective Rossi? This is Michael Preston—"

"Why am I not surprised?" Rossi drawled, dragging out the words. "First I get the pleasure of running into Nancy Drew, and now Magnum PI calls me on my private cell. Will wonders never cease?"

"You saw Beth at the Callahan crime scene?" The lump in Michael's throat swelled into a rock.

"I did, and I'll tell you what I told her: Stay out of police business. If there's any connection to the Lamar Doyle homicide, we will find it. We don't need any out-of-town gumshoes getting in the way."

"Yes, ma'am. I agree wholeheartedly and I have full faith in the Savannah and Tybee Island police."

"But…" she prodded.

"Beth may have gone looking for Bonnie Mulroney after she left you. I've been unable to reach her for hours."

Rossi blew out a breath of exasperation. "And she also could be at Taco Bell or having her nails done."

"No, ma'am. Beth wouldn't leave her phone turned off this long. According to Mrs. Doyle, Bonnie Mulroney lived with a Lenny Mulroney before she met Lamar. He might have something to do with this or he might not, but Mrs. Doyle described him as dangerous. We need to track this guy down."

Rossi mumbled something incoherent. "Look, Preston, I'm working a case right now. When I'm finished, I'll find Lenny Mulroney. If you find him before I do, your first call is to me, got it?"

"Got it. Thanks."

"Don't thank me yet. After we find your partner, I will personally make sure you two are headed back to Mississippi on the next plane, boat, train, or bus."

"I have a car, Detective. And I'm ready to go as soon as I find Beth."

"Good. Keep your phone turned on." Rossi ended the call, probably wishing for the good old days when a person could slam a handset into a cradle.

Michael went back to what he was good at, what he'd worked at for years, and what he'd aced in college—gleaning databases for that piece of information that could crack a case wide open. Yet he found no trace of Lenny, Len, or Leonard Mulroney east of the Mississippi River that would fit the general age and description.

There were no tax records, credit cards, or utilities in his name, no registered vehicles, and, no record that the man had voted in any election.

How does a person live in the twenty-first century totally off the grid?

Bonnie Mulroney, however, owned one registered vehicle—the yellow Honda, which listed the Bull Street address as home. Her previous car registration contained a bogus address, as was the address Bonnie had used on her job application at Cool Beans. When another hour ticked by, Michael dropped his head on his desk and started to pray—something he should have tried sooner. Never in his life had he felt so useless doing the one thing he loved.

Suddenly his phone rang, jarring him upright. "Tell me you found something, Kaitlyn," he said, after seeing her name on the caller ID. "I've hit a brick wall."

"Maybe, but we won't know until we get there. Beth seemed to think Bonnie hailed from Florida, same as me. I have a government friend who owed me a favor. There's a Leonard Mulroney registered with the Florida probation department who's currently living in Savannah. He'd been checking in with his parole officer once a month, but Leonard missed his last appointment. He said work wouldn't allow him the day off to drive down. The officer gave him a break but said if Leonard misses this month's appointment, a warrant would be issued for his arrest."

"What are the particulars on this guy?"

"Thirty-five, six feet two, one hundred ninety pounds, blond hair, blue eyes, all the usual scars and tattoos." Kaitlyn paused, drawing a breath. "He was paroled after serving three years for five counts of breaking and entering, theft, possession of stolen property, et cetera. He lives in a rental house out by Bonaventure Cemetery. He pays his rent in cash, and the utilities are paid by the landlord."

"Sounds like he's our guy."

"There's more. This particular Leonard Mulroney has been arrested twice for domestic violence, but both times the complaint was withdrawn. He seems to enjoy hitting women."

Michael felt the blood drain from his face. "We need to move. Beth could be the next recipient of his rage. Text me the address you got from Florida, and I'll meet you there. I'll call Detective Rossi along the way." He buckled on his shoulder holster for the first time since coming to Georgia and took his gun from the safe.

"Small problem. Beth has my car."

Michael hesitated, not wanting to delay.

"Picking me up would be out of your way," she said. "I'll take a taxi or Uber or something. Just go. The address is already on your phone."

He wasted no time getting out the door, punching the address into GPS, and calling the detective.

Rossi answered immediately. "I take it you have news about your missing partner?"

As succinctly as possible, Michael told her about Leonard Mulroney's criminal record and his penchant for violence toward women.

"Okay, Bonnie might not have gotten much of a better half, but do you have any reason to suspect he's holding Beth against her will?" While Michael struggled for an answer, Rossi continued. "I'll take that as a no. So I can't dispatch Savannah police to this address for a *possible* domestic complaint. They have real, ongoing crimes to respond to, not suppositions and possibilities. And they're already irritated about being dispatched to the Bull Street apartment for no good reason."

"I understand, Detective. You asked me to keep you informed, so I'm letting you know I'm on my way to that address now. I should arrive in sixteen minutes."

"Just hold your horses, Preston—"

"No, ma'am. I believe my partner's in danger. If Beth isn't

inside the Mulroney home, I'm simply a private citizen who got his signals crossed. They can sue me or have me arrested for trespassing, but you won't be involved."

Rossi again muttered something he couldn't understand. "Fine. Give me the address and I'm on my way. I'll call Savannah for backup, but I doubt they'll respond based on the priority code."

"Thanks, Detective."

"Listen to me carefully. You are *not* to enter an occupied dwelling. And for heaven's sake, don't draw your weapon. I'm twenty-three minutes away."

"Got it, but I need to end this call. Traffic is a nightmare in this town."

Actually, Michael hadn't *gotten it* at all. No way would he wait until Rossi drove in from Tybee Island, not with Mulroney's history of violence.

Of course, it was possible Beth was having her nails done, or chomping on burritos, or simply enjoying an evening away from him, but he couldn't take that chance. Because when you loved someone, you even risked making a fool of yourself to make sure they were safe.

When Michael arrived at the correct address, his bad feeling took a turn for the worse. He spotted Kaitlyn's Mustang parked in the lot of a church, so he knew Beth was close by. And because there were no coffee shops or delis in the area, he knew the only place she could be was inside the ramshackle house the Mulroneys called home. He left his car parked at the curb and approached the house.

The rooms facing the street were dark at Bonnie and Lenny's, but lights blazed in the rear of the house, presumably the kitchen. A yellow Honda was parked in the yard with a dual-axle pickup truck blocking it in. A gun rack mounted in the back window was never a good sign. While still twenty feet away, Michael heard voices—one male and one female—raised in anger. The female sounded whiny and young, not at all the sultry drawl of his beloved Beth. *Maybe she isn't here. Maybe this is just me confusing gut instincts for indigestion.*

"It's your fault she's here in the first place, Bonnie!" The man's profanity-laced accusation wiped any *maybes* from the slate. "She followed you, not me!"

Michael crept close enough to peer into the side window at a room in disarray. But it wasn't a lack of housekeeping skills that turned his blood to ice water. Beth sat in a straight-back chair, tied to a freezer, her hands bound behind her. A filthy rag had been jammed into her mouth, and a red welt across her face had already started to darken.

"Who watches their rearview mirror?" Bonnie wailed. "I have to keep my eyes on the road. That doesn't mean we need to do something stupid now."

"Just make sure you have everything packed. We're not coming back to this dump no matter what you leave behind."

"I already have everything right here, Lenny. I swear. Let's just leave Beth tied up. By the time she gets loose, we'll be long gone from this old city."

Lenny untied the chair from the freezer and dragged Beth roughly to her feet, the chair coming along with her. "Nope, we need the lady PI for insurance. If anyone tries to stop us, she'll be our bargaining chip to make them back off."

"What will you do with her then?" The desperation of Bonnie's plea almost matched his own apprehension.

Michael checked his watch. Fifteen minutes had passed since he'd talked to Rossi, yet there was still no sign of her or the Savannah police. Drawing his weapon, he couldn't wait any longer for backup.

"If you don't shut up and let me think, Bonnie, you'll get the same, whatever I decide."

Tears coursed down Bonnie's cheeks as she bobbed and weaved into Michael's line of fire.

"You think you can walk out of here with me tied up?" asked Beth the moment Lenny pulled out the gag. "I grew up in a neighborhood like this. Nobody *ever* minds their own business, especially not the way you two have been screaming at each other."

Please, Beth, don't rile the guy up more than he already is, Michael thought. Now she was between him and his target.

When Lenny pulled out a long hunting knife, Michael knew he had to act.

"You almost cut her loose!" Lenny shouted, slicing through the restraints easily.

"That's what I intended," snarled Bonnie.

Michael took aim, grateful that Mulroney was at least six inches taller than Beth. But before he could get off a shot, Diane Rossi hissed in his ear.

"I told you not to draw your weapon, Preston!"

Michael didn't take his focus off Mulroney. "The creep has two guns and a knife. I'm not taking a chance with Beth's life."

"He won't kill her between here and his truck. I'm going around to the front. Just let me handle this."

Michael didn't agree. He also didn't argue. He just aimed his Smith and Wesson at Mulroney and waited like the patient man he'd always been.

Lenny slipped the knife into his belt and jabbed the gun barrel into Beth's rib cage. "You're right about nosy neighbors. That's why you and me are walking out of here just like the sweethearts we are." He wrapped his other arm around Beth's shoulder. "And I wouldn't try anything if I were you. Grab my duffel and the cooler, Bonnie, and let's go!"

"Can I go to the bathroom first?" she whined. "Key West is a long way from Savannah."

"Hurry up!" he snapped. "Sometimes I swear you're still ten years old."

As Lenny paused just inside the threshold, Michael froze to the right of the door. Seconds passed as he waited for Rossi to come through the house. If he could get off a clean shot that wouldn't endanger Beth, he would take it, but he couldn't see well enough in the dark.

"What's taking you so long?" Lenny shouted. "I want to get on the road!"

Inhaling a deep breath, Michael wrapped both hands around his gun. If he waited for Bonnie to exit the bathroom, one more person might be in the way of Detective Rossi.

Just as Lenny muttered an obscenity, Michael yanked open the screen door and leveled his weapon at Lenny's forehead, less than a foot away. "Drop the gun, Mulroney, and release Beth. I'll say it only once."

"And if he misses, I won't." Detective Rossi's voice came from somewhere inside the kitchen. She jabbed Lenny between the shoulder blades with her gun barrel.

Lenny uttered a second foul phrase, dropped his gun, and pushed Beth down the steps. "She's all yours."

Michael grabbed Beth's arm before she fell. "There's a second weapon under his shirt, Detective," he added.

Beth regained her footing. "What do you bet ballistics will match it to the bullet that killed Mr. Doyle?"

"No doubt, but first I can't wait to hear how you ended up here, Kirby," Rossi said as she slapped handcuffs on Mulroney.

"That will make an interesting story for later." Beth moved out of the way while Michael relieved Mulroney of the second firearm and his hunting knife.

"You won't need these where you're going," Michael said in response to Mulroney's glare.

As Rossi read Lenny his rights, Michael dragged Bonnie from the bathroom, where she'd been hiding.

"Looks like I missed all the action," said Rossi's partner as he sauntered up the driveway. "Traffic on the Islands Expressway was the pits."

"You're just in time to say thank you, Fuller." Rossi patted Mulroney down for additional weapons. "These two out-of-towners just solved our homicide."

Michael wasn't interested in praise or gratitude. He was still worried about Beth. Turning Bonnie over to Detective Fuller, he walked to where Beth waited on the sidelines. "I have never heard you speechless this long, Kirby." He wrapped an arm around her shoulders. "I hope Mulroney didn't injure your vocal cords."

"Let's just say I'll choose my words carefully for a while." Beth spoke hesitantly, as though trying to regain her composure. Then, without warning, she collapsed in his arms. "Oh, Michael, just when I thought my number was up, you saved me!" She encircled his neck with both arms and kissed him long and hard. It was one perfect kiss. "I'm usually not afraid to die, but I didn't want to today. Not without telling you about the decision I reached."

Michael wanted to hear her decision more than anything, but four pairs of eyes were boring into them like lasers. He gently turned Beth's face toward their captive audience. "Why don't we let the detectives take care of business, and you can tell me later."

Beth nodded but didn't loosen her grip on his shirt one iota.

"Wow, how come you didn't react like that when I saved your skin?" Detective Fuller asked his partner.

"Hey, I bought your lunch the next day," said Rossi. "Be happy with that." The two detectives watched them for a few more moments until the sound of approaching sirens demanded their attention. "Looks like the cavalry has arrived. Bring Bonnie. We'll sort out what role she played in all of this down at the Savannah station." Rossi dragged Lenny none too gently down the driveway, while Detective Fuller followed with a rather reluctant Bonnie.

But Lenny wasn't finished with his five minutes of fame. "I can't believe you gave me up." He scowled at his sister. "We could have started over someplace new. I'm your family. I'm the one who took care of you, but you sided with this PI over your own brother."

Bonnie's explanation was short and sweet. "You killed my best friend. There's no overlooking that."

Suddenly, another voice called out, "Michael, Beth! Thank goodness, you're all right." Kaitlyn emerged from the shadows and hurled herself at them. "I was so worried about you."

Beth reached out to pull her into a three-way hug. "Thanks to my partner, I'm fine. How on earth did you get here?"

"Well, since you had my car, I had to use Uber."

"Sorry about that. We'll reimburse you…"

That caused Michael and Kaitlyn to laugh. What an incredibly inane thing to say in such an emotionally fraught moment. After a few seconds, Beth joined in. Then, as she wiped moisture from her eyes, she said, "Thanks for coming."

Michael gently extracted himself from the embrace. "Kaitlyn did more than come late to the party. She's the one who found Mulroney's address in the Florida parole database. I passed it along to Rossi, and the police were able to get here in time."

"Sounds like we make a great team," said Beth, ending with a sigh of exhaustion.

Michael grabbed her to lend support. "You look ready to drop. You can give a statement and retrieve your firearm tomorrow. Kaitlyn, please drive Beth back to the hotel while I talk to the Savannah police. I'll join you there as soon as I can."

"You got it."

"And I meant what I said before. I'm very grateful for what you did tonight."

Kaitlyn shot him a smile as she helped Beth into her car.

Michael watched until the Mustang disappeared around the corner, still shaken at how close he'd come to losing the love of his life. Anyone who went the extra distance for people she just met deserved a chance despite any skeletons in her closet. Even if he had to walk across hot coals, he would convince Nate that Kaitlyn was right for the job. Loyalty deserved loyalty in return.

THIRTY-SIX

*W*hen Beth awoke the next morning, for one brief moment she thought it all had been a horrible nightmare. But the rope burns on her wrists and the pain in her jaw brought her quickly back to reality.

Crystal was dead. Bonnie hadn't killed anyone. And her brother, in some twisted version of defending his sister's honor, had also killed Lamar.

She swung her feet out of bed and padded to the window. Dew sparkled in the autumn sun on the grass down below. *Michael saved my life.* Beth always thought of herself as the one in charge—the one to rush into a burning building or dive off a pier or wrestle the gun away from a felon. But if her partner hadn't shown up, Lenny Mulroney would have kidnapped and then killed her.

Last night after Kaitlyn dropped her off, Beth had taken a hot shower and then collapsed on her bed, waiting for Michael to knock on her door. But she'd apparently fallen asleep long before he finished giving his statement to the police. *Just as well. What do you say to a person after they risked their life to save yours?*

When the phone on the desk rang, Beth knew she'd run out of time. "Beth Kirby," she said in a voice she didn't recognize.

"Good morning, Miss Kirby," drawled Michael. He, on the

other hand, sounded normal, not at all like a knight in shining armor. "Isn't it about time you turned your cell back on?"

"Good grief. I was so tired I forgot about it."

"I decided to let you sleep as long as possible, but the Savannah police have already called twice. When we didn't come to the station this morning, they sent two officers to get us."

"They're downstairs now? What time is it?"

"It's noon, and they're in the breakfast area, unless they called for backup to surround the place." Michael chuckled.

"I'll be right down," Beth said before hanging up. She grabbed a clean outfit from the closet and flew into the bathroom.

And so began the longest six hours of her life. After she and Michael were questioned individually about the events leading up to her being taken hostage by Mulroney, they were grilled about their involvement with the Doyle homicide. Then everyone went to the Tybee Island station to talk with Detectives Rossi and Fuller. When Michael insisted on driving his car, one officer rode with him, perhaps to circumvent a sudden sprint for the Mississippi state line. At least when Rossi took the lead on Tybee, Beth and Michael were no longer treated like part of a sinister plot to scam and murder a local citizen.

Finally, the Savannah detectives rose to their feet. "I think we have what we need, Miss Kirby, Mr. Preston. We'll have these statements typed up, and you can stop by tomorrow to sign them."

"We'll be there," said Michael as Beth nodded in agreement.

After the Savannah detectives thanked their Tybee Island brethren in blue and left, Beth turned to Rossi. "Is that it? We're free to leave Chatham County?"

"The sooner the better, if anyone wants my opinion," Rossi said with a grin.

"Will we be called back to testify at Mulroney's trial?" asked Michael.

"It's possible, but the DA seems to think Lenny will cop a plea.

This is his third violent offense. Because the gun registered to Lamar Doyle was stuck in his belt, he doesn't have many options. Chances are ballistics will match the bullets to those that killed Lamar and Crystal."

"What kind of plea?" Beth gripped the arms of the chair.

"Relax. He'll plead to life in prison without parole to avoid the death penalty. He won't be coming after you in this lifetime."

"I was more worried about Bonnie." Beth unlocked her fingers.

Rossi's face softened. "You stuck your neck out for that girl. I'm not sure she's worth it."

"She's had few breaks in life with Lenny as her only family."

Rossi nodded. "As long as she cooperates fully, I don't see Savannah pressing charges against her. You went to that house of your own volition, and Bonnie had no control over her brother. She should be able to break free of Lenny at long last."

"Any clue how Mulroney entered the Doyles' enclave without passing by the security camera?" Michael stretched out his long legs.

Rossi paused, as though deciding whether or not to share. "One of their neighbors reported seeing a landscaping truck, loaded with mowers and implements, parked by the beach access gate. The neighbor assumed that a tree had toppled close to the dune line and a resident wanted it cleaned up immediately. Maintenance workers use a special beach gate to make sure fences are protecting nesting turtles and the fragile areas of the dunes. No one would question a landscaping truck being there. And unlike the main gate, there are no security cameras at the service entrance."

"Mulroney left his truck at the gate and walked down the beach to the Doyles'?"

"That's my theory. It's less than half a mile. Besides, people walk the beach at night. He wouldn't have drawn any attention whatsoever."

"Have you found a homeowner who made a middle-of-the-night service call?" asked Beth.

"I have not. And I checked the background of every employee of every landscaper who works on Tybee and came up empty. I never would have found Mulroney, because his boss has no contracts on the island and pays Mulroney under the table. So you two ended up helping after all."

"We were happy to assist, ma'am," said Michael, the voice of diplomacy.

"Does that mean we can stay a little longer?" asked Beth, the voice of living dangerously. "I haven't quite finished sightseeing."

Rossi nodded. "You can stay to sightsee, eat at our fine restaurants, and buy expensive souvenirs in the City Market. Heck, I'll even let you swim at our beautiful beaches on Tybee. But your firearms will stay locked in the hotel safe. Are we clear?"

"As a bell." Michael jumped up and pulled Beth to her feet. "Speaking of restaurants, I'm starved. Ready to go, partner?"

Picking up on his cue, Beth reached out to shake Rossi's hand. "Thanks for showing up last night. Please express my gratitude to Detective Fuller too. If not for you and Michael, I might have died from breathing toxic fumes. Mulroney needed a shower in a bad way."

They could hear Rossi's laughter all the way out of the station.

"Are you really starving, or did you just want out of there?" asked Beth.

Michael patted his stomach. "Eating is definitely on today's agenda, but I can hold off for now. What's on your mind?"

"I thought we could walk the beach a spell. I have something to get off my chest. Then I'd like to stop at Evelyn's house with the news. I want her to hear from us that she's no longer a suspect."

"Then we can eat?" Michael took her hand as they crossed the street.

"Continuously for the rest of the day if you like. After yesterday, I have a taste for just about everything."

When they reached the hard-packed sand—the tidal zone that would soon be underwater—Beth shielded her eyes and peered out to sea. Fishing trawlers bobbed in the waves, while gulls and pelicans wheeled on air currents searching for their next tasty meal. "It's really beautiful here."

"You sound sad that our case is wrapping up." Michael flung a sand dollar back into the surf.

"I am in a way. We haven't done half the relaxing we had planned."

"Nate can probably spare us for a few more days. After all, he's flying out tomorrow to meet the new hire, for better or for worse."

"What have you told him?"

"The bare minimum. I thought I'd let Kaitlyn explain what's going on, as much as she feels comfortable. I don't want to influence Nate ahead of time."

"While we sing her praises from the sidelines, right?" Beth said, pushing her long hair back from her face.

"Absolutely. I'll make it clear that Kaitlyn provided the info that saved your life. I was merely in the right place at the right time."

"*Waaay* too modest, Preston. You're still my hero, so get used to it." She wrapped an arm around his waist.

"We'll see how long I stay on your pedestal." He reached down to rescue another sand dollar. "You were the one insisting we remain on Mrs. Doyle's case, even though we'd been paid to find proof of infidelity."

"I made mistakes on this one—mistakes that cost Curtis pain and might have cost Crystal her life."

"Curtis created his own problems, and Lenny killed Crystal. Period."

"I assumed Mr. Scraggly Beard was Bonnie's old boyfriend that she abandoned when she met Lamar. My gut said he had nothing to do with our case. My gut was wrong. I should have tracked that guy down long ago."

"That's why you should keep your partner in the loop. A partner can often be more reliable than a digestive organ."

"I know that now. I'm sorry, Michael." She peered up at him.

"I forgive you, Beth. Now it's time to forgive yourself."

"What do you mean?"

"You've been pretty hard on yourself since we got here."

"I messed up several times. That's not easy for me to admit. I allowed pity for Evelyn to cloud my professional judgment. A good PI never lets that happen."

"Your faith in her was right on the money. Your belief in her innocence is what cracked the case. Considering all the evidence against her, a lesser investigator might have given up."

"But I betrayed her trust—"

"You made a mistake. Nobody's perfect. All we can do is our best. Sometimes it won't be enough."

"At least I did one thing right in Savannah." Beth started walking to hide her emotions.

"What's that? Fall in love with free food at the hotel's hospitality hour?" Michael fell in stride at her side.

"Nope, but I did fall in love."

"Really? Anyone I know?" He grabbed her arm to stop her forward progress.

"Yep. I'm in love with you, Preston. I wanted to tell you at the Mulroneys', but those people—the good guys and the bad guys—kept horning in on our privacy."

"You sure about this, Kirby?"

"It's what my gut says…and my brain, big toe, and most of all, my heart." She stretched up and kissed his cheek.

"In that case, maybe we'll give your gut one more chance." Michael kissed her softly on the lips. "Because I've been in love with you for a while now."

He leaned in for another kiss, but she stopped him. "Since we went to Charleston?"

"Nope. Before that." Michael came around from the other side, but again she thwarted his attempt.

"When we went to Wild Adventures?"

"Well before we arrived in Savannah."

"When, Michael?"

"It was the day you taught me to shoot at your uncle's farm. I simply can't resist a woman who looks like Mae West and handles a gun like Annie Oakley." He leaned in for his third try.

"There's no time for smooching." Beth started across the soft sand, dragging him behind her. "We need to get to Evelyn's before we faint with hunger."

They soon forgot their appetites once they reached Oleander Drive. Evelyn was sitting in a chair on the deck. A book lay in her lap, but her attention was definitely out to sea. She didn't notice them until Beth touched her lightly on the shoulder.

"Beth, Michael. What a lovely surprise."

"Sorry we barged in without calling first. Your maid told us where to find you. We have good news that couldn't wait a moment longer." Beth pulled a chair next to hers while Michael retrieved one from the lawn. Then she launched into an abbreviated version of the events of the last twenty-four hours.

For the third time, Evelyn's reaction wasn't the one Beth anticipated. Her eyes filled with tears, and a frown deepened the creases around her mouth. "How awful. That young man was so filled with hate he killed not one but two human beings who had done nothing to him."

"In his warped mind, Lenny thought he was protecting Bonnie," said Beth, squeezing Evelyn's fingers. "But now the police can stop looking at you as a murder suspect. Your name will be cleared."

"Am I free to leave the island?" Evelyn focused on the waves rolling in with relentless regularity.

"Of course, but word will soon get around that you had nothing to do with your husband's death."

"My name will never be clear on Tybee, but that's okay. I loved this island because Lamar loved it. I would rather live near my sister and her family."

Sitting between the prettiest house she'd ever seen and a vast expanse of deep blue sea, Beth couldn't resist asking, "Won't you miss all this?" She stretched her arms wide.

"I will. I love the ocean. But I can always vacation on Sullivan's Island, Kiawah, or at Myrtle Beach."

"Hilton Head is also very nice, ma'am," Michael said.

"Yes, it is, young man. You should remember that when thinking about honeymoon destinations."

Beth felt herself blush, a rare occurrence for her. "What will you do with this house?"

"Put it up for sale. It doesn't feel the same without Lamar."

"Of course not. Sometimes I say the stupidest things." Beth tapped the side of her head with her knuckles.

"Not at all." Evelyn patted her knee. "Part of me wants to stay right here to remember the good times we shared. It's a tough decision."

Michael scooted his chair closer. "The police said Mulroney parked his truck by the service gate and walked down the beach to your house. Nobody noticed him cutting through the dunes."

Evelyn held up a hand. "Please, no more details. I'd rather not put images of Lamar's last moments in my mind."

"Of course," Michael murmured. "Before I forget, the Savannah detective mentioned they recovered the twenty thousand dollars from Mulroney. For now it will be held in evidence, but eventually you'll get it back. Surprisingly, Lenny had spent less than a thousand of it."

"Could you please see that Miss Mulroney receives the money?" she asked.

"*Bonnie?*" Beth and Michael asked in unison.

"Yes. She'll need additional schooling if she's ever to stop needing a man to support her."

"That's very nice of you, Evelyn," said Beth. "Most women wouldn't be quite so charitable."

"Lamar and I chose that course of action together. If I hadn't met him, I might have ended up in circumstances similar to Bonnie's. This may provide her with the chance she needs."

"At least Lenny will be gone a long time."

"I know it's hard for you to believe, Beth, but Lamar was a very nice person. He made a mistake, yes, but nobody's perfect."

"That seems to be today's consensus." Beth winked at Michael. "I certainly know I'm not."

"What are your plans now that your work in Savannah is done? Are you eager to get home?"

"Actually, I'm not. I miss my parents, of course, but this town has really grown on me." Beth stole a glance at Michael.

"What about you, Michael?" Evelyn cocked her head to one side.

"I like Natchez. I like Savannah. I just want to be where Beth is."

Evelyn burst out laughing. "It sounds as though you two have decided your own course of action."

"We have. We're still in the preliminary stages, but I'll keep you posted." With that, Beth pushed to her feet.

"You'd better since I had a hand in this romance." The woman's smile filled her entire face.

"You did. More than you'll ever know." Beth buzzed a kiss across her forehead. "Right now I need to get food in this guy before he turns into a bear."

"Before you go, I have a small gift for all your hard work. Only I haven't wrapped it yet."

Beth shook her head. "That isn't necessary. We were well compensated for our time, and you have been a pleasure to work with."

The corners of her mouth turned down. "Truly, it would mean a lot if I could give you this."

Beth glanced from Michael back to Evelyn's expression of distress. "All right, if you insist."

"I'll wrap it and send it to your hotel tomorrow. Thank you for allowing me to show my gratitude."

"You're welcome. And don't forget what I said about staying in touch. Who knows when I'll need more relationship advice?" Beth headed down the steps to the grass with Michael close behind.

"Were you serious about wanting to stay in Savannah?" Michael asked before they reached the front yard.

"I was, although the idea just came to me recently."

"What about Kaitlyn? If we man the office here in Savannah, Nate won't need to hire anyone."

"That's the tricky part. Her assignment with the Industrial Commission was temporary, and without another job, she might have to return to Florida."

"Nate originally toyed with the idea of having a traveling investigator—someone willing to live wherever the case took them. But so much work started lining up here that he knew he needed a satellite office."

Beth stopped dead in her tracks. "Traveling around would be perfect for Kaitlyn, at least until she's ready to face what she's afraid of in Florida."

"Establishing another office would be perfect for a newlywed couple." Michael grinned at her as he clicked open the car doors.

"Aren't you getting a little ahead of yourself, Preston?"

"I know we must make Nate as impressed with Kaitlyn as we

are, but that shouldn't be too hard. How about Marlin Monroe's for dinner? We had a great meal there the last time."

Beth crossed her arms. "You know very well I'm not talking about her."

"Oh…do you mean about the 'newlywed' part?" he asked, sounding way too innocent to be believed.

"I am, and you're not getting off easy. I expect a true dog-and-pony proposal show."

When Michael stopped at a red light, he turned toward her with an impish smile. "Not a problem. Why do you think we're on our way to Marlin Monroe's? I'm sure we can improve the romance factor of our auspicious first date."

THIRTY-SEVEN

*B*eth, would you get away from there?" Michael whispered. "What if someone sees you with your ear pressed to the door? Let's go back to the pool and wait like we were told."

She didn't move. "How big is Nate's suite? I can't hear anything going on. What's taking him so long to make up his mind?"

Michael grabbed her hand and dragged her toward the elevator. "The longer the interview takes, the better things look for Kaitlyn. I'm sure she told him about her new identity by now."

Beth dug in her heels like an obstinate horse. "Are you sure she understood your instructions? I probably should've talked to her while you picked up the boss at the airport."

"She understood. When and if Nate starts talking particulars about the new Savannah office, she will send us a text and tell Nate we're joining the conversation."

"What if he feels manipulated?" Beth grabbed onto a post to hold her position.

"We're talking about Nate Price, who is the epitome of easy-going." Just as Michael picked Beth up to carry her like a sack of potatoes, the door to Nate's suite swung open.

"Preston, Kirby. What are you two doing?"

"Nothing," said Beth as soon as her feet hit the ground.

"We were just on our way in, sir." Michael tucked in his shirt with a dignified air as they slunk past the boss.

Across the room, Kaitlyn greeted them with a big grin. "I'm hired!" she crowed.

"Hooray! Wise choice, boss," Beth said, giving her official new coworker a high five.

Nate returned to the small conference table. "Except Miss Webb wishes to go wherever the case takes her, including Natchez. She seems to think one of you wants to stay in Savannah." He looked at both Michael and Beth as they sat down.

"We're hoping to work the office together," said Michael. "We fell in love with the city."

"Both of you? How would that work out?"

"It would work out *spectacularly*." Beth held up her hand and wiggled her third finger, where a diamond ring sparkled.

"You're engaged? To Preston?" Nate's shock was all too apparent.

"I am. Strange things happen in a romantic old town like Savannah." Beth hooked her arm through her fiancé's elbow.

"Especially when there's a full moon," said Michael.

"I will never understand women." Nate shook his head. "But getting back on track, are you both willing to go on assignment for a while? To wherever our next big case takes us? I thought one of my two veterans would be chomping at the bit to travel on the company's dime."

Kaitlyn's eyes turned round. "I've always wanted to see the world. What kind of case is this? If you put your trust in me, I promise not to let you down." She was practically levitating from her chair.

Nate held up his hands. "Don't get too excited. The case might only take you a few days. A woman who was adopted as an infant wishes to track down a natural sibling. She knows only that her birth mother gave up *two* daughters fortysome years ago."

"Isn't this something that could be handled through the court system without hiring an investigator?" asked Beth.

"Usually, yes," agreed Nate. "But the woman's husband is adamant about finding the sibling even if she doesn't wish to be found. If his wife doesn't receive a transplant within the next six months, she will die. There are no suitable matches in the organ bank, and none is expected due to certain rare genetic markers. A natural sibling is her best and most likely only chance."

"I'm the woman for the job," said Kaitlyn. "Did I mention I was adopted as an infant?"

"She's perfect, just like I told you, boss," Beth said somewhat smugly.

Nate narrowed his gaze. "All I have to say to you, Miss Kirby, is that the wedding had better be in Natchez. Or I won't be able to face my wife or Maxine or your mother when I get home."

"No problem," said Michael. "Beth wants a big wedding, and we know only three people here."

"And two of them already ordered us out of town."

Nate stood. "Save that story for another day. I would like to discuss salary and benefits with Miss Webb. So you two can go take a hike. We'll go to dinner later to celebrate your engagement."

Beth and Michael bolted for the door like children at the recess bell. "That certainly went well," she said in the elevator.

"I told you it would. Nate is a practical man. Should we walk to Forsyth Park?" he asked in the lobby. "I just love it there."

"That's fine with me, but if we stay in Savannah, what happens to your Ironman competition with your buddies from the gym? You've been training for months."

"My whole point was to get in shape. To prove to myself I could do it. Now that I have, I don't need to be better than anyone else. Curtis Doyle helped me come to that conclusion."

"*Curtis Doyle?* What does he have to do with this?" Beth snugged her arm around his waist as they crossed the street.

"Curtis blamed his father for all his miseries. Lamar picked up the gauntlet after their father died, and then Curtis blamed him. But when Curtis stopped letting Lamar support him, he finally gained peace of mind. Sometimes you win by refusing to play the game."

"Didn't somebody famous say that originally?" Beth asked.

"Only in her own mind...and in mine." Michael kissed the top of her head.

"Guess what, Preston? My toes are tingling!"

"How 'bout that? Mine are too." He moved in for another kiss but was thwarted by an interruption.

"Are you Miss Elizabeth Kirby?" asked a well-dressed young man. "I'm from Mrs. Hilda Gwinn's office."

"I am."

"I've been instructed to deliver this package to you." He held out a large yellow envelope.

"Am I being served a subpoena?"

"No, ma'am. It's a gift."

The moment Beth's fingers grasped the envelope, the young man hurried away. "How bizarre was that?" she asked, turning her gaze up to Michael.

"Open it, Beth. The suspense is killing me."

"Hold your horses." Beth extracted an elaborately wrapped box from the envelope. A sparkly silver cord had been wrapped around the box several times and tied with an elaborate bow. Inside the box were two pieces of paper, one a note and the other a document. She scanned the document first. "Good grief. It's the registration to the Lexus. Evelyn signed over Lamar's car to me. It's been witnessed and notarized, and apparently the tax has been paid, by all the notations."

"Mrs. Doyle gave you a sixty-thousand-dollar car? Read the note," Michael demanded.

Dear Beth, if you're staying in Savannah, you must have
your own car. A gal never knows when she'll be invited to
lunch in Atlanta. And don't even think of trying to return
this. Hilda Gwinn has rendered that virtually impossi-
ble. Blame yourself. You're the one who found me such a
talented lawyer. Best regards, Evelyn

Thunderstruck, Beth had a hard time forming the words.
"There go our insurance premiums."

"Not to worry, my love. I believe married couples get some
kind of break on the rates. We can call our good friend Joseph
Reynard, just to be sure."

Discussion Questions

1. Why is Beth so nervous about working on Evelyn's case?

2. At first Beth is put off by the wealthy Evelyn. What changes Beth's mind so that she becomes Evelyn's champion and protector?

3. Why doesn't Michael believe someone is trying to kill Evelyn?

4. Throughout the story, Evelyn's behavior toward Bonnie Mulroney confuses Beth. Discuss all the factors contributing to Evelyn's empathy for the young woman.

5. Michael and Beth seem to come from two different planets emotionally, but opposites attract romantically. What traits do the two partners have in common?

6. Why is Evelyn the police's chief suspect in Lamar's murder?

7. Curtis Doyle's life was hobbled by his father's lack of compassion. How did he finally break free and find true purpose and self-respect?

8. Bonnie's character and motivations become clear by the end of the book. Why does Beth finally find compassion for her?

9. What was standing in Beth's way of forming an emotional bond with Michael? How does he help her overcome this?

10. Kaitlyn Webb seems to be perfect for the new position at Price Investigations. How is she also her own worst enemy?

ABOUT THE AUTHOR

Mary Ellis is the bestselling author of a dozen novels set in the Amish community and several historical romances set during the Civil War. *Midnight on the Mississippi, What Happened on Beale Street, Magnolia Moonlight,* and *Sunset in Old Savannah* are books in a romantic suspense series, Secrets of the South.

Before "retiring" to write full-time, Mary taught school and worked as a sales rep for Hershey Chocolate. Her debut book, *A Widow's Hope,* was a finalist for a 2010 Carol Award. *Living in Harmony* won the 2012 Lime Award for Excellence in Amish Fiction, while *Love Comes to Paradise* won the 2013 Lime Award. Mary and her husband live in Ohio.

~∂

Mary can be found on the web at
www.maryellis.net
or
Look for Mary Ellis/Author on Facebook

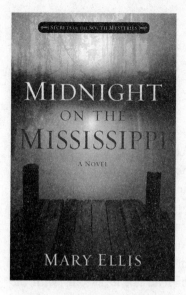

SECRETS OF THE SOUTH MYSTERIES

MIDNIGHT ON THE MISSISSIPPI

A NOVEL

MARY ELLIS

What Lies Beneath the Black Water of the Bayou?

Hunter Galen, a New Orleans securities broker, suspects his business partner, James Nowak, of embezzling their clients' money, but he's reluctant to jeopardize their friendship. After James turns up dead, Hunter realizes his unwillingness to confront a problem may have cost James his life.

Nicki Price, a newly minted PI, intends to solve the stockbroker's murder as she establishes herself in the career she adores. As she ferrets out fraud and deception at Galen-Nowak Investments, Hunter's fiancée, Ashley Menard, rubs her the wrong way. Nicki doesn't trust the ostentatious woman who seems to be hiding something, but is the PI's growing attraction to Hunter—the police's only suspect—her true reason for disliking Ashley?

As Hunter and Nicki encounter sophisticated shell games, blackmail, and death threats both subtle and overt, danger swirls around them like the mysterious dark water of the bayou. Only their reliance on faith and fearless determination give them hope they will live to see another day.

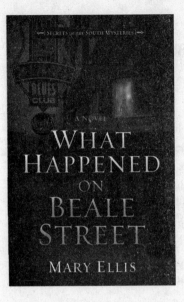

How Can Music So Beautiful Hide Something So Deadly?

A cryptic plea for help from a childhood friend sends cousins Nate and Nicki Price from New Orleans to Memphis. When these two private investigators arrive at Danny Andre's last known address, they discover signs of a struggle and a lifestyle not in keeping with the choirboy they fondly remember.

Danny's sister, Isabelle, reluctantly accepts their help. She and Nate aren't on the best of terms due to a shared past. Can they get beyond painful memories to find her brother?

And what on earth was Danny involved in besides becoming a rising star as a sax player? Nate and Nicki follow clues into dim and smoky clubs, trail potential stalkers, and challenge dangerous men with connections to underworld drug trafficking. To complicate things, the hotel they are staying in has its own secrets. Confronted with murder and mystery in the land of the Delta blues, the cousins and Isabelle will have to rely on their faith and investigative experience to solve the case and not lose their lives.

What Sinister Secrets Lurk in the Shadows of Yesterday?

Natchez, Mississippi—Private investigator Nate Price and his new wife, Isabelle, need a vacation. Their coworkers generously team up to surprise them with a belated honeymoon, but the happy trip turns sour when Izzy spies her ex-husband, who appears to have taken up his gambling addiction once again.

While the boss is away, Price Investigations remains in the hands of Beth Kirby, a former police officer, and Michael Preston, a former forensic accountant. Hardly a dream team, as Beth resents working with a man who has no experience in his new job.

But Beth and Michael must move past their differences if they hope to uncover the truth behind a beloved Southern preacher's demise. The preacher's widow suspects foul play, despite the evidence indicating suicide.

With tension escalating between these investigators and local law enforcement—and new threats arising on all sides—how will Beth, Michael, and Nate hold on to faith and bring the truth to light?

To learn more about Harvest House books and
to read sample chapters, visit our website:

www.harvesthousepublishers.com

HARVEST HOUSE PUBLISHERS
EUGENE, OREGON